MW00962778

Dragons
of
Earth

Book Two
of
The Dragons of Nibiru

Lorna J. Carleton

Published by
Nibiru Press
9556 Winchester Road
Vernon, BC V1H 2E2

ISBN 978-1-0861938-7-9

First International Edition June 2019

Illustrations by Danielle Hebert

To Vincent—
dearly loved, dearly missed.

CHAPTER 1

Earth

Vogelsberg Mountains, Germany
2018 A.D.

Fianna knew the time had arrived. She watched the priest approach from the far end of the cavern. "Celine!" the white Dragon called over her shoulder, "We must go. Are you ready?"

"Almost. Another minute," the girl replied. She worked intently to strap a crate of precious Dragon eggs to the saddlebags her winged companion wore.

At last, everything was well secured. "Okay. Let's go," said Celine. "Will you lead the way, Father Greer?" The old priest, who had been waiting patiently, nodded. He turned and began the long climb up the ancient mountain tunnel, up toward the hidden gateway to the outer world.

Walking a few paces behind the priest, Celine was soon lost in thought. She shuddered in apprehension; what lay before them was uncertain at best. Failure was grimly possible, even probable. As was death. And theirs were not the only fates hanging in the balance: The survival of a whole race of Dragon-folk was at stake.

The young girl struggled to return her attention to the present—to suppress the insistent memories of their harrowing, near-fatal battle with the criminal Soader and his two-headed fire-breather, just days before. It was no use. She shivered and nearly cried out at the thought of the hideous Rept-Human hybrid and the flaming beast he rode.

Finally, the trio reached the massive door to the outer world, and stood facing its elaborately carved inner panels. The tension was almost a physical presence as they awaited the moment when the great space vessel *Queen Asherah III* was due to appear above their mountain refuge.

Father Greer's fine old timepiece chimed softly. The moment had arrived.

Celine and Fianna edged closer to where the opening would appear. They glanced at one another, filled with anticipation—and a healthy dose of fear. The girl turned to the priest and nodded. He smiled, bowed, and turned his focus to the imposing grey doors before them. He spread his arms wide, then brought his hands to his chest and bowed as though in prayer. His low, droning chant reverberated through the rocky entry chamber. In moments, the portal whispered open; in rushed a gust of brisk evening air.

The old man stepped out onto the ledge beyond the doors, scanning the moonlit vista before them. "It is safe, my child," he assured Celine, who had followed close behind. "I will wait with you until your father's vessel arrives."

Moments later, the sleek, shining under-hull of a

spaceship appeared high in the sky, directly above them. At once Celine reached out mentally to contact Jager, who should be aboard the massive craft. The two were among but a few humanoids who still possessed this ancient ability, a kind of telepathy known as "menting"—mental communication. "Jager, are you there?" she called.

"Yes, Celine—right here," her young soulmate replied.

"Good. Good. Now, please tell me: Will *Asherah* be able to transbeam Fianna and me directly to Scotland?"

"I'm sorry, but no—we'll have to 'beam you aboard first, then back down to Loch Ness."

"All right. I was afraid that might be the case. Please listen carefully. I apologize for what I must do now. I..."

"Wait! What do you mean, 'apologize'?!" the young man broke in.

"There's no time. Listen to me! Father Greer has something for you. You must come get it, and give it to my father. Please, please do this for me. I *must* go now. I'll see you soon. I love you, Jager."

With that, she shut her mind against further contact and rushed to Father Greer, hugging the priest so hard it nearly cracked his poor old bones. Pushing a recorder button into his hand, she explained: "Jager will come for this. It's for my father. Thank you again—for everything."

She dashed to Fianna, leapt to the saddle and hunkered down tight, ready for the jolt when the Dragon took flight.

Then, just as Fianna crouched to make her skyward leap, the pair glimpsed a flashing blur of wicked scarlet above, and felt, more than heard, a screaming *whoosh* of rushing wings.

There it was—their worst fears come true: a scarlet, two-headed Dragon diving straight at them. A humanoid form stood in the black saddle strapped between the enormous wings, laughing hideously—the evil Rept-Human hybrid, Soader.

Before girl, Dragon and priest had fully registered what was happening, a new blur of black streaked into view from their right, on a collision course with the red fiend. Another Dragon! It closed the distance in a flash and slammed into its adversary with terrifying force.

The Dragons tumbled out of the sky, down, down to the mountain slope below, a shrieking tangle of wings, claws, gnashing teeth and slashing tails. Celine leapt from the saddle and rushed to the ledge's brink to follow their fall, Fianna right behind. It was no good, though—their immediate view was blocked by a rocky outcrop.

"Ahimoth! That was *Ahimoth!*" cried the white Dragon, half in amazement, half in terror at her brother's peril.

"Jager!" mented Celine, "There's a black Dragon somewhere on the mountainside below us. Can you shield him? It's Fianna's brother!"

"Yes, I believe we can. I see him on our monitors," Jager flashed back.

Jager turned to Major Hadgkiss, *Asherah's* second-in-command. "Major, can you put shielding around the black Dragon there on the mountainside, then on Celine and the white Dragon next to her?"

"*Dragon?!* Celine's with a *Dragon?*" bellowed Commander Rafael Zulak, the ship's captain—and Celine's father. "Major, what in all space is going on?? Bring her aboard! 'Beam her out of there! Do it *now!!*"

"No time to explain, Captain," the major replied. "Lieutenant Madda, shield the black Dragon, then the girl and white Dragon on the ledge above him."

"Yes, sir," Madda replied, running nimble green hands across the glowing panel before her.

"I asked what the hells is going on!" yelled Zulak, glaring at his bridge crew. "Bring my daughter aboard, this instant—or I'll have the lot of you up on charges." He strode toward Madda's panel.

"Sir, respectfully, please bear with us," replied Hadgkiss. "We'll 'beam them as soon as we can." He managed to speak calmly, knowing full well he was disobeying a direct order from his captain—and a fervent plea from his life-long friend.

Celine and Fianna raced along the ledge, trying to get a clear view of the slopes below. They saw no sign of Ahimoth, but spotted the red Dragon sprawled far below, both snakish necks limp. Soader lay close by, legs splayed almost comically in front of him. Then, to their astonishment, a scintillating swirl of energy grew around the distant figures, its intensity increasing until it vanished abruptly—taking their foes with it.

The girl and Dragon had no time to consider where their enemies had gone, or what it all might mean—for now, high above the mountain, a second ship flashed into view and wheeled to bring its blunt bow to bear on *Queen Asherah*; in seconds, it rammed the *Queen* amidships. Had her shields not been up at half-power, the impact would have been fatal.

Thrown violently to the deck, the *Queen's* bridge crew scrambled to resume their stations. Claxons blared and hazard lights flashed. Hadgkiss made a lightning assessment of the situation and roared out an order: "Shields to full power! Prepare to jump-shift out of here!" Turning, he came face to face with a horrified Rafael. "Don't worry, Raff. Celine will be okay. She's safer down there than with us. We'll come back for her directly."

But now Dino's eyes widened in a horror of his own. Over the commander's shoulder he saw Ensign Jager—his adopted nephew and the newest member of the bridge crew—screaming and writhing in a desperate struggle to escape a transbeam. The major lunged past Rafael toward the young man, but it was no use. Before he'd covered half the distance between them, Jager had vanished.

Moments later, the ship was rammed again. The bridge's lighting flickered, then switched to harsh red: they were on emergency backups. "Whoever that is, we're outmatched, and we won't survive another impact," shouted Dino. "Jump-shift for Erra—now!"

The helmsman slapped his control panel; a howling groan echoed through the hull as the jump-shift drive engaged, wrenching the already tortured vessel. Dino and Rafael's eyes met; both feared the worst...but it didn't come. Instead, the ship steadied, shuddered once more, then smoothly made the jump across light-years of space. In no time—quite literally—they were in orbit above their home port and planet, Erra. Gravely wounded, limping, but still alive.

CHAPTER 2

Alternate Plan

Their faces turned skyward, Celine, Fianna and Father Greer watched, helpless, as the immense spaceships battled high above.

Suddenly, Celine was rocked by a mental cry of angry surprise from Jager; she sensed his desperate struggle to escape the transbeam. "Jager? *Jager! What is it?!*"

There was another roar of rage, then terrible silence. Silence, and an aching vacuum. The girl cried out in anguish with both voice and mind.

A new mental voice entered her awareness: the Mentor, West. "What troubles you, child?"

"West! Jager's gone silent—I can't reach him! What's happened?"

"I do not know," West replied, her tone betraying deep concern. She paused, then continued. "He does not reply to my call. He is no longer aboard your father's ship, nor anywhere nearby. I fear someone has taken him; most probably the same agents who took the hybrid and red Dragon. And now the ships have departed—your father's jump-shifted moments ago; the other followed almost at once."

Turning her attention to the skies above, Celine saw it was true: There was nothing to see but a few early stars and some wisps of cloud, still roiling from the ships' sudden departure. "No! NO! I *can't* lose him again!" she despaired, slumping against Fianna's flank.

The Dragon swung her head round to press her muzzle against the girl's shoulder in reassurance. "Do not fear, my Companion. We shall find him. I know it. It is meant to be so."

Celine heaved a shuddering sigh, then reached up and gave her friend a grateful hug. "I hope you're right. You know such things. But it's...it's awful." Shaking off her near-overwhelming dread, she steeled herself and addressed the Mentor. "West, who could have taken him?"

"I do not know for certain, Celine, but I suspect the Brothers."

The girl could well have collapsed into a fresh bout of despair, but—to her own proud surprise—she reacted instead with adamant resolve. "You're right. Damn them to the deepest hells! It *had* to have been the Brothers. Either the Brothers or G.O.D.—the attacking ship appeared out of jump-shift. No one but the Brothers or the damned G.O.D. has jump-ships."

"Quite correct," West replied. "We know the Brothers want Jager. So does High Chancellor Scabbage. And Soader and his Dragon slave are minions of both. But the Galactic

Omniplanetary Democratum may also covet him for purposes of its own."

"Fine. So, we've got to go find the Brothers. Now. Or find Jager, at least."

"We must find Jager, yes," said West, "but my sisters and I are best equipped to do that—and do it we shall. Right now there is another task, equally urgent, which only you and Fianna can complete. You must journey to Nibiru with all speed, and lift the hex upon the Dragons' last eggs. To do that, you must travel to Scotland and enter the tube-chute, at once."

"You're right, West," said Celine, "but I'm worried about the chute. I don't think it's safe. I have a feeling whoever took Jager and Soader may be watching it. If that's true, and we try to use it, they could trap us."

"Your concerns are astute, child," replied the Mentor. "I sense you are correct, in essence. The tube-chute itself could not be compromised, but its vortex entrance at Loch Ness might be."

"So, the situation's changed," said Celine, frowning. "Fianna, we've got to call Nessie. Maybe there's a way she can keep the vortex safe. And we've got to make sure your parents made it safely through the tube-chute to Nibiru. If someone were waiting to ambush us, they could have interfered with your parents' passage, too."

Fianna gasped at the awful truth of Celine's words. Her parents could be in terrible danger.

"West, we should leave here right away," said Celine, "no time to talk to Nessie. Could you speak with her and relay all this? And find out if Fianna's parents have arrived on Nibiru?"

"Yes, I can, child," replied the Mentor. "And you are correct: Whatever Nessie may say, you and Fianna must hasten to Scotland, risk the vortex and travel the tube-chute yourselves. I see no alternative. You are no longer safe on Earth. And you must reach Nibiru soon, or the Dragons' eggs will perish."

A low voice came from the shadows behind them. "There is another way. You could escape through the Chalice Well."

"Ah!" said West.

"The Chalice Well?" said Celine. She turned to see Father Greer standing calmly near the tunnel entrance. "Is that the old mystic well in England? I've read about one there, in the south."

"Yes. In Glastonbury," replied the old man. "I do not believe it has been used for centuries, but it should still function. I foresee only one problem. The Well was designed to accommodate humanoid bodies. The spell which controls its working would have to be re-cast, to transport Dragons as well. Princess Fianna, are you willing to make the attempt, if we manage to amend the spell?"

"Yes, of course," replied Fianna, without a moment's hesitation.

"So be it, then," the priest continued. "A trusted friend and member of my order, Father Sinclair, lives beside the Well and tends it. I will converse with him, explain matters and solicit his help. I will also ask that he give you the Egg, a comm stone our brotherhood has used for centuries to converse with Pleiadean and other friendly vessels in the area. Use the stone to call for a ship, once Father Sinclair has transported you safely off planet."

"Off planet? Do you mean the Well won't take us to Nibiru?"

"No, no, dear one. It is not so potent as that. Only the tube-chute can carry you safely to Nibiru."

Celine nodded. "West, are you in agreement with Father Greer's suggestion?"

"Yes, Celine. I believe his counsel is most wise—the best and safest way to proceed. No one will expect such a move, certainly. It should buy you precious time, and take you safely away from Earth."

"All right. That's settled, then. We'll travel to the Well, and do as Father Greer suggests. But we can't just leave here without finding out what happened to Ahimoth!"

"Exactly so!" cried Fianna. All three hurried to the ledge's lip and began scanning the terrain below for any sign of the black Dragon.

"Ahimoth!" Fianna called, mentally. "Where are you? Are you injured?"

"I am here, sister," Ahimoth replied, "in a ravine far below you, hidden from your view."

Fianna turned quickly to Celine and the priest. "I have found him! Please bear with me, while I learn more."

The girl and older man nodded relief and agreement.

"Are you injured?" Fianna asked her brother.

"Yes, but not so very badly. Tell me, are Soader and that red Kerr still about? I should like another go at them!" A stifled groan betrayed his effort to make light of his condition.

"Hmph!" Fianna snorted. "I *am* greatly relieved to know you survived, but I don't for a moment believe you are fit for battle! You are fortunate, though. Our enemies are gone. Transbeamed away, though we know not where, nor by whom."

"Transbeamed? A perplexing development," the black Dragon replied.

"Perplexing indeed, but solving it must wait. Are you well enough to fly?"

"Yes, I believe so. Are we to return to Scotland?"

"No. We must travel to England; I shall explain as we fly. We must depart at once. Can you follow us?"

"Oh, yes, yes. Please! Even injured, I can out-fly *you*, my silly sister!"

"Hmm. We shall see about that. We shall depart momentarily. I can sense your location now. When you see us pass overhead, please follow."

"As you wish, Princess," he replied.

"He is injured, but able to fly," Fianna explained to Celine and Father Greer. "I have told him of our plan; he is waiting to follow us to the Well."

"All right. Let's go!" said Celine. She paused, then turned to Father Greer. With a deep bow, she addressed him. "We are forever grateful to you, Father, for everything you've done for us and for our cause. I hope you'll be safe here, and that our presence hasn't endangered you or your brothers."

Father Greer bowed, returning reverence to the girl and then the Dragon. "Your efforts are the greatest thanks my brothers and I could wish for. You are risking your lives to save Nibiru and all its peoples. That will benefit this planet, too—more than you may understand."

Celine gave a final bow, cupping her hands over her heart in a pose ancient priests once used to channel their mystic powers. Fianna bowed too, extending a foreleg as Dragons do.

The girl leapt to the saddle and snugged herself in for flight. Fianna spread her wings and dove headlong over the ledge's margin. The glistening creature swept downward and then outward, soaring over the spot where Ahimoth waited. After a quick flip of a wingtip in greeting, she swung upward again; pumping wings carried her high into the sky.

On the mountainside below, Ahimoth managed a faltering leap upward, caught the air with a pained but powerful downbeat, and slowly climbed after his sister.

Celine looked behind, following Ahimoth's flight. Sensing his struggle, she cast a spell to enwrap the injured Dragon in a bubble of calmer air, easing his efforts. She shifted in the saddle to keep an eye on him; if he should falter or fall behind, she wanted to know it at once.

CHAPTER 3

Flight to The Chalice Well

The trio flew silently westward and north, toward Britain. Celine concentrated on maintaining the spell she'd cast to ease Ahimoth's flight, but every few minutes spared some attention to call out to Jager. Her heart grew heavier as each new call went unanswered.

An hour into their journey, she sensed the area they'd reached was relatively safe. "Fianna," she asked, "would you circle down and land on that weathered ridge just ahead?" Down the Dragon spiraled, her brother following close behind. Soon they rested in the shadow of a rocky outcropping.

Near exhaustion, Celine was relieved to release her protective spell over Ahimoth. The big Dragon thanked her for her help, then turned his attention to Fianna. At last they had some time for each other, brief though it might be. The pair embraced, deep in mental conversation. Now and then, one would nuzzle or nibble the other's shoulder, or gently, rhythmically rub the smooth-scaled neck. Here they were—brother and sister, Prince and Princess of Nibiru; separated for decades until just days before, now nearly overwhelmed at how close they'd come to losing one another forever.

After a time, the Dragons spoke aloud again, out of respect for their Human companion.

"Celine," cried Fianna, "my brother has told me our parents' injuries have prevented them from attempting the trip to Nibiru. They are still on this planet! We should have considered their age and weakened condition before suggesting they travel the tube-chute so soon. But, if they stay much longer, I fear Soader or his minions may find and re-capture them! Oh, Celine, what are we to do?"

"I trust West and the Mentors to keep them safe," replied Celine, afraid to say more. Fianna nodded, and began to speak—then cut herself short when she noticed Celine staring blankly into the near distance. The Dragon knew this meant the girl was communicating with someone mentally, and would "return" when the inward exchange was complete.

Sure enough, in a few seconds Celine spoke. "West has been told your parents are about to enter the tube-chute. They should be back on Nibiru by this time tomorrow! She says we have Nessie to thank. The old girl has been working her healing magic on them, and she and her Water Dragon friends have woven a cloaking spell over the whole region. So, no one—not even Soader or the Brothers—could find them and interfere."

"Ahhh, that is wonderful news," Fianna sighed. "I only hope they make the passage safely."

"They will, my friend," replied Celine, giving Fianna's neck a huge embrace. "They will."

Now she approached Ahimoth, looking up at his towering ebon form—nearly a third again as large as his snow-white sister. "It's time to tend to some of your more serious wounds," she said. "You can eat while I do it—I won't be in your way.

"Then," she added gruffly, "I want to know why you're here, not with your parents as we agreed. And about what you did with the comm stone I gave you."

The Dragon-prince nodded agreement, and Celine went to work: She cast healing spells over the nastier injuries and applied herbal dressings and bandages.

Meanwhile, the famished creature gobbled the ration Celine took from Father Greer's provision. He hadn't eaten in days, but although the meal was meagre for a Dragon his size, he felt stronger and brighter at once. He suspected—correctly—that the old priest had employed more than a little healing magic when preparing it.

Ahimoth chatted with his sister as he ate. "I still marvel that you are here, and that our parents live," he said. "Until a few days ago, I felt certain they had passed away, and that you were held captive. But here you sit! And with a Companion, no less!"

Celine couldn't hold back a proud smile. It soon faded, though, chased away by thoughts of her own sister. How she wished she and Mia shared a bond as close and warm as Fianna and Ahimoth's.

She refrained from contacting West to ask for news of Jager, knowing the Mentor would share anything significant without delay. She knew West and the other Mentors must be completely absorbed in their search for the boy, and for

Soader and his awful mutant Dragon. Or perhaps in battling whoever had whisked them away.

As the Dragon-siblings continued their conversation, the teen finished patching up the worst of Ahimoth's injuries. It was far from a perfect job, but she'd done the best she could with the scant supplies on hand.

Though Celine knew Dragons considered interruptions ill-mannered, she felt compelled to cut into their good-natured chat; she wanted answers to her questions.

"I beg your pardon, my friends, but I think it's time we discuss something extremely urgent. Ahimoth, would you please explain why you returned to Germany before your parents left for your homeworld, as we'd agreed? And please, please, what became of the comm stone I gave you?"

"What are you talking about?" asked Fianna, stomping her feet in frustration. "What agreement? What comm stone?"

"Fianna, it's my fault," said Celine, facing her friend. "Remember, a couple of days ago, I went with Ahimoth to the tunnel entrance—when he was leaving for Scotland?" The white Dragon nodded. "Well, the two of us decided it would be best if he returned to Germany once your parents had entered the tube-chute, instead of going with them. They would be safely on their way, and he'd be back here to help in case Soader and his Dragon showed up again. You were still recovering down in the cavern, so we decided not to tell you about it right away. We didn't want to worry you— it might have slowed your healing, and there was absolutely no room for delay."

Celine knew she'd breached their cherished trust by letting the young Dragon believe her brother was far away, out of Soader's reach. She simply hadn't seen any safe way around it. There were far larger issues at stake. Celine stood silent, as did Ahimoth; both hoped for a mercifully measured response from Fianna.

The white Dragon said nothing. With a deep, thoughtful frown, her gaze shifted from Companion to brother and back again. Here were the two most important souls in her young life. Hearing that they had kept silent about something of such import was a shock. It seemed a betrayal, and betrayal was a new experience for her. All the more shocking since the apparent betrayer was her Companion. The two had been inseparable since first meeting, more than a year before. Neither had ever kept anything from the other.

Finally, Fianna drew herself up and cleared her throat. Celine and Ahimoth tensed, fearing the worst, hoping for the best.

"Indeed, I am deeply hurt to think neither of you trusted me enough to mention such a change in our plans," Fianna began. After another pensive pause, she continued. "Nevertheless, I know you must have felt you were doing what was best, for me and for everyone. And you were almost certainly right. If you had not done it, it is unlikely I would have been ready to travel today—and that would have been disaster. Stubborn little Dragon that I am, I would have insisted on attempting the flight to Loch Ness. That would have been a foolish choice—perhaps the death of us all, and ultimately the end of my race. If anything could ever be called unforgivable, *that* would be it."

Celine and Ahimoth heaved sighs of relief; huge smiles replaced worried frowns. Then the two exchanged a flicker of a sidelong glance. Quick, but not quick enough to escape Fianna's notice.

"And now, since we are being honest," Fianna said, "would

you please tell me about this comm stone you mentioned, Celine?"

"I would be very glad to. Major Hadgkiss recently gave me a magically charged purple crystal—a communication stone used for mental communication over limited distances. My father had asked him to pass it on to me, so we could be in contact. It couldn't reach between here and Erra, but I think it made Dad feel better to know I had it.

"One can also use such a stone as a sort of recorder—you imprint it with a message, and set it to relay that message to a designated person. The stone will repeat the message aloud, in the imprinter's voice—as though he or she were there in person. I imprinted my stone with a message for Orgon the Wise, back on Nibiru.

"I also imprinted it with a spell I learned from the ancient books we'd just recovered: a spell to sustain the last Dragon eggs on Nibiru until I could be there myself, to cast off the hex forever. In my message to Orgon, I asked him to place the stone among the precious eggs, all gathered in their safe Nursery Chamber. There it will chant the spell of sustainment, over and over until I arrive.

"I gave the stone to Ahimoth. He was to entrust it to your parents, to carry through the tube-chute and deliver to Orgon. But now we know your parents have only just begun the journey to Nibiru. That means the stone will not be in Orgon's hands until tomorrow. I fear by then it may be too late!" Celine fell silent, despondent. Fianna's look echoed her Companion's despair.

"There is no need for sadness, my rescuers," announced Ahimoth. "The stone is already on Nibiru, and I am certain the Old Wise One has followed your instructions with meticulous care. I have no doubt the eggs are safe, awaiting your return."

"What? But...how??" exclaimed both Fianna and Celine—in perfect unison and tonal harmony, a phenomenon quite common with Dragon-Companion pairs.

"I shall begin at the point we parted ways—that is, when I began my flight to Scotland. I had only been flying a short while when I was struck by a premonition that the two of you were in desperate danger. I felt compelled to abandon my journey and return at once to Germany. I knew I must *not* do so, but the feeling tormented me and grew more urgent with each passing minute. Twice I could bear it no longer, and turned back toward Germany. But, each time, the urgency of Celine's request made me turn once again toward Scotland and Loch Ness.

"When I arrived, I was devastated to learn that our parents were not yet ready to enter the vortex and return to Nibiru. They were still too ill and weakened from their recent ordeal. What was I to do? The stone must be delivered to Orgon with all speed, yet it might be days before our parents could carry it to him. And all the time, I was besieged by the dire need to return to Germany.

"I explained my plight to Nessie, and together we devised a plan. She and her Water-Dragon clan would open the vortex, and we would send the comm stone, with its precious message, through the tube-chute to Orgon on its own—ahead of our parents. We placed the stone in a small, sturdy case to keep it safe. We attached a note, saying the case must be delivered to Orgon at once, and that he and he alone must open it—immediately.

"The Water Dragons worked their magic. The vortex opened, and Nessie propelled the case toward it. It entered and was swallowed in a flash of liquid light. Nessie assured me the case would arrive safely on Nibiru before a full day had passed, and that it would be delivered safely and at once to Orgon.

"With the comm stone safely on its way, and our parents in Nessie's tender care, I made my goodbyes and took to the air once more, flying harder than ever I can recall."

"Oh, thank the Ancients!" gasped Celine and Fianna—in unison yet again. Celine *was* immeasurably relieved, but shot Ahimoth a look that told all too clearly how she felt about his failure to mention any of this sooner.

"I had no idea you could send objects through on their own," said Celine. "It's wonderful, but I'm still dreadfully worried. We've got to get to Nibiru ourselves, fast. I have no idea how long the comm stone's chanting will protect the eggs."

"Have faith, dear friend. We will arrive in time," said Fianna, nuzzling her. "I know we will. I feel it in my bones, and Dragon bones are seldom wrong. And do remember: Positive thoughts and emotions are ever superior to negative."

Now she turned to her brother. "Ahimoth, I am forever grateful you rescued us, but are you certain you are able to continue flying?"

"Yes, Fianna," laughed Ahimoth, "quite certain."

Celine was still a trifle peeved at the big black Dragon, but had to admit his solution had worked out handsomely. And if he had done anything else, where would they be now? He was the hero of the hour, and he'd earned some rest.

As the Nibiru prince and princess talked on, Celine repacked the items she'd used in treating Ahimoth's wounds, and reflected on the trio's current circumstances.

A loud laugh from the Dragons popped the girl out of her reverie. Seeing Celine look their way, Ahimoth addressed her. "Fianna was just complimenting me on my little warning voice—the premonition I had about returning to Germany quickly." A toothsome Dragon grin lit his noble face.

"Yes, that little inner voice of yours has proved helpful more than once," said the teen, with a wry smile. Her annoyance with the black Dragon had faded nearly away.

"Mmmmmm," Ahimoth rumbled. "Celine, I must tell you that your magic is strong. It has been only minutes since you tended my hurts, yet already I feel greatly restored." Rising to his full height, he unfurled and fanned his space-black wings. Powerful gusts blasted the area with each downstroke, hurling debris in all directions and churning up a thick cloud of dust. "I shall no doubt fly at speed again, and soon. I thank you!"

Shielding her face from the mini-gales and nearly choked by flying dust, Celine laughed. "You're welcome," she managed to croak, "I think!"

In minutes, the three were in the air again, driving toward Britain, keeping to cloud cover, where there was any to be had. Celine held silent as they flew, knowing the Dragons were menting non-stop. Not wanting to eavesdrop, the chestnut-haired girl closed her mind to her friend. Still, she maintained her healing and bubble spells; she would take no chances about Ahimoth reaching the Chalice Well.

She called West occasionally, to update the Mentor on their progress and reassure her of their safety. Were she to be honest with herself, though, her purpose was more to seek news of Jager. Sadly, there was none; her heart ached.

Celine also consulted the Mentor about the plan to use

the Chalice Well, rather than going directly to Loch Ness and then on to Nibiru. After all, the Water Dragons had managed to keep Fianna's parents hidden and safe.

West acknowledged the merit of the girl's question, but pointed out that Soader and the Brothers had somehow known exactly where to find her and Fianna, more than once in the past several days. This suggested some means of tracking—and the possibility that they could still track the trio to Loch Ness and ambush them. A stop at Glastonbury would not arouse the evil ones' suspicions, so escape through the Chalice Well still seemed the best option. Celine agreed, and the trio flew on.

Hours later, the three broke down through the cloud deck, low above the night-shrouded English countryside. They preferred night-time travel, not wanting to be seen by Earthlings. Even now, they returned to the cool, covering mist of the clouds as soon as they'd spotted enough landmarks to be sure of their location. Appearing so near the ground was a risk they had to take; there was no time to waste on diversions around populated areas. They must reach the Well quickly and get off the planet, until they could be certain it was safe to return.

"It's just a little farther, Fianna," Celine mented. "Are you two still doing all right?"

"My brother is weary and weak, but says he can continue a while longer," replied Fianna. They flew on in silence, too tired for talk. A few minutes later, Celine signaled Fianna to dip below the clouds once more. She guessed they should now be within sight of the relic tower on Glastonbury Tor— the landmark Father Greer had given them. All three were relieved to see the centuries-old tower below, barely visible in the pre-dawn darkness.

CHAPTER 4

Into the Well

At the foot of Glastonbury Tor lay a small stone farm-house and wooden barn, fronting on a tidy farmyard and adjoined by a low livestock pen. The Dragons tipped their wings and descended in a wide, graceful arc. As they approached, a man appeared from the cottage, holding a lantern aloft. A young lad followed at his heels.

"That must be Father Sinclair," said Celine. Advancing to the middle of the yard, the man waved the lantern in welcome, as though the arrival of flying Dragons was business as usual.

The Dragons came to Earth some ten paces from their hosts. Each gave a huff of relief as they touched down, then tucked up their weary wings.

Celine climbed stiffly from the saddle. Hoping their hosts wouldn't think her rude, she stretched elaborately. Marvelous though Dragon flight always was, it was delicious to be back on solid ground.

While the Dragons waited in patient silence, Celine collected herself and approached the gentleman and his young apprentice. The priest was advanced in age; he wore a voice translator similar to Father Greer's, fastened at his throat. "Hello, Father. I am Celine Zulak, and these are my friends, Fianna and Ahimoth. Father Greer sends his greetings. He said he would explain our situation to you, and that you may be able to help us."

"Welcome, Celine, Fianna and Ahimoth," said Father Sinclair, his voice unexpectedly deep and steady for one so elderly. "Yes, Father Greer has told me of your plight, and I will indeed be glad to help you as I may. Time is short, though; we must make haste.

"Food and drink await you in the barn. I would rather serve you in my home, but it hasn't room for such a company, as you can see!" He smiled, gesturing toward the tiny farmhouse. "My animal friends will help welcome you, though, and we can talk while you refresh yourselves."

As the tired travelers ate, Father Sinclair described the Chalice Well and explained its workings. His last words, however, worried Celine.

"Thank you, Father. I'm terribly concerned, though. You just explained the correct magic must be used, or the Well may fail, possibly with disastrous results. We cannot risk that. Too much is at stake!"

"I understand your concern, child, but do not fear. I am Master of the Chalice Well and skilled in its magic. My clan has passed the Well's secrets through centuries, and I will work them to see you safely on your way."

Celine relaxed at the priest's firm assurance, as did her

Dragon companions.

The old man went on: "The Well was designed and placed here to provide safe transport for its builders—and to prevent persons of ill intent from invading their safe havens.

"I see you have finished your meal. Are you prepared now to make the journey, or need you more rest before travelling the Well?"

"Rest would be wonderful, but I feel we should leave at once," replied Celine, looking to the Dragons for agreement. Both nodded earnestly.

"Very well," said the priest. "I believe that a sound decision. Let us proceed.

"First, there is something you must have." Reaching into his tunic, he produced a ball of wound black cloth, about the size of a plum. He carefully unwound the fabric to reveal a smooth, white, oval-shaped stone. "This is the Egg," the elder explained. "Simple though it may appear, it is a potent signaling device, precisely tuned. You may use it to contact any Pleiadean ship or station within a system's span of your arrival point. Enemies who may be in the area will not detect your call."

"Thank you, Father," replied the girl, accepting the stone from the man's gnarled fingers. She examined it closely as the old priest explained how to use it, then slipped it into a pocket inside her well-worn uniform tunic and secured the pocket's closure.

She exchanged looks with the Dragons; the time had come—they all sensed it was urgent they leave Earth quickly. They followed the priest out to the farmyard, then along a path toward a rock-rimmed pool of water, oddly red-brown in hue: the Chalice Well. It looked utterly unremarkable, but each of the travelers knew quite well how deceptive appearances could be.

Suddenly, Celine froze, struck by a chilling realization.

"Father Sinclair," she began, her emotions a buzzing, bewildering mix of fear and annoyance: annoyance at her own foolishness, and the priest's apparent omission of a crucial detail. "Perhaps I missed it in my eagerness to be on our way, but I don't recall where you said the Well will take us!"

"Mm, yes," replied the priest. "That, child, I do not know."

Shocked yet again, Celine could only open her mouth, then close it. No words would come.

"Again I must counsel you, Celine—you need not worry. The lore and history of the Well, as handed down from generation to generation, does not include any means of predicting where it will carry those who enter its waters. All we are given to know with certainty is that the Well is unfailing in its choice of the destination that is *necessary*."

Celine was silent for a time, considering the priest's words. Ahimoth and Fianna looked on, their polite outward manner concealing inner turmoil.

Finally, Celine's expression coalesced into one of calm resolve. "All right. If that is what the Ancients, in their wisdom, have handed down to us, we have no sensible option but to have faith, and to act."

Seeing their human friend's certain composure, the Dragons shrugged off their own worries. Turning toward her friends, Celine was relieved to see that they too were now resolved to act.

"Thank you, Father," she said. "Now we must go—and quickly! I sense someone approaching!"

Father Sinclair stepped to the side of the Well. "I will now begin to chant," he announced, "speaking the incantation to activate the Well. After several stanzas, you will hear a distinct pause. At that moment, the first of you—you, Celine—must enter the Well.

"Step boldly in. Do not hesitate. Step first onto the ledge you see here, just beneath the surface. Then step directly out toward the center of the pool. You will sink beneath its surface and descend for but a moment; then the Well will transport you to the destination it has chosen. As this takes place, I will continue my chant.

"Fianna, as soon as Celine's head has passed beneath the water's surface, take your position in the spot where she now stands. Soon you will hear the same pause in the chant; at that moment, you must do just as Celine did: Step first on the ledge, then straight out toward the Well's center. I realize this will be more difficult for you, owing to your size and bodily form, but have no fear. The Well will accommodate you. It will help you and keep you safe. It *lives* to help those who come to it in honest need and pure purpose.

"Ahimoth, you must follow Fianna in the same way she follows Celine. Step to the edge, await the pause in my chanting, then step into the pool—first on the ledge, then toward the center.

"I will continue my chant until you have all passed into the Well. From there, I can do no more. But I need not; you will be in the care of the Well, and the Ancients who give it power.

"Now, remember this, all of you: *Wherever* the Well may take you, it will be the *necessary* place. *Whatever* may befall you when you arrive there, seem it good or ill in the moment, it will be what is *necessary*—necessary to carry you toward fulfillment of your purpose. Your purpose is good, just and honest. Therefore, the Well shall not fail you."

The three companions nodded their solemn understanding. Celine took a moment to check the straps holding the packs and saddle snug to Fianna's graceful back. Then, with a loving smile—first at the white Dragon, then at the black—she stepped to the edge of the Well.

The priest had just uttered the first words of his incantation when Ahimoth cried out in alarm: "Look!" He pointed a foreclaw skyward; an enormous ship was breaking through the high cloud cover, descending toward them. Celine and Fianna gasped, eyes wide. The priest seemed oddly unconcerned.

Celine was the first to shake off this new shock. "Begin your chant, Father! Quickly, *please!*"

The old priest needed no further urging. Taking a steady stance, he began to chant. His resonant voice carried calm certainty, and the power of his purpose.

Tense with anticipation, Celine followed the chant, word by word, phrase by phrase, waiting for the pause the priest had promised.

Fianna, watching intently, broke her concentration for no more than a second to steal a look upward at the huge vessel, still bearing down upon them. "By the Ancients!" she thought, "we must *hurry!*"

Finally, there came a break in the old priest's chant. Celine stepped forward and down onto the ledge, just below the surface of the oddly colored water. With no hesitation, she brought up her right foot, out toward the center of the placid pool. Leaning ahead, she felt herself falling smoothly forward and downward—slowly, slowly, as though time itself were slipping into the waiting waters with her. Despite the evening's chill, the water was comfortingly warm as it rose almost languidly up to envelop her waist, then her torso, then her face, then...

THE INSTANT CELINE'S HEAD disappeared beneath the surface, Fianna stepped to the edge of the Well. Soon she heard the pause in the chant, stepped down onto the ledge and then outward. Just as the priest had counselled, the water seemed to help her—guiding the greater bulk of her Dragon's body and easing it into its depths...

BEFORE FIANNA HAD FULLY entered the pool, Ahimoth hurried to its side, ready for his turn. Glancing upward, he saw that the great craft was still descending, but judged it still to be a few thousand meters up. There would be plenty of time before it could arrive. He tensed, waiting for the pause in the old man's chant. It came, and the Dragon stepped forward. Misjudging the width of the ledge, his forefoot slipped, and he nearly stumbled headlong into the pool. But, just as it had assisted Celine and Fianna, the water itself seemed to catch and steady the great black creature, allowing him to recover his balance and continue smoothly out, down, in, and...

WITH HIS THREE GUESTS safe in the care of his beloved Well, Father Sinclair voiced his chant's final phrases and then fell silent. He smiled at the calm waters—the Well showed not even a ripple to mark the passage of the three beings it had just conveyed.

Looking skyward, he saw the enormous craft had halted its decent, a few hundred meters up. It hovered for a few seconds, then rose, heading back to space the way it had come. The old priest nodded, as if the ship had behaved exactly as expected. He watched the craft out of sight, then nodded again and turned happily toward his humble home, satisfied with his night's good work.

CHAPTER 5

Malfunction

Completely immersed in the Well's waters, Celine felt supremely comfortable, utterly at ease, body and spirit buoyed in warm tranquility. It was as though the severe tension and urgency of the last hour had never been. She felt suspended—not just in gentle liquid, but in time as well.

When Father Sinclair had described the Well and its workings, she had wondered if she would be able to hold her breath until she emerged from the mystic waters. Since the priest hadn't mentioned this detail, she assumed it wouldn't be a problem. Still, in the last moments before stepping into the pool, she had taken several deep breaths. Since that time, though, she'd given no thought at all to breathing, and had no slightest urge to breathe now. And, though the Well was presumably transporting her...somewhere, she had no sensation of motion.

Suddenly, the liquid tranquility ended. With a sharp jolt,

the sensation of floating suspension was gone. She was dumped—apparently from a height of half a meter or so—onto a cold, metallic surface.

Bright, artificial light blazed down from overhead fixtures; harsh, machine-processed air assaulted her nose and throat. Disoriented at first, she quickly found her bearings, sprang to her feet and began to assess the scene.

She stood on a circular platform, perhaps fifteen meters across and raised a dozen centimeters above the surrounding floor. She guessed this must be some sort of workshop or hangar, in a military or industrial installation.

"Now—the Dragons!" she thought. Where were they? Had they made it into the Well? If so, why weren't they here yet? Had it sent them someplace else?

An instant later, she received an answer. Fianna's white form appeared in mid-air, a half-meter above the platform and a few meters away. The Dragon fell at once to the floor with a sickening thud—and lay deathly still.

Celine called out to her precious friend, both aloud and mentally. No response. Rushing to the Dragon's side, the girl checked the neck for a pulse. It was there, but alarmingly weak. Fianna was breathing—barely. The worst sign of all was the near-total blank Celine encountered when she attempted mental contact. Something must be terribly, terribly wrong.

Though well trained in human first aid and emergency management, Celine had no idea how to assist a Dragon in such grave distress. What could she do?! In one way, though, her emergency training served her well: she did not panic, or collapse into useless despair. Instead, she was all business—serious, focused business. She examined the room again, looking for anything that might offer help.

She had scanned about half the area when there came another loud thud behind her. Wheeling around, she saw Ahimoth's black bulk, lying on the platform and as sickeningly still as his sister. Now she had two Dragons to rescue. And still no resources in sight. If she didn't find something soon, she would have to adapt human rescue techniques to the creatures.

Resuming her scan, her eyes fell on a welcome sight. A human! Standing in a doorway some ten meters away was a rather short, slight person, dressed in a jumpsuit of vaguely military style. His head seemed too large for his body, his hands were oddly paw-like, and his upper back was slightly humped, but he was clearly human. Or human*oid*, at least. By his bearing and features, she assumed him to be male. He stared at her, transfixed. Clearly, she was the last thing he'd expected to find here. Then, out of the corner of his eye, he caught a glimpse of Fianna, lying to Celine's left. And, not far from her, Ahimoth. His eyes went even wider, his jaw plunked nearly to his narrow chest, and he let out a long, low moan of disbelief.

"You there!" called Celine. "Please help! My friends need help!"

Montgomery had been stationed here—Transfer Station 428, in the south-eastern quadrant of Luna's spaceward side—for decades. In all that time, he'd never seen anything arrive on this platform—Platform 9. He had no idea why it went unused, but there had been none of the usual traffic. No souls, packaged for transfer. No bodies. And, by all the Gods and Goddesses, no *Dragons!*

"This can't be happening," he thought. Pulling open a lapel, he stared at the metal flask protruding from an inside pocket. The flask he was (mistakenly) sure his superior knew nothing about. "Okay," he announced to the universe in general, "no one can say I don't know when I've had enough." Gingerly extracting the flask, he held it at arm's length, as though it carried some dread disease. With his free hand, he plucked a grease-smeared rag from a hip pocket, draped it over the flask and unscrewed the cap. With a shudder, he walked the few steps to a waste bin, upended the flask and poured out the liquid it held. He peered at the empty flask for a few moments, then dropped it in to join its erstwhile contents.

Hoping desperately this unprecedented and profoundly virtuous act had broken the hex—since all of this *must* be a hex or curse or other cosmic punishment, meted out by the Gods for his many sins—he turned timidly round to face the platform again, hoping to find it mercifully empty.

No such luck. The girl was still there, as real could be. Fists on hips, glaring at him. And..yes. The Dragons were still there, too. One black, one white, both huge, both...*Dragons.* He took tiny comfort in the fact that they were very *still* Dragons.

Impatient, but not wanting to scare off a possible source of aid, Celine calmed herself and gently broke in on Monty's miserable musings: "Sir, please. My friends are hurt. Can you help us?!"

"Ahhh...b-buhh...mmmmm...," Monty offered.

"I see," said Celine, with all the patience she could muster. "Well then, could you tell me where we are?"

"Ahhh...buhh...TS. T-TS 428!" Monty stammered.

"TS? Oh! TS! A soul transfer station—is that right?" Celine ventured.

"Right!" Monty beamed, proud to be so extraordinarily helpful. "Transfer Station 428. Earth. Planet 444. Er, rather, Earth's moon. Spaceward side. You know—the side the Earthers never see. Unless they come up here, of course, but they mostly don't, you see, because it's..."

"Thank you. Thank you," Celine gently interrupted, with her most grateful smile. She turned her total attention to calling her Mentor.

"West! Please, West—are you there?"

"Yes, child. I am here," the Mentor assured. "What is your location? Are you safe? And what of Fianna and Ahimoth?"

"Oh, thank the Ancients. Yes—yes; I'm okay. But Fianna and Ahimoth—there's something dreadfully wrong with them. Must have been damaged by the Well, somehow. I think they're nearly dead, and I don't know how to help them. Can you come? Can you help them?"

"Certainly, Celine. You need only tell me where to find you."

"Oh. Right. We're on the Earth's moon. In a transfer station. TS 428. Oh, please come quickly. They can't die!"

"Thank you, child," soothed the Mentor. "We will be there as quickly as we may. Now calm yourself and stay close to your friends. Talk to them, reassure them. Though they may seem not to hear, your loving presence will sustain them until we arrive."

"I will. I will. Thank you, West. And please—hurry!"

The girl rushed to Fianna's side, dropped to her knees and embraced the noble creature's snowy neck, speaking reassurances in the most calmly confident tones she could muster. Then, assuring her friend she would be back momentarily, she rushed to the black Dragon to tell him the same. After a few trips back and forth, repeating her reassurances, she slumped against Fianna's flank for a few moments' rest.

It was only then that Celine noticed a new oddity: she was dry. So were the Dragons. Though they had all been completely immersed in the Well's mystic waters just minutes before, they had arrived quite dry. "Hmm. Another puzzle," she thought, ever curious about the ways of magic. "It will have to wait, though."

Through all of this, Montgomery remained where he was, frozen in amazement and uncertainty. What should he do? He didn't want to sound any alarms; that would just attract unwanted attention from Richter, the ill-tempered station boss. Richter despised him enough already; if he brought any of this up, he'd only be handing the big sociopath a fresh justification for making life miserable. And if this impossible situation were discovered, word of it was sure to reach Soader—a dozen times worse than Richter. No, he had to keep all this quiet, and find some way to get the strange arrivals the hells out of here, fast and undetected.

Wait, though. Maybe he was still just hallucinating! Ah, yes. That *could* be it! Ha. That home-made gin in the flask was the last of a really, really nasty batch. Maybe all this *was* just a worlds-class case of the deliriums. That *had* to be it. Had to!

Drawing a deep breath, he tucked chin tightly to chest, crossed all available fingers, muttered a brief prayer (just to cover *all* the angles), clenched his eyes tight shut, and waited—repeating the prayer again, twice over, for good measure.

A full minute later, figuring he'd given his clever rite ample time to do its work, Monty slowly, cautiously opened his eyes—just a slit!—and peered out toward Platform 9, hoping desperately to find it empty.

No!

Oh, no, no, no, no, *no.*

There they were. Still. Girl, Dragon and Dragon. Just as they had been.

So, it *wasn't* the gin.

A new moan escaped him, even longer and more despairing than before.

CHAPTER 6

A Voice from Afar

A week had passed since Fianna and her Companion, Celine, had travelled the wormhole tube-chute from Nibiru to Earth. Each day, Fianna's uncle and aunt—Orgon the Wise and his wife Tamar—had taken turns keeping vigil here, beside the tube-chute's Nibiru terminus at Dragon Hall.

Because the tube-chute was not active, the terminus was closed, and hidden by a cloaking spell. At the spot where the terminus—or vortex, as it was commonly known—would appear, there seemed to be only a sheer rock face, a natural section of the walls that formed Dragon Hall's grand courtyard. The only feature to distinguish the spot was a trickle of water—also an illusion: a feeble rivulet falling from a crack at the wall's upper edge. It stained the red-brown rock a darker hue, with cheery little patches of green moss here and there along its course.

One morning, as Orgon settled in to begin a new day's vigil, the false wall and trickle suddenly vanished, revealing what lay behind: a tall, V-shaped cleft, extending a couple of meters back into the real wall's face. Adorning the center of the cleft was a spritely waterfall, plunging from the heights above to churn and froth in a deep pool, before passing on down beneath the cliffs as an underground stream.

Tamar, about to depart the courtyard to rest after her night's watch, heard Orgon cry out in joy. Wheeling about, she saw the reason for his jubilation and rushed to his side. They waited eagerly for what they knew would come next.

First, a small, bright point of light appeared in mid-air, in front of the falling stream and at Dragon's-eye level. At once the dazzling point began to expand into an opalescent, mid-air whirlpool, filled with sparkling, flashing flecks, bubbles and bursts of color in every imaginable hue. The whirlpool—a virtual vortex of liquid light and color—grew steadily until, with a loud pop, it reached its full extent: nearly five meters across, and utterly dazzling to behold. It appeared to be the open end of a tube or tunnel of some sort, though there was no way to discern its depth or extent. In fact, it was an interdimensional passageway, defying the simple senses of creatures accustomed to living in a seemingly solid "here" and "now." This was the tube-chute vortex, the portal Fianna and Celine had entered just a week before, for their journey to Earth. Now it would be bringing them home! Orgon and Tamar watched and waited for nearly half a minute in breathless anticipation. Others who'd heard the vortex open began gathering too, fanning out on either side of the elder Dragons, watching and waiting.

To the Dragons' amazement, though, neither Dragon nor Human emerged from the vortex. Instead, it was a simple object. A small box. It shot straight out of the vortex's mouth, narrowly missing Orgon's left horn. Sailing across the courtyard, it arced down to hit the floor and slid to a stop at the foot of the Cynth Pedestal.

A collective gasp went up as the box came to rest.

Shaking off his surprise, Orgon turned and made his way to the pedestal. Raising a great, green wing, he gave a commanding "Hush!" to quiet the clamoring crowd.

He gingerly picked up the box, inspected it closely, and, discovering its simple but secure latch, carefully opened it.

Inside, nestled in soft felt fabric, shone a small, oval-shaped crystalline stone, beautifully polished and seeming to glow with an inner light. After gazing at the mysterious crystal for a few moments, he held the box out and swept it in a slow arc, so the gathered Dragons could catch a glimpse of the contents. Then he turned back to the pedestal and tenderly placed the open box in the center of its smooth upper platform.

Stirred to action by the Cynth Pedestal's energy field, the stone came to life. For several seconds, it glowed with a soft, lilac light. Then, to everyone's fresh astonishment, it began to speak—in Celine's voice, strong and clear!

"O, wise Orgon, uncle to my precious Fianna," said Celine, "I have much news. There is no time to relay it all, but here is the most important thing: Your princess and I have recovered the ancient Spell Books of Atlantis."

The crowd erupted in joyous cheering.

"Quiet! Please, quiet!" bellowed Orgon. "The message continues!"

"Fianna and I were injured after finding the Books," the stone continued, "but please do not worry—we are recovering rapidly and soon will travel the tube-chute home to you."

The stone was silent for a few moments; the swelling crowd was anything but. Thinking the message complete, they resumed their dancing and shouting. Even stately Orgon and Tamar joined in. Suddenly, someone dancing near the pedestal heard the stone begin to speak again, and gave a great roar—"Silence, all! It speaks again!" The jubilant throng was silent in a heartbeat, straining to hear.

"Wise Orgon," the stone had begun. "This stone carries one more message, more important than the first. I have recorded an incantation to protect the remaining eggs until we arrive with the Books, and the spell to break the horrid hex.

"I ask you to place the stone in the Nursery Chamber; set it high, so my voice can be heard to the farthest corners. When you have done this, speak three times the word, 'Commence.' The stone will recite the protective spell, repeating it over and over again until we return. Keep a small lamp or light orb close to the stone, always lighted. Its warmth will provide enough energy to keep the stone speaking indefinitely."

The gathered Dragons were speechless with wonder. Orgon took up the box and made his way toward the courtyard's exit, bound for the deep chamber where the last of his race's living eggs were guarded. Tamar and the crowd followed solemnly behind.

Coming at last to the Nursery Chamber, deep in the heart of the Dragon Hall's mountain home, Orgon paused. Only Tamar was with him now; the other Dragons had stopped to wait at the tunnel entry's guarded gate.

He called out to Lye, the Nanny keeping watch over the

eggs. Lye responded, and the two exchanged the ritual greetings, entreaties and responses required by ancient tradition before anyone, regardless of station or stature, could be admitted to the sacred chamber. At last, the rite completed, Lye bowed deeply as Orgon and Tamar entered.

There, in the soft light of the glowing orbs that ringed the chamber walls, rested the eggs. Each with a slightly different hue, each nestled on its own deep, soft, indigo cushion. Advancing to one of the shallow shelves that bore the many light orbs, Orgon carefully set the box and its crystalline purple stone next to the glowing sphere—near enough that the orb would keep the stone gently warm.

Turning, he met Lye's eyes, then his cherished Tamar's; then he focused on the stone once more. After a moment's silent contemplation, Orgon spoke.

"Commence. Commence. Commence!"

Filling the chamber, firm and full, Celine's voice began to chant…

CHAPTER 7

Transfer Station

Celine scanned the area for any threat. Safe for the moment, she drew her incant-baton from its sleeve in her bodypack and set to work casting healing spells over her Dragon companions. She *must* keep them alive until the Mentors arrived.

She completed the spells; both Dragons seemed to be breathing more evenly. Satisfied for the moment, she unlocked and unsealed the crate to check on the eggs. She sighed relief to see all were intact; she had arranged their cushioning well.

Next, she brought out her spell book and began to leaf through, searching for the far more potent invocation she'd have to attempt over the imperiled Dragons—without West's guidance and support—if the Mentors didn't arrive soon. She shuddered at the thought.

At last she found the spell she sought. Her heart sank at its complexity and demands: Perfect timing. Flawless intonation. Unwavering mindset and focus. Such was its power that a single misstep or hesitance might kill her precious friends. And herself along with them. All they had been through would come to nothing, and the Nibiru Dragon race would be lost.

West just *had* to come soon!

She rested her head on Fianna's faintly quivering foreleg and resumed chanting her first spell of healing. Maybe keeping it fresh and potent could buy them a bit more time. Somehow, she had managed to hold back tears, but now they welled up again and wouldn't be denied.

Suddenly there came the voice she'd awaited so desperately. "Celine. Child, we are here." There were no physical forms to be seen—the Mentors had come without bodies, as was their usual custom—yet Celine could sense their presence.

"Oh! Thank you! Thank you for coming!"

"Certainly. Now let us tend to Fianna and Ahimoth."

"Yes, please! They seem so far gone. Barely breathing, and they don't respond at all. I cast healing spells over them, but I'm so worried they may die..." She broke down in fresh sobs.

"Calm, child. Calm and peace. They shall survive," West soothed. "They are strong, stronger than you may know. Yet they need your strength as well.

"You have done well in making your magic over them. You no doubt saved their lives. Now let us bring a deeper power to bear."

Recovering a measure of composure, Celine responded, "I've found the spell I think we should use." She flashed a mental image of the one she'd chosen. "Is that the right one?"

"Yes, Celine," West replied. "You have chosen well and wisely. We will support you in its wielding—though in truth I am confident you could perform the task without us."

Celine blushed at the affirmation, but wished she felt the same confidence.

"Now, before we begin, there are preparations to be made," continued West. Celine nodded, and the Mentor went on. "First, move the eggs from the platform to a safer place. Keep an eye on the person by the door as you do this, and through the rest of your preparations. I sense no harm in him, but better to be vigilant just the same."

Celine re-sealed the crate, carried it to one side of the room and set it beside a group of larger containers. She glanced at Monty a time or two as she worked. He'd remained where he had first appeared, watching her with interest between wary glances at the Dragons.

"Good," West acknowledged, when Celine had secured the eggs. She gave Celine a new task, then another and another, thanking her as she completed each one.

As she worked, Celine was increasingly aware that she too must have been injured in the passage through the Chalice Well. But it had *seemed* so smooth and peaceful! Maybe all the strains and batterings of the past week were just catching up with her. In any case, she had quite a collection of aches and sharper pains, and they weren't going away. She shoved them out of mind, though, and carried on with her assignments.

She made a ring of white candles around the two Dragons—or as close to a ring as could be managed, with the small collection of candles in her bodypack. Next, Celine lit the first candle she'd placed, and said a brief invocation while sprinkling a pinch of powder—dried oak leaves and rosehips—over its flickering flame. After repeating the rite with each candle, she made a second circle—this one of small, translucent crystals—inside the boundary created by the candle ring. Next, she placed a pair of larger crystals on each Dragon's forehead: a white apophyllite healing stone, and a black epidote earth stone, which she'd been taught would assist in opening the third eye. Both crystals were meant to promote the flow of healing energy to the creatures' failing hearts.

West had then directed her to place a single white Lemurian seed crystal before each Dragon's snout. Rare and potent, their purpose was to enable and enhance a being's present-time access to past-lifetime knowledge and experience.

Finally, Celine placed a treasured talisman beside the Lemurian crystals—one talisman before each Dragon: In front of Ahimoth, her five-pointed star medallion of cherry wood and copper; before Fianna, her necklace bearing a carved white Dragon. As she gently placed each talisman, she kissed it and whispered a fervent invocation.

With all the preparations complete, Celine stepped off the platform. After a quick glance at Montgomery—still rooted to the same spot and watching with obvious fascination—she turned to face the Dragons once more.

"Beautifully done, child," said West. "Thank you. And now we shall begin. You know the words of power. Please commence, and lead us all."

Both humbled and amazed by the honor the Mentor had bestowed, Celine began the chant; the four Mentors joined in at once, sounding just as Celine imagined angels must.

Mother Dragon of the light
Father Dragon of the night
Your children suffer
The black, the white
Please aid our friends
In their deep, dire plight

The power of the light
The power of the right
Your children suffer
The good, the bright
Please heal our friends
And their souls set aright

The five continued their chanting until the candles were spent, and the last wisps of scented smoke spiraled upward.

Celine watched over the Dragons closely, noting every twitch and moan. Occasionally she took a quick glance at the strange little humpbacked man; he remained transfixed.

After a time, Fianna began to stir. "Fianna? Fianna?" called Celine softly, not wanting to jar or startle her friend. She knelt at the Dragon's side and asked aloud, "Can you hear me?"

"Y-yes, Little One," answered Fianna, her voice scarcely more than a whisper. She opened her eyes slightly and raised her head for a better look at her beloved Companion. "Ahimoth? My brother—is he here?"

"Yes, he's here beside you," said Celine, gesturing toward

the black Dragon. "Somehow, you were both gravely injured in our passage through the Chalice Well. By the grace of the Ancients, you are both still alive, but Ahimoth isn't yet conscious. He is breathing comfortably, though, and his worst distress seems to have passed. You'll both need more attention, but it appears you're at least out of danger."

"Thank you. Thank you," said Fianna, her voice stronger now. She lifted and turned her head to look at her brother. Just as she did so, Ahimoth stirred, raised his head slightly and opened his gold-and-ebon eyes. Celine breathed a great sigh of relief, and Fianna smiled.

Hearing Fianna begin a mental conversation with her brother, Celine turned her attention to West and the other Mentors. "I couldn't possibly thank you enough." Tears welled up and spilled down her face, but now they were tears of happiness and relief. "I don't know what I'd have done if you hadn't arrived. I can't imagine life without Fianna!" She slumped wearily to sit beside the platform. She was exhausted, and her injuries were wearing on her.

"You are welcome, Celine," replied West. "Both have been gravely injured, but I believe they will recover well. Their injuries make it clear that someone has interfered with the Chalice Well and its workings. This must be set right, but that is a task for another time. At the present, we must transport the three of you to a place of safety, where the Dragons may receive proper care.

"Despite its malfunctioning, the Well brought you to this transbeam platform. We will use the platform to transport you to our Mars outpost. The platform is of sufficient capacity to span such a distance—unlike any ship-born unit. Medical care can be had at the outpost, so that your recoveries may be swift. They must be, for the sake of Nibiru.

"Would you please tell Fianna of our plans?" West continued. "You may assure her that the transbeam will not harm her, or her brother. It is a reliable mechanism, and we know that it has not been compromised, as was the Chalice Well."

"Of course—and thank you again, West," replied Celine. She could hear Fianna and Ahimoth were still deep in conversation, and didn't want to interrupt. They must get to Mars though, and quickly. So much depended on it. And until the Dragons were in good hands on Mars, she couldn't give her full attention to locating Jager. She was going crazy with worry about him.

"Fianna, I am sorry for being so ill-mannered, but I must interrupt," Celine began. "The Chalice Well brought us to a Transfer Station on Earth's moon—Luna. There is a transbeam platform here. In fact, we're on it right now. West and her sisters will use the platform to transport us to the Mentors' outpost station on Mars. There are medical facilities there, where you and Ahimoth can be cared for and recover. We must get there quickly, for both your sakes, and for the sake of our mission. We can't risk travel to Nibiru until you are strong enough to use the tube-chute. West also wants me to assure you the transbeam is safe. It will not harm either of you, as the Chalice Well did. Do you understand?"

"Yes, yes, my Companion. I understand, and I thank you and your Mentor friends. If you have faith the mechanism is safe, I have no fear. I will tell Ahimoth of the plan. But I sense you intend to search for Jager while we are being cared for. I beg you not to attempt this alone. We have no idea where Soader and his mutant brute may be. It is also likely they are in the same place as Jager. I must insist on accompanying you in your quest. Please promise me you will wait, my Companion."

"I understand, and I won't go off looking for him without you," Celine assured the Dragon. "But please—we must hurry!"

"Certainly, Little One." Fianna turned her attention to her brother, while Celine looked on. Moments later, the Dragon turned again to Celine. "Ahimoth understands, and thanks you and the Mentors. We are ready for the journey. What must we do?"

"Just stay where you are, and rest. I'll get everything ready and then tell West we're set to go." She quickly gathered her belongings, brought the crate of eggs back onto the platform, and made one last scan of the area to be sure nothing had been missed. In the process, she noticed Monty, still watching. She waved and gave him a big smile. "We're leaving! Thank you for everything. I hope we didn't inconvenience you too badly!"

"Uh...no...sure! Bye!" Montgomery managed, with an uncertain wave.

Celine settled down beside Fianna, one arm across the Dragon's shoulder, one on the precious crate. "Okay, West, we're ready," she called.

Moments later, Monty found himself all alone in the transbeam chamber. "What a day. What a day," he thought, and turned to resume his duties.

Mars Outpost

The transbeam performed flawlessly, transporting Celine, Fianna and Ahimoth from Luna to Mars, some fourteen light-minutes away. The Mentors had set the 'beam to take them straight to the outpost's medical facility. Like the rest of the outpost, its design was compact and efficient, yet it was equipped and supplied for emergency care of all the sector's principal races.

"Are you all right?" Celine asked Fianna, as soon as they arrived.

"Yes," she replied, "at least, I am no worse than when we left Luna." She turned to check on her brother, lying quietly beside her. A few moments later, she announced, "Ahimoth was not troubled by the transbeam, but he still suffers badly from whatever happened in the Chalice Well."

"Please do not worry, Fianna," came West's mental voice. "Tell Ahimoth we shall care for you both."

Two beings approached the trio. Humanoid in form, they were cloaked in white gowns of a shimmering, satiny fabric. Their heads and faces were veiled in a diaphanous material that glittered slightly with silver- and gold-hued flecks. They moved with exquisite grace, seeming to float down the corridor toward the open medical bay. It was Celine's first meeting—physical meeting—with Mentors. It suited them to assume bodies for their current purposes, and so they had.

Sensing Celine's unspoken question, one of the figures spoke, her voice like soothing music.

"No, child, neither of us is West, though she will join you presently."

"Please be assured that your friends will be healed, and soon," comforted the second ethereal being.

"Have you injuries to be tended?" asked the first Mentor.

"A few, but nothing serious. I'll be fine for now. I'm just concerned about my friends—and finding Jager."

"Ah, yes. Yes. I understand." The Mentor paused to look past Celine, down the corridor behind her. "But look—here is West."

Celine gasped and spun around.

Yes. There was West. It could be no one else. Her appearance was nearly indistinguishable from the first two Mentors, yet there was no mistaking the being who had guarded and guided her for so many, many years. Celine rushed to embrace her. The Mentor welcomed the girl into her arms, and the two held one another, silent, for more than a minute.

Meanwhile, the other Mentors quietly approached Fianna and Ahimoth. Murmuring reassurance, they brought their delicate hands up before them, palms upward—then raised them slightly, in a gentle lifting motion. The Dragons rose several centimeters above the floor. Neither Fianna nor Ahimoth seemed to notice they were now floating in mid-air.

Flanking the Dragons, the Mentors began walking slowly toward a room that opened off the medical facility's main space; the Dragons floated along between them. Ahimoth, still only partially conscious, let out a low moan, then wrapped his tail more closely about him; there was still no sign he was aware of what was happening. Soon the group disappeared into the large side room, and with a whisper, its broad doors slid closed behind them.

Celine turned to West with a worried frown. "Jager?" she asked.

"We have found no sign of him yet," said West. "It is most unusual. We know his energy well. There should be no difficulty locating him, yet we see nothing. It is as though he were nowhere at all. Someone has taken him; that much is certain. They took Soader and his Kerr Dragon as well. Another certainty is that they have a ship with jump-shift drive. There is no other way they could appear, disappear and travel beyond the limits of our sensing so very rapidly. Almost instantaneously. I believe your suspicion of the Brothers' involvement is correct. There is also evidence the Brothers have infiltrated G.O.D., so someone within the organization may be acting at their orders."

"Xenu!" gasped Celine in sudden realization. "Soader works for the Brothers. *And* for High Chancellor Scabbage, and—and that means G.O.D., too. They must have grabbed him, and got Jager in the bargain."

"I believe you are correct, my dear," West replied. "Now it is a matter of finding them. No known cloaking or shielding can keep them from our sight for long, so we shall find them, and we shall bring Jager to safety. Of that you may be assured."

"I believe you, West. Of course. But I'm still so terribly worried!" The girl could feel the anxiety rising again, threatening to overwhelm her.

"I understand, dear, but you need not worry. And it is in your power to quell your worries. As Jager himself would counsel you, your energies would be better spent to examine the situation, and to devise and execute a solution. Call upon your strength, calm your mind, be in the present and focus your being on the task before you. I know well that you can do this. Many are the times you have demonstrated as much."

Celine settled for a moment, seeing the wisdom of the Mentor's words. "You're right. You're right. Thank you. Emotions have their uses, but the truth is, they're ours to use, aren't they? Not the other way around. Hm! I hadn't seen it that way before."

"There is the girl I know," responded the Mentor. "Your strength, your reason and your command of yourself grow ever stronger. It is wonderful to behold."

"Thank you!" Celine beamed, proud to have earned such praise from her life-long teacher. "Now, I should tell my parents I'm okay, and what's going on. I'm sure they're even more worried than I've been! Is there a comm link I could use to call them?" She knew the Egg stone Father Sinclair had given her was a comm stone, but he had said its range was limited.

"Yes, there is a comm link, in the quarters we have prepared for you." West went silent for a moment, her gaze

distant; then she returned. "Someone will be here presently, to guide you there. Reassure your parents, rest if you wish, and then we shall tend to your injuries. There will be time for all of this, while we help your Dragon friends."

Another Mentor approached, robed and veiled in shimmering white like the others. The figure indicated a corridor to Celine's left and began toward it, motioning for Celine to follow. The girl nodded, looked once more toward the room where Ahimoth and her precious Fianna were being treated, then followed the Mentor.

CHAPTER 9

Abduction

At Major Hadgkiss's order, Peggers jump-shifted the battered *Queen Asherah* away from the skies above Germany and back to orbit above her home port on Erra. With ship and crew safe—but for the missing Ensign Jager—Hadgkiss hurried the frantic Commander Zulak off the bridge and into the ready room. Chief Medical Officer Deggers came right behind them; the moment the door closed, he administered a sedative. Soon the commander lay sprawled across a cushioned bench, snoring softly.

"Doc, make sure he gets enough to keep him out until tomorrow morning, at least," said the major. "Then have him transbeamed to his home. But do not tell his wife anything about what's happened. Just that you had to sedate him. Not a blessed thing more! I'll take care of the rest. Understood?"

"Aye, Major," Deggers nodded. "I'll need to go get some additional sedative. Also, I recommend we 'beam him directly from here, rather than taking him to the transbeam bay."

"Agreed," replied the major, musing. "We don't want the crew seeing him like this. When you come back, bring Madda; I want her to go down with you."

The medic left, returning a few minutes later. Madda followed him into the ready room. "Remember, Deggers—and this goes for you too, Madda—the commander's wife is hot-headed. She's going to demand you tell her everything. You're just to leave him in her care and return. Not a word about what happened here, or on Earth. Assure her that I'll be in contact right away, to explain everything."

"Understood, sir," acknowledged the two officers.

"Thank you both," said Hadgkiss. He flipped on the comm link, gave a brief order, then watched as Deggers, Madda and the sedated commander vanished in a flashing swirl of light.

EARLY NEXT MORNING, well before dawn, Remi Zulak stood over her sleeping husband. "Wake up, Rafael! For the Ancients' sakes, wake up." She shook him, anxious and insistent. "Major Hadgkiss is here. Come on, dear, come on—*wake up!*"

"Wh...what th...? Wh...what happened? What time is it? Hells, what's going on?" mumbled Rafael, groggy, confused and desperately dry-mouthed. He shook his head, rubbed his eyes, then sat up and looked foggily around the room. "Home? I'm at home? How the...how did I get here? What's going on?"

"Hurry, get dressed," Remi whispered curtly, "and keep it down—Mia's asleep upstairs, and we don't want her all upset."

62   LORNA J. CARLETON

"Oh, Ancients forbid!" said Rafael, wryly. He knew his wife was right, though. He loved his elder daughter, but not her penchant for drama.

"Dino says it's urgent you go with him. He'll answer all your questions. I sure as hells can't—he's hardly told me anything! Come on, he's waiting in the lounge." She huffed out of the room, leaving Rafael to fend for himself.

Muttering and grumbling, Zulak donned his uniform and made his unsteady way to the lounge. His wife was already there, arms crossed and glaring up at a somewhat uncomfortable Dino. She was clearly unsatisfied with his answers—and non-answers—about what was going on. Both men knew if she was not satisfied soon, she'd go over their heads. She had lofty connections, and no fear of using them. She'd done it before.

"Commander, we're to report to Admiral Stock. There's been an incident," said Dino. He turned back to Remi. "Thanks for getting him up, Remi. We both know I haven't told you everything, but please trust me— I've told you everything that's safe to say, without jeopardizing anyone. We'll explain it all as soon as we can. Everything. Right, Raff?"

"Absolutely," agreed Zulak. "Of course, that means *I'm* going to have to find out what's going on. I trust you'll brief me in full, and fast. Yes?"

"Yes, sir," the major agreed.

Remi shook her head, then smiled at the two men. "You boys are such a piece of work. But I trust you. For the moment. Go do your duty. But I want my daughter back and I want answers and I want them soon. You do not want to trifle with me on this, and you darn well know it."

"Oh, we do—we do," Rafael agreed.

"No question there," said Dino, with a smile. "And thank you. We appreciate your understanding and support."

"Well, you'd better!" she scowled. "Wait a moment, though. I'll be right back. She disappeared toward the kitchen, returning a minute later with a big travel mug of teala, a wisp of steam escaping from its lid. Handing it to Raff, she said, "You look like you're in serious need of some of this." Then, to Dino, "*You* can fend for yourself. At least you were conscious when you arrived. Now go! Go! Both of you! Before I change my mind!"

Rafael accepted the mug, kissed his wife square on a scowling cheek, and headed out the door with Dino close behind.

Once in the shuttlecar and under way, Rafael checked the privacy setting to ensure their driver could not hear them, then addressed his second-in-command. "Major, exactly what is going on? Bring me up to speed."

Dino sighed, knowing what he was in for. "Right, sir. Here's the situation. High Chancellor Jin's daughters have been kidnapped. Both Bonafede and Dorte." Zulak opened his mouth to speak, but Hadgkiss held up his hand. "Just a moment." He touched the comm link in the panel beside him and addressed the driver. "Proceed to drop point A-3, as you were briefed."

"Aye, sir." The car veered left and accelerated.

"We're not going to headquarters, Raff," Dino said, "though we *are* going to meet the admiral."

Rafael bit back his protests and questions, settling for a head shake and a scowl. He knew Dino would explain, and trusted the man knew what he was doing. He didn't have to like it, though.

The shuttlecar settled to a stop in a deserted lot at the back of an ordinary office building. The two men exited, and the car sped away. In seconds, a new car appeared from around another building and settled before them, its passenger doors open. The officers climbed in, the doors slid shut, and the vehicle pulled up and away.

Resigned to the situation, Zulak sat back and sipped at his teala, taking no notice of their circuitous route: abrupt turns—often un-signaled, or contrary to what their signals indicated; multiple double-backs; ignoring "Route Closed—Detour" signs, and other evasions. Dino pulled up a viewscreen and scrutinized multiple video feeds of the roads and alleys ahead, behind and parallel to their course. He and the driver would take no chances about being followed.

Ten minutes into the journey, the commander broke his brooding silence. "All right, *that's it!* I've had it with waiting. What's going on, Major?" In truth, he was less annoyed at Dino's secretive behavior than at their latest course change—it had caught him by surprise, and he'd sprayed half a mouthful of hot teala over himself.

"Hey, hold on, would you?" Dino replied. "Sir." He added, realizing who he was talking to. "I assure you, we're on our way to a complete briefing."

Rafael bit back a retort and sunk into a black scowl.

The shuttlecar came to rest in front of a dilapidated building, in one of the city's more unsavory neighborhoods. "Damn it, Dino," growled Zulak, "why in all space have we stopped *here?*"

Dino gave a combat hand signal for silence, then indicated the commander should exit the vehicle. Rafael scowled ferociously, but followed Dino out onto the curb. The car slid off into the darkness. The major pointed to a shadowed entrance and motioned for Zulak to follow. Drawing a beam pistol, he stepped to the doorway. Once inside, he stopped, then turned to the fuming commander. "Look, I'm sorry for all this," he whispered, "but I don't know who's clean, or who may be watching. The kidnapping is clearly an inside job, and we've had almost no time to get organized. This is the best we could arrange on scant notice. Come on—the admiral's inside, waiting. Just hang on another minute."

Zulak reluctantly followed up four dimly lit flights of stairs. The place was a mess—random trash strewn about, broken fixtures and flooring to avoid, various vermin scurrying off into the darkness, a steamy swamp of unsavory smells. "Here we are," said Dino, stopping at a faded maroon door that announced "Massage" in cracked and dingy yellow.

"Dandy," muttered Rafael.

Dino knocked twice, paused, knocked three times more, then waited. A single knock came in answer, followed by a pause, then four more. He pushed open the door and the two entered.

The room was fairly well lit, but Zulak could see the windows on the far wall had been blacked out. It looked as though the place had been in the same grim shape as the corridors they'd just come through, but hastily neatened for this meeting. Admiral Stock stood in the center of the room, impeccably dressed as always. An armed aide was positioned at the far wall, near one of the covered windows.

"Rafael, I apologize for all this," began the admiral. "Major Hadgkiss, what have you told him?"

"Not much, sir; no time."

"All right. Rafael—please take a seat, son," the admiral

said, motioning toward an old, mustard-colored lounge chair.

"I don't want to sit. What's going on?" barked Zulak, protocol forgotten. He caught a look from Dino and forced himself to calm down. Barely stifling a few choice obscenities, he sat stiffly at the edge of the old chair's threadbare cushion.

"Thank you," said Stock, his tone suggesting he was about to break uncomfortable news. "This is what I know. Last night, someone kidnapped High Chancellor Jin's daughters, Dorte and Bonafede, from their beds. They left a ransom note, directing us to a web nexus for a message. We checked it; they promise the girls' safe return, on one condition."

"Right, right," Rafael said, straining to stay civil. "What's the condition? Why all this damned drama?"

Stock and Hadgkiss exchanged a look, then the admiral went on. "They're demanding an exchange—the two girls for your daughter, Celine."

Rafael sat stunned for a moment, but his gut had told him something like this was coming. "Xenu! Who did this? Where are they? What are we doing *here*, damn it to all the Gods-forsaken hells??"

"We don't know who did it. Not yet," answered Stock. "The note gave us nothing to go on, and the web nexus wasn't directly traceable, of course. But our analysts picked up clear indications Soader is involved. My guess is he orchestrated the whole thing."

"No doubt. Probably just his latest scheme to take revenge on me. Wonderful. And Remi's going to be absolutely impossible when she hears. That's my problem, though. What else have we got?"

"Someone inside Fleet has to be working with Soader.

There's no other explanation for his disappearance back on Earth, or how he even knew Celine had turned up again. Our people are searching for the traitor; they'll find him, and when they do, we'll extract everything he knows."

"Sir," said Dino, "may I suggest we also track down Ensign Jager—the young man taken from our ship? His abduction may very well be connected to all this—and his mental link with Celine could prove invaluable in resolving it."

"Mental link with Celine? What are you jabbering about?" demanded Zulak.

"I'll explain later, Rafael," answered Dino. "No time now. You'll understand, though." He turned back to the admiral; "Sir?"

"I agree, Major. I'll assign some people at once and direct them to you for briefing. But nothing takes priority over your return to Earth to recover Celine."

"You're damned well right!" concurred the commander.

The admiral paid no attention to his subordinate's breech of etiquette; Hadgkiss suppressed a grin. "The girl's own safety and that of the chancellor's daughters depends on it," said Stock.

"Exactly. Thank you, sir," Zulak replied. He turned and strode from the room without permission or salute—protocol abandoned yet again.

Hadgkiss and Stock's eyes met; Dino smiled an apology. Returning his smile, Stock gestured toward the door; "Dismissed, Major." Dino saluted and sped after his commander.

"And may the Ancients watch over you both," whispered the elder officer.

CHAPTER 10

Communication

Celine had been reluctant to leave Fianna and Ahimoth, though she knew they were in the best possible hands. Back in the room the Mentors had provided her, she gave way to exhaustion and the myriad pains she suffered. She longed to lie down and sleep, but wouldn't yield to the desire just yet. First she had some things to consider, resolve and do. She eased herself into a chair as gingerly as she could, but a groan of pain escaped her nonetheless. "At least West can't hear or see this," she thought.

Her most immediate challenge would be speaking to her parents. It was only right, for their sakes, to do that without delay. But first she had to settle on what she would say—and not say.

She recognized that though she was still young, she must be responsible for herself, and for her decisions and actions—and their consequences. She couldn't wish that responsibility off on anyone else. She was thankful for all the training she'd received at the Academy. The courses in evaluating data and situations were especially applicable right now. So was her training in leadership and its responsibilities.

She carefully reviewed recent events, everything she knew about the people and groups involved, and the options open to her. Then she saw it: the path she should take, and *the* thing she must do next. It felt so good and so right to be able to think clearly like this, and with confidence.

"Here goes," she thought. She sat up straight, smoothed her hair, and set the desktop comm link squarely before her. She switched off the unit's tracking feature so her location wouldn't be revealed, and spoke the sequence that would connect her to her family home on Erra.

"Celine! Oh, my Gods!" gasped her mother. "Wait—wait just a minute, dear!" Turning from the link, she called out, "Rafael! Hurry! *It's Celine!*" She turned to the screen once more; "Celine! Where are you? Are you okay?"

Rafael and Dino thundered into the study. Barely managing not to shove Remi aside, Rafael glared at the comm link and fairly yelled, "Celine! Where the hells *are* you?" The conversation with Admiral Stock still burned in his mind. Remi knew nothing of it, and he certainly couldn't drop it all on her right now. That would have to wait.

"I'm all right, Daddy," Celine replied, side-stepping his question about her whereabouts. She knew if he discovered her location, he'd come for her at once. That mustn't happen. Not now. "Just a few bruises—nothing serious. Hey, we found my friend Fianna's brother. Isn't that great? The bad part is, he and Fianna were badly hurt in a...a fall. I managed to get them to a place with decent medical help; now I just have to stick with them until I know they're okay. The doctors say it won't take too long. I know you understand. And I'll be home so, so soon!"

"Who's this Fianna?" demanded Rafael. "Is that the Dragon I saw you with? How in all the universes did you become friends with a *Dragon*?"

"Dragon? What are you talking about?" interrupted Remi. She glared at Celine in the comm link, then at each of the men at her side. No one replied.

Her daughter broke the awkward silence. "I don't get it. You two talk about Dragons as if there were something *wrong* with them! Yes, I know the old Erran bedtime stories and prejudices and such, but seriously—the Dragon races are people, just like we are. Just like *anyone* else. Sure, some planets have primitive Dragons that are dangerous predators, not civilized or sentient. But they're nothing at all like Fianna and her people. That should be obvious! So, what happened to all your talk about people being people, no matter their outward form? What about tolerance and acceptance and leaping to judgments?" she demanded, so indignant she forgot their *other* lessons about respect for elders—parents, in particular.

"All right. All right. You're right, and I'm sorry," said Rafael, chastened. He looked at Remi, who nodded agreement.

"That's right, Celine. I'm sorry too," Remi said, "but please understand—we've been absolutely sick with worry. And Dragons are...they're...they're just... startling!"

"Thank you, Mom. And you too, Dad. I do understand. Really I do. And I'm sorry I've been so bad about being in touch with you. Truly, though, I couldn't help it for almost the whole time. I promise I'll explain everything. Soon! I'm just glad *Asherah* made it safely back to Erra, Daddy." She wanted desperately to ask about Jager, but couldn't have explained how she knew he'd disappeared—much less their relationship. As far as her parents knew, the two had never met.

"I need to go look after Fianna now," she continued, in a sudden rush. "I promise I'll call the instant it's okay to come get me. Soon! Love you all. Bye!" She jabbed at the comm link, cutting the connection before they could object.

"Wait! WAIT!!! Where are you?" shouted Zulak at the blank screen. "*Blast* that girl! Get her back, Remi! Reconnect! Reconnect!"

"Don't you bark at me!" snapped Remi, with a menacing scowl. She bent over the comm link, feverishly poking at the screen. "It's no good. There was no location record on that call, and no reconnect link. And I have no more idea where she is than you do."

"Damn it, damn it, damn it to every last hell in all the bloody, bloody universes!" howled Zulak, pacing the room in angry frustration. "We have to get her back *now! Right* now!"

"Allll right. What, exactly, is going on?" demanded Remi, spearing her husband with a wicked-sharp look. "I want her back, too. Hells! It's more than a year since I've seen her! But she just *told* you she'll call as soon as she's ready. She's caring for her friend, and she said she would be home soon. We brought her up to do the right thing, and it sounds like that's exactly what she's doing. You should be proud! Instead, you're acting like the world is going to end if she doesn't get back here instantly. So, what is it you're *really* all worked up about? *What haven't you told me?* Out with it!"

CELINE CONTEMPLATED THE BLANK screen, glad to have survived the dreaded call. She rose carefully and made her way to a nearby recliner, her injuries throbbing. When the conversation just now had gotten heated, she'd had to resist the urge to stand. Otherwise, her parents—her mother, at least—would surely have recognized she was in pain, and become even more alarmed and unmanageable. She had kept calm, and navigated the conversation more smoothly than she'd hoped.

Her father was becoming more and more difficult to handle. She hated having to *handle* him at all, and realized her own dishonesty with him was behind the mounting trouble. She felt awful about lying to him, but couldn't see any way around it at the moment; it seemed the least of several possible evils. Well, when this was all over, she could confess, and set things right between them again.

It was a blessing her godfather was there with her parents. Dino understood the personalities in play, and the complex dynamics between them. He had always been so perceptive, so clear-headed, such a help in dealing with the family she loved so dearly—despite their fiery natures. She realized she'd been a fiery one herself, at least as her parents would see it. A super-heated handful, all too often. Raising her, they had stressed she must always try to do and say only things those around her could experience easily. But never—and this, they assured her, was even more important—never at the expense of her own integrity. At least she'd gotten *that* right!

Now that she'd made the call, Celine's thoughts turned again to Jager. Who transbeamed him? And to where? Was he injured? Or...worse? She *had* to clear her head somehow, so she could get into action. Right now!

"No," she thought, "that's backwards. I already know what I have to do—so I've got to get into action, and *that* will clear my head."

Energized, she started to stand. "Owww!" Fine. The pain would help chase away the worries and wonderings, too! Even more determined now, she made her way back toward Medical.

CHAPTER 11

Communications and Revelations

Celine hobbled down the hallway toward the lift, stopping several times to rest. It was strange, she thought; the aches and pains seemed to be getting worse. Most unusual.

She reached the elevator and rode it back to the main level. Moments after she stepped out into the corridor, one of the robed Mentors approached, greeted her warmly and led her to a treatment room. The Mentor who had brought her was replaced by two more, who gently examined her, asked a few questions, then began tending to her aches and injuries.

When asked earlier, she had lied about her condition. Brazenly. She didn't have just a few little bruises and bumps, "nothing to worry about." No, she'd racked up a fairly impressive catalog of injuries in the past day or two. Heading the list were three broken ribs and a broken finger, followed by a badly strained ankle, several lacerations that required sealing, and a dozen or so significant bruises and contusions. She'd received a wicked blow to her head—she had no clear recollection of when or where—which one of the Mentors explained was dangerously close to a concussion. The Mentor cradled Celine's head in her hands for a time, murmuring a healing spell. She then counselled the girl to be alert for any of a list of symptoms, and to tell someone at once if one or more should appear.

The Mentor left Celine lying on the warm, comfortable... "Well, what is this thing?" she thought. "It's too nice to call a table, but it's not really a bed...oh, what does it matter? It's just *nice*." She had nearly drifted off to sleep a few times during her treatments. And the Mentors...it was wonderful just to be in their presence. When they spoke, she felt almost mesmerized—as though she were afloat in a deep, warm resonance, centered on the core of her being. The Mentors even smelled wonderful, like springtime on Erra.

Erra. It seemed a lifetime since she'd been there.

As she lay quietly, she reflected on what had happened back on Earth; yesterday in particular, when everything had seemed to fall apart. Finding the Atlantean's secret treasure room in the tunnels beneath the little Turkish town had turned out to be the easy part. Carrying the precious spell books safely to Germany, then to England, and finally to this place, had been far, far more dangerous and difficult. She suspected the difficulties were a long way from over, too— which made her all the more grateful for this moment of peace and comfort.

"How could Soader have been flying with a Dragon?" she mused. She supposed it was true to the Rept-hybrid's poisonous character that he would befriend (enslave or subvert, more likely) a *mutant* Dragon. Life must be a constant agony for such an unfortunate creature.

Thinking about the red Dragon reminded her of Fianna and Ahimoth, battered and suffering when she saw them last. She hoped and prayed their treatment would prove as marvelously, mercifully effective as what she had just experienced.

"They would never have needed such treatment, if it hadn't been for me!" she thought, wracked with guilt. If they died, she could never forgive herself. "My magic. I should've used my magic to protect them. Some friend I turned out to be! To the Dragons, and to Jager, too. I'm just a walking *disaster!* They're all in trouble, and it's my fault." Tears welled up, then tumbled down her flushed cheeks.

At her side, a Mentor's silken voice said, "You are too hard on yourself, my dear."

"What?" said Celine, startled straight out of her puddle of misery. "What? Oh! West! *West!* Oh, thank you!" She sat up, her vitality returning. "Thank you for coming back!" Her tears evaporated, along with the soggy emotions that had spawned them. Such was the power of the Mentor's presence.

"Certainly," West replied, nearly laughing at the girl's abrupt mood reversal. "I see my skillful friends have worked their ways with you. I am pleased to find you more whole and healthy."

"Yes!" Celine replied. "Isn't it wonderful? I would give anything to study with them. There's so much to learn! And you know, you're right. Totally right. I *was* being hard on myself. I'll try to stop doing that."

West nodded, encouraging the girl to continue.

"All that shame, and regret, and berating myself—that

doesn't make *anything* better. Nothing. Ever! It just makes things worse. And it *stops* me from doing anything useful. I'm through with it. Forever." She folded her arms across her chest, raised her chin high and proud, and beamed.

"You are quite correct. Quite correct," the Mentor replied. "It warms me to see you recognize such truths. I know—as do you, I believe—that all your decisions and actions, these past few days and through your whole life, have been based on your belief that they were *right;* that they were the best things you could have decided or done at the time, and with the knowledge and resources you had. Is that not true?"

"Yes! Yes. You're right again," said the girl. Fresh tears welled up, but this time they were tears of relief and happiness. "I *do* do what seems right, with what I know in the moment. Sometimes something I 'know' isn't really true, so my actions turn out wrong. But those are just mistakes, really. I guess that's what people mean when they talk about 'honest mistakes.'

"I *don't* do or decide wrongly on purpose, or because I'm stupid or bad. Ha!" The tears ran freely, leaping off her happy cheeks to form a cheerful mini-pool on the floor.

"I don't have to plow myself into a shameful hole, or beat myself up. Over *anything*. Maybe I've just done that because I meant well, and someone gave me the idea...whoa!—the *false* idea—that you're *supposed* to beat yourself up. But it never, never helps, in the end."

Suddenly, the slightest of frowns darkened her face. She sat in silent thought for several moments, then lit up all over again, bright as before. "There's one more thing. Maybe more important than all the rest. Sometimes you're still going to do something wrong. Make a mess, hurt someone, whatever. You know—make one of those honest mistakes. That's just going to happen, once in a while. But, instead of beating yourself up or hiding yourself away, you could *do* something about it. Admit to yourself that it was wrong, and that you did it. Then take a hard look at *how* you went wrong. Find out what you 'knew' that wasn't true. And then use the truth to clean up the mess you made. It might take a lot of discipline, but if you could make a habit of doing that, no one could stop you. Not even yourself!"

West embraced the girl and held her close. "Ah, my special one," she whispered, "your vision and your deepening wisdom never fail to delight me."

Still holding Celine, West changed their conversation's course. "Fianna is mending well, as is Ahimoth. They shall be back to normal in a week, no more." The Mentor was glad at the girl's escape from emotional turmoil and self-recrimination, but was all too aware of what the brave young soul had yet to confront.

"That's so good to know—thank you, West." She wiped at her flushed face with a sleeve, then gave the Mentor another hug.

"Wait here for just a moment," said West. She crossed the room to a counter, returning with a small device. "This is a chip injector," she explained. If you will permit it, I wish to implant a new, long-range locator chip. The process is quite painless."

"Sure."

"Very good. I must ask you to turn, and face away from me." Celine complied; West placed the device along the side of the girl's left buttock, then pressed a circular stud near its center. Celine felt a momentary pressure, then West withdrew the device. "It is done. This will ensure my sisters and

I do not lose track of you again. You are too precious to misplace, my young friend! And, like the shorter-range chip in your left wrist, this one can neither be detected nor tracked by anyone but myself and my fellow Mentors."

Neither Celine nor West was aware the girl bore a third tracking chip, implanted beneath her left shoulder blade. Soader had placed it there while she was his captive, back on Earth. Her mother and sister bore similar chips. They could only be tracked by Soader and his minions.

Motioning for Celine to follow, West crossed the room and seated herself at a console along the far wall. Celine joined her, pulling up another chair. "Now," West began, "I must ask: do your parents know of your whereabouts?"

"No," Celine replied, sheepish. "I didn't want my father coming after me, so I switched off the comm link's locator."

"Very clever. I'm afraid I must ask that you not reactivate it, nor call anyone again until I indicate it is safe to do so."

"Okay. But why?" Celine queried, sensing something seriously amiss.

"I have been made aware of an incident which occurred early today." The Mentor had only just learned of the chancellor's daughters' kidnapping and the ransom demand. "I do not wish to burden you with the details, but it is imperative that you not attempt contact with your parents at this time, nor with anyone on Erra or in the Fleet. There is no need to worry for your family's or friends' safety, though."

West knew Celine would gladly give herself up to ransom the chancellor's daughters; however, noble though such a move might be, it would accomplish nothing useful. It would only strengthen the enemy's position. Immeasurably.

The Mentor continued, "For the moment, your location

must remain secret. I realize I am being vague and giving no clear reasons, but I believe you will trust me in this. Is that correct?" Celine nodded agreement.

"Thank you." Turning to the console, West passed her hand above it; a holographic projection of several sectors of the galaxy leapt into view. "As you can see, there are a number of indicators flashing. This one represents you." She pointed to a tiny ring of turquoise light, pulsing slowly. "The other indicators locate people we monitor—yet Jager is not represented."

Celine frowned grimly at the projection, as if to locate Jager there by sheer force of will.

"No sign has yet been found of him, nor of Soader. This is unusual, but do not fear—we shall find them. Skilled scouts are combing each sector. We assume both Jager and Soader are shielded from detection in some way, but even the best shielding known cannot defeat our detectors at close or moderate ranges.

"They shall soon be found. For now, you and your friends must rest and mend. And," she added with a smile, "I believe this would be an excellent time for you to enhance your skills at magic."

"What? No! Not *now!* I should be helping find Jager!" She began to jump up from her chair, but caught herself abruptly, with a wicked flinch and a groan. Grimacing, she eased to her feet and went on. "I know I have to recover, but searching needn't be strenuous. I had an idea: If I had a fast ship and followed a wide search pattern, I could try menting him all along the way. Maybe I could locate him that way. Anyway, no one else is getting anywhere, and I've got to do *something!*"

"I understand completely," said West, "but the risk is simply too great. You could be detected and taken, just as Jager has been—and then our troubles would be worse than doubled."

"Okay, okay. But look, if they did capture me, they'd almost surely take me to wherever they're keeping him. Then the two of us could work out a way to escape. I *know* we could."

"Again, a clever plan. Yet the risks remain. Our scouts can and will find him, child. Rarely have they been defeated in a search. And never in one so vital as this. Not in all the millennia.

"Right now, your time could not be better invested than in advancing your skills. Nothing bears more heavily on what is to come. If Jager were here, I know he would agree without question."

Caught up in a tangle of reason and emotion, Celine dropped back into the chair and stared at her restless feet. "Okay," she said at length. "But if he isn't found soon, I'm going to go search anyway."

"I would expect nothing less. Nor would Jager," replied the mage.

"Good. I'm glad we have an understanding," said Celine. She sat silent for a moment, then spoke again. "So, about my skills: if the past few days are any indication, two things are clear: I've got to do better at healing, and at fighting. What a disaster! When can we start?"

"Tomorrow, in the morning. Today, rest and visit with Fianna. But first, there are things you should know."

Celine tensed. "Oh. Okay. What?"

"Foremost, it is essential you know why and how you and Jager came to be the beings—the only beings—able to wield the most potent magic of the ancient Pleiadeans and Atlanteans."

The girl nodded; her restlessness had vanished. "We're the *only* ones?"

"That is correct. The enchantments contained in *The Book of Atlantis* and *The Book of Mu* can only be cast by you and by Jager—or, in some cases, by the pair of you working in perfect concert. Long ago, others could wield them as well, but when the Brothers horribly misused the grimoires to hex the Nibiru eggs, they also triggered an ancient curse, laid down by the book's authors to limit possible abuse. Now, the grimoires' spells work only for those supremely rare beings who have been gifted with the Dream of Atlantis."

Celine was stunned. "But, why us?"

"Because you are, each of you, descendants of The Ancients of Mu. And so was Schimpel."

"Does...does anyone else know we're the only ones who can use the grimoires?"

"Yes. And this is a matter of gravest concern. We Mentors know, as do you. The Brothers know. So do High Chancellors Scabbage and Pratt. We have explained the matter to Admiral Stock and Major Hadgkiss. And, most recently, we have also informed your father."

"What? *Dad?*" gasped Celine.

"Yes," replied the shimmering figure, her face alight. "He received the revelation well, saying it explained many things for him; not least, your fascination with magic.

"When you first were brought to your adoptive parents' home, we told your new father you were a uniquely important being, destined to play a pivotal role in the future of our worlds—and that one day he would learn the nature of your special difference. Years later, after Soader transbeamed you out into the cosmos, we came to Rafael again, to tell him of the ancient grimoires, and your role as a key to their use for the benefit of all. We wanted him to understand that *this* was the root of all that had befallen you. Not, as he had thought, the result of his past conflicts with Soader. The news was not as helpful as we had hoped; he was somewhat relieved, yet still blamed himself to a needlessly harsh degree.

"We did not reveal Jager's role at that time, and your father remains unaware of it, as far as I know. In any case, he has revealed the secret of your special nature to no one. Even your mother does not know."

Celine's face betrayed both amazement and a flurry of new concerns.

West gently touched the girl's arm in reassurance. "I am sorry to surprise you so, my dear, but we had to keep this information hidden, even from you. We feared that otherwise we might not have been able to protect you and Jager adequately. Alas, now you are both in grave danger, despite our efforts."

Celine sat silent, gazing in fresh wonder at her guardian angel. Now she realized why West and her sisters had devoted themselves to developing her knowledge and skills—and Jager's, too.

West began again. "It was necessary that your father understand who you are, to reinforce his inherent protective instincts. He needed to understand why it was necessary to keep you away from certain people and situations. Raising you was not easy for him, child; you must not judge him too harshly."

The girl nodded slowly. "It's all right, West. I appreciate

hearing this. It explains so much of what he's done and said."

"Good. Your father has his weaknesses, as do we all. Yet he has been fiercely loyal to you. He has dedicated his life to your wellbeing; to protecting and supporting you—for yourself, as his cherished daughter, and for what you mean to the future of all.

Your sister despises you—or, rather, the person she *thinks* you to be—because of your father's actions. Actions he took deliberately, reasoning Mia must remain apart from you, and resentful. She must not admire or want to be near you, as would have been her natural inclination. He had to do this to protect her from potential harm, should anyone come after you."

"You know, learning this just makes me love him all the more," said Celine. She reflected in silence on all she had just heard. "Thank you," she said at length. "I understand so many things more clearly now. I'm sure I'll see more and more as time goes on, too. I have one last question, though: Does Jager know we're the only ones capable of using the ancient books?"

"Yes. The knowledge gave him hope that somehow, because of your importance to the fate of our worlds, higher powers would be working to protect you. And it redoubled his resolve to find you."

Celine smiled. "I'm glad for that! Is there anything else I should know now?"

"Yes. There is one more thing. A supremely important one. Scabbage desires to capture Jager and use his body for a soul transfer. His own body is aging badly, and is not far from death. Jager is quite advanced spiritually, and has a strong, healthy young body. These factors would make it an ideal transfer target in any event. But Scabbage's desire goes a sinister step further. Knowing that you and Jager together may wield the power of the ancient grimoires, his plan is to drug Jager and then mentally and spiritually torture him into total subjugation. Once that is accomplished, Scabbage believes he can transfer into Jager's body and conceal himself there so thoroughly that no one—not even you—suspects his presence. Jager himself—the spirit—would still be present, but he would be acting under Scabbage's covert control.

"Scabbage believes he can then catch you off your guard, drug and torture *you* into subjugation, and then link with you—through his slave, Jager—in wielding the grimoires' power.

"You see, he is not satisfied with his position as high chancellor, master of a single sector. So insatiable is his lust for power that he means to subvert G.O.D. and rule all the sectors as supreme dictator. And then to go in search of new worlds to conquer, whole new sectors to bend to his twisted will. Insane and improbable as it may sound, he dreams of stretching his rule far, far beyond the known sectors. He means to rule entire universes."

Celine contemplated this new revelation for a few moments, then stood, her face set in a look of grim, steely determination. Scabbage would never succeed in his utterly deranged, unspeakable scheme. She would see to that. No force, no being in this or any universe would prevent her from smashing his plan.

"West," she announced, "it is time to recover Jager. Now." She turned from the Mentor and strode toward the corridor, all her aches and injuries forgotten.

"Celine. Stop," West commanded.

The girl halted abruptly, as though she'd struck a physical barrier. Her face remained grim, but her resolve had begun to crack: her eyes were welling with tears. She had trained long and hard as a cadet, as a worker of magic, as Companion to a Nibiru Dragon. She had won through perils few could even imagine, much less confront in the flesh. But still, she was a young girl, and the love of all her lives was in mortal danger. She knew what she must do, and she *would* do it. But her emotions were still a potent force. In truth, they were an integral element of her personal power, one of the keys to her surpassing strength.

She stood where she'd stopped, breathing heavily, her back to West, face flushed and tears flowing. After a pause, she slowly turned to face the graceful being whose gaze spoke of limitless understanding, care and compassion.

"Many Mentors seek him now," said West. "They are wholly aware of their mission's grave import. One will find him and send word soon. For now, please believe that your most valuable course is to add all you can to your prowess in magic. This is how you can best help Jager—in the present, and in all the time that lies before you. Do you understand?"

Celine clenched and released her fists several times. Then came a shuddering sigh; her bunched shoulders relaxed, and her stance softened. "Yes, I understand," she whispered, making her way to the console and steadying herself against it. The tears were drying on her still-reddened cheeks. "I understand, but I still want to help in the search."

"Certainly. And you can—from right here," West reassured, placing a hand on the girl's shoulder. "Call to him. Physical distance is no limit to your menting. And no one has a stronger connection with him; no one is more keenly attuned to him. For his part, there is no doubt he is striving with all his power to contact you. So, remain always open to his call. In free moments, call to him yourself.

"And have faith, dear Celine. In many ways, we Mentors are as strong as the evil Volac Forces that so bitterly oppose us. In some ways, we are stronger. Just as you are, and just as Jager is. He will return. When he does, together you will join us to end Scabbage and Soader's evil. And we will bar the Volac Forces from destroying our universe."

West paused, reflecting. "It would be the end of most of us if we were to fail. I know this is a heavy burden of responsibility to place upon you, but we must—and we would not do it, if we had not faith in you."

Celine, heartened to hear this, still felt a hint of guilt for sitting in this place, safe, while Jager was in such peril. He must have felt similarly when she had disappeared suddenly, more than a year earlier. She pondered this a moment more, then stood, passed both sleeves across her face, forced a smile and said, "Okay. I'll do as you ask."

"Thank you," replied the Mentor.

"I'll do it," Celine went on, "but I can't promise I won't worry. I'll dig into my lessons, call to Jager at every opportunity, and stay open to his call."

The two worked out a training schedule, then West departed to attend to other matters while Celine headed for the caves where Fianna and Ahimoth were recovering.

Celine arrived to find Fianna awake, lying quietly near her brother, her great white head resting on his space-black tail. Celine rushed to her friend, threw her arms as far round the Dragon's neck as she could manage, and heaved a trembling sigh.

"Hello, Little One," soothed Fianna. "Ahimoth and I are

recovering nicely. We shall be in fine form again, and soon. The eggs in our care are all alive and undamaged, thanks to you. You will be a legend for all time when they are returned to Nibiru, and you have cast off the hex that lies upon them. We shall be eternally grateful. You will have prevented our race's extinction!"

"I'm doing no more than you would do for me and my own people," Celine replied, easing her hold on the Dragon's neck to look into one of her large, gentle eyes. "I would do anything for you Fianna. Anything."

"I know this, Companion. And I am thankful nonetheless. Now, to business. Though I believe it will be soon, I do not know when Ahimoth and I will be ready to travel the tube-chute home to Nibiru. I take it there is no news of Jager."

"No, nothing yet."

Celine rose and began pacing, twisting a lock of her long brown hair. "Many Mentors are searching. West says that if the ship that took him orbits or makes planetfall on almost any inhabited world, a Mentor will know it and alert us at once. They are searching open space as well." A tear appeared and trickled down her fair-skinned face.

"What is it? What is wrong, Little One?"

Celine brushed away the tear; making a brave effort to appear stronger than she felt, she answered. "A transfer! A *transfer*. High Chancellor Scabbage wants Jager for a soul transfer. That hideous *Scabbage*, in Jager's body! I can't even bear to imagine it!"

Fianna lifted her head and nuzzled her friend. "That *is* horrible to contemplate. But see here—we must be strong and keep faith. We are not helpless, you and I, not while we draw breath! We must remain positive, to keep our strength high and our vision clear. The positive always vanquishes the negative, in the end. Always."

Celine smiled and hugged the Dragon's neck.

"Thank you, Fianna. You're right. Wallowing in negatives is exactly what Scabbage would want."

She curled up against the Dragon's flank and fought back another twisting surge of grief. "Can we rest now?" she asked.

"Of course. Of course."

Celine curled tighter, made a fresh attempt to contact Jager, then relaxed and drifted toward sleep. The Dragon arranged herself carefully, to comfort and protect her precious friend. Soon the pair slept soundly.

Little more than an hour later, Celine woke. Her first thoughts were of Jager, who she called to once again. She rose with care, not wanting to waken Fianna. Planting a gentle kiss on the Dragon's muzzle, she walked stiffly from the chamber toward her own quarters. She was still in pain, but there was a new determination in her step. Determination to do what must be done. And for her, that meant study. Hard study. For that she must be well rested. Within minutes, she was back in her own quarters, fast asleep.

CHAPTER 12

Family Ties

Celine woke to a mental call from West: "Celine, please come to the second level." She rose, stretched, slipped out of the light sleeping garment the Mentors had provided, and stepped into the shower. As the cool spray refreshed her, she called again to Jager. No reply. She would never get used to that awful silence.

Showered and dressed in fresh clothes, she followed the mental image West had sent and soon arrived at a spacious training facility. Its walls and floor were of the same smooth, cool, slate-like stone. At the far end, a raised platform stretched across the width of the room. A long table occupied the room's center, its top at the same height as the platform. Celine approached the nearer end of the table, where two large books lay open and side by side: *The Book of Atlantis* and *The Book of Mu*. A simple chair waited before them.

At the table's far end sat West, her graceful form seeming to glow from within. "Good morning, fair child. I know you have not yet eaten, but hope you will not mind if we begin your lessons at once."

"No, not at all," Celine replied.

"As you know," said the Mentor, gesturing toward the grimoires, *The Book of Atlantis* is a compilation of ancient spells, recorded in cryptic codes. *The Book of Mu* is its companion volume, containing a vast collection of mystic riddles and puzzles. To decipher and use any spell contained in *The Book of Atlantis*, one must first solve its corresponding riddles and puzzles in the Mu volume."

"Yes, I learned these things when I began studying the books with Father Greer."

"That is good news. Good news indeed," said the Mentor. "In that case, you may resume your studies from wherever you left off.

"Right now, we have two objectives before us. We must expand and enhance your magical skills in general. More immediately urgent is the task of locating and mastering the spell to break the hex upon the Nibiru Dragons' eggs. This you must accomplish before Fianna and her brother are fully recovered and ready to travel to Nibiru.

"Before you continue your study, however, there are a few more facts you should know. Facts about your own heritage.

"Your birth parents were natives of the planet Mu. Mu, as you know, was the homeworld of the beings we know as the Ancients; masters of the ways of magic—in fact, the originators of much of magic as we know it today—and creators of the grimoires before you.

"As I believe you also know from your schooling and

other studies, long ago the Ancients hid their planet, casting a cloak of imperception that rendered Mu undetectable, both by living beings and by any devices they employed. The people of Mu have maintained their self-imposed isolation for all the millennia since. They have enjoyed the peace and safety isolation brought, and they believe it to be for the greatest good that the powerful magic to be found on their world be kept secret—safe from those who might abuse and pervert it.

"Your parents loved their homeworld, but it was their conviction that it would be unjust for children to be kept in such isolation. They wanted the family they would raise to enjoy the freedom to experience other worlds and peoples, and to share some of the Ancients' precious wisdom for the good of all. And so, several years before you were born, they left Mu and settled on the moon of a planet in a nearby system. The place was peaceful and pleasant, and so were its people. Your brother was born less than a year after their arrival there. You were born some eight years later."

"Wait!" Celine nearly shouted in her surprise and amazement, "Brother?? I have a *brother?!*"

"Yes, child. Or rather, you *had* a brother. Allow me to explain. Your parent's first child was a boy, whom they named Alika. A name beloved by the Greeks of old Earth, as was yours. In their language, it meant 'guardian.' The name proved an apt choice, as you will see.

"We Mentors had been following you, from lifetime to lifetime, for millennia. We knew you to be a special being, recognized by the Ancients for your purity of spirit and your exceptional gifts of perception and ability. We also knew you were a direct descendant of another such being: Schimpel. And so, you see, your connection with Nibiru and its Dragon race is a long one.

"Very shortly after your birth in this present lifetime, one of my sisters visited your parents. She explained who you were, and your importance to the future of all peoples. Without censuring them for their decision to bring you up away from the safety of their homeworld, Mu, we explained that it was entirely possible that others—with evil motivations—might eventually become aware of your presence, and seek to capture you for their own unwholesome purposes. We asked whether, under such circumstances, they felt willing and able to assume responsibility for your safety, and, indirectly, the safety of all. We also assured them that, should they decide it would be best to give you up, we would convey you to safer circumstances and assist them to bear another beautiful child.

"They thanked my sister for her honesty, and for the true care our actions and promises displayed. Your parents considered long and hard, and finally concluded they were not properly prepared to assume such responsibility. They agreed to pass you into our care, asking only that they might enjoy your precious presence for a little while longer.

"After consulting with the Mentors most directly concerned with your care, my sister agreed to your parents' request, and said we would come for you in two months' time.

"Alas, this proved disastrous. Less than a month later, the Brothers, having detected your presence at the moon settlement, sent a band of vicious mercenaries on a mission to capture you and destroy your family, disguising their attack as a random space-pirate raid."

"Well, here I am, so obviously they failed!" Celine interjected.

"Failed in part, yes," replied West. "They failed to capture you. You have your brother Alika to thank for that. Somehow—we have never learned how—he sensed or knew you were in awful peril. Mere hours before the mercenaries attacked, Alika took you to a neighboring village, and told a family there—friends of your parents—that your mother and father had fallen quite ill. He begged them to care for you until they recovered. The good people agreed, and took you in.

"Alika returned home just as the 'pirate' raid began. The raiders scoured the small neighborhood, house by house, searching for you. They brutally murdered everyone they met, and blasted every home to ash.

"We Mentors had also learned of the impending attack, and rushed to the scene in hopes of preventing it. We arrived too late. Your parents, your brother, and all but two other families in your neighborhood had been annihilated. It was clear that the mercenaries still searched for you, though, and we sensed you were alive and somewhere in the region.

"We quickly captured and paralyzed every one of the mercenaries. Probing their minds, we learned who had hired them, then placed in their minds false memories: each now believed the raiding party had found you, as ordered, but that one of their group had accidentally killed you.

"After wiping from their minds all true memory of our arrival and their capture, we released the raiders. Knowing what would happen if the Brothers learned they had killed you, they fled at once, hoping to evade their employers' wrath. However, the devious Brothers had planted a tracking chip on their ship. They were hunted down, brought before the Brothers, and made to confess to what they had done—or to what they *thought* they had done. I won't ask you to imagine the punishments they received at the Brothers' hands.

"We were able to detect your presence at the home where Alika had left you. We visited the kind family who had taken you in, explained what had happened, and offered to care for you and keep you safe. They were horrified to learn what had been done to your family and village. And, sensing we were honest and sincere, they gladly agreed to turn you over to our care.

"Though heavy with tragedy, the whole incident bore two positive results. First, you were safe and in our care. Second, the Brothers now believed you had been killed, and ceased searching for you—at least in your current identity.

"In considering where and with whom you should be brought up, we consulted our old friend and ally, Admiral Stock. Together we decided to place you with a bright, imminently capable and responsible young officer and his extraordinary wife: Rafael and Remi Zulak. The rest of the story you know, but have you any question?"

After a pensive pause, Celine spoke. "Thank you. Thank you, West. Once again, you've made so many things clear, and brought light to questions I've had for ages."

"You are welcome, certainly," replied West. "And now, you have studies to attend to."

"I certainly do!" agreed Celine, "And after what you've told me, they'll have more meaning than ever!"

The Mentor rose, turned, and left the chamber.

Wearing a determined smile, Celine opened *The Book of Atlantis* to where she'd left off, back in Father Greer's chamber under the mountain. There was much to learn, and she must learn it well. And quickly, before it was too late for the Nibiru race—and everyone, everywhere.

CHAPTER 13

Disturbing Developments

"Remi!" bellowed Rafael, shaking his fists at the blank console screen they both faced. "Why did you let her go before she told us her location? How the hells can I go get her if I have no idea where she *is?*"

"Rafael Ramon Zulak! Who the bloody hells do you think you are, talking to me like that?" Remi blasted right back. "Dino, it would be safer for everyone right now if you got this idiot out of my home. If you don't, he might not see another sunrise." She stormed off toward the door to the garden solarium.

"Remi!" growled Rafael to her disappearing back, "you come back h..." She slammed the door behind her, cutting him off.

"Well, well, Rafael," said the major, "I would guess this has been one of your worst days ever! Come on, let's go down to Callaghan's. It's still early in the day, but under the circumstances, nobody would blame us for having a drink or two. Besides, right now you'll be safer anyplace but here."

Rafael snorted, yet had to admit his best friend was right. With a grumbling groan, he followed the major out the front door. Not to be outdone by his darling-but-dangerous spouse, he gave it a slam that nearly tore loose its hinges.

The men climbed into the waiting Fleet shuttlecar and settled in for the short ride to the pub. "Of all the…," began the commander—but he was cut off once again; this time, by an insistent beeping from the comm link on the car's console. There on the screen was Admiral Stock, looking gray and haggard. "Sir!" Zulak acknowledged. "I'm surprised to hear from you so soon. Is something wrong?"

"Yes," said the admiral. "Some strange events have transpired since we parted, earlier today. But look, I see you're in a car."

"Correct, sir."

"Damn it. How fast can you get to a secure comm link?"

"Not long at all—we've just gotten into the car, outside my home. Give us a moment and we'll go back inside. Just call again on my secure home line."

"Good. Good. But move it!"

"Yes, sir!" Raff and Dino exchanged surprised looks. This wasn't like the admiral at all. Telling the driver to stand by, they returned to the house, ran to Zulak's study, locked the doors, activated the room's electronic soundproofing and awaited the admiral's call. In moments, it came.

"Secure, sir," said Rafael.

"Good. To continue: It's now even more imperative we locate Celine and the chancellor's daughters."

"Sir, we just heard from Celine. She's safe with some, uh... friends," replied the commander. "Can you tell me what's happened, sir?"

"Of course—but, you heard from Celine! That's excellent. Where is she?"

"Ah...that I don't know, sir. Our connection...ah...ended before I found out. You know how bad interplanetary comm can be."

"That's too bad, Rafael, really too bad," said Stock. "In any case, you must track her down and recover her. You'll be on your own in this, I'm afraid. You should know that as of today, I've been forced into retirement."

"What!?" exclaimed Zulak and Hadgkiss together.

"That's right. The boot. Forty-eight years; then, with no warning, discharged. Honorably, I'm assured, but with no plausible reason or explanation. Something smells wrong, don't you think?"

"I would say so, sir," said the major.

"Mm-hm. After our talk earlier, I returned to my office," continued the admiral. "I found it in a shambles, everything ripped apart. The files on my Fleet computer had been hacked into and deleted. Everything. I checked the different backups, but those were gone or wiped, too. Someone knew exactly what they were doing. Broke into my safe as well; took everything. Even got the hard-copy file you and I discussed this morning, about the chancellor's daughters. Files on your daughter, too, Rafael."

"Not a good situation, sir," replied Zulak.

"No, it certainly isn't. Now to deal with it. Your first task is recovering Celine and securing her. At once. Under the circumstances, I can't offer any material assistance. Can't legally issue you any orders. Shouldn't even be using this comm link! So please regard anything I say as, ah...advice! Advice from a concerned and knowledgeable civilian."

"Yes, sir," acknowledged Zulak. "Oh. No. I mean, of course, Admiral...no. Ah! Sounds like a decent idea, Elias. Major Hadgkiss and I were just now working out details on how to, uh...bring Celine home. We'll manage it."

"Good!" said the older man. "Now, unless this is resolved otherwise, and very quickly, my guess is that Fleet and G.O.D. will decide it's best to hand over Celine, so as to get Chancellor Jin's girls back immediately. So, once you've secured your daughter someplace they can't find her, you'll have to locate and recover the kidnapped girls before this goes any further. All behind the backs of Fleet and G.O.D."

"Yes, si...I mean...oh, hells! Yes, *sir*, we're on it."

"Good. I trust you'll do a fine job of it, too." There came a sound off-camera; the elder man turned toward it. Someone could be heard speaking, but they were too far from the comm link for Dino and Rafael to make out more than random bits. As Stock listened, a strange look came over his face, then disappeared almost at once—but not before the two officers noticed it.

The off-screen speaker went on; Stock nodded now and then. At one point he made a furtive, worried glance at the comm link, then returned his full attention to the mysterious speaker. At length, he said, "Mm, okay. Very good. I understand. Give me the details as soon as you've got them."

The men heard a door close, but Stock's attention remained off-screen for a few moments—as though there were still someone there. He abruptly turned to the screen, took a moment to collect himself and then said, "Zulak,

Hadgkiss—uh, good news. Good news. That was one of my former staff, who's still loyal to me. He says Celine has been located, at least generally—somewhere in one of the Pleiadean systems. They'll tell me as soon as they've narrowed it to a specific star and planet. I'll relay details as soon as I have them."

"Thank the Ancients!" answered Zulak. "We'll return to the ship at once and make ready for departure. Thank you!"

Rafael wrote a short note for Remi, explaining that he and Dino were on their way to the ship, and that they would call her soon. Then the two men hurried back to the waiting shuttlecar and ordered the driver to take them to the Fleet base—fast.

On the way, Zulak reflected on all that had transpired since last night, and what would come next. He was thankful he'd been reinstated as *Asherah's* captain. Without a ship of her capability, he'd have been hard pressed to carry out what they'd planned. He was certain Soader was behind the Jin kidnappings, just as the Rept had kidnapped his precious wife and daughters. He vowed to himself that once Celine and the chancellor's daughters were safe, he would hunt Soader down, no matter the cost. Hunt the psychopath down, and kill him.

Back aboard the ship, the men split up: Dino to attend to launch preparations, Rafael to his ready room to make the call he'd promised Remi. He sat down at his small desk-console, opened a secure line and punched in her code.

No answer. "Well, no major surprise there," he thought. He tended to a few launch-prep tasks, then tried her again. And again. At last, someone opened the connection—but their camera was off, and the only sound Rafael could hear on the line was measured breathing. Knowing better than to say anything, he sat back and forced himself to wait in patient silence. Finally, an image appeared: Remi, standing with arms locked across her chest, rigid and fuming.

"What do you want?" she growled through clenched teeth. "Wherever you are, you might as well stay there. You are not welcome here."

"You're right, Remi. I've been a first-class Lunndein ass lately. As I am far, far too often," said Rafael. He was sincere; he had at least some idea of how difficult he must be to live with. "I don't know how I could make it up to you, Remi, and I'm sorry for that. I do have some fantastic news, though. Celine's been located, and we're on our way to bring her home."

"What!" gasped Remi, grabbing the comm-link screen in a death grip. "Where is she? Is she all right? I want to go with you! Come back—I'll be ready to go by the time you get here!"

"Yes, dear, as far as I know, Celine is all right. She's on a planet somewhere in one of the Pleiadean systems." Rafael was enormously relieved his wife was talking again, but dreaded her reaction to what he had to say next. "I'm awfully sorry, though—there's just no way you'd be able to come along. Regulations, you know. Besides, I desperately need you to do something right here at home—something that will ensure Celine's safety in the future. Yours and Mia's, too."

"No bloody way!" yelled Remi. She reassumed her previous angry stance, arms crossed and glaring. "You send Dino to get me right this bloody minute, Mr. Zulak, or you can move out permanently."

Rafael groaned. "This is going to be difficult," he thought. He'd have plenty of amends to make once the girls were safe

and Soader was history. "I want you here beside me for this, dear—please believe me. But it would be a severe violation, and I've only just been re-assigned to command. On top of that, I can't do what must be done here, while I'm away. I don't trust anyone with it but you."

"No!" barked Remi. She stepped forward and jabbed at the comm link's connection switch; the screen went blank.

"Xenu!" muttered Zulak. He tried to re-establish the connection. No go, of course. He waited a minute and tried again. On the fourth try, Remi allowed the connection.

"Well, am I going with you or not?" she demanded, with an icy stare. Rafael made no reply. He sat looking at her, expressionless. He had already made his case, and there was no more to be said.

Remi's stony resolve softened. There was something unusual about her husband's gaze. She could see he hadn't told her everything he knew—and he would not, could not say more. Recovering a bit of objectivity, she reviewed what he'd told her. He was right about the regulations. There really wasn't any getting around them. Not right now, anyway. And she hadn't even tried to find out what he wanted her to do here. She was acting like a spoiled child. A hormone-crazed teenager, in the grip of raging emotions. She heaved a sigh and sat down, resolved to be an adult; the strong, responsible wife of a Fleet Commander. Yes, the past couple of years had been terribly hard. For both of them. That made it even more important to back him up.

The couple quietly regarded each other, both wishing things could be as they'd been before: in love, loving their darling daughters, making a happy home and a better world.

"I'm sorry, dear," she said, with a wry smile. "I guess I've been acting like Mia on one of her more dramatic days!"

"Well, that makes two of us," her husband replied. Both laughed as they envisioned their eldest in the throes of one of her infamous tantrums.

"Okay. So, I will stay here and do whatever it is you need, Raff. But as soon as you have our daughter safe, you'd better call, or I'll out-Mia Mia by light-years. And you *know* I can, too."

Rafael gave a wide smile, which she returned warmly. "Oh, and be assured I'm going to make sure Dino knows about this, too. He'll hold you to it."

"All right! All right!" Zulak smiled, "I promise." Sometimes he so enjoyed the games Remi played. He knew they'd patch everything up when he returned. Everything between the two of them, and their daughters' strained relationships, too.

All of that would have to wait for just one more thing, though. Once Celine was back and he'd secured the family in a safe and secret location, another task would become his most pressing priority. He would hunt down and terminate Soader. Alone.

There was always the possibility he wouldn't return from that particular mission, though, so he would have to give some serious attention to tidying up loose ends and ensuring the family would be well provided for—just in case.

Shaking off his momentary reverie, Rafael turned his attention back to Remi. "Thanks, my darling. I can't tell you how much I appreciate it. May I tell you what I'm hoping you'll help me with?"

"Of course. Please," she replied, suddenly all business.

"Perfect. Here it is. Pack bags for an extended trip for the

two of us. Informal. Off-world, but mild climate, no special needs. Then persuade Mia and Hyatt to do the same. Oh, and pack for Celine, too—she won't have time to do it herself.

"I don't know precisely where we'll be going yet. I will soon, but even then, I'll only tell you. It must be kept completely secret, and I can't trust Mia or Hyatt to maintain security. We'll tell them some plausible location, but it won't be our true destination. Ideally, we'll all be home safe in a few weeks, and they'll never even know where we actually were. In other words, we're going to go hide out for a bit."

"Hide out for a bit?" barked Remi. She shook her head, rolled her eyes and launched a fresh barrage. "Are you *daft?* The wedding! What about the wedding? It's only four weeks away! I wouldn't be able to get Mia to agree to a bloody *day* trip, let alone spending weeks in *any* location, so close to the wedding. Exactly what are you thinking? Or is *thinking* against regulations now, too?"

Rafael bit his tongue, concentrated on his breathing, and silently counted to ten. Back under at least a semblance of control, he responded as diplomatically as he could manage. "You're absolutely right, dear. It *is* quite a lot to ask. And I don't think there's anyone but you in all the universe who could pull it off.

"I'll tell you what I thought might work, but I'm really just looking for your advice. In our special team-for-life, you're the expert on this kind of thing. Anyway, my idea was to tell Mia and Hyatt the trip is one of several early wedding presents. Tell them it's a pre-honeymoon of three weeks' rest, relaxation and indulgence at a totally secluded hideaway. A place so super-exclusive that no one will even know where we are. The old Pleiadean pre-honeymoon tradition calls for just one week, but they're such a special couple that, the way we see it, nothing less than three weeks will do. Then, when it's all over—and I pray it *will* all be over in three weeks—we can go ahead with the wedding as planned. There'll still be a whole week for the few little final preparations.

"Oh, and it also occurred to me we've got to reassure Hyatt that I got his commanding officer's approval for the extra weeks of leave. Now I'll have to remember to actually *do* that! His C.O. is an old friend, though, and he owes me a couple of favors. It won't be a problem."

Remi sat quietly, deliberating. After what seemed to Rafael like an eternity, she answered. "Well, I think that actually might work. Mia responds instantly to extravagance, so two extra weeks—at a 'super-exclusive place,' as you put it—ought to go over very well indeed."

"Right!" replied Zulak. "There really are such places; I'll just have to find one that's suitable. Hey, you could also tell Mia we wanted a chance to spend extra quality time with them before they begin their life together. It will give us a chance to get to know Hyatt better, too. Mia should love that. It's true, too—I barely know the boy."

"All right. It sounds feasible. Let's hope it works!" said Remi. "I'll get right on it. Oh—and when you're making transport arrangements, bear in mind Mia will want to take an inordinate amount of luggage."

"Ohhhh, yes. I'm glad you mentioned it. Oi! All right, then. I'm off to handle the logistics. I'll call as soon as I can, with details of when and how we'll pick you up. And do call me if you need anything at all."

"Thank you, dear. I will," Remi replied. "And...I'm sorry we fought. I got out of hand, I know. But... Well, no. No buts. I do know things have been difficult for you, and I appreciate your taking care to work this out, on top of everything else. I also know you're not telling me everything—as usual! I'm sure you believe it's for my own good, but it makes me so bloody angry sometimes. I don't understand why you won't trust me with the whole story."

"I'm sorry too, Remi. And you're right, I'm not saying everything. Part of that is just military mindset, spilling over into personal matters. But, damn it, a bigger part of it is basic, basic security—it's for your safety, and for the kids. You're all too precious to me to take unnecessary chances. And sometimes that means keeping certain details under wraps."

"Okay. I understand, Mr. Zulak. I really do. I don't like it one tiny bit, but I do understand it."

"Thank you, Remi. That's just one reason I love you so. You do understand, and you don't let your emotions rule you." She smiled. "At least, most of the time," he joked. She gave him a mock look of fury and took a vicious swing at the comm link—carefully missing, but only by millimeters. They had a good laugh, then signed off.

Zulak called for Hadgkiss, who entered the ready room moments later. "The ship and crew are ready, sir."

"Good. Thank you, Major. Sit down. You and I need to figure out a few details before we head out. We still need Celine's location, too. I haven't heard from Stock, and assume you haven't either."

"Correct. It might be smart to call him—not as a nudge, but just to make sure he's okay. Something bothered me about that last conversation."

"Good idea," said Zulak. "And you're right; there was something odd going on in that office of his. Something we weren't supposed to know about."

Stock didn't answer their first attempt to reach him, so they tried his former driver, his home, and his lapel comm pickup. No response. The men exchanged worried looks.

"Now I'm concerned for sure," said Dino. "We already know someone in Fleet must be working with Soader. So maybe they got to Stock and threatened him or something— and that's what was behind that odd conversation."

Zulak nodded. The two attended to various tasks for another half hour, then met up again in Zulak's ready room for another attempt to reach the admiral. Still no response, from any location. "I don't like this," said the major. "I think we'd better get off-planet right away."

"I agree. Ready the ship," replied the commander. "We can try reaching him again from space."

CHAPTER 14

Resort

Less than an hour later, *Queen Asherah III* orbited Erra, awaiting final clearance to depart the system on a routine patrol. "Routine" as far as the crew knew, at least. A select few senior officers were briefed on their true objective: locate and secure Celine Zulak, as part of the effort to recover High Chancellor Jin's daughters.

After several failed attempts to re-contact Stock, Zulak and Hadgkiss agreed they could delay no longer: To protect the commander's family and free him to concentrate fully on Celine's recovery, they must move Remi, Mia and Hyatt to a safe location. Immediately, and in secret—without their crew's knowledge. There were too many signs they had been infiltrated to risk any other course. They had no choice but to transport the family aboard *King Hammurabi*.

Hammurabi was a retired Fleet corvette—a small, highly maneuverable, lightly armed and armored warship capable of extreme velocities. Decades earlier, and acting through trusted intermediaries, the Mentors had arranged to purchase the ship. They refitted it with the latest, most advanced equipment and technologies, then had it upgraded as new developments arose over time. Unlike most ships of its class, *King Hammurabi* was jump-shift and transbeam capable. But one factor made the *King* truly unique. It could travel cloaked: invisible, and undetectable by even the most powerful sensors.

Shortly after entrusting the infant Celine to Rafael and Remi Zulak's care, the Mentors had stationed *King Hammurabi* on one of Erra's tiny moons. They housed it in a secret and undetectable cavern, attended by a trusted ground crew who kept the ship in constant readiness. Aside from the Mentors and its ground crew, the only people who knew of *King's* existence—and the only ones who could operate it—were Rafael Zulak, Dino Hadgkiss, and Madda. The ship's sole purpose was simple: to protect and defend the beings now known as Celine Zulak and Jager Cornwallis, crucial to the Mentors' crusade against evil.

Their decision made, Rafael and Dino acted. Dino rapidly researched and located a suitable, ultra-private resort planet, and reserved accommodations. Zulak contacted Hyatt's Commanding Officer and, calling in a favor, secured an extension of the young officer's upcoming wedding leave. Hyatt was now free to fly off to a three-week pre-honeymoon.

Next, Rafael gave Madda temporary command of *Asherah*. She was to captain the ship on its assigned patrol of the Pleiadean systems, while he and Major Hadgkiss tended to another urgent matter, under sealed orders from Fleet High Command. In the privacy of his ready room, he also briefed Madda on their true plans, and promised to maintain

contact through his secure channel.

An hour later, with every detail attended to, Zulak and Hadgkiss transbeamed down to the secret moon base where *King Hammurabi* lay hidden. Madda herself was at the transbeam controls—and the logs showed the two officers were 'beamed back to the Fleet base on Erra. At last, under Madda's command, *Queen Asherah* headed for deep space and her scheduled patrol.

On arrival at *Hammurabi's* base, Rafael and Dino inspected the ship. The ground crew had been meticulous and thorough: *King Hammurabi* was fully fueled, fully provisioned, fully prepared to take them anywhere they might want to travel. "Well, here we go," said Zulak to his life-long friend and ally. He opened a secure comm link and called Remi.

His wife answered at once. "Hello! I'm surprised to hear from you so soon."

"Hello, darling. I'm surprised to be calling so soon—events have moved forward quicker than expected. Now, I'm sorry for the sudden change in plans, but we're already prepared to come pick you up and head for the resort planet."

"No need to apologize, dear. After all you told me, I've been worried. The sooner we leave, the happier I'll be."

"Me, too. I'm guessing you and Hyatt are packed and ready, but what about Mia?"

"Naturally, she fussed and dithered over what to bring, but I managed to jolly her along and help her with decisions. She's just now finishing the last of her packing; we should all be completely ready in less than half an hour."

"Perfect, because that's about how long it will take us to launch, and get there safely and unnoticed. Thanks for handling everything so quickly, Remi. I don't know what I'd do without you."

"Well, as long as you behave, you're not *going* to do without me, so don't give it another thought. You and Dino just get here fast. We'll be ready and waiting."

"Okay. I'll call when we're in position to transbeam you up. You and all Mia's luggage. I just hope the ship is big enough."

"Ha!" Remi laughed. "I think you'll be impressed with how economical I convinced her to be. To her credit, she did seem to understand the practicalities, and limited her extravagance. By the way, it's wonderful you'll be here so quickly, but how? In what ship? Surely Fleet hasn't reassigned *Queen Asherah* as your family transport."

"No, no. Nothing like that. Something even better—and safer. I'll explain when you're aboard. You'll like it, I promise. And it's about as exclusive as any ship could be, so Mia should love it, too."

"I'm intrigued! I'll let you go, though. You shouldn't be talking to me, you should be getting under way."

"Aye-aye!" Rafael joked, and closed the comm link.

In just under an hour, *Hammurabi*—fully cloaked—slipped into orbit around Erra. Zulak called Remi to confirm his arrival; she assured him everyone was ready to go. Rafael asked her to assemble the three travelers in the center of their home's lounge, with their luggage close beside them. In less than a minute she signaled they were in position. Hadgkiss activated the transbeam, and in moments Remi, Mia and Hyatt stood on *King Hammurabi's* platform.

Seeing her husband waiting beside the console, Remi flashed him a warm and just slightly conspiratorial smile.

Mia leapt from the platform and ran to her father's waiting arms. "Daddy!" she cried. "This is wonderful! Three *weeks* at an exclusive resort?! You're the best *ever!*"

Hyatt remained where he'd materialized, looking slowly around at the transbeam bay and equipment. He let out a low whistle of appreciation; everything here was clearly top-of-the-line, efficiently laid out and in perfect order.

"Remi, Mia, Hyatt," Rafael began, "meet *King Hammurabi*."

"Welcome aboard," spoke the ship, in a deep, firm, but friendly voice. "I am at your service."

Rafael, Dino and Hyatt grinned at the astonished looks on Remi and Mia's faces; though they had heard of AI ships, neither had ever been aboard one.

"Thank you," said Remi, quickly adapting to the concept.

"H...hello?" said Mia.

"Hello, Mia. I am pleased to make your acquaintance. You may address me as Hammurabi, if you wish—or simply say "ship" and I will respond. If there is some other way you would prefer to address me, please do not hesitate to say so."

"Okay, Hammurabi. Thank you," replied Mia. She found she liked the idea of a talking ship. And it said it was at her service. "Hm," she thought, "I wonder what kinds of things it can do for me."

Remi gave Rafael and Dino a hug, and the senior officers shook the young ensign's hand in the traditional Fleet grip.

"Dino," said Rafael, "take us out of orbit and plot a course for the resort planet. I'll give our guests a tour of the ship and brief them on protocols and security."

"Aye, Captain," said Dino, and he left to carry out his orders.

Rafael lead the newcomers on a tour of the spaces they would be able to access, explaining the ship's equipment and capabilities as he went. The tour ended in the lounge, where he invited the group to sit while he explained what they could expect during the voyage, and the few simple rules they should observe for their safety and comfort.

Finally, he took up the matter of security. He explained that *Hammurabi* had been made available to him as a special favor, and asked that they not mention the ship or their voyage to anyone, at any time. Fortunately, all three had years of experience with Fleet matters, so they understood the necessities and demands of security.

"While we're talking about security," he said, "I'll go ahead and brief you on security at the resort where we'll be staying. The place is exclusive in the extreme. It is frequented by VIPs of various kinds, and the resort guarantees their complete privacy. As part of their security and privacy rules, you won't be able to use your comm devices for any off-planet transmissions, in or out. Don't worry, though. Major Hadgkiss will set your devices so they can't be traced, hacked, or accidentally activated. We'll still be able to use them to communicate amongst ourselves and with resort staff, but that's all. Oh! I almost forgot. We'll be able to make image-captures, but only of the scenery, wildlife, and members of our party. We're quite unlikely to encounter any other guests—that's how private the staff keep things—but if you happen run into anyone, no images. Any questions?"

There were none, so Zulak concluded the briefing, showed them where they could find snacks and drinks, and excused himself to attend to the voyage.

Joining Dino on the bridge, he said, "They're all briefed. I'm glad the kids have been through cadet training. Otherwise I doubt we could trust them to keep security when all this is over. Remi's an old hand at this sort of thing, too; no worries there."

"Right," agreed Dino. "Here's our status: I took us out of Erra orbit, and plotted a course for the resort planet. We're ready for jump-shift when you give the word."

"Excellent," replied Rafael. "I'll get the others strapped in for the jump, and call you when they're ready. I'm going to stay with them—this will be Mia's first jump-shift." Dino nodded acknowledgment. It was a smart move; jump-shift could be a harrowing experience, no matter how many times one went through it. For some, the first jump bordered on traumatic. It would be good for Mia to have both her parents close, just in case.

Minutes later, Rafael spoke into his comm pickup: "All secure for jump-shift, Major. You may engage the drive."

"Aye, Captain," acknowledged Hadgkiss. He made one last check of coordinates and settings, then tapped out the sequence that would engage the drive. Starting below the level of human hearing, but building rapidly, a deep hum filled the ship. Zulak noted its frequency was different from *Asherah's*. No surprise—this was a ship of a different class, with the very latest in drive technology.

Thanks to *Hammurabi's* speed and jump-shift capability, the ship announced their arrival at the resort planet only a few minutes later. Much to Mia and Remi's relief: Neither was accustomed to the physical stresses and sensations of jump-shift travel, or its mental and even spiritual disorientation.

From space, the resort planet was pretty, but nothing out of the ordinary. About half the surface was covered in deep-blue ocean. Much of the land visible on this side of globe was clad in varying shades of green, broken up here and there by the reds, yellows and browns of arid regions, and the grays and whites of a few snow-capped mountain ranges.

Hadgkiss guided the ship down toward the surface. The resort itself, situated on the western coast of a continent and roughly thirty degrees north of the equator, had its own private spaceport. The *King* came to ground and the party disembarked to a warm, cheery greeting from two resort staff.

The planet itself was just as welcoming: temperature and humidity gentle and pleasant, air clean, fresh and graced with the sweet and spicy scents of lush plant life. The sky was a deep, almost violet blue, dotted here and there with billowy blue-white clouds.

One of the staff, whose name was Moana, showed them to their suite of rooms. Another saw to their luggage; to his credit, he barely batted an eye at all the items destined for Mia's room. He had encountered more than a few of her type during his years here.

Once the guests had settled in and freshened up, they met once again with Moana. She explained she would be their private concierge, completely dedicated to their comfort and enjoyment.

Moana led them on a tour of the facilities; all were beyond fabulous, but in a relaxed and gracious way. The tour included a "refresher" on the security and privacy briefing they'd received before arrival. They would encounter no off-planet media, nor any paparazzi or other potential privacy violators. There would be no contact with guests outside their party, though they may occasionally see other visitors off in the far distance. There could be no open off-planet communications sent or received, excepting only secure comms the military members of the party might require. The staff, Moana explained, were all vetted and bonded for utmost security.

She detailed the wide range of activities available,

including hiking, swimming, water sports, riding, exploring, wildlife viewing (on land and at sea), pampering in the spa, exquisite food and drink, and just plain lounging—whatever might take their fancy.

In short, this was the ultimate haven of peace, pleasure and privacy. So discrete and private, it didn't even have a publicly mentioned name.

Mia was ecstatic. All through the tour she busily compiled a mental "to-do" list for the weeks ahead: exploring the resort's gorgeous grounds and lavish facilities, sampling the superb cuisine, delicious hours in the hands of the spa's staff, and days of pre-honeymoon fun and romantic adventure with her darling Hyatt. Her only complaint was the absence of other guests. There would be no one to show off to (or make envious). No one but the staff to fawn over her. No media teams to follow her around, begging for interviews and photo ops. She shrugged it off, though, sure she would still manage to have a marvelous time.

"It's perfect," Remi purred, throwing her arms around her husband and hugging him tight. "Even better than I'd imagined. And Mia's beside herself; she's in love with the place. There's so much for her to do, she'll scarcely miss being the center of a crowd's attention. I hope Hyatt can keep up with her!"

"It is nice, isn't it," agreed Rafael, trying his best to sound enthused. The resort truly impressed him, but more serious matters gripped his attention: Celine and the high chancellor's daughters.

"'Nice' scarcely begins to describe it," said Remi, "though I do understand you're concerned about Celine. I am too, believe me. But you said it yourself: There's nothing we can do until the admiral's people give you her location. So, unless they make an unexpected breakthrough, we have a week almost entirely to ourselves. Maybe more. I think you know how precious that is to me, Rafael. And I hope it's as precious to you."

"It is precious, my dear. But you're absolutely right: I'm worried for Celine." She was more right than she knew, and for reasons he couldn't reveal. "I promise you, though, we're going to make the most of this time. You deserve it." She hugged him again, and pressed against him in a long kiss.

In the days that followed, the resort and its staff worked their charms on the guests. Mia and Hyatt dove into a whirlwind of activities, but always returned to their favorite: swimming and sunning on the resort's pristine beach. Remi indulged herself poolside and at the spa, and caught up with some long-neglected pleasure reading. Best of all, she spent happy hours with her husband, renewing their relationship—hours she would treasure the rest of her life.

Mother and daughter enjoyed a girls' spa day; the skilled staff pampered them to the limit while the pair chatted about their men and the serious business of husband-management, and put the finishing touches on plans for the wedding soon to come.

Rafael and Hyatt shared quality man-time on the hiking trails, climbing a highly rated cliff face and fishing in the surf. Zulak was pleased and proud to learn more of his future son-in-law's character: a well-grounded, able young man, full of potential for a distinguished career. The elder man's only concern was Mia's possible mis-influence on the lad, with her self-absorption, her demands for attention and special treatment, and her preoccupation with trivialities. Still, there was always the hope life's challenges would mature her. She was not stupid, after all, and had Remi and

Celine's fine examples to look up to. She could bear healthy children, too, and was openly eager to do so—there was much to be said for that.

The time passed pleasantly, but twice each day, Zulak and Hadgkiss turned their total attention to the serious business never far from their minds: Celine. They conferred with Madda, who provided status reports and updates. She had little to report; the patrol was proving routine and uneventful, and there had been no word of Celine or Jin's daughters. The men grew increasingly agitated, and harder pressed to conceal it from the family. Word *had* to come soon. Time had grown perilously short.

CHAPTER 15

Temporary Captive

Jager examined his new surroundings. He was in a cell, maybe three meters by four, and nearly three meters high. Floor, ceiling and three walls were smooth, gray metal. The fourth wall was some sort of hard, transparent, glass-like material. It was ventilated with round holes, a couple of centimeters in diameter and arranged in a grid pattern that stretched from floor to ceiling, each hole about half a meter from the next. In the center of the transparent wall hung a door of the same clear material, in a gray metal frame with stout hinges and an electronic locking mechanism. The cell's only furnishings were a simple bed platform with a thinly cushioned top, a small metal sink and toilet in one corner, and a tiny table and bench, bolted to the floor in the center of the space. Two Repts, armed with beam pistols, stood a few meters from the transparent wall, facing their prisoner.

Suddenly, the guards spun around toward the corridor

behind them. Someone was approaching, and the guards' body language made it clear they feared him. It was a Rept—short, ugly even by Rept standards, much fatter than average, and decked out in official finery: High Chancellor Deebee Scabbage.

A retinue of Grey servants followed the creature. One fawningly fanned him, two more lugged an assortment of official-looking shoulder bags and satchels of who-knew-what, and a fourth followed behind, struggling to hold up the end of the long cape that completed the outfit's garishly pseudo-regal look. As the procession approached, a wicked stench assaulted Jager. Scabbage stunk. Badly. "Ugh!" Jager thought. "If only the one with the fan would get the breeze going the other way!"

"Well, well. At last I get to lay eyes on my new body," cooed Scabbage, in his native Rept language. "Oh, it is simply lovely! Remove your clothes, boy, and take a turn around that cell. Slow and pretty, so I can see how I'm going to look."

Jager put on a quizzical expression, pretending not to understand.

"Oh, come, come. I know you understand me, laddie-buck. Don't think me stupid," barked the Rept, flecks of spittle flying. "And don't try my patience. You've one more chance to do as I say. Now. Now, or you'll *wish* you had. Oh, yesssss."

With an innocent shrug, Jager again feigned incomprehension.

Scabbage snorted and waved a hand at one of the guards, who touched the screen of a handheld remote. Blue-white arcs leapt from metallic studs set in two of the cell's walls, enveloping Jager in a searing, crackling network of raw

energy. The young man collapsed in agony, screaming and thrashing on the hard cell floor.

"Hmm. Seems like enough," suggested Scabbage. The Rept touched his remote again, and the torture ceased.

"Har! Now that you know exactly who is in charge here, do as I said," smirked Scabbage. "Remove your clothes and give us a show."

Still severely shaken, Jager rose unsteadily to his feet, turned his back on his captor and began removing his white Fleet uniform. He worked slowly, neatly folding each item and placing it on the bed. At last, wearing only his trunks, he stopped, still facing away from the Rept.

"No, take it *all* off!" insisted Scabbage. The young man gave an exaggerated yawn, then removed his trunks and placed them on the bed. "Turn around, gods-damn it!" barked Scabbage. Jager shrugged, then turned a full 360 degrees, again facing the back of the cell. "Stop playing stupid!" roared the Rept. "Turn and face me!" The boy complied; he turned to face Scabbage, but with eyes averted. "That's better. Now look at me. I want to see your eyes."

Jager, who had been chanting a spell under his breath through the last stages of his little performance, lifted his head and glared straight into Scabbage's beady reptilian eyes. The creature gasped, threw up his hands as if to ward off a blow, and stumbled backwards, gagging. His entourage shrank back in horror, but no one made a move to help the Rept. When the fit finally passed, Scabbage turned abruptly and stormed back down the corridor, his minions scuttling along behind.

He hadn't gotten far before he doubled over, seized by another fit of gagging and coughing. His servants made a few feeble attempts to help, fanning him and offering hopeful suggestions. One produced a flask and offered the Rept a drink, but was angrily waved away. Watching from his cell, Jager had a chuckle at the pathetic spectacle.

With Scabbage gone, Jager dressed and lay down on the bunk, crossed his legs, clasped his hands behind his head and idly surveyed the cell's ceiling. Spotting two tiny button cameras, he smiled broadly and gave each a cheery wave. A while later, one of the Rept guards left the cellblock, then returned with a shallow metal dish of food. He motioned for Jager to move to the back of the cell. When the young man had complied, he opened the cell door, placed the dish on the table and said, "There's yer chow, Human. Make the best of it; won't be bringing any more 'til tomorrow."

When the guard had gone, Jager sat at the table and ate the meal. It was standard ship's fare: not exciting, but not awful. He lay down on his bed and—expecting the usual negative result—tried calling to Celine, then to West. His expectation was met: silence. "This is how Celine must have felt, stuck on Nibiru," he thought. "I hope she's all right. Fianna, too." After a few minutes of quiet musing, he turned over and went to sleep.

Some hours later, a loud *clang* from down the corridor jolted Jager awake. He rose from the bed, stepped to the front of the cell, smiled at the guards and examined the cellblock beyond. There were cells like his along both sides, six on each side. At its far end, the block opened onto a wide corridor. He could see people passing by, alone and in small groups; some carried, pulled or pushed loads of different kinds. He gasped; many wore *Fleet* uniforms. What in hells was going on? Then it struck him. No wonder the details of his surroundings seemed rather comfortably familiar. He was aboard a Fleet ship! But, how could that be? Now he truly had a mystery on his hands.

The mystery would have to wait, though. He had to find a way to escape from this cell. He jumped back up on the bed and sat, back against the cold wall, to work out how.

Being aboard a Fleet ship worked to his considerable advantage. Fleet vessel designs and layouts had been standardized centuries ago—so this one would be similar to those he'd studied and trained on. With any luck, it was nearly the same as the one he'd served on for the past year: *Queen Asherah III*. He'd spent most of his free time exploring her. And with his near-perfect memory, every detail was mentally "on file" and readily accessed.

He reviewed all he had seen and heard since waking up here—the design and dimensions of this cell, its configuration relative to the others he could see, and the glimpse he'd had of what lay beyond the cellblock. And then he smiled. He was sure of it: this ship wasn't just similar to the *Queen*. It was of the very same class, and therefore identical in layout, basic furnishings and equipment.

That meant once he found a way out of the cell, he'd have little trouble evading pursuit and setting himself up in a serviceable hiding place, from which he could execute whatever plans he cooked up next.

The first barrier to escape was the Rept guards. From their chatter, he knew there were three pairs of them, standing rotating shifts. There were also the button cameras in and around the cell. He assumed they were always on, but, like most such systems, probably not well monitored in real time. He considered several options, then settled on a plan.

Next day, when the guard left to get his food, Jager

slumped down on the little table-side bench and stared blankly toward a corner of the cell. To all appearances, he was lost in the deepest of apathetic funks. In fact, he was seriously but silently busy: busy chanting a spell.

Soon the guard returned, entered the cell, set the new bowl on the table and picked up yesterday's empty. Jager looked listlessly up at him, smiled vacantly and then said "thanks," in a pleasant, soothing tone. He modulated his voice in a way he knew would stimulate the Rept's brain centers for calm and contentment.

It worked! The guard paused, lulled by the sound, and looked down at Jager with a faint Rept-smile.

Jager looked directly into the Rept's eyes and said, in a soft but compelling tone, "Sleep"—the word that activated the spell he'd been weaving.

At once, the guard's eyes went glassy. His body swayed for a moment, then slumped to the floor in a heap.

Jager jumped up in feigned shock and amazement, crying, "Oh! Oh!! What *happened?!*" The second guard rushed into the cell. Jager turned to him, careful to keep his voice and body language submissive and frightened. "Look, look! He just fell over! Is he sick? Is he okay?"

Momentarily disarmed by the young human's tone and manner, the guard still managed a half-hearted gruffness. "Fell over? What do you mean, he fell over? What are you up to, Human?"

Jager gasped in shocked innocence. "Up to? *Me?*"

The guard cocked his head slightly and looked straight into Jager's eyes, suspicious. The boy returned his piercing look and repeated the spell's trigger-word: "Sleep."

The Rept's face went slack, his body teetered briefly, and

then he collapsed, half on top of his partner.

Jager smiled, but there was no time to admire his handiwork. Though these guards would be out for hours, the button cameras in the cell and corridor would be recording everything. It was only a matter of time before someone at a monitor panel noticed the scenario and sounded the alarm.

Frisking the guard on top of the pile, Jager found and snatched his pass key, a knife and a light-orb. He was about to grab his ID badge too, but realized it would contain a chip; if he took it, they'd track it and find him in no time. The guard's blaster looked awfully tempting, too—but it was certain to be chipped as well.

Shoving the heavy Rept aside, he frisked the second, taking his key and knife. No time for anything else. He stepped out of the cell and swung the door shut, testing to be sure the locking latch had engaged. Then he dashed down the cell-block corridor, stopping just before he reached the opening to the larger corridor beyond.

He took a moment to compose himself, consciously moderating his heart rate and breathing down to a calm normal. He checked his endocrine state, too—he didn't want to be emitting any alarm pheromones that might arouse someone's suspicions, or any security sensors. Satisfied, he stepped out into the passing foot traffic, mimicking the posture and pace of the other Humans he could see. Since his Fleet uniform was identical to most of the passing crew, and a fair percentage shared his coloring and build, he blended right into the scene. No one even lifted an eyebrow at his presence.

CHAPTER 16

A Universe Away

Jager expected to hear an alarm's blare at any moment. It didn't come, though. Puzzling, but there was no time to give it a second thought. He had to get out of sight, fast.

He passed a work party unloading crates from a power cart and carrying them into a storage room. As he went by, he caught a glimpse of one of the crate's labels, and barely managed to keep from stopping to stare. It said *"Queen Morrighan."* Maintaining his pace, he casually looked back to be sure he'd seen correctly. Yes, he had. There were several more in the stack with *"Queen Morrighan"* clearly visible, in official Fleet script.

"Queen Morrighan!" he thought. "She's been missing for years. Word was, she'd been destroyed. Hmmm. This is getting interesting." Up ahead he saw an open lift, filling with crew; he joined them. The lift's doors slid shut, there was a sensation of controlled falling, and the doors reopened,

revealing the parts and supplies storage area, at one end of the engineering deck. "Perfect," Jager thought. A couple of the crew stepped off the lift and headed to the left. Jager followed them out, but turned to the right instead. He headed down the corridor, deeper into the storage area.

Spotting a hand computer hanging outside one of the storage compartments, he stopped, took the device off the wall and pretended to study it, swiping the screen from time to time. Anyone who saw him wouldn't give him a second thought. Just another crew member going about his duties.

Jager kept up his show of ever-so-purposeful computer study, glancing up now and then until he saw the corridor was deserted. He set to work at once, repositioning some crates that were stacked along the wall beside an empty compartment. He put three just inside, then stacked the rest so they almost completely obscured its opening. After a last look up and down the corridor to confirm no one could see him, he squeezed through the narrow gap and adjusted the crates to block the entry completely.

Relatively secure at last, Jager sat down on a crate and heaved a sigh. "Whew!" he thought. "Now for step two. Whatever that is!"

First things first: He called out to Celine and West, hoping only the cellblock was shielded, not the entire vessel.

"Jager? Jager! Thank the Ancients!" both responded at once. "How are you? *Where* are you?" asked Celine.

"I'm fine, but please—I have to be quick. I'm aboard a Fleet ship. *Queen Morrighan*. Very strange. She disappeared years ago, presumed destroyed. I think it was Scabbage who brought me here, but can't be sure of that. Whoever it was, they 'beamed me straight off *Asherah's* bridge. Unfortunately,

I have no clue as to our location. They locked me in the brig, but I just now escaped. I'm hiding in a spot where they won't likely find me for a while.

"I'd love to capture the ship and return her to Fleet, but that's probably just a tad unreal. So, West, can you sense my location, and somehow get a ship within range to transbeam me out of here?"

"Yes, Jager," replied West, "that should be possible. One moment while I locate you..."

"Oh..." said the Mentor, perplexed. "Another moment, please."

After a pause, she went on. "I am sorry, Jager. I do not understand how this can be, but you are no longer in our universe. You and the ship which carries you are located in the Serpens Universe."

"Serpens Universe? But..." said Celine.

"Great," said Jager. "Just wonderful. Another universe. What in hells do we do with *that*?"

"*Morrighan* could only have crossed between universes through dimensional jump-shift," said West. "The technology to shift small masses between universes has existed for quite some time, but I have never heard of it being done with anything as massive as a Fleet capital ship. It would seem, though, someone has done just that."

"Would it be possible to transbeam me back to the Phoenix Universe?" queried Jager.

"I suppose it may be possible—technology continually advances—however, I know of no one with the knowledge or capacity to do so at this time."

"No!" said Celine. "There *must* be a way. He *got* there, so there *is* a way for him to get back."

"Right," said Jager. "And I'm aboard a *ship* that got here. It must have jumped from this universe to ours, then jumped right back after snatching me off the *Queen*. So, the answer to how it was done must be right here. *Someone* knows how."

"Astute, young one," said West.

"Thank you. And, since I'm here, and you're unable to join me, it's up to me to find out. Fair enough! I like a little challenge now and then."

"That is true, to an extent," said West. "Still, someone else in this universe may know how—someone friendly, and willing to share the knowledge.

"This is what I recommend," the Mentor continued. "You seek the solution there. Learn how to return *Queen Morrighan* to this universe, if you can. Or, at the least, learn how to return yourself."

"Right. And if I can't bring the ship back, I'll sabotage it before I leave, so they can't use her for any more mischief," added Jager.

"As you see fit," replied West. "While you work on that, I shall consult my fellow Mentors, and a host of additional resources, to learn whether a solution can be found here."

"Perfect," said Jager and Celine, in unison.

"Very well," said West. "Keep us briefed on anything you learn. We shall do the same in return. Even if neither of us finds a complete solution, our individual discoveries may combine to reveal a total answer."

"Agreed," said Jager and Celine, again in perfect harmony.

"Excellent. And now, perhaps the two of you would care to share a private moment?"

"Yes, West. That's thoughtful! Thank you," replied Celine.

"Yes. Thank you, West," added Jager.

The Mentor quietly departed, withdrawing her mental presence as well, and leaving the two in privacy.

"Listen, Ensign Jager. I agree with this whole plan, but I don't like it one little bit. The thought of you stuck there, a whole universe away...it just makes me want to cry. If it weren't for my training, I'd be a complete mess."

"I understand. But please—there's no way I'm going to let a little thing like being stuck in a different universe stop me from collecting that kiss you owe me!"

"This is no time for jokes, Jager," said Celine, grimly.

"Okay, okay. I don't like it either, sweet cheeks. I'd far rather be right there, with you in my arms. I have to admit, though, it's a terrific challenge. And our first kiss will be the perfect reward!"

"All right. Just get out of there safely. Bring the ship back, if you can. But what I need—what this whole universe needs, whether it knows it or not—is you. Here. Alive."

"Okay, Celine. Now, I've got to get to work and figure all this out before they find me."

"All right. Do what you have to do, and be quick about it. I want that kiss!!"

"Yes, ma'am!" replied Jager, with a snappy Fleet salute— even though Celine, a universe away, couldn't see it.

CHAPTER 17

The Brothers

Neither was aware of it, but at the same moment a transbeam deposited Jager aboard *Queen Morrighan*, another 'beam placed Soader in a different part of the same ship. Moments after Soader's arrival, his two-headed Kerr Dragon appeared beside him, unconscious.

Shaking off his astonishment, Soader surveyed his sudden new surroundings. "Must be a cargo hold," he thought. But what ship? Whose ship? His eye fell on a nearby stack of freight containers, and his mouth fell open in shock and confusion. Their labels informed him he was aboard a Fleet vessel—*Queen Morrighan.*

"How in all the hells can that be?" he asked aloud. He knew *Morrighan* had been given up for lost, years ago. Well, she'd obviously been found. But who had found her? The Fleet? Someone else? And whoever it was, why had they brought him here?

One of the hold's immense doors slid open, cutting short his musings. In strode a tall Human, dressed in the garb of a high-level G.O.D. official—complete with flowing robes. "Soader!" the man intoned. His voice was a sonorous tenor, but with a sneering edge. "So nice to see you. Come. Come with me." He turned and left, not bothering to look back to see whether he was being obeyed. He was accustomed to unquestioning compliance with his every command. "Oh, and do be sure the door closes behind you. We wouldn't want your pet getting loose. That would be *too* annoying."

Without even a thought of disobeying, the mystified Rept-hybrid followed. He knew the cargo door was set to close automatically, but he stopped to check it anyway. He followed down a long corridor, then through a series of turns at connecting corridors. They passed a number of crew members; several races were represented, but most wore Fleet uniforms. A few glanced at the robed gentleman, but no one paid Soader the slightest attention.

The two came to an open lift, apparently waiting for them. The tall man stepped in, Soader right behind. As they rode the lift upward, the man spoke. "Someone will attend to your Dragon, Soader. We'll feed and water it, and treat its injuries. I hear it took quite a fall. But then, you know that—you were aboard. Heh-heh. That little witch and her Dragons turned out to be craftier than we expected." Soader muttered an acknowledgement.

The lift doors opened and the man stepped out, gesturing down the corridor to their right. "Come, we need you mended. They're waiting to see you."

Soon they came to Sick Bay, where the tall man left the Rept-hybrid in a nurse's care. For an unpleasant while, the medical staff peered at, poked, prodded, pinched and punctured him, but in the end Soader felt considerably improved.

"You'll need more sessions to fully heal that broken arm," explained one of the medics, "but everything else should be fine in short order." An indifferent grunt was all the thanks Soader offered.

After a brief wait, the tall gentleman returned and led him to a rather elaborate-looking door, guarded by two Repts. The man nodded, and one of the guards jumped to open the door. "Come right in," he invited Soader.

They entered a large, well-appointed room. Lounging on richly upholstered divans beside two low, round tables were a pair of grotesquely obese Repts: The Brothers.

The tables held wide platters, piled high with meats, fish and fowl, all drippingly raw. And, from what Soader could see and smell, a fair proportion of the meat was human. Another, larger table stood to one side, groaning under the weight of even more dead flesh. A nearby pedestal held an array of beverages, and glasses and goblets of various sorts.

The Brothers' mouths were stuffed full, and they were busy chewing—quite visibly and quite messily. One held a goblet of crimson liquid. "Earthling elixir," guessed Soader, "or I'm an Auripian toad."

The smell in the room—a miasma of decomposing flesh mixed with Rept at its rankest—was almost overpowering. As was the stifling heat.

"Ah, Soader, it's been such a long time! How *are* you, you old half-breed bastard?" said one of his hosts, past a mouth half-filled with gore. "I heard you took a nasty fall. Isn't it fortunate we happened to be there to cushion your land-ing, and rescue you before Zulak blew you to some dismal

hell? I do believe you owe us a debt. Yes. Yes, I do," sneered the bloated Rept. "But here, what sort of hosts are we? Eat, eat!" he insisted, waving a bloody bone toward the capacious, food-filled table where the tall man now stood, filling a platter.

The Brother who'd spoken was Lancaster; the other was his twin, Dodd. These weren't their original names, though. They'd acquired them when they had tortured and killed a fabulously wealthy Rept family—the Barbdews of the planet Bali—nearly a century before, and then taken over the bodies of the two young Barbdew heirs, Lancaster and Dodd.

The Brothers' own Rept bodies had been near the end of their useful lives, so when the Barbdew lads finally succumbed to torture, the Brothers had their own souls transferred into the still-warm and revivable bodies.

The feature that had fascinated them about these particular bodies was their sadly unusual nature: They were conjoined twins, attached at the hip. This oddity had enormous appeal to the Brothers' perverse, twisted mentalities. And, in the perverted circles in which the Brothers travelled, conjoined twins were regarded as a sexual delicacy, in enormous demand. When the opportunity arose to assume conjoined bodies, they simply could not pass it up.

Decades later, the conjoined Brothers had grown bored with all the sexual antics, and fed up with the endless irritations of living in such unrelieved proximity. After an especially vicious argument, they had decided to split up—literally—and sought the services of a competent surgical team.

Though they annihilated the true Barbdews, the Brothers shamelessly continued using their famous and fashionable family name.

Platter in hand and looking over the tasty-looking smorgasbord, Soader was speechless—a historic event. "What in all the hells are the Brothers doing aboard a Fleet ship?" he wondered as he filled his platter. "Could they have been behind *Morrighan's* disappearance? Hmmm." His platter full, he turned again to the Brothers.

"Nice selection you've made there; awfully nice," said Dodd, his voice a near duplicate of his twin's. "Now sit, sit! Right here beside Pratt, won't you?"

"Pratt?" thought Soader. "Pratt??" The only Pratt Soader could imagine the Brothers entertaining would be High Chancellor Pratt, of the Rept's home sector. But Pratt was a Rept, of course, and this person was Human.

The Brothers laughed at Soader's obvious befuddlement.

Pratt looked up from his platter and smiled a sardonic smile, as if he could hear the Rept-hybrid's thoughts. "Yes, Soader. Pratt. High Chancellor Pratt. But sit, please! And do shut that mouth of yours, if you're not going to use it. Gawping is quite gauche, you know."

Soader quickly closed his mouth and made his way to the empty divan. "So!" he thought, "Pratt must be a Chameleon Rept."

"To answer the obvious speculation, Soader, yes—Pratt is a Chameleon Rept," said Lancaster. "And he's been extremely useful to us, haven't you, Pratty-Boy?"

Pratt nodded, smiling slyly.

"Yesss, he has," Dodd said. "He managed to perfectly duplicate the appearance, voice and mannerisms of a high-level G.O.D. official, after the poor fellow suffered a most unfortunate...accident." With an evil grin, he went on. "Every so often, Pratt here would slip away from his duties as high

chancellor, transform himself, and report in at G.O.D. headquarters, just as if he were the man himself. Attended official functions and all that. Because the dear departed gentleman represented one of the more remote sectors, he hadn't appeared at headquarters often anyway—so no one was bothered when his 'replacement' showed up infrequently, too. The man's inside information sources and high-level signing authority have proven ever so useful, though. Invaluable, I'd say."

"Heh-heh," said Pratt, so full of himself he nearly slipped back into true Rept form.

"Mmph," said Soader, deeply impressed, but not wanting to seem so.

"But enough about Pratt," said Lancaster. "Business. Business. Pratt-my-lad, thanks to you, we now have the boy, Jager."

Astonished, Pratt nearly dropped a half-eaten haunch. "Wha...?"

"Mm-hm. Right here. In our very brig. An information source you so kindly provided told us where he was stationed. Oh, and by the way, Soader, he was aboard your dear chum *Zulak's* ship."

Soader gawped again in fresh astonishment.

"That's right," continued Lancaster, amused at Soader's surprise. "The queen bitch *Asherah*."

"*Queen Asherah III*," clarified Dodd.

"Be quiet and finish your liver, brother dear," said Lancaster.

"As I was saying, Pratt," he went on, "we knew where the young gent was stationed. We received word they were soon to jump-shift to Earth—a nice, out-of-the-way spot for an ambush, don't you agree? So, we watched and waited until they made the jump, then jumped there ourselves, right behind them. As we were snatching the boy—right off their bridge!—we were surprised to see a stirring aerial battle in progress below, between Soader here—riding his two-headed freak of a Dragon pet—and a most handsome black Nibiru Dragon!

"That wasn't all, though. Right there beneath us, on a mountain ledge, was the Zulak girl! With a white Dragon beside her, no less. A more perfect jackpot I couldn't even begin to imagine!

"We tried to grab the girl, but something or someone blocked our 'beam—and nothing we could do would break the block. We were forced to settle for snapping up Soader and his flying flame-out of a Dragon, who'd been knocked right out of the sky by that magnificent black."

"The black was down, too," grumbled Soader.

"Shut your meat hole, half-breed," snapped Dodd. "At least *he* was awake and getting to his feet. You and Mr. Cherry-Red Two-Head were sprawled all over the landscape like roadkill, out cold."

"Exactly so," said Lancaster. "Now, where was I? Oh! Yes. While we were treating the damned Fleet ship to a hearty battering, we made one more try for the girl. Still couldn't get a 'beam on her. Meanwhile, the Fleeties turned tail and jump-shifted out of there, spoiling a perfectly good fight.

"We couldn't stick around for them to return with reinforcements, so we left, too. Jumped back here with our prime target—the boy—in hand."

"And Soader," added Dodd.

"Whatever," said Lancaster.

"How intensely interesting," said Pratt. "Now, what shall we do next?"

"*We* shan't do anything next, Mr. Putty-bod," said Lancaster.

"Why...what do you mean?" said Pratt, suddenly stern.

"What he meeeeeans, Pratticus-old-fruit, is that you have had your day in the sun," explained Dodd. "You have served your purpose. Your show is over. It's the final curtain. You have outlived your usefulness. You are, to use a quaint phrase from I've-forgotten-where, toast. History. Archival. Finished."

"Now, see here!" objected Pratt, rising to his feet in indignant bluster. "*I* am a high chancellor! You can't simply dismiss me like some...some peon!"

"Peon! Peon! What a wonderful word. So apt!" cheered Lancaster. "Apt, because that's exactly what you are, as far as we're concerned. A peon. A sub-peon, third class, actually. So, here's what's in store for you, Prattapotamus: First, so you can't shift your shape and weasel your way out of here, you'll be paralyzed."

As Lancaster spoke, Dodd looked up at a camera button on the wall above and behind Pratt, and gave a brief nod. Before Pratt could launch a fresh objection, a guard stepped into the room, raised a weapon and fired at the Chameleon Rept, immobilizing him.

"There! Isn't that pleasant?" said Lancaster. "All nice and comfy-still. At least it'll be nice as long as you don't get an itch, eh?" His twin brother laughed, splurting half-chewed gobbets of some poor creature's kidney.

"Now that you've, uh, calmed down," Lancaster jeered,

"we'll take you to the transfer station on Earth's moon. There you'll be extracted from that body and channeled right on down to a lovely *new* body on the planet below. A lovely new *primitive* body. In as dirty and degraded a crap-hole of a place as can be found.

"Now, you *do* know what happens to a soul as advanced and able as yours, when its memories have been wiped and it's lodged in a primitive body. Yes? Yes, of course you know. You'll have none of your skills, none of your precious intelligence and cunning. You'll be stuck. Forced to scrabble your way to maturity, if you can. And breed, and grow old—if the teeming diseases and lurking criminals and incessant, senseless wars don't get you first. And when that body dies, you'll get to do it again. And again and again and again, on and on. Mmm. Dreary, eh?

"The only happy note in the whole sad story will be that you'll be too pathetically unaware to appreciate just how dismal your existence truly is. So, there! You have at least *that* to look forward to!"

Pratt said nothing, being completely paralyzed. His thoughts weren't paralyzed, though, and they were racing, in screaming, terrified high gear.

"Take him to the brig and see that he's hooked up to life support. We'll dump him at the transfer station next time we visit the Phoenix Universe," ordered Dodd.

The guard who'd paralyzed Pratt saluted, then spoke into his lapel comm pickup. A fresh pair of guards entered, picked up the Rept's immobile body and carried it—like a piece of furniture, one at each end—from the room.

Soader sat paralyzed, too: frozen with awe at the sheer ruthlessness he'd just observed. His respect for the

Brothers—or whatever passed for respect among such irretrievably evil beings—had tripled.

When the guards had toted off the former high chancellor, the Brothers turned their attention to Soader.

"Ahhh, Soader," Dodd began, "we're disappointed in you. So awfully disappointed. Once again, you've let the Zulak female and her Dragon escape. That was not clever. Not clever at all."

"I almost had them," defended Soader, "and if you hadn't..."

"No, no, no. Please! We've no interest in your excuses, and certainly not your attempts to blame *us* for your failures," jumped in Lancaster. "*You* were an idiot, so she is still free, and she has the spell books. Both spell books. Which she is no doubt learning how to use. And that's going to make it harder than ever to apprehend her."

Soader wanted to stand up to the cruel pair, but he was utterly at their mercy. They controlled the ship; a ship that wasn't even in his home universe! His only weapon was a knife. True, he might use it to kill one of them—possibly even both—before the guards shot him dead. But these swine weren't worth losing his life over, no matter how much he hated and admired them.

Lancaster was right, too. He *had* been an idiot. Of course, that was *only* because of the draining, mind-numbing influence of the fools he was forced to associate with—like his dimwitted guards and assorted minions, and that doubly addle-brained red Dragon. If not for them, he'd have been in peak form all along, and the girl and her cursed white would have been his prisoners.

"You're right, you're right," he said, putting on his best feigned contrition. He lifted a goblet from the table and raised it to the Brothers in submission. "I've been a colossal idiot. Failed to deliver. Caused us awful setbacks. I assure you, though, I'll set it all straight. And fast. I *know* this girl, see? She reacts and responds just like her father, and he's someone I understand so, so well. I know how to predict all her moves, and plan around them. Trust me."

"Trust you?!" roared Lancaster, incredulous. "*Trust* you?! That's all we've *been* doing. Trusting you! Trusting an idiot! What would it make us, if we went *on* trusting you? Even bigger idiots. Hard to conceive, but true.

"But, wait. Let me keep my emotions in check here, no matter how thoroughly justified they may be. We *do* wish to be rational beings, and always to be fair and even-handed in our dealings." He stared off into the distance for several moments, brow furrowed as if he were contemplating the weightiest of concepts.

Turning to his brother, Lancaster continued. "Well, brother Dodd, what do *you* think? Should we end this miserable wretch's life right here and now? Or, out of supreme and perhaps damnably foolish mercy, grant him a final chance to bring us the girl and the ancient books, and so end this bloody debacle?"

"Hmm," mused Dodd, nodding sagely, then gazing at Soader for a long moment. He shook his head briefly, then leaned close to his sibling and began speaking, too quietly for Soader to hear. Soon the pair were deep in whispered conference. Soader caught only occasional words and fragments of phrases. He waited.

Finally, the Barbdews nodded to one another and sat back, regarding their captive as they might a naughty child.

Lancaster spoke. "All right, friend Soader. We have agreed

to be lenient, much though we fear we'll regret it. We shall grant *one* final chance to bring us the Zulak girl. If you do not produce her—and the Dragon, and both spell books, intact—within two weeks, you might as well flush yourself out an airlock and save us the trouble of destroying your sorry ass. You know we can, and you know we will. And you know there is nowhere—*nowhere*—we can't find you. Not in this or any other universe. And when we have you, before we've barely even begun, you'll wish you *had* killed yourself while you had the chance. Your fate will make Pratt's look like divine mercy. And that's putting it *ever* so gently. Are we clear? Eh?"

"Yes, we're clear. And your offer is quite fair. Thank you."

Though he'd agreed, Soader had no illusions. He knew once he met their demands, the Brothers would kill him on the spot. He knew it with certainty, because it was exactly what *he'd* do. His plans would just have to include killing *them* first.

"You're welcome," said Lancaster. "Or, rather, you *will* be welcome when you've captured the girl and Dragon, and secured the spell books."

"Guards!" called Dodd. "Please show our guest to his quarters." Two guards entered, saluted the overstuffed Repts, and escorted Soader to a small but well-furnished room. They left him alone, though he knew very well he was still under close, close watch.

He flopped down on the bed and took stock of his situation. It wasn't good, not by a long, long way. He'd gotten out of worse fixes, though, so he ought to be able to get out of this one. Unfortunately, this wasn't a simple escape situation. Somehow, he had to get out from under the Brothers' control, grab this Jager kid everyone wanted so badly, get back to his own universe, then find and capture Zulak's brat and the damned spell books. From there, it would be easy: sell the kids and books to the highest bidder, and go live somewhere nice and remote, in anonymous luxury. Oh, yes—and kill Zulak. Kill him very, very dead.

For hours he lay in deep thought, considering every detail, every angle, every possible opportunity, every potential pitfall. Then, gradually, gradually, he began to form a plan.

CHAPTER 18

Solutions

Fresh from breakfast and her morning exercise, Celine settled in at the table she'd left the night before. "Today is the day I find that spell," she thought. "I've been at this long enough. Time for results!" She stroked the exquisitely crafted cover of *The Book of Atlantis*, then opened to the page where she had left off.

She worked hard, occasionally taking a break to stretch a bit, or to fetch a drink from down the corridor—sprinting there and back as fast as she could, just to keep from going soft. She felt a little self-conscious about this, and her other occasional physical outbursts. They were hardly in keeping with the calmly businesslike, almost serene conduct of the Mentors and others working here. She didn't much care, though; she knew if she let herself get out of shape, it could be fatal. And not just fatal to her—there were so many people—even races—whose futures hung on what she would do, or fail to do.

Sometime in the early afternoon, she found it: the spell! The incantation that would—once decoded and precisely rendered—reverse the hex laid upon the Dragons of Nibiru and their precious eggs, centuries ago. Wanting to be sure, she looked over the spell's cryptic description again, and then once more. Yes! This was definitely, definitely the one.

Leaping up from the table, she capered about the room in a little dance of joy, singing merrily to the universe in general. Then she called to West, Jager and Fianna to share the fabulous news. The three were thrilled, and lavish in their praise of her accomplishment.

Celine happily accepted their accolades, but then sobered slightly. "Of course," she said, "this is really only a *description* of the incantation. Finding it was just the first step. Now I've got to decode the spell itself using *The Book of Mu*, so I have its exact words and steps. And then I'll have to practice performing it, so I know I'll get it right when we reach Nibiru."

Her friends' enthusiasm wasn't dampened in the least. "Yes, yes," Jager acknowledged. "But look, sweet cheeks—smart cheeks, I should say!—you've decoded plenty of incantations, and never had any problem. This will be easy for you. I just know it!"

"Jager is quite right, my Companion," agreed Fianna. "I have no doubt whatsoever. You will solve the code in short order. In fact, *I* am now the one who is under pressure! Pressure to heal without delay—to heal sufficiently that we may make the journey home to Nibiru. I have no worries about that, however. I do believe this good news alone will speed my progress ten-fold!"

"Well done, child. I could not be more thoroughly proud of you," added West. Then she addressed the others. "Now, friends, we must leave our brilliant Celine to her next task."

"Thank you!" said Celine. "Thank you all for your encouragement and praise. Now I'll decode the spell, and make you even prouder!"

Beaming, she returned to her study table, took her seat, and carefully, lovingly opened the elegant, imposing *Book of Mu*. Concentrating on her breath for several moments—slowly, deeply in...out...in...out—she centered herself. "Here I go," she thought. And so she set to work.

From time to time she would pause in her efforts, to stretch, have a quick drink or snack to keep her energy up, and—of course—to check in with Jager. She always found him in good spirits. "Hello, beautiful! Working on my escape plan," he would say. Still, though, there was a tiny, persistent knot of worry at the back of her mind. She shoved it aside and returned to her sacred task.

Later that evening, West came to her. "Hello, Celine. I must apologize for leaving the decoding work entirely up to you, rather than sharing the task. I am confident, though, that you will complete the work handily."

"Oh, please don't be concerned! I understand," replied the girl. "I never even thought about it. I know you and the other Mentors must attend to so many different matters, probably important beyond what I could even imagine. I'm just so very grateful for all you've done for me, and for all of us. So grateful, I can't even put it into words," she went on. "But then—ha-ha!—you probably don't *need* any words from me. You know me and my thoughts and my heart so well. Maybe better than I do myself!"

The girl had a hearty laugh, then continued. "Besides, I promised Fianna and her people I would help them, so the task is really mine after all. That's what the legends say, too." She drew herself up and struck a serious pose; in a stuffy, professorial voice she declared, "It is written that a descendant of Schimpel, together with a noble Dragon to whom she has been made Companion, shall save Nibiru."

"Yes," acknowledged West, smiling. "That, too, is why I have asked that you help them."

"I know," said Celine, sighing. "Hey, I've good news. I'm making great progress on the spell. I've got several of its words and directions decoded already. What's really exciting is that it looks like it may not even be all that difficult an incantation. Pretty basic, so far."

"This *is* wonderful news. You continue to make me proud."

"Thanks," said the girl, humbly. "Since I'm nearly ready with the spell, it seems like we should go back to Scotland as soon as Fianna and Ahimoth are able. That is, if it's safe to go there now."

"I believe it should be safe, yes," replied West. "We shall examine the area closely, though, just before you travel there. Once you complete your work on Nibiru, you may return here, to assist in recovering Jager—though I am confident he will be back with us before then."

"Ha! That's exactly what I wanted to suggest!" laughed Celine.

"Certainly it is," replied the Mentor. Though she never smiled—the body she animated always wore an expression of supreme serenity—the faint glow surrounding her brightened momentarily, and its color shifted slightly, from golden to a sort of merry yellow.

"Was that a Mentor laugh?" wondered Celine—then laughed afresh at her own wondering. Even though Jager was still in danger and a universe away, she was more cheerful and hopeful than she'd been for days.

Most of Celine's conversations with Jager were extremely brief. Both would have loved to talk longer, but each was focused on a supremely important task, and eager to complete it so they could be together—soon.

In one of their longer exchanges, Jager reported good progress on his escape plans. His goal was to find a way to deliver *Queen Morrighan* into Fleet's hands, rather than simply getting away himself. He knew he couldn't simply take over the ship and fly her home single-handed, but there were other ways to accomplish what he had in mind.

He told Celine he hadn't yet uncovered the secret of *Morrighan's* universe-to-universe jump-shift capability. "Not that I think I'll be jumping her myself," he clarified, "but I ought to know how it works. If I can't manage to bring her home, at least I can come back with the universe-jumping technology. That would mean the end of the advantage these guys have at the moment."

"Smart. Very smart!" said Celine. "But there's one thing I don't understand. How do you manage to gather such information when you're hiding out in a storage bay?"

"Ah! I'm glad you asked, young cadet!" he joked. "I just go to Engineering and look it up, of course."

"How awfully clever of you," she said, wryly. "Come on, though. You know what I mean. How do you get around the ship at all? You're an escaped *prisoner*—they must be scouring the place, trying to find you!"

"Yes, I'm an escaped prisoner. But they're not searching for me. Not anymore. They think they found me, and tossed me back in the brig. You see, I've been practicing a bit of the old magic."

"Okay. So, what did you do, exactly?? Would you please

stop playing with me?"

"Well, I'm not about to stop *that*," he joked, "but I *will* explain, pumpkin."

"Wait. 'Pumpkin?' What's 'pumpkin?'"

"Oops. Sorry. Earth talk. It's a kind of gourd that grows there. Big and plump and orange-colored, with a thick, gnarly stem and grooves running from top to bottom."

"Sounds just lovely," she said, sarcastic. "And this is what you call your devoted girlfriend? You think of me as a fat, orange gourd?? Perhaps you should rethink ever returning to this universe, Ensign."

"Nooooo!" he protested. "I do *not* think of you as a gourd! Well, okay—not *usually*," he kidded again. "Seriously, though—it's just a pet name people use where I grew up. A term of endearment. I swear! You only ever use it for someone impossibly cute and very, very dear to you. Is that better, pumpk...er...sweetie?"

"Well, if that's really the case, okay. But be warned: I'm going to be investigating this further. You'd better hope your story holds up...pumpkin!" They laughed, then Jager continued his explanation.

"Here's how it went. Once I'd set up my little hide-out, I returned to the brig area. Strangely, the same guards were on duty. When one of them left to go fetch something, I caught up with him and managed to put him to sleep with a nerve grip—just like a super-popular character in an old Earth entertainment program.

"I propped him up against an equipment cart in the corridor and bent over him, as though I were tending to someone who'd fainted or gotten ill. I got into his mind and left some false memories. When I was done, he believed he and the other guard had heroically captured me when I'd tried to escape—so quickly that I'd never even made it out of the cellblock. They'd thrown me back in the cell and taunted me for my pathetic attempt to evade guards as quick and clever as they.

"While in his mind, I discovered why they'd never sounded an alarm. They were too terrified they'd be punished for letting me escape, and hoped they could catch me themselves, as soon as their shift was over—and before anyone noticed. They'd have to pay off the guards that came to relieve them, but that was a small price to pay. Pretty routine, too. Apparently there's a thriving pay-off economy among the crew here, covering their butts for all sorts of infractions and misadventures.

"When I finished planting the fake memories, I told him, mentally, to go about his business, but not to return to the cellblock until ten minutes later. Then he was to tell his partner to take a break, and to "go blank" himself—seeing and hearing nothing—for another fifteen minutes.

"I made my way back to the cellblock and waited in the corridor, pretending to be inspecting an electrical panel near the block's entry-way. The first guard returned, and did as I'd instructed.

"When the second guard came out, I went through pretty much the same routine. Followed him, put him to sleep and planted the same memories I'd given the other guy. But this time there was a bit more to be done. I made him return to the cellblock area with me, and let us both into the little control booth where the automatic monitoring equipment is set up. This part was tricky—I had to mentally guide him through the steps of tampering with the equipment and recent recordings.

"He—well, I, actually—erased the recordings back to just before the point where I'd escaped. Then we set up a loop, so the recorder continually re-recorded the *previous* day's routine, over and over. So, if anyone were to check the recordings, they'd see me in the cell, safe and secure, and the guards going through their regular routine—including feeding me and taking away my empty dish.

"To top it all off, I left him with the idea he and his partner had tampered with the equipment so no one would know about the 'escape attempt.' I even gave him the idea of going to collect my food every mealtime and delivering it to the cell, as usual—but then to eat it himself, so no one in the galley would be suspicious. They hadn't thought of that. He was supposed to share 'his' clever plan with the other guard, too.

"There was one more detail to deal with. The guards on the other shifts! I waited until just before it was time for the next shift to come relieve the pair I'd tampered with. I slipped into the cellblock just ahead of them, and put the first guards back to sleep. They got a lot of sleep that day! Anyway, I nerve-pinched the new guards, got into their minds, and set it up so they would always think they saw me in the cell, and would never be suspicious. Then I woke everyone up and slipped away again.

"After repeating that little exercise with the third shift of guards, I was all set. What a lot of messing around, eh?"

"No, it's brilliant!" cheered Celine. "*Typically* brilliant, I should say. That's my brave and intrepid Ensign Jager." She sent him the mental equivalent of a kiss on the cheek.

"Aw, it was nothin' special, Miss," joked Jager. "Actually, it *was* pretty slick, I'll admit. I just don't know how long it will be before someone discovers it, and they really *do* start searching for me. So, I've got to get back to work and get out of here. I miss my own universe—*and* my sweetheart. That's you, you know. Pumpkin!"

After another good laugh, Celine said, "You're right. You should get back to work, and so should I. What's really sweet is we have the best-ever reward waiting for us when we've finished. We'll be together!"

"I'm for that, one-thousand percent. All for now, then. I love you, Celine."

"And I love you, Jager. And don't you forget it, no matter *what* universe you're in. Bye, now!"

Both returned to their tasks with fresh outlooks and new energy.

CHAPTER 19

Solved!

Consumed as she was with decoding the Atlantean spell, Celine still thought of her parents often. She didn't dare call them, though. It tore at her conscience to keep them in the dark like this, but it couldn't be helped. Not now. Too much was at stake. She just hoped they would forgive her when it was all over and they were reunited at last. She'd have a lot of making-up to do.

After two long days of diligence, Celine made a careful note about the riddle she'd just solved, set aside her hand computer, and gazed at the beautiful old book for a thoughtful minute. Then, abruptly, she burst from her chair and danced around the room, elated. "I did it!" she crowed. "I *did* it!!"

And she *had* done it. With the last of the riddles solved, she had the spell she needed, complete.

Though far away, Fianna and West were nearly knocked

over by the spiritual force of the girl's exultation. They knew at once what it meant. As soon as Celine had quieted down a bit, they cheered and congratulated her with admiration and praise almost as intense as her own joyful outburst.

"Thank you, thank you!" she answered. "And you both know very well I could never have done it without you."

Then, just as abruptly as she'd broadcast her jubilation, she fell silent and serious.

"What is it?" asked Fianna, aghast at the change. West said nothing, sensing what troubled her young charge.

"Jager," the girl said. "Where's Jager? You two heard me just now—and he must have, too. But he's said nothing. And now he doesn't answer when I call. West, do you know what's happened?"

"Not with certainty, child. However, moments before your celebration, I learned that *Queen Morrighan* has re-entered our universe. It is now in orbit above Earth. But Jager does not appear to be aboard—and I cannot locate him anywhere. Neither here, nor in the Serpens Universe."

"But the ship is in our universe—that's wonderful," said Celine. "He *must* be aboard. Where else would he be? Maybe he's just laying low for the moment, while he executes some part of his plan. Maybe he's the one who brought the ship across!" She called to Jager again, but there was no reply.

"I, too, have been unable to make contact," said West. "It may be that he is in an area shielded against thought. In any case, he is smart, strong, and exquisitely skilled. Whatever his circumstances, he will emerge and restore contact as soon as he can do so safely. He knows we would be concerned at his silence, and would weigh that factor in deciding upon any course of action."

"Yes, you're right," agreed Celine. "But he may also be in danger, or injured...or worse."

"I have not discounted those possibilities, child," said the Mentor. "And I have asked all Mentors to be alert for his presence, and to render assistance, should he need it.

"Meanwhile, the urgency of your own mission has not lessened. Rather, it has grown, and grows with each passing hour."

"You're right, West, but I can't help worrying. He's all alone. He could be in awful danger. I can't just drop my concern."

"I understand," replied West, "truly I do; but I must ask you to trust me. Be assured, dear child, I know what I ask of you is not fair in the least; still, I must advise that you put feelings aside and do what is necessary." She glided to Celine's side as she spoke, and gently touched her shoulder. The girl pulled away, still caught up in a tangle of emotions.

"I realize it will be difficult," continued the Mentor, "but you must go to Nibiru and complete your task. Otherwise, the Nibiru Dragon race will cease to be; that is inevitable. I am certain Jager would understand, and he would not want to be in your boots, facing this decision—but he would go. I believe you see that, do you not?"

Celine bowed her head; a few tears fell. She sniffed and ran a sleeve across her face, then looked up at West. "Yes, I see it. And I understand what you're saying and what you ask. I'll do it, but please, West, promise me. Promise you'll find him and keep him safe."

"Yes, certainly," West replied. "We will find Jager. Most likely he will be waiting here when you return from Nibiru."

"All right," replied Celine. She sat up straighter, her

composure returning. "Thank you. I guess the next order of business is Fianna."

"Yes, my Companion?" came Fianna's mental voice.

"Hey! Are you listening in on all this?"

"No, I have not been listening, but you said my name—aloud, and through our connection, too. We are closely attuned, you and I!"

Celine managed a half-smile. "We surely are. So, now that you've joined the conversation, I have a question: How soon can you be ready to travel the tube-chute? Be honest—no over-optimism. We can't risk it if you're not completely ready."

"I am prepared to make the journey at once. I say this with no over-optimism. A few stiffnesses and aches remain, but those are from lying around so long. I need to *move*. If there were a proper atmosphere here on Mars, I would go outside and have a good aerial workout."

"Well, that's good to hear," said Celine.

"It most certainly is," added West.

"And I have you both to thank for such a fine recovery," said Fianna. "You, and the other skillful, kind and caring people here."

"You are most welcome, Fianna," said West. "Now, would you be good enough to meet us in the training room?"

"Yes; I would love to. If Celine will be so kind as to show me the way, I shall join you directly," the Dragon replied.

"Excellent," said the Mentor.

Celine gave Fianna a mental image of the route; she arrived a few minutes later, Dragon-smile alight. Celine rushed to wrap her in a heartfelt hug. She was pleased and

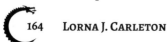

relieved to see her beautiful friend—and craved the comfort of her presence. She hoped it would help dispel her worries over Jager, and make it easier to focus on the demands before her. A shudder passed through her, and she hugged Fianna all the tighter.

"Errooo!" cried Fianna; she sensed her friend's inner anguish and hoped to lighten her mood. "Take care, Companion! I have only just mended!"

Celine chuckled in spite of herself; Fianna joined in, and West's subtle glow brightened to cheery yellow. Celine noticed the Mentor's change at once. "She *does* laugh," she thought, "Ha!"

"Though I will not understand it, may I see the incantation meant to break the hex?" Fianna asked.

"Sure," said Celine. "I need to look at it again, too—just to make certain of the items we'll need to cast it properly." She moved to the table, sat down in the chair she'd occupied almost non-stop for days, and opened the big *Book of Atlantis* with loving care. Fianna and West followed, taking up positions behind the girl and looking over her shoulders.

"Here it is," Celine announced, pointing to a paragraph of beautiful script. Taking up her hand computer from beside the ancient volume, she pointed to a paragraph on its screen. "Here is my decoded version. And down below, you can see the list of things we'll need. Tall, tapered black candles. And white ones. Sixteen of each. Next, a white bowl and a black one, broad enough that half the candles will fit around the rim of each." She paused for a moment, mentally reviewing the small inventory of magical supplies remaining in her bodypack. "I only have a little white salt left, so I'll need some more. Black salt, too—I'm completely out of that. A few grams of each will be enough. Oh—and a small mirror;

preferably circular, but any shape should do." She paused, musing. "Wait. No. Let's not take any chances with this. The mirror should be circular. That's everything, though. Pretty simple, for something so important."

"Very well. I shall provide these things shortly," said West. She turned to the Dragon; "Fianna, in your estimation, will Ahimoth be well enough to journey to Nibiru with you?"

"I believe so, yes. If we were to ask him, he would undoubtedly say so. In this case, we could believe him."

"I believe you are correct," said the Mentor. "I have just consulted his caregivers; they are prepared to release him, provided he promises to attempt no battles with larger Dragons for at least seven days."

Celine and Fianna laughed—and Celine thought she caught another flicker of that bright yellow laugh-glow from West.

"Wonderful!" said Fianna. "I shall go to him at once and deliver the good news. When should I say we will leave?"

"I suggest you depart tomorrow morning," replied West. "That would allow you a good night's rest, and place you at Loch Ness in plenty of time to assist Nessie in preparations for the vortex opening."

Fianna and Celine nodded agreement. "I'd rather go *now*," said Celine, but we would still have to wait until evening, for the vortex ceremony. I guess this gives me more time to practice the spell."

"Very well," said West. "Celine, by morning you will have the items you requested for your incantation. I will..." The Mentor broke off abruptly and turned her head to one side, as though listening to an unseen speaker. A few moments later she returned her attention to Celine and Fianna.

"I am sorry. I must leave at once. There is other pressing business to attend to. Good evening to you both." She rose and left the chamber, in as close to a rush as Celine had ever seen in a Mentor.

"Thank you!" Dragon and Companion called after her.

"Something serious must be happening," said Celine to Fianna, "I've never sensed such urgency from her."

"Yes," Fianna agreed. "It concerns me, too. Well, we know what we must do. Sleep well, my friend." She gave Celine a fond nuzzle, then exited the room, ducking carefully to avoid bumping herself in the doorway.

Celine picked up her hand computer, then carefully wrapped the precious books for their journey to Nibiru. She returned to her quarters and set to work repacking her bodypack and Fianna's saddlebags. At last she was finished: everything was ready for an early-morning departure.

After one last attempt to reach Jager, she sat down on her bed with a sigh. She'd almost laid down to try to sleep when she stopped, thought for a moment, then rose again.

Leaving her room, she made her way to Fianna's chamber. Entering quietly, she found the Dragon nearly asleep, tail wrapped up around her as usual. Careful not to disturb her most precious friend, the girl knelt down and arranged herself for sleep at the Dragon's side. Without fully waking, Fianna stirred; her great tail uncurled a bit, just enough for Celine to snuggle up close to the smooth, white flank. When the girl was in position, the tail tucked gently around her, and the Dragon gave a contented huff. In moments, the two were fast asleep.

Their sleep was not fast enough, though. Before long, both were tormented by brief but awful, frightening dreams.

Dreams of being trapped in a never-ending tube-chute. Dreams of a pleasant flight turned nightmare by a vicious Dragon attack. Dreams of falling, falling, falling from unimaginable heights—unable to recover. Dreams of drowning in the ruddy waters of the Chalice Well. And more, and worse. Suddenly both woke—Celine sweating and disoriented, Fianna trembling, nostrils flared and claws extended as if for battle. They looked at each other, dazed, but relieved their nightmares had ended.

"Dreams?" queried Celine.

"Troubling dreams, yes," replied Fianna.

"Why?" said Celine.

"I do not know, my friend."

"I don't have such dreams often," Celine continued. "I almost never dream at all, really. I never know where the bad ones come from. Someone once suggested they come from eating something you shouldn't. I've heard other ideas, too—even less likely. I do wonder about it sometimes."

"There are similar explanations among my people," said Fianna, "just as improbable."

"Well, we know that at least one good dream—The Dream of Atlantis—is caused by good beings. Maybe evil dreams are somehow caused by evil beings—or at least by troubled ones," Celine mused. "Maybe some of them get a sort of sickly satisfaction out of causing upset or fear or worry. It's hard to imagine anyone being so mean, but we certainly know people in our waking world who are. Like Soader. Sometimes I almost feel sorry for him. What an awful way to go through life."

"Hmm. That is a more reasonable-sounding explanation than any other I have heard," said Fianna. "But who knows for certain? Not I."

"Nor I," agreed Celine. "But let's suppose it really is the reason. And let's suppose those unhappy bad-dream-causing beings can hear us, or receive our thoughts. What if we told them to shut up and leave us alone? Do you think they might stop and go away? Or at least be quiet and let us sleep?"

"It would be worth a try!" said Fianna. "Let us do it. It certainly could not cause harm."

"Right!" agreed the girl. "Let's try. I think we shouldn't be emotional about it, though. No anger, for sure. That might just antagonize them. And I guess 'shut up and go away' isn't the best thing to say. You know, maybe it would work if we just acknowledged them—if there really is any 'them' at all! This whole idea is just a guess, after all. But you know what I mean about acknowledging. Like when someone is talking and talking, and you really let them know you've heard and understood them. They sort of relax and feel better—and like they don't have to continue."

"Exactly. You are a wise one, my Companion. Let us try it. You first."

"Okay," agreed Celine.

She took a moment to settle herself, still her mind and become fully present. Then she thought—calmly, intentionally, but without emotion, positive or negative: "Thank you."

She smiled. "Well, that was that. I hope 'they' got it."

"That was very good, I think," offered Fianna. "If anyone is present, I am certain they did get it."

"Well! Thank *you*," Celine said with a chuckle. "But now it's your turn. Go ahead."

Fianna smiled her warm Dragon smile, then did as Celine

had done. When she felt fully at ease and present, she thought, calm and firm, "I have heard you."

Now she smiled broadly. "I think that was good! Do you?"

"Yes, I do. Nice!" said Celine. "Now, let's complete our little experiment and get back to sleep. We have a lot of traveling ahead of us. And not the easy kind."

The Dragon agreed, and they curled up again, in their favorite sleeping position.

"Sweet dreams," said Celine. "Or no dreams at all!"

"And the same to you, Little One."

In less than a minute, both were fast asleep once more. They slept the rest of the night straight through, in quiet peace.

CHAPTER 20

Preparations

E arly next morning, rested and refreshed, Celine returned to her own room. There she found the items she'd requested of West, laid out neatly on her bed. With them were some food packets, a change of clothes, and a surprise—a few toiletries a girl would appreciate if she found herself in a far-away place—Nibiru, for instance—longer than expected.

And then she noticed one more item, and an even better surprise: West had left her an image-capture. At first, she didn't recognize the people it depicted: a handsome young man, his arm around an athletic-looking boy of perhaps seven or eight years, and a lovely, chestnut-haired woman with a baby girl in her arms. The baby was smiling brightly and reaching toward the camera with fingers spread wide.

"Oh!" said Celine, aloud. "It's my family! And me!"

She gazed in wonder at the happy group. Then it struck her—she knew her brother's name, thanks to West, but not the names of her parents. On a hunch, she turned the image-capture over, hoping. Yes! There on its info panel were their names. Sloan and Fagan Beghe—her birth parents. And her protector-brother, Alika Beghe. Alika *Ronit* Beghe, to be precise. And there was her name, too: Celine Olivia Beghe. "Olivia!" she thought. "Ha! I never even knew I *had* a middle name. I like it! Thank you, Mother and Father!"

After drinking in the image a few moments more, she held it close to her chest, then placed it tenderly in a protective pocket in her bodypack. She couldn't stop smiling—and a few happy tears trickled their way down her cheeks.

"Okay," she thought. "Back to business!" She finished her packing, made a final survey of the room to ensure she'd left nothing behind, and headed for the transbeam room.

As she strode through the corridors, she made a hopeful try at contacting Jager. No go. Apprehension welled up at once, but Celine pushed the feelings and thoughts away. "I need to act like I'm a cadet on a vital mission," she thought. "Heck, that's exactly what this is. I have my orders. I must execute them. I need to believe in West and the Mentors. They will find him. He'll be right there at the transbeam platform when we return, mission accomplished. And then he's going to get *such* a kiss. I hope everyone else there will be totally embarrassed! What was it Jager told me Earthers say when a couple get all smoochy in public? Oh! That's right. 'Get a room!' Ha!"

Ahimoth and Fianna were already in the transbeam room when she arrived, deep in animated mental conversation. Catching Fianna's reply to something Ahimoth had said, Celine gasped. "What?! There are Nibiru Dragons on *Earth?*"

"Well, good morning to you, too!" said Fianna, merrily. "And yes, my brother has learned there are more of our

people on Earth. They have been there, carefully hidden, for quite some time."

"It is true," confirmed the black Dragon. "Allow me to explain. Through all my years of captivity in Soader's deep cavern, I had an odd sort of friend. A presence who spoke to me from afar. It had no name that I could discern, but it was there and it was friendly, keeping me company, reassuring me, boosting me up if I began to despair.

"It was this little voice-friend who helped me find the means to escape Soader's prison, and prompted me to follow the evil wretch to Germany. There I finally learned whose voice it was. It belonged to an elderly witch, living in a remote valley less than an hour's flight from Father Greer's tunnels and caverns. She asked that I not attempt to visit her hidden home, fearful someone might see and follow me. But she said she was a friend—a Dragon-friend—and that there were other Dragons living on Earth. Nibiru Dragons."

"That's wonderful!" cried Celine, amazed. "Maybe we can go look for them—once we've found Jager."

"Well," said Fianna, sheepish, "that is exactly what we were discussing. You see, it is not necessary that Ahimoth be on Nibiru with us when we reverse the hex, so he prefers to remain on Earth, and seek out the Dragons of whom his witch friend spoke."

"That's a good idea," said Celine, "but is it wise, when Soader and his Dragon might return at any time?"

The Dragons exchanged a brief look, then turned back to the girl. "Well, that is a possibility, but...well..." began Fianna.

"Okay, okay. Never mind. I see there's more going on here than you're eager to talk about. And that's fine with me. I'm sure you have your reasons, and I won't pry any further. So!

Shall we get on with our journey?"

The Dragons smiled thankfully and agreed. "Yes! Let us be off!" said Fianna.

"An excellent plan," chimed in West, entering the chamber. "If the three of you will step onto the platform, I will send you on your way."

"Of course, of course!" said Celine and Fianna, in harmonic unison. Ahimoth nodded agreement as the trio mounted the platform.

"Good luck," said West. "And please, Celine, when you arrive on Nibiru, secure the grimoires. Orgon will know how to keep them secret and safe. I know you will agree, we do not want to have to go looking for them ever again. And, when you have completed your sacred mission, return to Earth and call to me—I will bring you back to us here."

Celine nodded agreement, but then her determined smile dimmed. She opened her mouth to speak, but before she could form even a single word, the Mentor said, "Yes, my child. We will find him. Find him and bring him back."

"Thank you, West. Thank you!" said Celine.

In the next moment, she and her Dragon friends vanished in the transbeam's light.

THE TRANSBEAM BROUGHT CELINE, Fianna and Ahimoth to the shores of Loch Ness, in the Scottish Highlands. It had been less than two weeks since they'd stood at the same spot, but it seemed like half a lifetime. And, indeed, that brief span had been filled with enough events and adventures to fill any ordinary lifetime.

Orienting themselves, the three scanned their

surroundings—and stopped in utter astonishment. In a grassy meadow, not a hundred meters away, were the Dragons' parents: Neal Tawni Uwatti, King of the Dragons of Nibiru, and his Queen, Dini Amara Uwatti! The royal couple hadn't noticed they had company; they were enjoying the afternoon sun and fanning their wings to strengthen them.

"Mother! Father!" cried Fianna. Ahimoth was still too surprised to speak. At their daughter's call, the elder Dragons turned. Now it was their turn to be astonished. In a twinkling, astonishment turned to joy, and they rushed to greet their children. Ahimoth and Fianna sprang forward too, meeting their parents half-way. The four merged into an exuberant mass of happy Dragon-folk, embracing, nuzzling, filling the air with sounds of elated greeting.

"How can you be here?" asked Fianna. "West told us she heard you had traveled back to Nibiru."

"Ah. I'm afraid West was mislead," said her father. "You see, when West called to Nessie to inquire after us, Nessie perceived her urgency and concern, and sensed West might be with you, as well. Nessie also knew there was not sufficient time for a full explanation, and for adequate assurances of our safety. She chose to report that we were safe and well—which was true—and phrased her assurance so as to imply we were about to be on our way to Nibiru. As I am sure she will tell you when she joins us, she felt terrible to have been less than completely honest—but she felt it the best course, under the circumstances. She was also sure West would understand, as would all of you."

"Thank you, Father," said Fianna. "I do understand, and appreciate Nessie's quick judgment. She was correct—our situation at that time was stressful in the extreme. Hearing you were still on Earth, without knowing all the reasons why, would surely have distracted and delayed us, perhaps disastrously." Ahimoth and Celine nodded agreement.

"But, please," said Ahimoth, "why had you not entered the tube-chute?"

"We were not sufficiently recovered to do so without dire risk," replied Dini. "We truly needed more time, and more of Nessie's care, to prepare for the ordeal. Further, she had shielded the entire area so that no one—not even Soader or the Brothers—could have detected our presence. We were as safe as could be hoped. And it has proved a blessing: We are marvelously healed, and well prepared for the journey. Moreover, you are now here to accompany us."

Fianna, Ahimoth and the girl could not be angry, as everything made sense. Besides, they were overjoyed the royal family was safe, and back together again.

"And now," said Fianna, "Celine and I have something to show you, dear parents."

Celine smiled; "Indeed we do!" She strode to Fianna's side, reached up, and uncovered and unlashed a crate. The crate. The elder Dragons were silent as she lifted it down, set it before them, and opened its lid to reveal the contents: Neal and Dini's precious eggs, all safe and whole.

The royal parents showered the girl with heartfelt thanks and praise, then bowed to her, each with a foreleg forward in respect and gratitude.

Celine, a trifle embarrassed at all the attention, thanked them sincerely, then excused herself to walk along the lakeshore. She wanted the Dragons to have time to rekindle and cherish their family bonds, still strong despite agonizing years of separation.

As she walked, the girl looked back, now and then, at the

delighted family. She was glad the royal couple had not yet left for Nibiru after all; it was deeply touching to watch the loving group. She pushed away thoughts of her own family—or rather, families: the Muian family of her birth, and the kind Errans who had adopted her. She tried instead to focus on the journey and tasks ahead. Inevitably, her attention turned at last to Jager, who still had not answered her calls. Her heart began to sink.

"Wait!" she told herself, shaking off the creeping sadness. She turned back toward the happy Dragons and broke into a run, eager to rejoin them and immerse herself in preparations for the journey ahead. She ran so hard that she didn't notice Water Dragons had begun to surface offshore. Dozens of them, all headed toward the spot she herself approached. Leading the living flotilla was Nessie.

Ahimoth was the first to notice the oncoming clan. "See there!" he called out, pointing. "Our water-cousins approach!"

The other Dragons turned as one and sang their greetings to Nessie and her followers. Still running hard, Celine noticed the commotion, stopped, and called her own greeting.

Nessie arched her head higher above the waters and trumpeted a cheery reply.

Celine rejoined her friends just moments before the first of the Water Dragons arrived. When the flurry of greetings had finished, Nessie clapped her forefins twice and announced to one and all, "It is time to prepare for the vortex-calling. Evening approaches, and everything must be in readiness before twilight!"

Eager to get on with it, Celine and Fianna thanked her warmly. Nessie turned to her people and issued instructions;

heads bobbed agreement, and they turned to their assigned tasks.

"And now we have a bit of time," said Nessie to the Nibiru Dragons and their Human friend. "Please, tell me what has happened since last we spoke."

The big Water Dragon listened in fascination as the party took turns recounting their catalog of adventures—aerial Dragon battles, recovering the ancient grimoires, Father Greer's hospitality, the encounter with the Chalice Well, and the events at the transfer station and Mars outpost.

At last the tales were told and eager questions answered. Just in time, for evening was nearly upon them.

CHAPTER 21

Sacred Mission

Everything, everyone was ready. The Water-Dragon clan was gathered near the shore, all in precise formation with Nessie at their fore. Pungent herbs, flowers and oils floated on the waters around them.

The floating elements were unique Water-Dragon adaptations of certain ancient rules and rituals of magic, which demanded such items be precisely placed, in working a spell or incantation. Or, more often, methodically sprinkled into open flames. Fire-making was a serious challenge to these lake-bound folk, so they had evolved alternative methods and means.

Celine was fascinated. In her extensive studies of the magical arts, she had read about the aquatic clan's clever adaptations—some uniquely powerful—but she had never witnessed them in practice.

While the Water Dragons were preparing for the

ceremony, Celine asked Nessie if she might contribute by building a small fire at the waterside, and casting in certain potent elements as the rite progressed. Nessie graciously accepted the offer, and thanked the young Human for her wisdom and willingness.

Working quickly so as not to delay the ceremony, but still with the utmost care, Celine drew the appropriate elements from her bodypack, laid them out in a precise array, and built a small fire on a flat rock close to the water's edge.

Meanwhile, Ahimoth—who would not be entering the vortex with the rest of the travelers— bid his parents a tearful goodbye. All planned to reunite soon, but the parting was painful nonetheless; their age-long separation was still too fresh in mind.

With her preparations complete, Celine bowed to Nessie once again, to indicate all was in readiness; Nessie bowed her graceful neck in return. The youthful witch knelt before her fire, and the Nibiru dragons stepped up to flank her, two on either side.

Nessie scanned the carefully arrayed assembly behind her, then met the eyes of each of her guests in turn. Lifting her muzzle to the sky, she sang out: a high, pure note. The ceremony had begun.

The Water Dragons began a chant, soft at first but rising swiftly in intensity. Celine joined in; at the same time, she sprinkled an herb-and-oil mixture above the flames. Richly scented vapors filled the air, mingling with those rising from the herb-strewn waters.

The chant went on and on, excitement and anticipation building with each repetition:

Gods and Goddesses of the light
Guide our people through this night
Guide them safe, hear our song,
Guide them now, and all night long.
Land them gentle at the end
Guide them safely
Home again.

After a time, a pale mist formed in the air above the assembled group. Then, at the center of the mist, a disc appeared, black as black and growing slowly to a diameter of several meters. The vortex was opening! A sparkling drizzle of water began to fall from the opening, like a gentle magic rain.

The Water Dragons closed ranks, maintaining their precise pattern but drawing closer together. Their muzzles pointed straight up toward the vortex on long, lithe necks. Nessie lead the group's chant to a higher pitch. The falling drizzle became a stream, then a rushing torrent, plunging into the lake and churning its surface to foamy froth.

After a few moments of this, Nessie dipped her great head down, down. She kissed the lake, then whipped her neck skyward once again, and called out in a powerful tone of command.

The thundering torrent ceased at once. Though nothing now fell from the disc above, it was filled with a whirlpool of liquid, foam and bubbles, spinning counter-clockwise in a dazzling swirl of blues, greens and purples. At the center of it all spun a splash of intense pink, shining as if lit from within. Here was the vortex, mesmerizing in its mysterious beauty.

"Just as gorgeous here as it was on Nibiru," gasped Celine. "If we visit Father Greer again someday, we'll have to make a painting of it in his caverns!" She and Fianna shared a laugh. It seemed like ages since she had suggested making just such a painting in the white Dragon's cave back home. It was hard to believe it had really been just two weeks since that day.

"True! True!" laughed Fianna. "But the vortex will not remain open long. We must enter. Mother, Father, are you prepared?"

"We are," Neal replied.

"We could not be more so," added Dini. "Our hearts ache to see our homeworld and our people."

"Very well," their princess-daughter answered. "Follow us now, and you shall see them soon."

Nessie still lead the chanting, steady, steady—holding the vortex open, ready to bear whoever dared enter.

"All right, Fianna. Let's go," said Celine. She gripped the saddle horn fiercely and braced herself.

Fianna crouched, inhaled sharply and sprang upward, wings tight to her flanks—her leap alone would carry her into the vortex's mouth. All below watched as the Dragon and her Human Companion vanished into the swirling color-maelstrom. With a last, loving nod to Ahimoth, Dini and Neal followed their daughter and her Companion.

An instant after the Dragon-king's tail-tip had disappeared, the vortex's Earthly manifestation vanished. Nothing remained but the evening sky, spangled with stars. Nevertheless, the Water-Dragon clan continued its chant, as they would throughout the night. By day they would anxiously anticipate the next evening's moonrise: the sign that their friends were safely home.

—— ❧ ——

TRAVELING THE TUBE-CHUTE was just as harrowing as Celine and Fianna remembered. For the elder Dragons, it was worse; moments after entering the vortex, Dini and Neal cried out in anguish. Celine cast a spell at once, enveloping each in a bubble of calm air and easing their passage. The grateful pair mented Fianna, asking that she relay their thanks to her brilliant Companion.

A few minutes later, Dini exclaimed, "Nessie and her clan are helping us, too! I sense their strength and their presence, supporting us. We will make the journey safely; I know it."

Rushed along in the rowdy current, the Dragons kept constant contact, alert for anyone in distress. Celine kept her spell fresh, chanting quietly. Occasionally, one of the group was buffeted off balance, but the others were always quick to right them.

After what seemed like days, the jolting and swirling gradually eased to a gentler, even flow. The weary travelers were delighted at the change, but it didn't last for long. Just minutes later, the harrowing journey ended abruptly: the vortex dumped them (in a most undignified heap) on a cold, hard surface. There they were, on the rocky ledge behind Dragon Hall's Cynth Pedestal. Home!

The group untangled themselves and rose unsteadily to their feet—only to find they had company. Lots of company. Crowded around them were Dragons, Dragons and more astonished Dragons, with Orgon the Wise at the forefront.

The two groups stared at one another for no more than a breath before the whole crowd erupted in wild, elated celebration. The cheering, dancing and capering went on and on. Dragons jostled for the chance to greet their long-lost king and queen, and welcome back Princess Fianna and her Companion.

After the tumult subsided a bit, Fianna reared up on her hind legs and trumpeted for attention. "My friends and clanspeople! A moment's quiet, if you please!"

The crowd fell still, wondering.

"As you see, we have returned with our beloved king and queen!"

This was obvious, and no longer news, but everyone gave a huge new cheer, just the same.

"That is not all, though! Oh, no!" said Fianna. "My dear Companion, Celine, has something else to show you. A gift to all our people, from my royal parents!"

Though they had no idea what the something else might be, this new bit of news prompted another full minute of cheering. Fianna waited out the commotion as patiently as she could manage. Meanwhile, Celine unstrapped the crate from the Dragon's back and set it carefully before Orgon. Neal and Dini came forward to flank the crate, one on either side.

When the noise had subsided, Fianna cried, "Behold!" as Celine lifted back the crate's cushioned cover. Every Dragon present jockeyed to see what it contained.

"Eggs!" boomed Orgon. "Six precious, beautiful eggs! And they all live!!" Neal and Dini beamed with regal pride.

Now it was twenty minutes at least before the wild celebration was spent. For here were the first new, living eggs to be brought forth on Nibiru for more than a century.

Fianna reared again, and swept the throng with her gaze.

"There remains one final wonder to reveal," she intoned, dramatic. "Celine, would you show them, please?"

Celine had been reveling in the Dragon's excitement, but an anxiety had been building in her for many minutes now. She knew that soon—very soon—she would be called upon to perform the most important work of magic of her life. But that time hadn't yet come. Without flourish or ceremony, she drew forth and unwrapped the ancient grimoires, then held them up for all to see.

"The books of the Ancients!" cried Fianna. "*The Book of Atlantis* and *The Book of Mu*. Herein lie the secrets to casting off the curse upon our eggs; the means to restore our future as a race!"

There was no cheering this time. Only gasps and "Ohhhhhs!" Then reverent silence. All knew well that these events and this day would live forever in legend and song.

"It is true. The end to our curse is near. Our brave and skilled Celine has found and learned the secret spell we have sought so long. And upon this day, she shall cast that spell, and break the hex forever!"

Again, the Dragons were speechless, scarcely daring to believe what their princess had revealed.

"Now!" Fianna went on, "There is not a moment to lose." Turning to Celine, she asked, "Companion, must you be in the Nursery itself, in order to work your magic?"

"No," Celine replied, "The spell is of such power that it will reach every Dragon's egg, no matter where it may lie on all of Nibiru. All I require is a bit of soft ground, and a few meters of space."

"And must you work in seclusion, or may the Dragons gathered here look on and bear witness to the miracle?"

Celine hesitated for just a moment. This would be the most important spell she'd ever cast, and certainly not the simplest or least dramatic. And she had rarely worked before an audience—let alone royalty! The thought made her nervous for an instant, but she cast the feeling aside and replied: "Princess Fianna, I should be deeply and forever honored if you, your royal family, and all those gathered here, were to witness the work I am about to perform. Your presence will support me in my work, and your support and loving energy will contribute immeasurably."

"Very well, then!" said Fianna. "There is a small glade just outside this Hall: Linglu's Glade. Its ground is fairly soft, and there is room for all to gather round." Now she addressed the elder green Dragon. "My dear Uncle Orgon, would you lead us to the glade?"

"I would be honored to do so, Princess—but only with our gracious king's leave. After all, I am but the steward of our land and people." He bowed deeply. "My noble brother Neal is our king!"

"Thank you, my dear brother," said Neal, returning Orgon's bow. "By the look of our fine people gathered here, and the perfect condition of this, our sacred Hall, I judge that you have born your duties beyond what any king could hope or expect. For this, my queen and I thank you from the bottom of our hearts. Now please, please! You have my leave and blessing! Lead us to the glade!"

All the gathered Dragons cheered. Orgon began making his way toward the glade; Fianna followed, with Celine close behind. Next came King Neal and Queen Dini, bearing the six precious royal eggs. Everyone else filed along, excited and eager.

In minutes, the grand procession reached Linglu's Glade.

On arriving, Celine indicated the area where she would do her work; the Dragons gathered round as she took off her bodypack and began the preparations, calm and careful. Meanwhile, at Fianna's request, two of the waiting Dragons went off to gather wood for the small fire Celine would build; another left to fetch a pitcher of water.

The Dragons waited patiently, watching in wonder as the young Human worked.

Orgon quietly addressed the king and queen. "Fianna and her Companion have come not a moment too soon. Dear old Haggis is near death; he may not live out the night. Without a hatchling at hand, we would lose his spirit. Now there is hope!"

With the utmost mindful care, Celine drew out each necessary item, arranging them precisely before her. Next, she used her incant-baton to mark out a large circle on the ground. She asked the king and queen to bring their six eggs, and indicated where they should place each one, at precise locations near the circle's center.

That done, she picked up the two bowls, one black and one white; she filled each with water and carefully dried their rims, all the while humming softly to herself. Next, she took up two white candles, lit one, and used it to heat the base of the other. Once the base was soft enough, she pushed it onto the rim of the white bowl, then held it until the wax hardened enough for the candle to stand on its own. She repeated this until the rim was ringed with white candles, then did the same with the black bowl and candles. Finally, she set the bowls before her, a half meter apart, with the circular mirror lying face-up between.

Next, she sprinkled a portion of white salt into the black bowl, then black salt into the white bowl, chanting softly:

"With salt this water is pure. I give it power to heal and cure."
Continuing the chant, she lit each candle.

Celine gazed into the flicking flames for a time, contemplating the malicious power that had cursed the Dragon race for so long—the power of the evil Brothers.

Now she used a small atomizer bottle to puff a mist of rosemary oil over the flames, making them sputter and spit. With the remaining oil, she anointed the six eggs that lay close by, chanting quietly as she smoothed it over their fine-textured surfaces. Next, she carefully draped the eggs with a black cloth and scattered a mixture of herbs on and around it.

At last, the preparations were complete. The moment of truth had arrived: time to begin the spell itself. In a voice that rang of wisdom and power which seemed beyond such a young person, Celine began:

Gods and Goddesses of the sky

A spell was cast

that Dragons would die.

With poisonous will

a web was spun

Before us now

see the damage done.

The dying of eggs,

I wish to undo

and so, I now

appeal unto you.

Spell, spell, spell be gone
back to the Brothers
to whom you belong.
A wish, a favor,
I must ask in return,
I gladly do now:
Send the Brothers
to burn.

The youthful witch repeated her chant nine times through, then sat in silent contemplation. At length, she drew her knife from its sheath at her side; the graceful white handle, exquisitely carved in form of a Dragon, seemed to glow in the candlelight.

The polished blade glinted as she raised it high, and then—to the astonishment of the watching Dragons—she slowly, methodically cut off her long, lustrous chestnut-brown hair, handful by silken handful, laying it in careful coils on the mirror before her.

Next, she placed two treasured possessions atop the silky coils: her five-star medallion and carved white Dragon necklace.

Rising, she approached Fianna and knelt before her. Aloud, she made a respectful request: might she have just two of her friend's exquisite scales? The Dragon smiled and nodded assent, then solemnly drew two scales, snow white and lily smooth, from the curve of her left flank. Celine accepted them with a bow and returned to her magic circle, where she placed the scales alongside the medallion and necklace.

Taking up her knife once more, Celine held her left hand over the mound and made a firm, deliberate cut across its palm. There were gasps from the watching crowd as blood welled forth, to drip over the hair and carefully placed talismans.

Hand held steady and blood still flowing, Celine chanted a new chant, nine times through:

My intentions are good
My intentions are strong
Now transfer the spell
from these eggs: be it gone!
Transfer it all
To the Brothers, to their fall
Transfer it whole
one spell-phrase and all.

O Gods and O Goddesses, in mercy so great
Break this cruel, hateful spell; all its power negate
I offer you treasures in token of faith
And ask in return a dear measure of grace:
Please grant all these eggs
And the fair Dragon race
The right to live on in their rightful strong state!

After a silent pause, Celine called upon Fianna for help. While the girl bound her own wounded hand with a clean white cloth, the Dragon used her powerful foreclaws to dig a neat, round hole, just inside the magical circle. When the work was complete, she neatened the mound of soil she'd extracted, then withdrew from the circle and resumed her place beside her brother and parents.

Bowing once again in thanks for Fianna's help, Celine blew out the candles that ringed the two bowls, then gently poured the salted water from each into the hole, chanting as she worked. She followed the water with the candle stubs, sixteen black and sixteen white. Next, she lifted the mirror, with its blood-soaked burden of hair, medallion and necklace, and lowered it carefully into the hole, softly voicing a chant only she could hear.

Now she took up the black cloth that had covered the royal eggs, twisted it to resemble a rope, tied its ends, and arranged it in a neat circle atop the items in the hole. With her right hand, she scooped and pushed the upturned soil to fill in the hole, then stood to tamp it firm with her feet. At the girl's invitation, Fianna approached and tamped the soil as well.

Finally, their work complete, the pair bowed their heads and intoned a Chant of Conclusion they had practiced earlier.

Turning to the watching throng, the girl and Dragon announced, as one, "It is done!"

The glade was rocked by a resounding cheer from the whole assembly. A cheer that echoed through Dragon Hall, down the long valley and out across the broad plains to the mountains beyond.

Suddenly, the cheers of elation were cut short. Gasps and cries of wonder took their place—then utter silence. One of the six eggs inside Celine's magical circle had stirred. As they watched, it quivered again, then rocked to one side and back, with urgent energy. It was going to hatch! The cheering resumed, redoubled...then ceased again, more abruptly than before.

Celine had collapsed at Fianna's feet.

CHAPTER 22

Mission Accomplished

Celine woke to find herself in her bed, in Fianna's comfortable cave home. This was the same home they'd shared since her arrival on Nibiru a year ago. Sensing Fianna nearby, she called out, "What happened to me?"

"Ah, Little One, finally you are awake," replied Fianna, sauntering in from outside. "You were overcome from exhaustion, we assumed. Moments after you completed the incantation, you collapsed. Though I could not detect anything seriously amiss, you had me worried! How do you feel?"

"A bit groggy and weak, but all right." She sat up, happy to see sunbeams shining cheerily in through the cave's entrance. "How long have I been asleep?"

"Nearly a day and a half! If you slept much longer, I planned to throw you in the river, just to see if that would help." Fianna laughed as the girl tried to swat her before she could duck back outside. Celine followed her out into the freshness of the day and took a long, fond look at the beautiful scene all about them.

"Time for a swim!" she declared, crossing to the river and diving straight in. She swam across and back several times, bucking the current to stay abreast of the cave. Thoroughly refreshed and blood pumping nicely, she climbed out, gathered her clothes and strolled back to the cave in search of something to dry off with. And even more important, something to eat! She was utterly famished.

"I do not know if you remember it, but one of the eggs in your magic circle began to stir, just after you finished the invocation," Fianna called from outside, where she basked in the sun. "Though I was tending to you, some of the others took the wakening egg to old Haggis. You should have seen the tears! Songs by the score will be written about what you have done, my Companion—and for years and years to come."

"You mean Haggis took up the hatchling?" asked the girl, chomping on a brattle from her bodypack.

"Yes! He was able to leave his old body and enter the young one before it hatched. I suppose he was in a hurry—it is customary to wait until the hatchling has emerged. But what an incredible event! We watched as the old body sank toward final sleep—then suddenly the little egg doubled its lurching and rocking. A crack appeared, then widened, and out popped a little snout! As Haggis's proud old body exhaled its last, he mented his sister Tamar, who was there among us. 'He is in the egg—struggling to get out!' she cried, and everyone cheered.

"Life is such a wonder!" Fianna exclaimed. "I had never witnessed a birth before. I shall never, ever forget it."

198   LORNA J. CARLETON

"I'm so happy for Haggis—and all of you," replied Celine. "Will he use the same name?"

"No, he wanted to have a special name, in celebration of the first hatching in so many, many years. He asked to be called Alika, an old Greek name from Earth—like yours. He said it means 'guardian,' and that you would understand why he chose it."

Amazed at what she'd just heard, Celine ran out of the cave to give her dear friend the tightest hug she could muster, tears streaming down her cheeks.

"Little One, have I said something to upset you?" the Dragon asked.

"No, no. Not at all. It's just that Alika was the name of my own brother. I only just learned I'd even *had* a brother when we were at the Mentors' Mars outpost. True to his name, he was a guardian; if it weren't for him, I wouldn't be alive today!" Drying her tears, she went on; "Life is definitely full of surprises; terrible and wonderful all at the same time. I just wonder how Haggis could have known. Well, I suppose that's a mystery for another day!"

Fianna smiled her Dragon smile, and the pair sat together in silence, enjoying their favorite place on all of Nibiru.

Over the days that followed, more elder Dragons abandoned their old bodies to take up new ones, as more eggs quickened and hatched.

Hatchlings! They meant new life for the world and renewal of its ancient Dragon race. All living things, from the birds and fish and animals to the trees and plants of forest and field, seemed happier and more vital. No one could remember a happier time.

———✦———

Celine had grown restless. She ached to travel back to Earth, and from there to the Mentors' Mars outpost, where she could join the effort to recover Jager. Driven though she was, she dreaded the thought of another passage through the tube-chute. She would gladly have borne it at once, but there was one final factor in play: Fianna.

No matter how the Dragon princess might protest the notion, she could not be permitted to travel the tube-chute again so soon. She had been through hell in the past few weeks—not one but two tube-chute passages, a near-fatal experience with the sabotaged Chalice Well, several high-speed, long-distance Dragon flights and a catastrophic battle with Soader's far larger, more powerful Dragon-slave. No, Celine would not allow Fianna to make another tube-chute passage just yet. After another day or two of rest, perhaps. And even then, only if it was eminently plain that her beautiful white friend was truly in fine condition.

When she explained all this to Fianna, the Dragon was apologetic. "I am so sorry, Celine. I am holding you back—keeping you from your urgent, urgent mission. You deserve so much better, after all you have done for me and for all my people!"

"Oh, I understand. And I thank you for your concern. But really, there's no need at all for you to feel badly. None! After all, we're a team. We're far more than any ordinary team. I'm your *Companion*, and I wouldn't dream of going off anywhere without you! Being sensible about it, I have to admit waiting a day or two isn't likely to make any difference anyway. It's nowhere near as important as knowing you're back in top form, ready for whatever craziness we get ourselves into next!

"Besides, the *Mentors* are searching for Jager! What could

be better than that? Ha! We joked about it before, but it's probably true: by the time we get back to the Mars outpost, he's going to be there at the transbeam platform to greet us. He's probably already there, chatting up and charming all the Mentors!"

They shared a good, long laugh at the idea of Jager surrounded by shimmering, white-and-silver-draped Mentors, gazing at him adoringly as he recounted his daring exploits.

"I don't suppose Mentors can really be chatted up or charmed," said Celine, "but if anyone could manage it, it would be Jager!" They laughed again, pushing aside darker thoughts of what the young man might be confronting.

In the end, Fianna needed two full days of rest and recuperation before she could honestly claim to be back to normal. To quell her anxieties during the wait, Celine immersed herself in a project she'd contemplated for many months: adding to the wall-paintings adorning Fianna's home.

First, she painted a stunning rendition of the open vortex, as it manifested itself at its terminus in Dragon Hall. The work covered nearly all the remaining open space on the cave's rear-most wall. Fianna was amazed at how her friend had captured the gateway's enthralling beauty.

When this first grand image was complete, she added a few smaller works to other unadorned spaces. One showed Nessie and her clan of Water Dragons; another depicted the Mentor, West, as she had appeared to them in physical form. When Celine finished, the two friends sat for a long while, contemplating the new images and the older ones as well. They couldn't have said why, but both experienced the wistful, faintly sad feeling that these might be the last paintings Celine would ever make in this special place.

The next evening, Fianna and Celine were enjoying what they thought would be a quiet visit with King Neal and Queen Dini, in their spacious and comfortable quarters at Dragon Hall. Suddenly there came the sounds of some sort of commotion outside. "Hm," said Neal, "I shall see what this is all about." He rose, went to the entrance and stepped outside. Fianna caught a glimpse of her mother suppressing a grin, and wondered what was going on.

Neal re-entered the cave. "Well, it seems a few people heard you might be stopping by here tonight," he said, pretending no more than mild interest. "Perhaps you would like to come out to greet them. Of course, if you would prefer it, I shall thank them and send them on their way."

"No, no!" said Fianna and Celine, in unison.

Everyone had a chuckle at this increasingly common phenomenon, then Fianna went on: "We'll be happy to greet whoever has stopped by, and wish them a pleasant evening."

"Very well," said Neal. "They are just outside." He led Fianna and Celine toward the entrance, Dini following behind.

As they stepped out into the cool evening, they were greeted with a resounding "SURPRISE!" There in the courtyard was a huge throng of Dragons, leaping, trumpeting, fanning their wings and cheering.

The remainder of the evening—and well into the wee hours—was taken up with a joyful celebration, honoring Princess Fianna and her marvelous Companion—rescuers of the Nibiru Race.

The two were pronounced Heroines of Nibiru; speeches were made, new songs sung, and new dances danced. Inscriptions of their names at the base of the Cynth Pedestal were unveiled—an honor bestowed on only two others before them: Princess Linglu and her Companion, Schimpel.

Ahimoth's name had also been inscribed, and it was announced there would be a fresh celebration to honor him, once he returned from Earth.

The following evening, Celine and Fianna sat outside their cave home, enjoying the sunset. They had awakened just an hour before; it had been nearly dawn when the party finally came to a close, so they'd slept the day through.

Fianna had hoped to spend more time on her homeworld, especially now that her parents had returned. She was well aware of Celine's anxiety over Jager, though. And after all the girl had done for her, and for her family and race, the Dragon knew she owed her Companion a deep, deep dept. She felt well rested and fully recovered now, too; there was no need to delay their departure any longer.

Knowing Celine was straining to avoid the subject, Fianna decided to broach the matter herself. Just after the sun dipped below the horizon, she asked, "My dear Little One, are you ready to return to Earth now, and rejoin the search for your soulmate?"

"Yes! Yes!" Celine practically shouted. Calming herself, she went on: "I mean, yes—of course. But not unless you're completely certain you're up to it. We both have to be at our best, you know. Who knows what we'll be getting ourselves into next?"

The Dragon laughed, "You are certainly right about that! But please—I feel well rested and fully fit. And in truth, I do not think I could bear another hour of celebration. Could we leave this very evening? The sun is gone, and I know Orgon would arrange to call the vortex for us."

"Yes. That would be perfect. I won't even have to pack—I

packed yesterday, and ever since then I've been checking and rechecking everything to make sure it's all there and ready to go. Let's go find Orgon and be on our way."

"Splendid. But I will ment my mother of our plans; she can ask Uncle Orgon to make preparations. That will save us some time."

"Perfect!" said Celine, and she gave her dearest friend a happy hug.

But, as the pair tidied up their homey cave to leave, each was haunted once again by a strange sadness. They loved this place—but how long would they share it?

Soon they were satisfied that all was in order; it was time to depart. As she was climbing into the saddle, Celine said, "Hey, before we go, I'd love to say goodbye to little Alika. Could we do that?"

"Yes. I would like that, too," replied Fianna, "and I am sure the hatchling will love the attention. Are you ready to go?"

"Ready!"

The Dragon crouched, then sprang into the air, her Companion clinging tight in the saddle. Climbing upward, she wheeled over the river and headed for Dragon Hall and the Nursery Chamber that adjoined it.

Arriving at the nursery, Fianna called out to Lye, the nanny. Suspicious as always when it came to visitors, the old Dragon huffed and grumbled as she made her way up the passage from the inner chambers, wondering who thought themselves important enough to call her away from her precious charges. When she emerged to see Princess Fianna and her Companion, her attitude softened. Here were the people who had saved all the eggs from death! To Fianna's great surprise, the tough old nanny even smiled!

Fianna greeted her with gracious formality, and Celine bowed to her in respect. Then Fianna asked if they might be permitted a moment with one of the hatchlings, Alika.

Lye's suspicious nature got the better of her for a moment. "No..." she began—then caught herself before continuing. "No problem at all," she finished. "You are always welcome, my Princess. And your fine Companion is welcome as well. Come right this way, if you please." She turned and walked toward the nursery's entrance.

Celine and Fianna followed, both smiling; they sensed the nanny's natural reluctance, and her efforts to calm her powerful protective instincts and be cordial.

As they made their way toward the chamber where new hatchlings were cared for, Fianna recognized they would be passing the Egg Chamber. "Dear Lye," she asked, "might we be permitted a few moments to look into the Egg Chamber?"

Lye hesitated, then gave her consent. "Yes, Princess Fianna. I would be honored to show you the chamber. Your very presence may encourage more of the young ones to awaken and break out to meet the world." Celine had to stifle a laugh when she noticed Lye's furtive, still-suspicious glance in her direction. Well, the old girl certainly took her job seriously!

The three came to the side-tunnel that led to the Egg Chamber, and Lye led the way to the chamber's entrance. With great pride, she stepped aside so Fianna and Celine could look inside. There were the eggs—the priceless legacy of generations past, and the only guarantee of a future for the Nibiru Dragon race. Each egg was nestled in its own velvety cushion, bathed in the gentle, dim glow of the light-orbs that ringed the chamber, set on small ledges at about Dragon-shoulder height. Some of the eggs seemed to pulsate faintly. From time to time, one would quiver or twitch. It was plain to see these were living things. In the Dragons' eyes, they—and the hatchlings to come—were the most precious living things in the universe.

Soon Fianna thanked Lye for bringing them to see this wonder, and indicated they were ready to go on to visit the hatchlings. Lye bowed (as well as she could, in the confined space), then led them back up to the main tunnel and onward toward the Nursery Chambers.

The distance wasn't great, and they soon came to the first of the chambers—one of a dozen spacious enclosures where hatchlings were cared for. Each had its own smaller side chambers and compartments, meant for storage and other purposes. There had been a time, long ago, when this was a busy, busy place. All its chambers had been filled with hatchlings and young Dragons, still too small to live at home with their parents, according to ancient custom.

Now, all but one of the Nursery Chambers was empty. Only one was needed to accommodate the few hatchlings just arrived. But everyone on Nibiru was now filled with a joyful hope: that soon, every chamber would soon be crowded with Dragon infants; a new generation of their ancient and noble race.

With Lye's permission—and under her intensely watchful eye—Fianna and Celine entered the occupied Nursery Chamber. They spotted little Alika at once. And, to their delight, he spotted them, and let out a joyful chirp. An astonishingly loud chirp, for one so small.

Celine crouched down to talk to the hatchling. "Fianna and I are going on an adventure tonight, and I wanted to say goodbye before we leave. It might be a long time before we return." The baby Dragon could not yet speak, but he began

a sort of buzzing purr, and nuzzled Celine's leg. "I think he understands," said the girl, "and it feels like he's thanking me."

"Yes, I believe you are right," replied Lye. "And he seems to like you!"

"How sweet!" said Celine. "I feel he's asking me to take care of Fianna, too."

She addressed the tiny Dragon. "It is a pleasure to meet you as well, Alika. And I promise to take care of your Princess so she comes home safely, to watch you grow big and strong."

Alika chirped again, seeming to appreciate the girl's words. Lye made a small sound to get her guests' attention, then nodded as if to say, "Enough." They got the message.

"It is time for us to go," said Fianna. Celine nodded agreement; Lye smiled approval. Before rising, Celine took Alika in her arms... (was that a stifled gasp from Lye?) ...and kissed his tiny, golden-hued muzzle. The little Dragon made his purring noise again as Celine rose, shooting Lye a quick, sharp look before smiling cheerily. Yes, the Nanny Dragon was boss here, but Princess Fianna's Companion was not to be trifled with.

Their happy business at the nursery concluded, the girl and white Dragon thanked their host profusely and prepared to make the short trip on to Dragon Hall. Just as Fianna was preparing to take flight, Celine spotted another Dragon spiraling down toward them: King Neal himself!

The Dragon king landed, greeted Lye with a bow of respect, then addressed his daughter and her Companion. "Queen Dini told me of your plans. I have come to escort you to Dragon Hall, so that we may see you safely on your way."

"Wonderful!" said Fianna and Celine, in unison once

again. Neal beamed, delighted to witness such a beautiful bond in action.

Without further discussion, Neal turned in the direction of Dragon Hall and launched himself upward. Celine hunkered down against Fianna's great neck, and Fianna followed her father skyward.

Moments later—the distance was not great—they approached Dragon Hall's majestic courtyard. Celine and Fianna could see they'd been expected—arrayed around the spot where the vortex would open was a teeming throng of Dragons. King Neal spiraled down to land, and they followed close behind. The Dragon-king trumpeted their approach. As one, the waiting crowd began to stamp and cheer; then they drew back, to allow ample room for landing.

Safely on the ground, with his royal daughter and her Companion just behind him, King Neal spread his great wings up and back, acknowledging the crowd and asking for silence. He waited patiently for their compliance; it wasn't quick to come, so great was their excitement.

When Queen Dini had advanced to stand beside him and the audience had settled at last, the king spoke.

"Tonight, our princess and her Companion—newest heroes of our people—travel again to Earth. Though they have other important business to conduct there and elsewhere, when next they return, our Prince Ahimoth shall accompany them. With his arrival, the royal family will be united once more!"

The crowd burst into fresh cheering, trumpeting and stamping. Celine and Fianna were a bit embarrassed at all the exuberant attention, but smiled, bowed, and waited patiently for the tumult to subside.

At last the crowd grew quiet. Fianna turned to Celine; "Are you ready, Companion?"

"Yes!"

"Then let us begin our next adventure." Turning to her uncle Orgon, who had advanced to the front of the expectant crowd, she asked, "Dear Uncle, would you lead the chanting to call the vortex?"

"It will be my honor, dearest Princess!" Now he turned to the crowd, raised his great green wings for attention, and began to chant. The gathered Dragons joined in at once, following along in the ancient ritual and watching for the vortex to respond to their magical call.

Gods and Goddesses of the light
Guide our dear ones through this night.
Guide them safe, hear our song
Guide them now, and all night long.
Land them gentle at the end
Guide them safely
Home again.

As the chant continued, Celine climbed into the saddle, and Fianna made ready to leap into the vortex. She didn't have long to wait; after just a few repetitions of the chant, the vortex opened in its familiar but ever-amazing beauty.

With a cry of "Off we go!" Fianna leapt forward, into the luminous whirlpool of light and color.

Moments later, the vortex disappeared. The Dragons concluded their chant, and their king led them in a final, fervent invocation for the travelers' safe return.

As soon as the vortex engulfed them, Celine drew her incant-baton and cast the bubble spell that would ease their passage. Still, they had to steel themselves to ride out the tumultuous, jostling journey.

Hours later, the tube-chute vortex abruptly opened; the pair found themselves in mid-air, high above Loch Ness and tumbling earthward. Fianna oriented herself, spread her wide wings, caught the air and eased into a gently circling descent—down, down to just above the lake's moonlit surface. Leveling off, she made a graceful turn toward the shoreside spot they'd left just a few days before.

The two had expected to find the place deserted. What they saw instead made them gasp in amazement.

CHAPTER 23

Joli

L ong, long years in the past, Ahimoth's childhood love, a lively young green Dragon named Joli, was killed by a lightning strike. Ahimoth was devastated by the loss—particularly since it occurred while Joli was watching a battle *he* had instigated, between himself and a rival for Joli's affections: a handsome young blue Dragon, Vin.

Forced to abandon her hopelessly shattered body, Joli—in spirit only—had traveled Nibiru for days, seeking a Dragon egg on the verge of hatching. Should she find one, she would stay close, wait for the baby to struggle free of its eggshell, and join with the hatchling body. Assuming the infant Dragon-body as her own, she would dedicate herself to its care, health and long, happy life. But unless she could find such an egg, she faced oblivion most permanent; she would be lost to the world.

Bodiless though she was, Joli tried calling to her suitors,

but neither could hear her. She reached out to Orgon the Wise and even her young friend Fianna; still she could not make herself heard. She spent much of her time haunting Dragon Hall, wishing to be close to her people in spirit, even if unable to be with them in body. Proximity to her people meant sharing their sorrow over their fate as a race. Unless the hex upon their eggs were somehow undone, they were doomed.

On occasions when Ahimoth or Vin visited Dragon Hall, Joli's pain was redoubled. Theirs was a special sorrow and suffering. They shared their people's anguish for the future, as well as a pain even more personal and immediate: the loss of their beloved Joli.

When Ahimoth and Vin made a pact to travel to Earth in hopes of finding Joli's spirit, she was horrified. They were much too young to risk traveling the tube-chute. And, because she was here, not on Earth, their journey would be in vain. She made a supreme effort to communicate with them, but without success. They did not hear her. The poor Dragon-spirit's despair became nearly unbearable until, on the day the young Dragons were to depart, she hit on an idea that gave her at least a small measure of peace: she would follow them to Earth! There she could continue her efforts to contact them. Even if those efforts still proved futile, at least she would be near them.

So, when the two heartbroken Dragons leapt into the vortex, she "leapt" in with them, and made the journey to Earth. Though she had no body to be buffeted and battered by the tube-chute's currents, the trip was still disorienting and unpleasant. Watching, helpless, as her two companions suffered through every moment of the transit only added to the trouble.

When the tube-chute brought them at last to Earth, Joli was relieved the trip was over. Her sorrows were far from over, though. First, there was Vin. He had suffered awfully in the passage, and was so near death that Ahimoth was certain he'd lost his friend and former rival. Joli took small comfort in being able to support and encourage Vin's struggling spirit. Even though he never became fully aware of her or the aid she gave, her efforts prevented his almost-certain death. In her heart she knew this, and took pride in her decision to come to Earth.

Soon after the Dragons emerged from the vortex, Soader detected their presence and rushed to the scene. He was delighted to find the pair so battered by their journey that he could capture them without a struggle.

Joli could see at once the Rept-hybrid was up to no good. She screamed and hammered at him, desperate to drive him away from her helpless friends. All she managed was to give Soader a vaguely uneasy feeling, as though someone were looking disapprovingly over his shoulder. Undeterred, he hauled the Dragons into his ship and flew off toward his underground complex in New Mexico. Though close to apathy at her failure to stop him, Joli followed. If she could do nothing else, at least she could watch over her dear Vin and Ahimoth. She stayed with the two young Dragons for several years, visiting one and then the other, back and forth, in the caverns where Soader imprisoned them.

As time went on, Joli became aware of a sort of mental voice that spoke to her from time to time, usually in the quiet hours of the night. At first, she wondered whether she might just be going crazy. But the voice seemed so real, and its messages of hope and reassurance were so welcome, she couldn't help but accept it. It was a living presence, and it acknowledged her own existence and life; that was enough. More than enough.

The voice praised her for so faithfully watching over her friends, and said her devotion would one day be rewarded: she would help them more directly.

A month or so after the voice first came to her, it suggested she travel to a region it called Germany. Joli had heard of this place before; it had been one of the favorite destinations of Nibiru Dragons visiting Earth. In recent times, it had become increasingly difficult to avoid the native population, so the area had fallen out of favor. There were so few safe places left on this lovely planet!

Still, the voice encouraged her to come. There was a secret place there, it said, where she would be safe and welcome. More important, if she came, there was a chance she would discover a way to rescue her friends from their awful imprisonment.

That was enough for Joli. If there were such a chance, no matter how remote it might seem, she would take it.

She visited Ahimoth and Vin one last time, bidding each an unheard goodbye. Then she moved off toward Germany. Unencumbered by a body, she could have *decided* to be in Germany, and she would have appeared there instantaneously. However, she often found it comforting to act as if she had a body, especially when traveling from place to place. So she "flew" upward out of Soader's prison-caverns, crossed the North American continent, soared over the Atlantic and the shores of Europe, and came at last to the green German countryside.

Guided by her voice-friend, Joli traveled up a remote valley and made her way to an isolated cave, its opening flanked by a stand of stately trees. An old woman stood before the cave's entrance, looking directly at her—just as if she could see the bodiless Dragon-spirit. Indeed, she *could* perceive Joli's presence, and quite clearly.

The old woman spoke. "Welcome, my friend. My name is Dagmar. I am so pleased you have come!"

Joli was nearly overcome by a warm rush of pure joy. This was the first communication she'd received from a living, bodied person in years! Ever since her own poor body had been destroyed, in fact. "Thank you! Thank you!" she thought, though she knew she couldn't really be heard.

"You are welcome, most welcome," said Dagmar, aloud.

Again Joli felt unspeakable relief and joy. She had the vivid sensation of hot, happy tears welling up, and a tight lump in her throat—even though she had neither eyes nor throat to well or tighten.

"There now, child. It is all right. I am ever so happy to see you, too. Now, see what I have here for you." Dagmar held up a woven basket, lined with a thick white cloth. Cradled in the soft folds was an egg. A *Dragon's* egg!

Joli was so astonished she nearly lost consciousness. "Is it...?" she began to form a question, but dared not complete it.

"Yes," spoke Dagmar, "it is a Nibiru Dragon's egg, and it is quite alive. Quite near to hatching, too. You have arrived just in time. Very well done!"

This was more than Joli had ever, ever hoped for. An egg! About to hatch! And an impossibly kind friend to help her. The joyful spirit-tears were welling again, even stronger than before.

"Watch now," whispered Dagmar, taking a seat on a low

stone bench and setting the basket before her. Joli moved up beside the woman's ear for a better view. The new friends gazed at the egg in eager expectation. There! It quivered! And then again. And then came a series of tapping sounds, each stronger and more insistent than the last.

The egg rocked sharply, and a small crack appeared. Dagmar began a low, rhythmic purring; the new life inside the egg seemed to respond, rocking in rhythm to her purrs.

The crack lengthened, running completely up the side of the shell and over its upper end. Suddenly, a small starburst of cracks appeared, and out poked a tiny snout. There came the sound of drawn breath, followed by a sigh. A wisp of vapor puffed from the little nostrils and rose in the cool evening air.

Joli was both mesmerized and ecstatic. She was watching a Dragon's birth! *Her* Dragon. Her new body! She said a silent prayer, dedicating herself to take perfect care of this beautiful creation; to safeguard and grow and nurture it, to make it strong and healthy, full of grace and skill.

"You may enter now, Joli—it's quite all right," whispered Dagmar. Joli needed no urging. In an instant she was inside the hatchling body. It seemed to welcome her, with a sort of primal awe at her wisdom and certainty.

Taking control of the body's movements—*her* body's movements!—Joli poked and shoved at the shell, struggling to widen the opening with her snout and straining at the walls with tiny wings and limbs. At last the egg burst apart. Out fell the hatchling, flopping over onto her side among the shell fragments.

It would be some time before Joli gained full control of her new body, but now she managed to open her eyes and turn her head to gaze at Dagmar's kindly old face. Others might have seen an ancient, toothless witch of a Human; Joli saw the most beautiful being she'd ever encountered. She smiled a hatchling smile and greeted her dear benefactor with the happiest sound she could muster—somewhere between squeak and shrill squawk.

Dagmar replied with the purring encouragement she'd used earlier. Joli made a wobbling attempt to stand, but fell over again and again, until at last she got all four spindly legs arranged beneath her, and her tiny wings folded none-too-neatly out of the way. She looked up at Dagmar with a proud smile...and then began to collapse once more. Catching herself just in time, Joli managed to keep from ending in a heap. Instead, she wound up sitting. With a smile at the old woman, she squeaked as if to say, "I *meant* to sit down! Pretty good, eh?"

Dagmar laughed. "Nicely done, nicely done, little one!"

Joli nodded proudly, then squawked—insistent this time. She was hungry. Very hungry!

Dagmar cackled, rose from the bench and took her tiny new friend into the cave, basket, eggshells and all. Setting down the basket, she returned to the entrance, closed her eyes, bowed her head, raised her thin arms, and chanted a low chant that would double the protective shielding she maintained over and around her valley. Knowing of Soader's frequent presence on the planet, and that he possessed a Dragon-location device, she tailored her shield-spell to prevent the evil wretch from learning of Joli's presence. Ever.

Joli grew quickly, and in the months and years after the hatching, she developed an inseparable bond with Dagmar. The woman's full name was Dagmar Arnbjorg; the same name born by her mother, her grandmother, her great-grandmother, and on down a long family line. All the way back to the time of Deet, last earthly Prince of Atlantis. In fact it had been Deet who had bestowed the name on the first of that long line of wise and powerful women. "Dagmar," as he explained to the first, means day maid. "Arnbjorg" combines "arn"—eagle, and "bjorg"—protect, help, save, rescue.

The name had not been handed down the generations without ample reason. Dagmar and all her predecessors commanded magic most powerful. As one small example, despite being a humanoid, Dagmar could link with Joli—or any other Dragon she chose—and communicate through menting. Such connection was possible for only a vanishingly few normal Humans, and then only through precise and complex rites.

Dagmar's valley was lush and beautiful, enjoying (thanks to her magic) a climate much milder than the surrounding country. Her magic also kept it perfectly hidden. Anyone who ventured near its boundaries, whether by land or in the air, would become curiously distracted and disoriented. They would wander harmlessly away, utterly unaware that anything unusual had happened. As the outside world had developed increasingly powerful detection and guidance technologies, Dagmar had kept pace, enhancing the valley's protections to ensure it remained undetected, untouched and unsuspected.

Under Dagmar's care, Joli blossomed. True to her basic nature, she became a strong, intelligent and thoroughly charming Dragon. Gentle in spirit, it was plain she could yet be a formidable foe if threatened. Her strength and wisdom grew with each passing year, as did her bond with her beloved teacher.

As part of her engaging physical, mental and spiritual

regimen, Dagmar insisted Joli work on her flying skills each day. In good weather and bad, the Dragon took to the skies, learned new skills, sharpened old, and continually built strength and endurance. Dagmar was adamant on these last two points; more than once she'd explained that Joli would one day need all the flying strength and stamina she could muster.

Ordinarily, Joli replied to Dagmar's reminders with loving respect, but one day her young-Dragon curiosity couldn't be denied. "Teacher," she said, "you have often reminded me I would someday need strength and stamina. I do not doubt you. But, is there something in particular I'll need them for?"

"Yes, dear, there is. One day—and not far in the future— your friends Vin and Ahimoth will depend upon you for their lives. You must be prepared to fly on and on without rest, perhaps for days."

"Oh! Then I shall work all the harder to improve. But...you know of my old friends?"

"Yes," replied the elderly witch. "Since their arrival on Earth, I have given Vin and Ahimoth such comfort and counsel as I could. I come to them as an "inner voice"—much as I reached out and encouraged you to join me here.

"You see, to serve, guard and protect good Dragon folk is the purpose and reason for my being in this world. And to rescue them, should it come to that. As the name we have shared through the centuries suggests, this has been the purpose and tradition of my family line since the days of the Atlanteans. It is our pride, our honor and our sacred duty to fulfill it."

Awed and humbled, Joli bowed before her teacher. "I am honored, my teacher, my dearest friend. I scarcely feel

worthy of such care and devotion, and I could never thank or repay you adequately."

"There is no need, child," replied Dagmar. "Your happiness and well-being are more than thanks enough, and always shall be."

"Thank you all the same," said Joli with a loving smile. But then her visage darkened. "I've got to go!" she blurted. "If Ahimoth and Vin need rescue, I must do it *now!*"

"Calm yourself, Joli," said Dagmar. "I understand your desire, but it is not yet the time."

"No!" came Joli's sharp retort. She leapt to her feet, stamping and snorting, wings spread wide and high. "I can't just hide here, safe and comfortable in this beautiful place, while they suffer in that awful cavern!"

"I do understand," replied the kindly Dagmar. "But hear me well: Dire though their situation may be, the time is not right for rescue. Should you attempt it, your efforts would be for nothing, and worse than nothing: The three of you would perish. To have any hope for success, you must wait until the stars show the time is right."

"But, but I..." Joli began.

Dagmar raised a gnarled finger for silence. "Until the stars decree it," she said, stern, "I say no. You may ignore my warning if you wish—your life and your choices are ever your own—but there are times when waiting is the wisest choice. I tell you this is one of those times. Think on my advice before you choose."

Joli demurred, realizing she had been foolish and impetuous. She bowed her head low, contrite.

"There now—no need to withdraw," said Dagmar. "I understand all that you are feeling. I was once young, too—though that may seem difficult to believe!" She laughed, and Joli knew she'd been forgiven.

"Now!" the witch continued. "You've not yet practiced your flying today. To work, child. To work!"

ON A COOL MORNING several weeks later, Dagmar woke, rose, and made her way out into the small yard before her home. The day had dawned gray and damp; a bank of fog was rolling its way up her secret valley like a great, pillowy caterpillar, immune to the powers that turned lesser visitors aside.

After tasting the air and taking in the scene, the woman straightened, closed her eyes, centered herself, and stilled her mind. She was simply present: doing nothing, thinking nothing. After a time—or perhaps no time at all—she opened her eyes, raised a hand to her sharp old chin, and nodded. Yes. The stars had spoken. The time had come. The time was now.

"Joli," she called softly.

The Dragon awoke from her dreamless sleep, rose from her bed among the trees flanking Dagmar's cave, stretched briefly, and approached her teacher. "Good morning! Did you call me?"

"Yes, child. I have news you perhaps will like. The stars have had their say. It is time. Time for us to free your friends."

"Oh!" cried Joli. "Oh!! Wonderful! I'll leave at once. No—wait—I should eat first, so I can fly without stopping. And then..."

"Peace, Joli," Dagmar gently interrupted.

"What?"

"It is not yet time for you to fly. First, I shall attempt to free your friends myself. If I succeed, there may be no need for you to risk the journey to New Mexico. It is not a flight to be attempted lightly, or without dire need."

"But, I..." began Joli; then she paused, considering. "Well, no. Never mind. What you say makes sense. And I know Vin and Ahimoth: They would be furious if I took a needless risk. They have lost me once already; I should not take a chance of putting them through such a loss again."

"There! There is the wisdom I have seen in you," said Dagmar. "Thank you, child. And now, please excuse me; the time to attempt their liberation is here, and I must go inside to concentrate upon the task."

With that, Dagmar returned to her cave, settled on a woven mat before her small hearth, and composed herself. After chanting a preparatory invocation, she reached out across the wide world to the deep caverns of New Mexico, where Ahimoth and Vin were held. There she discovered Ahimoth in a rage, after an encounter with the cruel Soader. She spoke to him—his familiar "little voice"—making a gentle suggestion; just a hint of an idea. The clever Dragon seized on the concept at once, and set about exploring it.

Satisfied the black Dragon would succeed and make his escape, Dagmar turned her attention to Vin. What she found pained her greatly. The once-handsome blue Dragon lay unconscious on a rocky floor, tethered to his prison-cavern's wall by a massive chain and shackle. Scarcely two hours before, one of Soader's minions had beaten the poor Dragon nearly to death. Even if the witch were to free him from his chains, he would be utterly unable to escape the caverns. Vin's rescue would have to come another day.

Dagmar rose and stepped outside; Joli greeted her,

anxious to know what had transpired. The Dragon was delighted to hear Ahimoth should soon be free, but the news of Vin's sad condition and continued confinement dashed her enthusiasm at once.

"You need not fear, Joli," Dagmar comforted. "We will free Vin yet. This was simply not his time."

"I understand," said Joli, "but it's still so sad to hear how badly he's been treated. If I could fly there today, I would tear that Soader to ribbons and feed him to the cave rats! But Ahimoth is free; I should concentrate on the positive. Do you know where he will go? I'll fly there now and meet him!"

"I am sorry, Joli. I must counsel you to wait a while longer. Now that he is free, there are tasks Ahimoth must attend to. You must not go to him yet, nor should you attempt communication. He would be overjoyed to learn you are here and alive, but the knowledge would distract him from his immediate purpose—and that could well prove fatal."

"Ohhhhhhhh!" wailed Joli. "Waiting and waiting and waiting again! It's tearing me apart!"

"It can be difficult, oh yes," said Dagmar. "And yet there are times when patient waiting is the wisest course."

"I see the sense in what you say," agreed Joli. "At least I've learned to listen to you and trust your words. You have never steered me wrongly, but I can be such a silly hatchling when my emotions take hold. All right. I will wait until you say the time is right. But please, please, while I wait, could we double my lessons to keep my poor mind busy?"

Dagmar laughed heartily and assured the young Dragon her lessons could most definitely be doubled. If not tripled! The time would pass quickly, *and* she would be better prepared for whatever might come.

CHAPTER 24

Schemes

While Joli, on Earth, prepared to meet unknown dangers, Soader was a universe away: aboard *Queen Morrighan*, busy with preparations of his own. But, unlike Joli's, his had sinister goals. Goals like murdering Rafael Zulak, betraying and killing the Brothers, and destroying the Earth before G.O.D. could carry out its all-important soul-harvest there.

He gurgled and chuckled at the images he conjured up. A shattered Earth, reduced to a flying mass of debris and molten rock while its billions of inhabitants, suddenly bodiless, screamed in soundless horror or shivered in numb disbelief. Thousands of G.O.D. officials in utter shock at the news—and the fury and hatred of the billions those officials "served," when they learned their hopes for a fresh start in a vital and vigorous new body were over. The Brothers' helpless terror as he gutted them and force-fed them their own entrails. "Lovely, lovely!" he crowed. But he set aside the cheery daydreaming; it was time to get real and hammer out all the details.

First, he thought, he should get more familiar with his resources—like that Earthling kid everyone was so hot to get their hands on. That scumbag Scabbage wanted to transfer into the boy's body before his own died. And there were others who wanted it for the same purpose. Well, he would get there first, grab the body and sell it to the highest bidder!

Ohhhhhhhh! But he could do better than that! He would transfer into the body himself! That would keep all the other scum from getting it—and keep him completely safe in the bargain. No one would dare harm him while he occupied that body—they *couldn't* hurt him without ruining the very thing they were after!

Whoa. This got better and better. The kid was a Human. For some stupid, stupid, stupid reason, only Humans could pair with Nibiru Dragons, and so gain access to their accursed planet. But, if he were inhabiting the boy's body, he could subvert and pair up with a Nibiru Dragon, travel to Nibiru and seize their fabulous treasure! "Ha!" he gloated, "The gods have delivered the answer to just about everything—straight into my hands! But what's really amazing is that no one has thought to do it before. Just proves my truly exceptional brilliance!"

What Soader didn't know was that someone *had* thought of—and tried—the same gambit before. A particularly devious Rept had once tried exactly what Soader now proposed to do: transfer into a Human body, find a Nibiru Dragon vacationing away from its homeworld, become its Companion and travel with it back to Nibiru. Unfortunately for the Rept, his little plan had a flaw. A fatal flaw. Literally. For even when a Rept soul transferred into a fully Human body, certain characteristics and wavelengths associated with having inhabited Rept bodies and worlds would trigger Nibiru's planetary shielding, and kill the imposter before he ever set foot on the planet's surface. But, for Soader, that would have to be a lesson for another day.

Oblivious to the deadly error in his planning, Soader set to work. An hour's search on the ship's computer turned up next to nothing about Jager. Nothing useful, in any case. "Very strange," he thought, "for someone all these high-and-mighty types are so obsessed with." Well, no matter. Their interest and willingness to pay were the only things that counted in the end. He decided to go have a look at the over-hyped little twerp, and headed off toward the brig.

Arriving at the cellblock entrance, Soader sauntered in, approached the guard at the block's monitor station and announced, "I'm here to have a look at your guests."

Just as the Rept expected, the guard gave him a "who-the-hells-do-you-think-*you*-are?" look, sneered his most dismissive sneer, and replied, "Is that so? And who might you be?"

"And where might *you* have learned your gods-damned manners?" Soader growled, whipping out the badge the Brothers had given him, granting free access to nearly the entire ship.

Seeing the badge's clearance level—and who had authorized it—the guard's demeanor changed instantly. "Yes, sir! Of course, sir. All the monitors are right here, sir."

"Of course they are, idiot. Let me see them."

"Yes, sir. Right away, sir. Here—you're welcome to use my chair, sir."

"That won't be necessary—I just want a look. Get out of my way."

"Yes, sir!" The guard jumped aside, giving Soader a clear view of all the monitors.

"What, is that it??" Soader demanded. "There are only two prisoners in the whole block??"

"Yes, sir, at the moment, sir. Just the one there in Number 3—he's paralyzed—and the young one in Number 7. He's sleeping."

Soader could see the prisoner in Number 3 was Pratt. The Chameleon Rept was still in Human form, just as Soader had last seen him. And with the same open-mouthed, dumb-founded look he'd been wearing when the guard paralyzed him in the Brothers' chamber. Well, it served the idiot right for trusting the Barbdews.

The Human in Number 7 must be the oh-so-precious runt Scabbage and everyone else had gone ga-ga over. Jager, they called him. The sleeping figure on the monitor had its back to the camera and was mostly covered by a blanket; Soader couldn't see anything but the back of his head and one shoulder. No matter. He'd seen all he needed in the data files. Just another scrawny Human, ugly as the rest of his pathetic race.

"Nothing more to see here," he thought. "As you were," he said to the guard, condescending.

"Yes, sir. Thank you, sir. A good day to you, sir," mewled the guard, trying his best to look sharp and efficient. All for nothing; Soader had already stalked off down the corridor.

"Too bad I can't cash in on the money Pratt was ready to fork over for the boy," thought Soader, making his way back toward his quarters. "That's just small change, though, com-pared to where I'll be sitting when I'm through."

Soader's next stop was the cargo bay where his red Dragon

was held. He made his way down two levels and into the cargo hold area, found the right bay, and flashed his badge to the nervous guard on duty.

"Yes, sir. What can I do for you, sir?"

"Oh, nothing. I just thought I'd stand around outside this cargo bay for a while."

"S-sir?"

"Open it up, lint-for-brains!!"

"But...but, sir! There's a D-D-Dragon in there, sir! With two heads!"

"No kidding? What a surprise! Now open it, dolt!! It's my stinking Dragon!"

"Oh. Oh! Yes, sir. That is, if you're v-v-very sure you want it o-opened, sir," stammered the guard, now doubly terrified: first of Soader, and second of what was behind the bay door.

"YES, damn it to all hells! It's MY Dragon, and I'm going in there. Open the damned door. I'm waiting!!" Soader stood before the door, crossed his arms over his chest, set his feet wide and scowled like a thunderstorm.

"O-okay, sir. Whatever you say, sir!" The terrified guard backed away to where he could just barely reach the panel, extended a trembling hand, jabbed at the "Open" button and then, with a shriek, dove for the wall—a desperate attempt to get as far away from the opening as he could.

The door slid open. For a moment, nothing could be seen in the darkened interior. Then, FLASH! A huge gout of blue-white flame burst out the doorway, singeing Soader's face and uniform and faintly charring the opposite corridor wall.

The guard shrieked again and dashed away down the corridor in blind panic.

Soader was more surprised and angry than hurt—his tough Rept hide could take a lot of abuse. Far more than his hyper-bloated ego could bear. With a roar, he charged through the door and straight at the big Dragon, intent on throttling the creature with his bare hands. He hadn't stopped to consider how he was going to manage throttling a creature with two heads, but he was enraged beyond reason.

Before the furious Rept had gotten two steps into the bay, the ship's fire-suppression system kicked in, showering the whole bay, popping on the emergency lighting and slamming the door behind him.

There they stood, master and Dragon-slave, faced off and fuming with mutual hatred. But drenched, bedraggled and dripping.

"What in all the flaming hells did you do *that* for, you useless lizards?" bellowed the Rept. "You ever pull anything like that again and I swear I'll strip your home planet's atmosphere clean off. Boom. Everybody dead—including your precious mommy. Nothing and no one to go home too. DO I make myself clear?"

The Dragon—both heads—skirted the question: "Oh, yes, mister half-breed. We hear you, loud and clear." They'd heard, but they had every intention of pulling something like that again. Next time, though, it would be something ever-so-fatally effective.

In an un-hypnotized moment, Narco and Choy had made a pact to destroy the wicked Rept the first chance they got. The only thing that had kept Soader alive this long was regular renewal of his hypnotic hold over the pair. One day he would get careless, though…

"I hate you!" both snarled.

"So? Tell someone who cares. I hate the both of you, so we're even."

"Well, what the hells do you want?" Narco growled.

"Thaaaat's better," purred Soader. "I'm here to inform you we're leaving tomorrow, to find and capture that blasted girl and her white bitch. You know—that dainty little white Dragon? The one who kicked your oh-so-fearsome ass? Hey! You should be cheerful as hell at that bit of news! You've got a chance to redeem yourselves and regain some of your lost face. Or should I say 'faces'?!" He almost collapsed in laughter at his own lame joke.

"We can't," spat Narco.

"What the hells do you mean, you can't?" bellowed Soader. "You do as I say, and I say we leave tomorrow."

"Go right ahead. But you'll have to find another way to get around. We're still banged up and damn sore after that last encounter. The one with the big, buff black Dragon. The one we knocked straight out of the sky, remember? The one whose ass we were about to kick, before you turned tail and got us 'beamed out of there.

"So, no—we're not hauling your disgusting bulk anywhere, or fighting any more of your battles for you. Not until we're all healed up and ready. You may be a suicidal lunatic, but neither of us is. Three days. We can go in three days. Take it or leave it."

"We don't have three days to spare," Soader replied. "We've got just two weeks, as of this morning, to turn over the bloody girl and her stupid magic books, or the Brothers are going to terminate us. Slowly and as painfully as they can manage. And they're universe-class experts in all things painful, so this is not something we want. Clear?"

"Clear. Clear, but twisted. The Brothers have no quarrel with Choy and me. No reason to threaten us. In fact, they came by here yesterday to check us out, and we had a very nice chat. Including mention of possible future employment. No, their beef is with you. And I think your threat is just more lying manipulation—the only field where you could claim universe-class expertise. So you can go get stuffed."

The Dragon was right, and Soader knew it. He snarled, spat and stalked out of the cargo bay. "Damn it," he thought. "They're right. And I can't afford to risk another fight if they're not in good shape. Ah. I know. An extension. The Brothers can be reasonable and willing to deal. I'll explain the situation and ask for three more days so the Dragon can heal. A simple and sound investment." Off he went toward the Brothers' lounge, where he'd met with them just hours before.

"Soader! What a surprise," said Dodd, when the Rept had been ushered back into the Brothers' presence. "We didn't expect to see you again until tomorrow. What brings you back so soon?"

"Dodd, Lancaster," said Soader, bowing to each brother. "Thank you for agreeing to see me again."

"Well, now we *are* in trouble," said Lancaster to his brother. "He's being polite. A dangerous, dangerous sign!" The two had a good laugh, then Lancaster went on. "Oh, you're so much fun, Soader. Truly, you are. But cut the phony nice-nice. What are you after?"

"I assure you I'm most sincere—as I said earlier, your skills and your ruthlessness are unparalleled. But, if you wish to dispense with honest pleasantries, so be it—I'll come right to the point. Earlier, you set the time limit for turning over the girl, her Dragon and her books at two weeks. I've been to see my Dragon, who plays a crucial part in the plans I've devised. It takes a Dragon to beat a Dragon, as the old saying goes."

"I don't recall any such saying," said Dodd, "but go on, go on."

"My Dragon has been through several heated battles in the past week, and sustained a number of injuries. To recover sufficiently to do battle again, he will need several days' rest and recuperation. In light of this unforeseen factor, I humbly request that three days be added to the limit you set."

"Haaaaaaaaaaaa!" laughed Dodd. "Can you believe this guy, Lanny? You must admit, he's entertaining."

"That he is. That he is. But allow me to respond to his question, if I may."

"Of course, brother Lancaster, of course."

"Thank you, brother Dodd." Turning to Soader and smiling broadly, Lancaster went on. "After careful consideration, Soader, our response to your 'humble' request is, 'of course...'"

A victorious smile began to take shape on Soader's face.

"...NOT," finished Lancaster. "As in no. No, no, no, no and no."

Soader opened his mouth to launch a protest, but Dodd raised a claw and cut him off.

"Don't even start. And oh, here's another little factor to consider in your precious plans, buck-o: Because we are currently located in the Serpens Universe, annnd because you cannot return to the Phoenix Universe by any other means than this ship, annnd because this ship will not return to the Phoenix Universe until three days from now, your time limit is effectively shortened, not lengthened: You can't *begin* until three days from now."

Soader didn't even attempt a retort. He'd hung up completely on Dodd's revelation that they were in the Serpens Universe. How could that be??

"What? Not even a nasty crack, half-breed?" Lancaster sniped. "My, my. That's certainly out of character. Something got your attention, hm? Or perhaps you've just had a little seizure! Mmm, yes. Perhaps so. Better scuttle on down to Sick Bay when we're through here; have them check you out.

"But just in case you missed it, allow me to reiterate: the answer to your absurd request is no. N. O. No. And allow me to say that the penalty we will be oh, so delighted to mete out, should you fail to produce the girl, her Dragon and the musty old spell books by two weeks from this morning, is death for your sorry old mongrel of a body, and transport to RPF113 for the crusty little cinder that serves as your soul."

"Transport *and* indefinite detention, I might add," said Dodd. "'Indefinite' as in 'until every last hell has frozen over.'"

"Correcto, brother! Ha!" Lancaster chimed in, chomping away at some sort of raw flesh. "But, Soader! Look at it this way: Since we won't be back in our home universe for three days, your faithful donkey...er, Dragon will have the recovery time it needs after all! No, no—there's no need to thank us. I assure you, our benevolence in this matter is strictly coincidental." Lancaster chuckled at his own cleverness; his brother grinned.

"All right, then," said Dodd. "Let's review this one last

time. You'll correct me if I have any of the details wrong, won't you Lanny?"

"Oh, absolutely, dear brother," smirked Lancaster.

"As of this morning, friend Soader's little countdown started at fourteen days, yes?"

"Indeed, it did," replied Lancaster, reaching for a glass a nervous servant offered.

"So, tomorrow the count will be down to thirteen. And by the day we're to return to the Phoenix Universe, the count will have reached ten, correct?"

"Correcto, brother. When we reach the old home universe, Mr. Soader here will have ten days to find the witch-bitch, subdue her—*and* her flying white horse-lizard—and present them to us, along with the spell books. Quite simple, really? Don't you agree, Soader?"

"Uh..." grunted Soader, his mind still digesting the fact he was in the Serpens Universe.

"Mmm, eloquent," said Dodd. "We'll just take that as a yes. Now, there's one more thing for us to decide, brother Lanny. Where should our enterprising friend meet up with us? Where shall we be, fourteen days from today?"

"Ah! Good question, Dodd, good question. A crucial detail! Let me see," said Lancaster, tapping his chin with two claws. "You know, Dodders, this is the time of year I just love to watch those adorable Stenerson females perform their traditional mating dances. What say we head for Farseya IV and take in the shows?"

"What a perfectly splendid idea!" cheered Dodd. "Then, if Mr. Soader doesn't arrive with the goods, we'll at least be able to drown our disappointment in, uh, how shall I put it? Cultural enrichment! I just despise being stuck in some dreary locale while waiting for bumblers to perform their assigned tasks; your idea takes care of that most handily. There are no finer females than the Stenersons, nor any more eager to provide—how did you put it?—cultural enrichment! So, if Mr. Soader-pop here fizzes out on us, at least the trip won't be a complete waste."

"I agree, I agree," Lancaster affirmed. "Farseya IV it is. Soader, does that meet with your approval?"

Soader, still half-dazed, said nothing.

"Soader? Soader!" shouted Dodd. "You were following along, I hope."

"Uh..." managed Soader. "Uh...yes. Yes, yes. Farseya fourteen, three weeks. Right. Got it. I'll be there."

"Tut, tut," said Lancaster. "You were *not* listening. Why I am not surprised? No, it's Farseya IV, in two weeks. Shall I repeat that one more time? Would you like me to record it for you? Perhaps a hypnotic implant? Tattoo it on the back of your hand?"

"No—sorry—yes. Yes, I heard you. IV, two weeks. I'll be there, with the girl and all that."

"Good, good! That's the spirit, Soader," laughed Lancaster. "You're free to go now. Run along." With that, the Brothers resumed their earlier conversation—and their endless chow-down.

Back in his quarters, Soader woke the desk computer and began a search: "Lizzy, how does this ship shift between the Phoenix and Serpens universes?"

It took some skillful maneuvering to find the information, including a devious hack using codes he'd blackmailed out of a Fleet security officer just a couple of months before. But there it was: the secret to *Morrighan's* universe-jumping.

While ransacking a sacred temple on Levin, the Brothers had run across a long-lost grimoire of spells from the Serpens Universe. Using threats of unspeakable acts against an orphanage under her care, they had coerced a priestess to translate and explain the spells. The one that delighted them most enabled the user to shift an object of any size, from a pebble to a person to a planet, between universes. After trying out a few of the translated spells, they were satisfied the priestess hadn't been lying. They thanked her for her service, then killed her, destroyed the orphanage and added all the children to their capacious larder.

Contemplating what he'd found, it suddenly dawned on Soader that the Brothers had been playing him for years and years—in a major, major way. They'd known his fondest, wildest dream was to rule the Serpens Universe. This had given them a sure-fire way to keep him occupied, and located where they could keep an eye on him.

They had convinced him the key to reaching and returning from the Serpens Universe at will was the Titan Portcullis, locked in orbit around the largest of Saturn's many moons. Operating the portcullis required vast amounts of energy; the Brothers had informed him that it must also be a very specific type: emotional energy, captured and stored in a system of batteries and condensers. Deep grief, despair and raw terror—especially in Humans—were the most effective emotions for the purpose, which suited Soader perfectly. He and his minions had been capturing and "milking" Humans of these energies for years, using a series of unspeakable techniques and "treatments."

The Brothers' calculation had been correct: Soader had accepted their lies, and the energy-gathering project had kept him occupied and easy to locate ever since. It was his pet project; no matter what other misadventures he got into, he'd never strayed from it for long.

Now Soader saw that it had all been a lie. They'd had him tethered, in effect. And they had no doubt had many a good laugh at his devotion to the bogus project. Hell, they were probably planning to profit from his efforts, too—all that stored energy wouldn't ever be needed to operate the port-cullis, but it *would* fetch them a handsome price on the black market.

Soader rapidly flipped from surprised to dismayed to furious. He desperately wanted to smash, kill, burn or explode something. Anything! After a minute's silent rage, he regained some composure and found a channel for his fury.

"So!" he thought, "They figured they could trick and outsmart me!" The thought was accurate enough, since that was exactly what they *had* done, for decades. Such factual details didn't faze Soader, though. "Big mistake, biiiiig mistake. It's always a mistake to underestimate me. And now they've brought me aboard their fancy universe-jumping ship! That changes the whole game. I'll bring them back what they want, all right. And then I'll kill them and take over their little ship—and full access to the Serpens Universe right along with it!"

CHAPTER 25

Return to Earth

The next morning, as close to cheery as he ever got, Soader headed for the cargo bay where Narco and Choy were held. He gave them the good news they would get a few days to recover after all—and the warning that they'd better make good use of the time, because this was the only break they were going to get.

With that little errand out of the way, he decided to check in on Jager again. Maybe this time the kid would be awake, so he could get a look at him. Maybe even have a little talk-talk with the lad, to size him up and get familiar with his speech patterns and mannerisms. After all, once he took over the body, there would be times when he'd have to pass himself off as the real Jager, when dealing with anyone the kid might know.

Approaching the brig, Soader encountered a flurry of activity. Guards and ship's police were arriving or hurrying away, quite intent and serious. Outside the entrance to the cellblock were two high-ranking officers, questioning a very nervous guard. "What's all this?" Soader wondered aloud. He retreated around a bend in the corridor, out of sight of the cellblock entrance, and waited. In less than a minute a guard hurried by; the Rept fell in behind him, caught up and tapped him on the shoulder. "Hey, what's going on?" he asked, feigning a crewmate's concern.

"Oh, Xenu—a prisoner's escaped," replied the guard. "Turns out he's been gone for days, and nobody knew. Don't ask me how *that* could happen! Lucky for me, he wasn't in my block. Hells, from all the fuss, it must be someone important, too. They won't tell us any details, though. Just that he's gotta be caught fast, or heads are gonna roll."

"Whoa! What a screwup," Soader said, pretending comradery. "Good luck catching him, mate."

"Yeah. Thanks. Gotta go." The guard rushed on up the corridor.

"Interesting!" thought Soader. "The little weasel escaped! Must be some way I can turn this to my advantage." Musing all the while, he made his way to a crew mess hall, got himself a mug of teala and sat down to think it through.

He reasoned that since this was—or had been—a Fleet ship, and since Jager, being a Fleetie, knew ship life and protocol well, all the kid had to do was go with the flow. He could go almost anywhere he wanted, as long as he kept a low profile. He couldn't risk staying in any one place too long, though, and couldn't stay in regular crew quarters. So, he'd have to have a hiding place. The trick was figuring out how to find and quietly nab him, then knock him out and hide him. Then, once they were back in the Phoenix Universe, he could smuggle the kid off the ship, get him to a transfer station and take over the body. There! All planned out, nice and neat. Except for the first little detail: finding and nabbing the stupid twerp.

The next morning, as he was gobbling breakfast in his quarters, Soader jumped up in mid-chew and yelled, "I've got it!" He'd reasoned Jager had to be eating somehow, and even if he didn't eat in the mess hall, he'd have to go there to pick up food. It would be too dangerous to risk pilfering from ship's stores or the commissary; ships—even pirate ships like this—were notoriously careful about such things, and severe in their punishments. No, the boy would realize it would be far safer to have meals like any other crew member. Just more blending in and going with the flow.

After one last mouthful, Soader headed for the mess hall. He got there just in time—they had opened only a minute or two before, and the first diners were only part-way through the chow line. Soader grabbed a cup of teala from the big urn near the entrance and found a table at the back of the hall, just beside a column. He positioned himself so the column partially hid him, but still gave him a view of everyone entering and moving through the line.

He didn't have long to wait. Minutes after he settled in, his quarry appeared. Jager, uniformed like almost everyone else, entered the hall and got in line. He had a computer tablet in hand, which he studied intently, avoiding interaction with the crew. He quietly collected a tray of food, then headed for a table in a part of the hall that was still sparsely occupied. He ate rapidly, but studied his tablet intently at the same time. To any casual observer, he was just a busy crew member grabbing a bite while reviewing some job-related material. No one would pay him any notice.

"Clever lad," thought Soader. "And he got here early

enough to finish eating and be gone before it gets crowded. Not quite clever enough, though. Ha!"

When he finished his meal, Jager got up to leave. Soader followed, careful not to be obvious about it. By all accounts, the boy was quite alert and perceptive; he'd have to be careful with this one. He maneuvered himself to be just behind Jager when they reached the exit. Jager went through the doorway, glanced up and down the corridor, then turned right. Soader followed several paces behind. Before long there was only one other person in sight in the corridor—a man in an engineer's jumpsuit, coming toward them. When the man had passed and gone out of sight down the curving corridor, Soader made his move. He quickened his pace and moved off to Jager's left, as though he were suddenly in a hurry and intended to pass the boy—nothing alarming, a normal occurrence in shipboard life.

When he came to just a pace behind, the Rept brought up the knife he'd been holding and stepped quickly to the boy's side, pressing the knife point against his ribcage; one quick thrust, and he'd pierce both lung and heart—and he knew the boy was smart enough to know it.

"You're a clever one, Jager. No doubt about it. Just keep walking now, and go where I direct you. And not to worry—your little secret is safe with me. I'm no more interested in your being tossed back in that cell than you are."

Though he'd never been face to face with the Rept, Jager recognized Soader at once. He fought down the burning impulse to attack—an impulse born of his fury at what the evil wretch had done to Celine, her mother and sister. He was not surprised to find Soader in the company of Deebee Scabbage, but he had no idea what the cross-breed was up to. He would bide his time for now, learn all he could, and

244   LORNA J. CARLETON

factor Soader's presence into his own plans. Justice could wait a while longer.

Soader led the Earthling toward his quarters. As they approached the entry, he scanned ahead and behind, checking the corridor—he didn't want to be seen taking the kid into the room. There was no one in sight, so he hastily keyed the door and escorted Jager inside. Guessing the kid was skilled at close-quarters combat, Soader took no chances; as soon as they were through the door, he whipped out the blackjack he always carried and gave him a vicious whack across the back of the head. The boy slumped to the floor.

Soader inspected the inert form, musing. What could be so special about this scrawny Human, that so many major players were willing to pay big for his body. Pure-bred Humans had always seemed ridiculously ugly, and this one was no different—so beauty wasn't it. Must be something else. Well, a little research could answer that in good time. Right now *he* had the body, and he was going to make damned good use of it.

He dragged the boy into the sleeping room, gagged him, bound hands and feet with restraint strips, shoved him into a closet and locked the door.

A few minutes later, Jager regained consciousness. From the pain at the back of his head, he guessed what had happened. A quick assessment of the sounds and smells and the bit of light coming under the closet door told him where he must be. He found Soader's actions more interesting than anything else. What could the Rept want? Well, no matter— he would watch and wait and make the best of the situation, confident he could turn this new development to his advantage.

With his prisoner secured, Soader ate a quick snack to

make up for his interrupted breakfast, then got ready to do a little more exploring. He meant to make this ship his own, and wanted to learn all he could about her—how she was run, what she could do, and what black-marketable tech, equipment and supplies might be aboard. He was about to leave when the door chime rang. "Crap!" he growled, not caring if he was heard. Well, he'd get rid of this stupid annoyance and get on with *important* business. "Who is it? Can't you see I'm busy? What the hells do you want?!" he yelled.

"It's your humble hosts! Here to inquire after your health and comfort, and make certain your accommodations are adequate," came the reply.

"Crap!!" said Soader, this time to himself. "Dodd. And Lancaster. Crap, crap, crap and crap. What now??"

"Open," he commanded, and the door slid back to reveal the Brothers, smiling their best reptilian pseudo-smiles and decked out in ostentatious finery. The pair sashayed straight past Soader, followed by an entourage of attendants, secretaries, servers bearing covered platters, and a couple of general-purpose toadies.

"So!" began Lancaster. "We haven't seen or heard from you in nearly two days. We became worried something dire might have befallen you, and came to see if we might be of service."

"Exactly so," confirmed Dodd. They leered at the Rept, awaiting a reply.

"Uh, no, I'm fine. Just fine. Everything is fine," mumbled Soader, taken aback—and completely taken in—by his hosts' faux-gracious show of concern.

"Oh, splendid! I'm so very glad our fears were for naught," said Lancaster.

"We also wanted to let you know," said Dodd, "that we have returned to the Phoenix Universe."

"Quite so," said Lancaster. "Further, you may be interested to learn that, as we speak, the ship is entering orbit around Earth. Directly above your little semi-secret base of operations, in fact. Dulce, I believe the primitives call it?"

"Uh, splendid," said Soader. "Yes, Dulce—that's it." This was a terrific turn of events—so good, it made him wonder if there was some devious motive behind it. "I'll get right onto finding that girl and her creature, then. Nice. Very nice. Very, uh, thoughtful of you."

"We try, Soader, we try," said Lancaster. Now his voice took on a more threatening edge. "We're pleased you appreciate our efforts. And we hope they convey how deadly serious we are about getting our hands on the girl, the Dragon and the spell books—fast, before anyone else can. Oh, and did I mention we were *deadly* serious?"

"Yes, brother," Dodd affirmed, "you certainly did."

Despite the thinly veiled threat, Soader was relieved—the shift in their tone probably meant the twins' "thoughtfulness" was just self-interest after all.

Jager, cooped up in a closet a room away, could tell Soader had visitors, but the sound was much too muffled to make out any details of their conversation. Soader's tone seemed faintly deferential, but that was all Jager could determine.

"All right, then," Lancaster went on, "when you and your flying battle-behemoth are ready to go, contact us. We've set our comm-link channel to allow you to call directly, just this once. We'll meet you at the transbeam station—number two—and send you on your way."

"More of your thoughtfulness. How nice," Soader replied.

The Brothers bowed and departed.

Soader hauled out the spacer's trunk he'd arrived with and began rummaging through it, tossing aside non-essential items and putting vital ones in a separate pile. From among the essentials he took out a hypo-spray kit, selected a vial and loaded it into the injector gun. Carrying the hypo, he opened the closet door, dragged Jager out and gave him a dose in the thigh. In seconds the boy was out cold. "There," muttered Soader, "that'll keep you quiet until we're planetside."

He hefted the inert body, dumped it into the empty trunk and covered it up with his pile of "keeper" items. After a few more minutes' preparation, the Rept was ready to depart. "I'm leaving," he said aloud to the ship, "but don't you worry, Queenie. I'll be back soon. And not long after that, you'll be mine. We have a lot of work to do, you and I! Haaaaarrrrr!!"

"Orderly!" he called into his comm link. "I need an antigrav up here. Be quick about it."

Minutes later an orderly—a Grey—appeared at his door with an antigrav unit. "May I ask what you need transported, sir?" he asked, clearly intimidated by the big Rept's size and surliness.

"The trunk!" Soader said, pointing. "Idiot. Do you see anything *else* here I'd need you for? Xenu, they must be desperate for recruits these days."

"Yes, sir. I mean no, sir. The trunk, sir. Right away, sir." The Grey hurried to the trunk, clamped on the antigrav and activated it. The heavy box floated upward a few centimeters, and the orderly looked at Soader expectantly.

"Follow me," grunted the Rept, and he led off down the corridor.

When they arrived at the cargo bay where the Kerr Dragon was housed, Soader stopped and took out his key card. The Grey recognized where they were and spoke up. "Uh, sir, we're not going in *there*, are we?"

"Of course we're going in there, dolt. I didn't come down here to loiter around the corridor. What? Are you afraid of my pet or something?"

"Yes, sir. Begging your pardon, sir. You can keep the antigrav, sir. Just leave it wherever you want when you're finished!" He turned and scurried off down the corridor, desperate to get as far away as he could before the bay door opened.

"Heh-heh," chuckled the Rept. "A free antigrav! How nice. Could come in handy." He keyed open the bay, guided the floating trunk inside and shut the door, locking it.

Narco and Choy had been sleeping, but now the big Dragon rose and lumbered forward, just out of the shadows at the back of the bay. Seeing how the antigrav'ed trunk moved, he could tell it was even heavier than when they'd arrived. "I hope you're not thinking we're carrying that again," Narco snarled. "It was bad enough before, but now you've loaded it up even more. How the hells do you expect us to fly—let alone fight—carrying all your crap *and* your own ridiculous bulk?"

"Quit your blasted whining and get over here so I can strap this on. We're 'beaming down this morning."

"We'd love to, but you're going to have to haul it over here. This is as far as we can go. Or had you forgotten you shackled us to the wall?"

"Moan, moan, moan. You two are unbelievable. Just a minute." Soader steered the trunk to the Dragon's side and manipulated it up to the saddle he'd left strapped to the creature's broad back. Soon he had it securely lashed in place, ready for flight.

He climbed up and plopped into the saddle—ignoring Narco and Choy's groans at his weight and jarring motions. Activating the comm pickup on his lapel, he rattled off the code the Brothers had given him. Dodd answered. "Ready?"

"Yes. Packed and loaded and ready."

"Charming. We'll send a couple of people to run ahead of you and clear the corridors. No sense scaring the crap out of the crew with that mutant monstrosity of yours."

"Whatever."

"Now, now—don't get grumpy on us. We're giving you quite the opportunity here."

"Heh! More than you know!" thought Soader. "Well, don't think I don't appreciate it," he replied aloud.

"As you should," said Dodd. "But remember—the deal cuts two ways. Bring us what we want in ten days, and you'll make out very well for yourself. Fail, and you and your two-headed friend there will spend the rest of your worthless existences on RPF113. Or worse."

"Uh-huh," said Soader.

Overhearing the conversation, Narco and Choy were instantly alert. What kind of "deal" had their twisted master made with the hideous twins? Better play along with whatever Mr. Half-Rept wanted, at least for now. The Brothers were clearly serious, and Soader was a Kerrian puffle-fly next to those two.

Minutes later, a pair of Ship's Police officers arrived at the cargo bay; one explained Soader should follow them in one

minute, and ever-so-diplomatically added that because of the Dragon's great size, they would have to stick to the main cargo corridor between the bay and the transbeam station. "Obviously, crap-for-brains! How stupid do you think I am?" snarled Soader.

The guard suppressed the urge to answer honestly, and hurried up the corridor to clear the way.

Soader and the Dragon arrived at Transbeam Station 2 without incident. Lancaster and Dodd were waiting for them inside; they smiled, bowed, and pointed the way to the transbeam platform with sweeping gestures. Soader gave a pained smile in return, as he and the Dragon stepped up onto the platform. "Ready," said Soader.

"Excellent," said the Brothers.

"I *hate* this," thought Narco and Choy.

At a word from Lancaster, the technician on duty activated the transbeam, and Soader and the Dragon disappeared—then materialized deep inside the Dulce complex, seven miles below the New Mexico countryside. "Very nice!" Soader said aloud, "'beamed us right to the holding cell area, just as requested. Perhaps the old Bro's are starting to see the light about me. Maybe they *can* recognize true genius. Hm!"

Spying two Greys crossing the nearby concourse, loaded down with equipment of some sort, Soader shouted out, "Hey! You! Put down that crap and get over here!"

"Wha' d' ya mean, crap?" one yelled back. "Can't ya see we're busy??"

The second Gray recognized Soader and hissed at his companion, "Shut it! That's the boss!"

"Oh, Xenu. I'm screwed," whispered the first worker. Both

dropped their loads at once and hurried toward Soader.

"Sorry, sir! Very sorry. Didn't recognize you at first, sir. No offense meant, sir. How can we help you, sir?"

Soader just glared at them for a long moment, letting them contemplate how horribly their lives might be about to end. "That's better," he growled. "Now, move that trunk to the first cell in that cellblock." He pointed past the trunk toward a row of cells. Looking up, the pair now noticed the enormous red Dragon standing in the shadows.

"Gaaaaaaaaaahhhhhhhhh!" they screamed, and spun around to flee.

"STOP," commanded Soader. The Grays skidded to a halt and turned back toward the Rept, trembling in horror. "Oh, stop it!" yelled Soader. "Pay no attention to the damned Dragon. He's not going to hurt you. Not as long as you do as I say. So, get on it!"

The poor pair stood shaking for a moment longer, then cautiously approached the trunk—never taking their eyes off Narco and Choy. Guiding the big container with the antigrav, they pushed it to the open cell and maneuvered it inside.

"Now unload it," Soader demanded.

"Yes, sir. Right away, sir. But, it's locked, sir."

"Enough of your senseless complaining!" Soader barked, pulling out his key card and releasing the trunk's multiple locks.

The Grays hurried to open the trunk and began to empty it, stacking the contents neatly to one side. When they'd worked their way down to Jager, they stopped, uncertain what to do next.

"The Human, too," Soader said. "He's out cold. Will be for another day or so. Just haul him out and toss him over there." He pointed to the back of the cell.

"Yes sir," replied one of the workers, and they did as he'd instructed.

"Now re-pack the trunk and take it to my quarters. And don't even think about swiping any of my stuff, or my Dragon might get an unexpected snack. Harrrrrr!"

Narco snorted in disgust, but the Greys took it for eager interest. Shaking almost uncontrollably, they managed to repack the trunk and trundle it down the corridor toward Soader's rooms.

When the Greys had gone, Soader entered the cell and poked Jager a time or two, to make sure he was still out. Satisfied, he exited and locked the cell, setting it to respond to his key card only.

"Okay, you," he addressed the Dragon, "your little vacation's over. Back to your nice cavern."

Much as they hated captivity, Narco and Choy were relieved to be returning to their subterranean prison-cavern. At least they'd have plenty of room, plenty of food, and plenty of blessedly Soader-free time to do as they pleased.

Nearly two days later, Jager came out of his drug-induced sleep, sore, badly brain-fogged and with an awful taste in his mouth. He got up, stretched, and started to examine his surroundings, working to clear his head and get oriented.

He was in a cell, obviously. From the smell, the qualities of the air, and the nature of the rocky walls and floor, he guessed he was back on Earth, far underground. "Probably Soader's compound in New Mexico," he guessed. "This should be interesting. I wonder what he has in mind." His only regret was that he hadn't been able to learn how *Queen Morrighan* was able to jump universes before they'd left her. Well, now he knew that it *could* be done. He could continue his search for the tech of it some other time.

After more stretching and a few minutes of exercise, Jager settled on the floor near the cell door to watch and wait. He tried to contact Celine and West, but found his menting was blocked. That was consistent with his guess about being at Dulce; Celine had told him the place was blocked when she was held here. Little did he know that his soul-mate and her mother and sister had been imprisoned in this very cell, little more than a year before.

After waiting patiently for a while, Jager came up with a more pro-active plan. Returning to the spot where he'd been lying unconscious, he re-assumed his earlier position. He reasoned that if it seemed he hadn't awakened, any guards or other personnel nearby might speak freely, allowing him to learn more about his situation.

His move was just in time. The guard on duty on the detention block returned from a visit to the facilities (and a shady errand or two) and resumed his post with a bored sigh. Less than half an hour later, another guard came by and the two got into a chat.

Much of their talk was idle gossip, of little use to Jager. There was one mention of Dulce, though, confirming his guess.

"Ha!" one of them said. "Did ya know the stupid Earthlings call this place 'Dulce?'"

"Yeah, heard that. What of it?"

"Means 'sweet' in one of the languages they use 'round here. They got thousands of languages, ya know."

"Hah! 'Sweet!' Nothing sweet about *this* dump."

"That's th' truth. And what would they call it if they knew we were down here—a whole damned base, all burrowed in under their 'sweet' little crap-hole of a town. And hauling their people down here for 'experiments' whenever we want! Haaa!"

The guards' chat ended, but Jager stayed where he was, silent and still, for a few more hours. At last he decided his ploy had served its purpose. He stirred, groaned, and put on a convincing show of regaining consciousness. The guard never suspected a thing.

Next morning (Jager guessed it was morning, from the bits of passing chatter he overheard) Soader paid him a short visit, accompanied by a uniformed Rept underling and a few subservient Greys.

"So, finally up from your little nap, eh?" grumbled Soader, clearly in a foul mood. "Well, sit tight and try not to get into trouble, would you? I've no use for you now, but I will in a couple of days. Oh my, yes."

Soader had good reason to be disgruntled. Shortly after securing Jager a few days before, he had returned to his offices and discovered a plot against him. It seemed that Orme, his second-in-command at the Dulce complex, and in charge of operations whenever Soader was away, had been taking advantage of the boss's absence. He'd been sowing discontent among the crew, with tales of Soader's misman-agement, incompetence, disregard for the crew and down-right cruelty. Not a difficult task for Orme—most of what he'd spread was gospel truth.

He had also been currying the crew's favor by granting special favors and putting on entertainments whenever

Soader was absent. One such entertainment was an arena spectacle, scheduled for that same day; no one had expected the boss to return so soon. The main event was to be a big fight between Soader's captive blue Dragon and a mean, massive rodeo bull, stolen from a ranch up on the surface. It wasn't something many would make bets on—the Dragon was almost certain to win the fight, in the end. But the battle would be spectacular nonetheless, and everyone was excited.

Hearing about the event and Orme's treachery, Soader decided to put the traitor in his place. He scoffed very publicly at the "silly kiddie show" Orme had promoted, and announced his own event to replace it: free food and drink for all, and a *real* battle, worthy of his loyal, industrious crew. The blue Dragon would fight, all right. But he wouldn't be up against a single earthling bull, easily dispatched. No, he'd face *three* bulls—all three fitted with electronic goads, guaranteed to drive them into blind, demented fury. The fight would be one for the record books, the fiercest ever—no doubt about it.

The bloodthirsty crew loved it; they talked of nothing else the rest of the day. And now it was very much a betting proposition! Bookies could scarcely keep up with the wagers flooding in. In the crew's eyes, Orme was reduced to a cheap, small-time schmuck, and all Soader's sins were suddenly forgotten. He was the real thing. The Boss. The *Rept*.

CHAPTER 26

Reunion

On a chilly morning two days before Soader's return to Earth, Dagmar sat tending a small fire outside her cave-home. She called young Joli to come sit beside her.

"What is it, Teacher?"

"I have news of Ahimoth," the old woman replied.

"Ahimoth! Oh, tell me, please!"

The witch smiled. "Not long ago, he was here in Germany, though many miles from our secret valley."

Joli broke in, "In *Germany?!* Ohhhh! Why..."

"Patience, dear," Dagmar continued. "I would have told you of this when it occurred, but the time was not yet right. While here, he was injured in a battle with a mutant red Dragon. He..."

"No!" gasped Joli. She leapt up and flared her wings wide in alarm. "I must go to him!"

Dagmar fixed her young charge with a stern look, as if to say, "I will continue when you've remembered your manners."

Joli caught her teacher's look and settled at once. "Patience?" she said, apologetic.

"Yes, dear. Patience and calm. Patience and calm. As I was saying, Ahimoth was injured in battle with a mutant red Dragon. Before the battle was ended, one of the Dragons— the red—disappeared. I can only surmise it was taken by one of two large star-craft which appeared overhead during the fight. A short time later, Ahimoth flew off to the west with his sister, who was also here in Germany at that time. I do not know all that has transpired since, but tonight I have learned Ahimoth will return to Germany in two days' time.

"That's *wonderful!*" cried Joli.

"Yes, child. And he comes with a purpose dear to his heart. He comes in search of you."

"Oh! But... Oh! I..."

"Calm, child. For years upon years—ever since your previous body was destroyed, Ahimoth has harbored the fervent hope that you would find a hatchling body to assume. That is the reason both he and Vin traveled here, though he eventually abandoned any hope of finding you, on Earth or anywhere else. He resigned himself to the idea you were lost forever. However, just in the past few days, he has learned that there are Nibiru Dragons living on Earth—and though he believes Vin to be dead, killed in their attempt to pass the tube-chute, he dares to hope that you may be here, alive in a new body.

"To begin his search, he will travel first to Vogelsberg, the location of his battle with the red Dragon. You must be there waiting when he arrives." She flashed her young student a mental image of the place, so she could find it when the time came.

"Yes teacher! Yes!" Joli exclaimed, leaping up and capering about the clearing like a giddy hatchling. "This is so exciting! To think I will see him again!"

The old woman laughed at the spectacle and cheered the delirious Dragon on. "See him you shall, young one. And then, together, you must go rescue poor Vin."

"Of course! *This* is why you have been so insistent about my training!"

"You are quite right, child. Quite right. That which lies before you will be dangerous. Dangerous and difficult beyond words. But you are strong, strong; and your skills in magic are formidable. I have faith that together, you and Ahimoth shall achieve what you seek."

"I know we will. I know it! But it will only be because of all you have done for me. How could I ever hope to repay you?" said Joli, now sobered.

"But you have, my dear. You have! With your love, with all you have achieved, and with the living hope of what you can and shall achieve. Remember, it has been my life's purpose to guide and assist Dragon-folk here upon the earth. I shall always remember you, through all the lifetimes to come. My fondest hope is that we shall meet again in the next."

"Well, meet we will, then. At least if I have anything to say about it!" replied Joli—though she had not fully grasped all that her dear mentor's words implied.

Dagmar's lined old face creased even more deeply in a wide, warm smile. Tired after a long day's efforts, she rose now, kissed Joli on her graceful green muzzle, and hobbled off to her cave-home and her waiting bed. Joli curled up beside the dying fire; her mind raced with thoughts of Ahimoth, Vin, and all the possibilities their future might hold.

Next morning, Joli woke to a strange silence. "Something is missing," she thought. "But what?"

Then it struck her: Throughout her life here, the sounds of Dagmar going about the day's first chores had been part of every morning's fabric. Today there were no such sounds.

Rising, Joli crossed the little clearing toward Dagmar's door. No smoke rose from the chimney-hole in the rocky hillside above. There was no sound of sweeping or washing or putting things in order.

Joli tapped gently at the door, not wanting to startle the old woman, if she were simply dozing. There came no reply, no half-cheery, half-impatient "Just a moment, just a moment!"

Fearing she'd guessed the answer to this small riddle, Joli pushed the door open and peered inside.

Sadly, the Dragon's guess had been correct. On her low bed, snug in a natural alcove along one wall, lay Dagmar's body. Her hands lay folded upon her breast; her head turned to one side, the eyes open as though she were gazing at the fire. Her silent lips formed a smile of perfect peace. There had been no pain or struggle here; the dear old woman had departed willingly, knowingly.

Joli took in the sad tableau, then turned away, caught up in a surging wave of grief.

She spent near half the morning crying, sobbing, letting the pain of loss have its way. At last, when her immediate sorrow had ebbed to a dull ache, she picked herself up, took

a few slow, deep breaths to steady herself, and made her way to a small copse of Daphne bushes at the edge of the clearing. They were Dagmar's favorite; she'd been tending them since long before Joli's happy arrival. Each spring they put on a spectacular show: luxuriant sprays of pink-and-white flowers, their heady scent drifting through field and forest. Dagmar had explained that when she one day passed away, she would like her old body placed here for its final rest. The body would nourish her old friends as it gave itself back to the earth.

Joli carefully dug a grave, just the proper size and depth. Then, with a sigh, she returned to the cave and gently bore back the empty shell that had served her beloved teacher so long, so well.

With the body safe in the earth, wrapped—at Dagmar's request—in nothing but her simple habit of linen and wool, Joli stood vigil the rest of that day and on through the night. At times she was silent, contemplating. At others she sang songs of praise and thanks to her dearest friend, and the forces that had brought them together.

The Dragon slept the next day through, waking just as the sun was setting. Refreshed and over the worst of her grief, she wanted to take to the sky at once in search of Ahimoth. She refrained, remembering Dagmar's instructions: she must wait two days, then go to Vogelsberg and watch for the black Dragon's arrival. Well, one day was gone; only one more to wait.

To pass the time, Joli threw herself into a vigorous aerial workout. Then, after a successful hunt and satisfying dinner, she reviewed and practiced the spells and charms she thought might prove useful in rescuing her long-lost suitor, Vin.

When the time to travel to Vogelsberg arrived, Joli spoke a final invocation over Dagmar's grave, then took to the sky. She covered the distance to the Vogelsberg range in well under an hour. And, thanks to Dagmar's careful description, she had no trouble locating the mountainside ledge at the entrance to Father Greer's caverns. Landing on the ledge, she chose a spot with a good view outward and upward, and settled down to wait and watch for Ahimoth.

The day wore on. Though she mainly scanned the skies, she occasionally took time to admire the valley below, with its woods, meadows and meandering streams.

The sun was dipping toward the horizon when at last Joli sensed, rather than saw, another Dragon. Her heart skipped a beat, then raced, a wave of anticipation sweeping over her. She strained to catch a glimpse of the approaching Dragon— and there he was! Just a tiny dot at first; he had been flying at high altitude to avoid detection by earthly eyes, but now descended rapidly toward her. In moments, she could make out his color: beautiful, ebon black. Ahimoth! It must be he! She fanned out her wings, then held them high in welcome. Ahimoth spotted her, and answered with a quick wing-flare.

He dropped so quickly Joli feared he might crash into the mountainside, but he was far too skilled a flier (and too much of a showoff) for that. At the last possible moment, he flared his wings hard, gave a mighty downstroke and halted in mid-air, just a few meters above the ledge. Then he touched down in a more graceful, more perfect landing than Joli had ever seen.

"Joli!" he called. "Joli! Oh, it really *is* you!"

"Ahimoth!" she cried, rushing to embrace him before he even had a chance to furl his broad wings. They held each other, speechless, for a long while. At last Joli broke the silence. "Thank you, thank you for coming to me. I am so sorry for all that has happened, and for my foolishness—look what it has cost you, and cost Vin! How can you ever forgive me?"

"Shhh," replied Ahimoth. "All is forgiven. You are here, now. Alive. That is all that matters."

Joli sighed. Tears of relief began to flow. Then, abruptly, she tensed. "Vin!" she cried. "I...I can sense him. He is in peril—right now!" She had no idea how she could perceive Vin so vividly, but there was no denying it. "Oh!" she thought, "It's Dagmar! Just days ago, she said that when we parted, as part we must one day, she would pass to me gifts—gifts that would reveal themselves when they were needed most. This perception must be one of them!" And she was quite correct.

"Ah, but Joli," Ahimoth interrupted her thoughts, "it pains me to have to say so, but Vin is lost to us. He was overcome during our passage through the tube-chute, and passed away shortly after we arrived here on Earth."

"No, no," said Joli. She broke from their embrace and held him away from her, then continued in earnest. "I do not doubt it seemed that way, but our Vin is not dead. I know it. He narrowly survived the passage. That horrible Rept found both of you and took you to his caverns before you regained consciousness. Think: was it the Rept who told you Vin was dead?"

"Yes!" gasped Ahimoth, incredulous. "And I *believed* the treacherous monster!"

"Part of his foul scheme, I am certain," said Joli. "He wanted each of you to think the other had been killed, knowing you would blame yourselves for each other's deaths—and so feel all the more alone and at his mercy."

Tossing his head skyward, Ahimoth roared in pain and anguish.

"I am so sorry, dear Ahimoth—but look at the wonder of it: Vin *lives!* He is beaten and chained, but he lives! And we know where he is, so we can free him, and all together have our vengeance upon the Rept."

"I believe you, Joli, but how do you know these things?"

"I sense he is alive, as clearly as I see you before me. But it was my dear friend Dagmar—she who helped me find a hatchling, then raised and taught me—who told me what the Rept had done, and that Vin has recently been badly beaten. That is why she could not help him escape the caverns, as she did for you."

"Your *teacher* helped me? Can it have been her voice that gave me aid and comfort through the years of my captivity?"

"Yes. That is what she explained to me."

"Mmmm! I see a story unfolding here," said Ahimoth.

"An amazing story, yes." And so she told Ahimoth of all she had experienced since the awful day of her old body's death.

"And now, we must go to rescue our friend," Joli concluded.

Ahimoth was speechless, gazing in wonder at the beautiful green Dragon before him. The things she had been through, the things she had done—and her dear devotion to him and to Vin, even after their senseless battle of stupid, stubborn pride.

"Yes," he said, at length. "Yes, we must help Vin. But I will go. It is a long, long flight from here to where he lies imprisoned. A flight of *days.* Days of hard, grueling work. It is a labor neither Vin nor I would ever dream of asking you to undertake. He would forbid it, I know. As do I!"

"Forbid it?" said Joli, astonished. "*Forbid* it?? What could give either of you the right to forbid such a thing? My life is my own. My purposes are my own. My decisions are my own. The tasks I set myself are my own.

"I do understand your concern and your care, but I must tell you: You do not know me. You do not know my strength, or the strength of my purpose. If you think me too young or too weak for such a task, you are mistaken. Dagmar trained me and drove me for years, in preparation for this very day. Many were the times I wanted to quit—it was painful and hard. I did not understand why she insisted so, why I must endure so much. But I trusted her, and I pushed on. Now I know why. So now I will go to Vin. *We* will go to Vin, you and I, and we will rescue him. Together."

Ahimoth was awed at the young Dragon's resolve, but he could not help but laugh. "All right! All right! I see it would be worse than useless to argue. But now I have a new concern: Will I be able to keep up with you?"

They both laughed—then stopped, each looking deep into the other's eyes, burning with purpose.

"Are you ready?" asked Ahimoth.

"Yes!" Joli cried.

"Then we're off!" shouted the black Dragon. He wheeled toward the ledge's rim and leapt into flight—out over the sweeping valley and up, with Joli just wingstrokes behind.

As they flew west and south, Ahimoth asked, "You are able to sense Vin—can you also communicate with him?"

"I don't know," said Joli, "I hadn't even thought to try." She was silent for a moment, then said, "Yes! Yes, I can speak with him!"

"Wonderful!" said Ahimoth. "Will you tell..." He stopped,

seeing the intense concentration on Joli's face; she must be talking with their captive friend.

After a while, Joli brightened and said, "Vin is quite surprised to hear from me. At first, he thought he was in a delirium, 'hearing voices,' but I told him a bit of our story, and he believes me now. He is overjoyed to know we are alive—and blood-furious at the half-Rept for his wicked deceptions.

"Let us hope he gets a chance to vent that fury, eh?" replied Ahimoth. "I look for such a chance myself!"

"If that chance should come, may I be there beside you both. I have my own fury to let fly!" answered Joli.

The pair flew a steady course onward, until they neared Spain's southwestern shores.

"We are making fine progress;" said Ahimoth, "you are an admirable flyer—just as you promised." he laughed. "But it is time we rested."

"No!"

"I know—I desperately want to push on, but rest is the wisest course. From here we must fly across the wide ocean, with the winds in our faces. We should rest a while, then make the crossing fresh."

"All right," said Joli. "It burns me to stop, but I bow to your judgment. You have made this journey before, after all."

Ahimoth lead the way to a small, deserted island off Spain's coast. Here they could land and rest without being seen. They caught some fine fish for their dinner and drank deep from a fresh island stream, then bedded down for a few hours' rest.

Before lapsing into sleep, Ahimoth pondered the situation. Joli lived! He was thrilled, yet not entirely surprised.

Through all the aching years of her absence, he had never fully believed her gone forever.

He thought of Vin, shackled in Soader's cavern. His joy at the news of his comrade's survival was tainted with a guilty misgiving. Vin had also been his bitter rival for Joli's affections. Joli had returned, but she could not be his without resolving that old rivalry. And their last attempt at resolution had ended very, very badly. Well, he thought, when the subject arose—as it surely must—he would content himself with Joli's decision. Her life and her choices were her own, just as she'd said. If she chose to be with Vin, so be it.

After a few hours' rest, the Dragons awoke, refreshed and eager to continue their mission. Within minutes they were in the air, winging westward across the Atlantic.

Joli called again to Vin, reassuring him they were on their way. "Ahimoth says we should reach you in two days."

"That will be wonderful," replied the blue Dragon, "but there may be a problem."

"What is that?"

"A few days ago, I learned I am to fight an earthling bull in the arena here. Part of an entertainment for the crew at the station where I am held. Today I heard that Soader, the Rept in charge of the station, has returned from a long absence. He has declared that instead of one bull, I am to fight three. Fighting one bull would not have been a pleasant thing— they are noble animals, but I can overcome one, even in my sorry condition. Three bulls is another story. I fear they will overcome me, instead. So, you see, I may have perished before you and Ahimoth can arrive."

"NO!" cried Joli—aloud, startling Ahimoth. "No, no, *no!!*"

"What is it, Joli?" inquired Ahimoth.

She explained Vin's predicament.

"That is awful!" he agreed. "But no more than can be expected from that wretched Rept. It is awful, but we cannot wish it away. Please tell Vin we are distraught at his news, but we shall come to him nonetheless. If he prevails in the battle—as we pray he will—then we shall free him, just as planned. If he should be defeated and his body broken beyond repair, still we shall come to him, and lead him—a spirit—away from his prison, then do all we can to help him find a hatchling to assume."

Joli relayed the message, then spoke to Ahimoth. "He thanks us, and agrees with your plan. But oh, I do hope he can defeat the bulls! I do not know how we could ever find him a hatchling!"

"I understand," said Ahimoth, "Vin faces an awful challenge. But do not worry. I have reason to believe it might not be so hard to find him a hatchling, if that should be our task."

"But, how?"

"I should not say more now—we must give all our energy to our mission. I will explain soon, though. I promise."

Joli was mystified, but agreed with her confidant. Right now, all their thoughts and energies must be channeled to the task before them. They flew on in determined silence.

Nearly two days later, the exhausted Dragons arrived above the mountains near Dulce. It was night, so there was little chance of being noticed by Earthlings as they glided in to land, just below the crest of a secluded ridge. "Have you tried again to reach Vin?" asked Ahimoth.

"Yes, but there's still nothing. Nothing since just before he was to enter the arena. I'm so worried!" said Joli.

"So am I," Ahimoth responded, grimly. "But before we go

to him, we should rest. Who knows what we will encounter down there, or how we will free him? We must be as fresh and alert as we can manage." Joli agreed, and they settled down for a few hours' sleep.

Dawn was still an hour or so away when the Dragons woke, rose, and stretched their flight-weary muscles. Though they could have used much more, they were glad for the rest and eager to press on.

CHAPTER 27

Rescue

Ahimoth explained his plan to Joli. "I escaped from this place not long ago. Fortunately, I had the sense to look behind as I flew away, fixing the place in my mind. I never wanted to return here, never in my entire life—but somehow it seemed important to remember it well. If you will follow me, I will take us to the shaft I used in my escape. We should be able to follow it back down under the mountains and into the caverns Soader uses as his Dragon-prison. Though I do not know how we will proceed once we are down there, at least we will be close to Vin."

"Ah, but I know exactly how to find him!" said Joli. "You forget I have visited him here many times, though not with a body. Once we are under the mountain, I will take us to the cavern where Soader has kept him."

"Wonderful!" said Ahimoth. "You are right—I forgot you had been here." He paused, smiling warmly. "You still amaze me, you know." She could see his smile well, even in the pale moonlight. She blushed a Dragon's blush, and tried to push aside the thrill his smile gave her. This was no time for such feelings—they had a mission to fulfill!

Their plan established, the pair took to the air. Ahimoth led the way, hugging the crests and ridges until they came to the mouth of the shaft he'd emerged from, in his flight to freedom.

Both Dragons tested the air wafting up from the caverns below. "I smell no danger, but take care just the same," said Ahimoth. He entered the shaft, easing cautiously down along the rocky wall; Joli followed closely.

Some twenty meters down the shaft, there came the metallic snap of a triggered mechanism, and Ahimoth found himself entangled in tough, unyielding netting. He had tripped a snare Soader had placed to keep his red Dragon prisoner from flying up and out, unless Soader was with him to disarm the trap.

With Joli's help, Ahimoth soon managed to wriggle free of the treacherous web, and the two continued downward.

They reached the bottom of the shaft and found themselves in Narco and Choy's underground cavern-prison. Ahimoth shuddered, his mind suddenly filled with painful images of his long subterranean captivity. Looking around to get oriented, he quickly came back to the present. "All right," he said to Joli. "You are now the guide; lead on, and I shall follow." Joli smiled, and started off on a path that would take them to Vin's cavern.

They hadn't gone far when a new obstacle sprung up. A large, two-headed, scarlet-scaled obstacle: Narco and Choy, right in their path, feet planted and ready to launch a double-headed blast of flame.

"Dragon-crap!" said Ahimoth, all decorum forgotten in his surprise.

"Ha. Think nothing of it," said Joli casually, as though it were a baby bunny they faced. She uttered a phrase—a potent spell, in fact—and their oversized red cousin collapsed in a heap.

"What?! How..." said Ahimoth. He stared at Joli in utter astonishment.

"Well, flying wasn't the only thing Dagmar taught me. Quite a few good spells, too." She gave him a coquettish smile, proud of stopping the Red, and just as proud to get such a reaction from the big, tough Prince of Nibiru.

"Mind you, that wouldn't work under most circumstances," she explained. "In a fight, for instance. In this case, he was overconfident—surprising us on his own turf. It was the last thing he expected."

"You are the one who is full of surprises, Joli," Ahimoth replied. "How long will he be in that state?"

"Oh, hours and hours."

"Splendid! I just hope it is long enough for us to free Vin."

"Me, too," said Joli. "I don't think it would work a second time, and I have no interest in a Dragon fight today."

She led off again, stopping before a wide, tall cleft in the cavern's rocky wall. "This is the way to Vin's cavern," Joli explained. The cleft goes back several meters, then we come to a tunnel opening. The tunnel leads to the next cavern—all part of the whole, huge system of caverns and caves down here. There we'll find Vin."

On they went, to the back of the cleft and into the tunnel.

It was quite dark inside, lit by only a few dim light-orbs at wide intervals. Plenty of light for Dragon eyes, though. The tunnel narrowed and narrowed until they had to go single-file, nearly crawling at one point. Then it widened again, and finally opened out into a cavern—spacious, but far smaller than the huge space where Ahimoth had been held, or Narco and Choy's big prison. Joli led along the cavern wall to their right until they came to a large opening, a sort of alcove cutting back into the tall rock face.

There, lying motionless in a crusted pool of dried blood, his leg shackled and chained to the wall, lay Vin.

He was barely conscious, and a battered wreck. There were great patches of raw skin, their scales missing. What scales remained were dirty, pale, mottled and dull, a far cry from their native state: deep, rich, glistening blue. His right hind leg had been worn raw and bloody at the ankle, ringed there by a heavy, cruel-edged shackle. The Dragon's eyes were open only a slit, but his rescuers could see they were glazed and dull, nearly devoid of life.

"Vin! Oh, Vin!" cried Joli, bending to gently embrace his ruined form. Tears fell from her eyes—a rare event among Dragons—leaving trails through the filth that coated Vin's tarnished scales.

He let out a moan, then uttered a few halting sounds in an effort to speak. "Shhh, Vin. No need to speak. We are here to help you. Ahimoth and Joli. Be still, save your strength. We will take you away to a place where you'll be safe—where you can heal."

"Uhnn..." groaned Vin.

"He understands," said Joli to Ahimoth. "But how shall we get him out of this place?"

"The first step is to unchain him," he replied, "but how are we to do that? We have no tools, and my flames are not focused enough to burn through the chain."

Joli thought for a moment, then spoke: "I have an idea. I think I may be able to modify an incantation Dagmar taught me, and turn your flames into a cutting torch."

"All right," said Ahimoth. "I see no other choice; let us try it. What should I do?"

"Stand right here," said Joli, pointing, "and direct your muzzle so that your flame will shoot toward the shackle. I'll perform an incantation. It may take a minute or so before I get it just right, but please be patient and watch the space in front of the shackle—about two meters from the end of your muzzle. You should see a sort of whirling ring appear there, in mid-air. When the ring has reached the proper intensity, I will nod my head sharply. That's your signal to send a brief blast of fire straight at its center. If possible, the flame should not be wider than the ring's borders; it need only be of moderate strength. Do you think you can direct your fire that accurately?"

"Yes, that should be easy. But, what will happen? Won't I burn Vin's ankle?"

"No, Vin should be perfectly safe. The ring will act as a sort of lens. With it, I will focus and direct your flames' energy quite precisely, right at the link that joins the chain to the shackle. I think you'll be impressed with the result!"

"All right, my friend. I will do as you ask. I must admit this makes me nervous, though. I have no desire to hurt Vin any further, even accidentally. But I trust you completely. I am ready!"

"Good. Good. I'll begin the incantation," Joli said. She

composed herself, closed her eyes briefly, opened them again and began to chant softly. Ahimoth aimed his muzzle at the spot she had indicated, and prepared to release a flame-blast, the moment Joli gave the sign.

After a minute's chanting, Ahimoth saw the manifestation Joli had described: a spinning ring of what looked like violet-hued lightning, perhaps twenty-five centimeters in diameter. The Dragon shifted his muzzle slightly, so his flame-stream would be perfectly centered on the ring. As he watched, the ring grew in brilliance and appeared to whirl faster and faster.

Now Joli brought her forepaws together in front of her chest, palm facing palm and a dozen centimeters apart; she arched her claws, as though she were gripping a ball in each paw. Next, she shifted their positions this way, then that, gauging distances and directions. At last she was satisfied; without taking her eyes off the ring, she nodded her head two times, sharply.

Instantly, Ahimoth released his flame-stream. His aim was true: the brilliant red-and-orange fire lanced out precisely at the center of the spinning ring. Just beyond the ring, the column of fire transformed into a pencil-thin jet of blazing blue-white light. It struck the stout link joining chain and shackle, vaporizing it with a flash and a sharp pop. The brutal chain clanked to the floor. Vin was free!

"Perfect!" said Ahimoth. His jaws were still open, but now in amazement.

Joli beamed with pride. "There! What a team we make, eh?"

Ahimoth turned his gaze toward his young friend and smiled in fond admiration. "A powerful team indeed. Yes indeed," he said.

"That's solved," said Joli, "but now we must get him out of here, somehow."

"Exactly so. And I have an idea how we might accomplish that," said Ahimoth. "Wait here with him. Do what you can to comfort him. I will return as soon as I may." He turned and hurried back the way they had come.

Soon, Ahimoth was back in the red Dragon's cavern. He ran out away from the tunnel entrance and vaulted into the air, flying hard for the shaft through which they'd entered. He passed over Narco and Choy, still inert in a heap on the ground. He reached the shaft and flew up to where he'd tripped the net-trap. Using claws and teeth, he methodically tore the netting from the trap mechanism, then rolled and wadded it into a ball as best he could. He didn't want stray ends to catch on the rocky walls of the shaft or tunnels, as he carried it back to Vin's cave.

At last he arrived where he'd left Joli and his old rival. Joli cried out in happy relief at his return—then eyed him quizzically, wondering what it was he carried.

Ahimoth smiled and unrolled a meter or two of the netting. Suddenly, Joli understood: they would use the net to carry their friend to freedom! She leapt to help Ahimoth unravel the netting and spread it on the cave floor. As they worked, she quickly explained that while Ahimoth was away, she'd been using healing spells to ease Vin's pain and begin the healing process. Ahimoth could see the blue Dragon was resting more easily, his breathing stronger and more regular.

"Brilliant!" he said. "You are a miracle and a wonder."

Joli blushed, and bent to their task with new vigor.

Soon they had the net neatly arranged beside their friend. "Relax, Vin," said Joli, "We're going to move you now. We'll place you in a net, then use it to carry you out of this horrid, horrid place."

"But you cannot do that," Vin protested, weakly. "I am too heavy. How will you ever lift me? And Soader—Soader will come and kill you both."

"Shh, shh. Be still, my friend. You'll never be too heavy for us. And Soader? Let Soader come! I, for one, would welcome the chance to rend him to bloody bits."

"A pleasure you would be obliged to share with me," put in Ahimoth. "And you, Vin, would have a prime view of the spectacle."

The blue Dragon grunted assent, still too weak to argue.

Soon the pair had positioned Vin as well as they could in the netting, forming it into a hammock-like arrangement. They each took an end in their jaws and lifted the Dragon off the ground. It took a bit to gain confidence and make adjustments, but they soon found they could carry him along at a fair pace—at least where the passage was reasonably wide.

Down the tunnel they headed with their precious burden. When they came to narrow stretches, they had to adjust their technique to make it through. At one point, Joli had to go ahead on her own; Ahimoth followed, then used the net to pull Vin through the passage as gently as he could.

When they reached the main cavern at last, they paused to rest. The greatest test lay before them: could they fly, carrying Vin between them? They had no idea—Joli had never attempted any such thing, and Ahimoth had team-carried only smaller loads.

"Well," said Ahimoth, "there is clearly only one way to do

this. We must fly abreast, with the net and Vin between us. It is fortunate the net's tethers are long—that gives us room to fly side by side without our wings clashing." Joli nodded. "We will probably find we need to trade sides from time to time, to keep from overstraining our muscles. We should also communicate mentally to coordinate our actions—it is far faster than speech."

"Smart thinking," said Joli.

Ahimoth smiled. "Thank you. And now, are you ready?"

"Yes."

"Off we go, then." Taking the tethers in his foreclaws, Ahimoth positioned himself to the left of their cargo and spread his wings, ready to take off; Joli readied herself on the right.

"We fly when I count to three," mented Ahimoth. "One, two, *three!*"

As one, the Dragons beat their wings downward in a tremendous rush. Then beat, beat, beat, matching each other's speed and thrust. They rose, and their burden rose between them. They could do it! They flew upward, gaining speed and confidence. Then, at Ahimoth's mented cues, they cautiously turned—first right, then left, learning to maneuver in this completely new way.

After several attempts and considerable menting back and forth, the pair felt they could maneuver adequately. It wasn't very graceful, but it would serve their needs. Ahimoth piloted them toward the shaft that would take them up and out of the caverns to freedom.

On the way to the shaft, they overflew Narco and Choy, still unconscious. They almost pitied the big mutant: captive here under Soader's sinister sway, forced to take part in his wicked schemes, and with little hope of escape.

They came to the shaft and faced a new challenge: the natural passage narrowed in places, so they had to adjust their positions and tighten their wingstrokes to avoid running into the walls. They narrowly escaped disaster at several points, but finally emerged into the open air. Not without a nasty collection of scrapes and bruises, though. Fortunate for Vin, he was unconscious through most of the ordeal, and suffered nothing worse than a few jostles and bumps.

Once clear of the caverns, the Dragons flew for several minutes along a mountain ridge, then set down for a rest. From here on the flying would be easier: With no walls to restrict them, they could fly wide to either side of the net-hammock and open their wings fully. The challenge now was sheer distance; it would be a long, long flight to Scotland.

And a long, exhausting flight it was. They were forced to land and rest many times along the way. Vin remained unconscious through most of the flight, though from time to time he would waken and watch the landscape slipping by below, or take a brief drink when they rested beside a lake or stream.

One of Ahimoth's rest-spot choices proved especially fortuitous. The weary pair gently set down their burden on the sandy margin of a rushing stream, then plopped to the ground themselves and fell almost instantly asleep. A few hours later they were wakened by a curious chorus of splashing, flipping and flapping sounds. They raised their heads and looked about, wondering what the noise might be. Looking toward the stream, they had their answer: a salmon run! Hundreds of salmon on their way upstream to mate, leaping from the water in their battle against the churning flow.

"Dinner!" cheered Ahimoth. Despite his weariness, he was up in an instant and into the stream, deftly catching fish after fish and tossing them ashore. Soon there were more than a dozen of the silvery creatures flapping and flopping in the sand. Joli grabbed one; with a flick of her head she tossed it straight up, then opened her jaws wide. Down it dropped to a darker destination.

"Yum!" she said, and called to Ahimoth to come eat quick, before she finished off his whole catch.

The big Dragon joined her, and the two soon satisfied their hunger—hunger they hadn't even noticed, in their determination to reach Loch Ness. Joli gently nudged Vin, holding a smaller fish close so he could smell it. His eyes opened a crack, then popped wide. Fish! He gratefully accepted Joli's gift, then another—but that was as far as his appetite stretched. Hardly a hearty meal, but Joli was happy to see him eat at all.

CHAPTER 28

A Bullfight and A Blessing

At last, Ahimoth and Joli set their friend down on the green, grassy banks of Loch Ness. "Thank you, thank you, my dear friends," said Vin. The depth of his gratitude was clear, though his voice was still sadly weak.

Nessie had sensed the Dragons approaching from far off, so within minutes of their landing, she and a pod of her Water Dragon clan arrived to greet them. Ahimoth introduced Joli and Vin, then gave a brief account of his old friends' history, and the daring rescue mission.

"Thank you, Ahimoth," said Nessie. "We welcome you all, and stand in awe of what you have done. I have never heard of such a feat as you and Joli have just achieved; it is truly the stuff of legends. But now, please allow us to tend to Vin—his condition remains grave."

"Certainly," agreed Ahimoth.

"Yes, please," said Joli. "I did all I could during our journey, but he needs more powerful help than I can provide."

"You have done well, Joli," said Nessie. "I judge that he would have been lost, if not for your care." As she bent down to examine Vin more closely, a cry went up from the Water Dragons.

"Look! Look above!! They return!"

Nessie, Joli and Ahimoth looked skyward at once—barely in time to see the mouth of the vortex closing. Just below it was Fianna, tumbling earthward with Celine clinging desperately in her saddle.

In a flash, the white Dragon righted herself and arced into a graceful glide. The instant they were in smooth, controlled flight, Celine made an anguished attempt to contact Jager. She nearly screamed at the empty silence she encountered.

Next, she called to West, desperate for any news. Again she met horrid, horrid silence. "West must be busy with something critical," Celine thought. She would try to reach both of them again as soon as she could. She *must*. Not knowing Jager's fate was driving her insane. She closed her eyes, breathed deeply, and brought her attention to the present moment as completely as she could.

Fianna's sweeping turn brought the pair in sight of the spot they'd left just days before; they were startled and amazed at the scene that greeted them. Instead of a quiet, deserted shore, there was a crowd of Dragons! In the water just off shore were Nessie and several of her friends. Close by were black Ahimoth, a lovely green Dragon they did not recognize, and a terribly battered blue Dragon lying at their feet.

"Hail, Dragons!" called Fianna, lighting gently before

them.

"Hello! Hello!" called Celine. Mercifully, the excitement of the moment made it easier to avoid her anguish. She leapt from the saddle, bowed quickly to Ahimoth and Nessie, then looked inquiringly at the newcomer Dragons.

"Hail, Sister-Princess!" replied Ahimoth. "Greetings, Companion Celine. Please allow me to introduce my friends. This is Joli..."

Celine and Fianna gasped. Fianna had been close to Joli in their youth; she recognized the Dragon-spirit the moment her brother uttered the name. Celine had heard the sad tale of Joli's death, and knew well her significance in Ahimoth's life.

"...And this is none other than Vin, my one-time rival and life-long friend," the black Dragon continued. "You have come at a most opportune time. Vin has suffered awfully; I hope you can help him."

"But...Joli? Vin? How?" asked Fianna, still astonished.

"The tale is a long one; I will tell it soon, my sister, but we must tend to Vin. I fear for his life. There is one thing I would know first, though: Were you and your Companion success-ful in your mission on our homeworld?"

"Yes, my brother. Celine has broken the hex on our people. Eggs are hatching—many eggs—and more are being brought forth. Our race has new hope for the future!"

"This is..." Ahimoth bowed his head, speechless. At last he looked up again. "This is..." another pause, then a shake of the great black head. "I am sorry. I have no words." He rushed to embrace Fianna. The Dragons—prince and prin-cess of their people—held together for a long moment, then Ahimoth drew gently back. "You must give me the whole account, every detail, but it must wait. Right now, Vin needs our help."

"Of course, brother," said Fianna. "Celine, can you and Nessie tend to Vin?"

"Certainly. Let me confer with her a moment." She went to the water's edge; Nessie came close and the two spoke quietly for several minutes.

Nessie turned and spoke softly to the waiting Water Dragons; they nodded their heads, and she turned to address Ahimoth and Joli. "Friends, would you move Vin as close to the water as is safe? Then Celine and I will set to work."

The Dragons did as she asked, using their improvised net to move Vin as gently as they could, then stepped back to rejoin Fianna. Nessie nodded to the Water Dragons, who began to chant. She smiled at Celine; the girl laid her hands on Vin's battered flank. Nessie arched her long neck downward until the tip of her snout touched the blue Dragon's shoulder. Now the two began a chant of their own, harmonized with that of the Water Dragons in tone and rhythm. The chanting went on and on, rising and falling in volume, for nearly half an hour. Then Nessie raised her head and said, "Thank you, friends." The chanting stopped. "Thank you. That is enough for the moment. He rests in greater comfort now; his heart beats quiet but strong, his breath is even and easy. Now he needs rest.

"He owes his life to you, Joli, for the aid you gave him on your journey to this place. He owes his life to both of you for making that remarkable journey."

She thanked her clanspeople; they bowed their necks, then turned and swam off the way they had come, submerging slowly as they went.

Ahimoth, Joli, Fianna and Celine all came to the water's edge. Ahimoth and Fianna flanked Nessie, each extending a wingtip across the water dragon's back. The others did likewise on shore, to form a living ring. Nessie led them in a prayer of thanks to the Ancients for all that had taken place.

Ahimoth and Joli carefully moved Vin back away from the water and settled him under the canopy of a nearby oak. Night had nearly fallen, with highland air taking on its customary chill. The Dragons went to gather fuel for a fire.

As soon as they had departed, Celine made another attempt to contact Jager, then West. Neither responded. And again, she forced her attention back to the situation before her.

She took a small, tight packet from her bodypack, opened it, and spread it out into a broad blanket—much larger than the packet's size suggested. She had just laid it over the sleeping blue Dragon when the wood-hunters returned. Soon they were all gathered around a cheery, warming fire. The friends talked long into the night, recounting the momentous events of the last several days. At last, after tucking Celine's blanket snuggly around the sleeping Vin, they joined him in a well-earned rest. All but Celine. After unanswered calls to Jager and West, she lay in fevered torment. Where were they? When would she know?! It was more than an hour before she brought her emotions under control, and fell into a fitful sleep.

Next morning, the five friends awoke to a surprise: Vin, wide awake, head erect and watching them with a faint but grateful smile.

"Vin!" Joli broke the morning stillness, jumping up to embrace the blue Dragon—gingerly, mindful of his condition. Everyone joined in, bombarding the poor creature with greetings, asking how he felt, was he hungry or thirsty, and on and on.

"Friends! Friends!" said Vin, his voice happy but still weak. "I feel...well, I can feel! I mean, I can feel my limbs and wings and head and all, and tell one from another, and how all the parts seem to be faring. Before, it was all just one dreary mass of pain, pain and pain. So, thank you, thank you." The five cheered, and hugs were exchanged all round.

When the mini-celebration was over, Ahimoth addressed Vin. "Days ago, you told Joli you were to fight three earthling bulls in Soader's arena, and we were deeply worried—afraid for your life, in fact. Can you tell us now what happened? Or should we let you rest a while longer first?"

"No, no—I feel rested enough for that, at least," Vin replied. His four companions settled down to hear the tale. Celine took the opportunity to call out to Jager again. And again, there were no replies. She shuddered, then forced herself to listen to the blue Dragon's tale.

"As I told Joli a few days ago," Vin began, "I was to fight three bulls as an entertainment for Soader's crew. Having been chained for so long, and after so many beatings from Soader and his minions, I feared I had no chance; I was far, far from fighting condition. The time for the fight arrived, and armed guards led me to the arena. The place was crowded with rowdy spectators; they all roared when I was led out into view, leaping up and down and screaming for blood. From what little I could make out, it was plain many of them had bet heavily on the outcome—most in favor of the bulls.

"Then there came a new disaster. Instead of being allowed to fight free, I was shackled and chained to the arena's stone wall, with little more than two Dragon-lengths of chain. Not nearly enough to properly maneuver. My heart sank.

"The fight was announced, the bulls were released, and the crowd's noise tripled. I have never seen people so blood-mad. Where did Soader find such a lot?

"The bulls paced back and forth, out of my reach, sizing me up. Then they began charging, one or two at a time. I dodged and leaped, clawed, battered and bit them, but still they managed to gore me; you have seen my wounds. Soon the arena's sand was thick with spattered blood. Much of it was the bulls', but as the fight went on, more of it was mine. They were winning, and I was nearing despair.

"Then an idea came to me. I could not hope to defeat all three directly—but if I could somehow turn their fierce energies against each other, I might have a chance.

"With a series of lunges, taunts, sidesteps and feints, I managed to get two of them positioned on opposite sides of me. Because of my size and position, neither could see the other—all they could see was me, and all they wanted was my final blood. I snapped my head back and forth, taunting first one and then the other but preventing them from charging. At last, both reached a blind peak of fury. I gave a final roar of challenge—and it worked: both abandoned all caution, lowered their heads and charged.

"At the last possible instant, I leapt upward and back, out of their paths. Their heads were down, confident of their target and lusting for the kill, so they never even noticed their target had vanished. They collided head-on, massive skull to massive skull, each with more than a ton of hurtling mass behind it. The sound of it was horrible. So horrible that the screaming crowd fell silent at once; they watched in sick fascination as the two great beasts collapsed, dead in their tracks.

"There was another moment of awed silence, and then

the crowd exploded, screaming and cheering. This was not the outcome they had expected. Not at all. It was *better!* Even those who had bet the bulls would win cheered and shouted their hearts out.

"That was all well and good for me, but it only bought me a moment's rest. There was still the third bull to contend with, and I was near the end of my wits and strength.

"The remaining bull had been watching my encounter with the other two, biding his time, looking for a chance to make his own move. With his rivals for my destruction neutralized, I was all his, and he was hot to end the fight—and my life.

"The two dead bulls lay between him and me, so he moved to his right for a clear path to my left side. He charged. I dodged at the last moment, biting him on the left shoulder— but he managed to hook his head to the right, goring me in the right shoulder. We both roared in pain and anger, and he backed off, out of my reach, to consider his next move.

"I took advantage of the pause, dragging one of the dead bulls to my left, the other to the right. My attackers had become, in death, my defense. For now there was only one way for the third bull to approach me: straight on. I had left enough room between my bull-barriers to move to either side, so I was not entirely boxed in. I could still maneuver and fight, but more on my own terms.

"The bull positioned himself to confront me, head on. He huffed and blew mightily and pawed the sand, preparing himself for a new charge: the charge that would end the fight in his favor, he hoped. As he saw it, he needed only to charge straight ahead. If I dodged to right or left, he would only need to turn in my direction and thrust with his horns, pinning me against the dead bull on that side. If I should try to leap upward and out of his way, he would stop, point his horns straight up, and impale me as I came back down.

"What he had failed to notice was that I had, while moving the second dead bull into position to my right, looped my restraining chain around one of its horns. I'd then positioned the chain across the opening between the two vanquished animals, and taken up most of the slack, leaving just enough that it still lay in the dust. Then I stood in the gap, facing the hostile creature, waiting.

"At last he lowered his head, pawed the earth twice more, and charged directly toward me—certain he could counter any move I might make.

"He was almost upon me, his front hooves coming down toward the ground at the end of a bounding stride; they would hit the earth just in front of the chain. The instant his hooves touched down, I spun to my left, yanking hard on the chain. Anchored by the dead bull's great weight, it snapped up taut, just above the charging bull's knees. Seeing my move to his right, he instantly veered in that direction, mid-stride.

"But before he could wheel to deliver a fatal goring, his knees struck the taut chain, and stopped. The force of the impact nearly tore my leg off, but I held fast. That same force and the bull's momentum caused him to flip upward, hindquarters flying up and over his head. He struck the wall behind me, his head downward and the full weight of his body above. Forward motion blocked by the wall, the huge mass had nowhere to go but straight down. It crashed to the ground, snapping the neck and killing the poor creature instantly. His body convulsed once, twice, then lay still.

"The crowd went berserk. 'The Dragon wins!!' they screamed, then chanted. Many a crew member lost good money on that outcome, but few regretted it—the spectacle and its impossible outcome were well worth the price. Those who had bet on me, against outrageous odds, were delirious. Many would take home more money that one night than they would earn in the whole year to come."

Vin chuckled. ("Well, that's a good sign," thought Celine.) "There was one person present who was delirious in a most negative, nasty way," he said. "Soader. He lost the hefty sum he had bet on the bulls. Worse, he knew the treacherous Orme had bet heavily on the Dragon, willing to take a loss just to spite his hated boss—and now he had won a tidy fortune instead. Finally, and worst of all, Soader had been utterly humiliated before the crew he meant to impress and win to his side. He screamed and raged at me as I was led from the arena, battered, bleeding and barely able to walk. I dreaded what I was sure would come next.

"In his rage, Soader killed two Grey orderlies that night—or so he informed me a few hours later, as he beat me mercilessly with an iron bar and a length of chain. Beat me into a black coma. The next thing I remember is...is..."—he turned to Joli—"is your lovely face, and the music of your voice calling my name."

With that, Vin laid down his head and lapsed into sleep, a smile of peace on his lips.

Hours later, Vin awoke to find his friends, new and old, still gathered round, watching over him.

He raised his head, looked around at all the friendly, inquiring faces, and smiled. Tears welled up and tracked down his scaled cheeks. "Forgive me," he said, "but I have not been surrounded by such kindness and good will since...since I can ever remember."

All the group thanked and reassured him. Then Celine

asked what everyone was wondering. "How are you feeling, Vin?"

"So much better, it is hard to express," he replied, "and for that I am grateful. There are still many hurts, though, and a deep and aching weakness. I fear it may be some time before they pass. And yet I know they *will* pass, all thanks to you."

"Of course they will," responded Fianna, and everyone chimed in with similar assurances.

"Will you all excuse me?" Celine asked, "I want to speak with Nessie about what we should do next."

"Certainly," said Ahimoth; the others nodded agreement.

Celine went to the water's edge, and she and the Water Dragon moved off to confer. A few minutes later they rejoined the group. "Nessie and I have an idea," Celine announced. "We would like to know what you think of it. Especially you, Vin. We believe the quickest route to a full recovery would be to send Vin to the Mentors' outpost on Mars. That is, if West and the other Mentors agree and are willing. They are far better equipped, materially, magically and spiritually, to care for Vin and speed his healing."

All eyes turned to Vin. "I have little knowledge of the Mentors," he said, "but what I do know is only positive, and I trust your judgment completely."

"Excellent," said Celine. "Then, it is decided. I will call to West, and ask if the Mentors are willing to do this. I have been trying to contact West since the moment Fianna and I emerged from the vortex, but without success. I hope she will hear me now." She bowed her head and called out to the Mentor.

"I am here, Celine," came West's mental voice. The girl nearly cried out with relief.

"Oh, West! I've been trying and trying to reach you and Jager! Please, please, tell me you've found him!"

"No, child. We have not found him yet. I am sorry."

At the horrible news, Celine collapsed, spiritually. West had anticipated just such a response, and prepared for it. Before any of Celine's friends could perceive the girl's plunge into despondency, West reached out and enveloped her in a gentle but powerful energy field—in effect, a globe of peace and reassurance. The field also prevented those around her from sensing the change, and becoming alarmed. As far as they could see, Celine was simply conversing mentally with the Mentor, a phenomenon most had observed before. They continued to talk among themselves, unconcerned.

Celine soon began to respond to the Mentor's efforts. She climbed gradually upward from the black depths of her despair; West comforted and encouraged her as she rose. At last, Celine was able to shake off the worst effects of the news, and face the present once more. West praised the girl's strength, courage and resilience, and assured her that Jager *would* be found and recovered; it was, and always had been, meant to be so.

To Celine, the ordeal had seemed to last hours and hours. In the physical world, and to those around her, only a minute or so had passed.

Ready to carry on at last, Celine recounted to West what had transpired since her return to Earth, and quickly summarized Vin's condition. "May we ask your help in restoring him?" she finished.

"Yes, child. We will be glad to transport your friend to our Mars outpost, and to heal him," said West. "Simply tell me when he is ready to make the journey; we will bring him, using the transbeam device."

"Thank you, West. Thank you and all your people there." She turned to the waiting group and told them the good news. Everyone cheered, and those who had met the Mentors assured Vin he was in for the experience of a lifetime.

"Well, I have had some dramatic experiences in this lifetime," he responded, "more dramatic than most, I would hazard to say. And more than a few experiences I would rather forget! But I understand what you mean, and I look forward to meeting these wonderous beings."

"Are you ready to go, then?" asked Celine.

"Yes," he said. "I believe I am. I long to be whole and healthy again—and then to rejoin you all."

The group cheered again, and began to bid him farewell as Celine called to West with this new news.

"Wait!" Vin called out, silencing the happy assembly. "Please wait a moment. There is something I must say before I go."

Looking first at Ahimoth for a long moment, then turning his attention to Joli, he went on. "Joli, long ago and far from this planet, you were the love of my life. The love of my ever-friend Ahimoth's, as well. And I know you loved him, too. Who would not!

"Now here we are, together again. It is still the greatest wonder of my life to see you, young, strong and fair as ever you were. This, after the unspeakable horror and sorrow of seeing your body broken beyond mending, and no hatchling on all Nibiru for you to assume.

"I have never ceased loving you. I never will. But I also see what a great love burns between you and the friend who was once my rival."

Joli blushed and turned away from Vin's fond and earnest gaze. Ahimoth was struck with a deep pang of conflict, but did not flinch.

"Now," Vin went on, "I no longer wish to be a rival. Joli, Ahimoth, I know in my heart you are meant to be together. Together for the rest of your long lives."

Jodi and Ahimoth looked at one another, then back at Vin, overwhelmed with astonishment and caught in a whirl of emotions—as if the vortex itself had opened inside them.

"But..." began Ahimoth.

"Vin, I...I...you..." stammered Joli.

"You see?" laughed Vin. "I knew I was right in what I saw. Now, please: Quiet. Both of you!" He laughed again.

"Besides," he said, addressing Ahimoth directly, "I rather fancy the look of that sister of yours, old friend."

Taken completely by surprise, it was Fianna's turn to blush.

Celine almost laughed at the sweet but silly lot of them, but her own worries still loomed too close for laughter. She called to West, and gave the word that Vin was ready.

Laughing still, the blue Dragon vanished in a flurry of transbeam light.

CHAPTER 29

Convergence

L ate in the evening of their sixth day at the resort, Rafael
and Dino sat in Hadgkiss's comfortable suite. Hoping
for good news, or at least an update, they were about to call
Elias Stock on the secure comm link. Zulak had just begun
entering the call code when the link lit up with an incoming
message.

"Good evening, Commander," came Stock's baritone.

"Good evening, sir," said Zulak and Hadgkiss, startled.
"We were just calling you."

"I have news for you, gentlemen. News I think you'll welcome." As always, the man's voice was imposing, but now
it carried unmistakable overtones of extreme fatigue and
stress. Dino thought he glimpsed a faint glistening of sweat
on the elder officer's brow. What was going on?

What the monitor did not reveal was a Rept, positioned
just to Stock's left, with the muzzle of a beam pistol pressed

tight against the man's shoulder. Nor did it show the recently-used syringe lying at the admiral's feet.

"Yes, sir. What is it?" replied Zulak.

"My people finally came up with an exact location for Celine. You'll receive coordinates shortly, by secure packet transmission. I'm not going to reveal the location over this line, for obvious reasons."

"Thank you, sir. Understood. This is excellent, sir."

"Yes, it is, Commander."

There it was again—Stock addressing Zulak by his rank; he hadn't done that for decades, except in the most formal or gravely serious situations. Something *must* be amiss here. Both men noticed the oddity, but they also knew better than to comment. If there really were something wrong, to show suspicion could easily make matters worse. Perhaps another tactic could net them more information without compromising Stock.

"I'm curious about one thing though, sir," said Rafael.

"Yes, Commander, what is it?"

"You recently informed us of your retirement. Should we be welcoming you back to active duty?"

"No, no—nothing like that. Because of my familiarity with the situation, I was invited to consult—temporarily—on the matter of High Chancellor Jin's daughters."

"Ah. That explains it. Thank you, sir."

"The coordinates will have been transmitted by now, to your secure comm account aboard *Queen Asherah*. I urge you to depart at once, rendezvous with the *Queen* and proceed to Celine's location. You must secure the girl before whoever is behind all this can grab her. If they get her first, they'll have

no more need for Jin's daughters; there's no telling what they might do then."

"Understood, sir. We'll contact the *Queen* and depart at once."

"One last question, sir, if I may," said Dino. The admiral nodded. "Ensign Jager, sir—do you know if he's been located?"

"I'm sorry, Major, but I'm told there has been no sign of the ensign. I understand he is a fine young officer, and your nephew as well—hence your concern."

"That's right, sir. Thank you."

"You should both know that there has been no new word on the Jin girls' location," the admiral said, "but we've received a new demand from the kidnappers. They've set a deadline; we're to hand over Celine by one week from today, or the hostages will be killed."

"I see," said Rafael. "We'd better get on it, then. We'll depart at once, sir."

"Very good," replied the admiral. "Good luck, and may the Ancients guide you. Signing off." The monitor went blank, but not before it showed just a glimpse of Stock looking to his right, an expression of pain and anger on his face.

"Something's wrong," said Rafael.

"Absolutely. He was trying to tell us something. All that "commander" business, and speaking formally," answered Dino.

"Exactly," said Zulak. "We have to assume he's been compromised. Nothing we can do about that right now—we've got to get to Celine. But, as soon as she's secured, we go to the admiral. I just hope we won't be too late."

"Agreed. And for now, we'd better be doubly cautious. If Stock has been compromised, who knows what might be waiting for us."

"Well, we'll deal with it," said Rafael, grimly. "Let's go. You ready the ship and plot a rendezvous course. I'll go say goodbye to Remi. She's known this was coming, but it still won't be easy."

"Aye, sir" said Hadgkiss. He was eager for action, but his friend's parting words sparked a gnawing unease.

Soader was furious. He sat at his office desk, surrounded by empty plates, trays, glasses and goblets. All liberally spattered and splotched with the remnants of a Rept-style eating-and-drinking binge: mostly blood, bones and scraps of raw flesh.

Why were the gods-damned gods suddenly all against him? First, he discovered his "faithful" second-in-command at the Dulce compound had been plotting against him and subverting his crew for ages. Then he lost a fortune betting on the "best" bulls this stinking, rotten planet had to offer, only to have them beaten by that total blue wreck of a Dragon. Impossible! Impossible!

That was just the bloody, bleeding start, though. After beating the piece-of-crap blue as close to death as any creature could get, he decided to end his day on an up note by beating his gods-blasted black Dragon into a coma, too. But what had he found? The black was GONE. How in all the bleeding hells in all the universes could THAT be? It must have been Orme. Yes. Orme must have freed it. Well, Orme was going to die for it. Slowly and painfully. Maybe publicly, too! That would make it clear to one and all what happened to people who dared mess with Soader. Yes, sir!

At least the black's disappearance answered a question that had plagued him for many days. When he'd gone to Germany to finish off the white bitch-Dragon and her little witch of a Human, he'd been attacked by a black. A big one. He'd had no idea where it could have come from. Everything had happened so fast, he hadn't gotten a look at the thing, but it must have been *his* black Dragon. What it was doing in Germany was just another question, but it didn't matter.

Next in the chain of disasters was his Dragon detector. When he had discovered the black missing, he'd returned to his office and turned the thing on, to track the escaped creature down. The device turned on as usual, but registered nothing. Nothing at all. The black hadn't shown up—okay, so maybe he was hiding somehow, but it should have shown the stupid, stupid, bull-murdering blue. He'd just seen the creature with his own eyes—and pounded the hells out of it with his own hands. It should have shown up on the detector, down in its prison-cave. But there was nothing. It didn't even show the enormous, pain-in-the-ass red!

So, the detector wouldn't detect a damned thing. Useless. He almost dashed it against the wall in his anger, but stopped himself at the last moment. The things were hideously expensive. And this was the only one in the whole sector. It would take weeks and weeks to get another. No, he'd get his people to fix this one. Meanwhile, he was blind, Dragon-wise. Damn it, damn it, damn it, damn it, damn it!!

Next day had come the crowning blow. When he'd arrived in his office, he had switched on the Dragon detector, just in case it had fixed itself. ("These things happen with electronics," he'd "reasoned.") Still nothing. Damn it to hells again.

Grumbling and growling all the way, he made his way

down to the prison-caverns, to check up on Narco and Choy. They weren't in their den, but that wasn't all that unusual—they often roamed around the huge cavern, hunting or fishing or whatever Dragons did in their spare time. "And the big stupid-ass red's got *plenty* of spare time," he had thought. "Harrrrr!" Soon he spotted the big Kerr out in the middle of a wide, open space, fast asleep. "Typical," he thought. "Lazy piece of crap!"

Soader continued on to the cave where he'd left the blue the day before, bleeding, battered and knocking at death's door. No doubt the thing was still lying there in a coma. But NO. The blue was gone!! Impossible! IMPOSSIBLE! Its chain had been burned clean through, as if with a plasma torch, and it was gone, gone, gone. Soader's screams of rage reverberated up and down the cavern complex.

He stormed out of the blue's cave and headed for the spot where he'd seen Narco and Choy. The pathetic creature was due for a good beating, and he was going to provide it, ohhhhh yes. He'd nearly reached the still-sleeping Dragon when his comm pickup beeped, summoning him to his office to receive a secure call from Scabbage. "Scabbage?! Just what I need! A call from that gods-damned conniving runt!" he thought. There was a slim, slim chance the idiot might have something important or useful to say, though, so he headed on back to his office, fuming all the way.

"What do *you* want?!" Soader snarled, when Scabbage's call was connected.

"Well! Aren't we cordial today!" Scabbage replied, sarcastic. "If you're actually doing something useful for a change, I can call back some other time."

"Cut the crap and tell me what you want, slime."

"Oh, well! If you *insist*, I shall. I thought you might be interested to know that right now your old pal Zulak is headed to a remote little spot, far from Fleet backup. But if that's not important to you, I'll leave you to your..."

"What the hells are you talking about?! Where?!" demanded Soader.

"Tut, tut. Be civil, can't you? Let me lay this out for you slowly, so you'll have some dim chance of grasping it. As even you may be able to comprehend, Zulak has been a constant annoyance, and will only become more so when we've captured his little Dragon-riding spawn, Sireen or Cosmoline or whatever her name is. So, I had the brilliant idea of taking him out of the picture—and an even more brilliant idea for how to do so. I presented my idea to Lancaster and Dodd; naturally, they approved it, wholeheartedly and at once.

"Putting it in the simplest possible terms for you, I arranged for doddering old Admiral Stock to be compliance-drugged into helpless mush, then forced to tell his hopelessly subservient minion, Zulak, where the missing daughter can be found. The idiot is so pathetically devoted to his sorry little family that he'll go there at once, no questions asked, to rescue the brat. Needless to say, she won't be there. Someone else will, though, and that someone will eliminate his meddling ass. Oh, and just for neatness's sake, we've ensured that his will be the only Fleet vessel in the area. No tedious evasion necessary, no messy space battles to be fought.

"Having arranged all that, I thought, 'Who better to snuff the good commander out of existence than dear, dear Soader?' And the set-up is so simple and so air-tight, even *you* would be hard pressed to muck it up.

"So! Are you interested, or shall I find someone else to

send on this little errand of joy?"

"Don't be absurd. I'll do it, and you know it. Where is Zulak going? When?"

"As it happens, he will almost surely be on his merry way in less than, oh, let's see—five hours from now. The location is the planet Scobee, in the Pleiades Sector. A lovely place, I'm told, but quite secluded, well off the usual travel corridors. I'll send you the exact coordinates Zulak will have. If you don't dawdle, you can be there to meet him."

"Crap! To get there that fast, I'd need a jump-capable ship—and you know damned well I don't have one. Are you just messing with me, damn you??"

"Now, now. Please attempt to control yourself. I'm well aware you have no such ship, but I, with characteristic foresight, efficiency and generosity, have arranged to have a jump-ship come for you. In fact, since you've agreed to undertake the task, it should be there for you within the hour. Imagine! A jump-ship sent half-way across the sector, just for you! But wait—don't thank me. I'm just doing what's best for all of us, as always."

"Yeah. Right. Whatever. Okay, I'll be ready. But listen: If this is some kind of elaborate prank, be assured I will find you and pound you into paste, dearest cousin."

"Prank? Oh, please! Only you could be so petty as to pull such a prank. No, Zulak will be there. Count on it. Now, I'm busy—so unless you want me to repeat everything again, more slowly this time, we're through here."

"Ass. We're done." Soader broke the connection, then hastily set about preparing to leave.

"Well!" he thought, "Maybe the gods don't have it in for me after all."

CHAPTER 30

Scobee

Queen *Asherah III* burst out of jump-shift above Scobee. In minutes, she settled into a parking orbit directly above the surface coordinates transmitted earlier to her captain.

"Jessup, scan the area. You're looking for an adult Human female," ordered Rafael.

"Aye, sir."

"Well?" said Zulak, a few moments later. "She's supposed to be right there."

"I'm not getting anything but a few small animals, sir. No Humans. I'm progressively widening the search radius, in case the target has moved."

"All right. Thank you. Just find her, damn it!" snapped the commander, instantly regretting his harshness.

"Y-yes, sir!" replied Jessup, taken aback.

"Damn it. I'm sorry. You're doing your job. Carry on."

"Yes, sir!" A few moments later, he spoke again. "Sir, I'm out to ten kilometers; still no Human in sight. However, I adjusted frequency parameters and did a new scan at the target coordinates. It looks like our scan may be being selectively filtered at that location."

"Can you work around the filtering?" Rafael asked.

"I believe so, sir; just a moment. Just a moment..yes. I'm reading a Human, average size and mass for an adult female."

"Got her! Thank you. Now maintain your scan. Tell me at once if she changes location."

"Aye, sir!"

What Jessup did not know—and what Rafael was too eager and anxious to suspect—was that the whole "filtering" and then "appearance" of the target was a machine-generated illusion—a ruse. Soader had arrived first and arranged it, not wanting Zulak to think finding Celine was going *too* easily, and so suspect a trap.

Zulak keyed his intercom. "Transbeam Station 1, this is the captain. There is a Human at the coordinates I'm sending you now." He tapped a few keys on his console. "Do you have them?"

"Aye, sir."

"Good. Lock onto her and 'beam her up at once. I'll be there shortly."

"Aye sir, but... Sir, I've located the target, but I can't get an acceptable lock. Something's interfering."

"Understood. Do not attempt to 'beam, then. Stand by."

Turning to Dino, he said, "Major Hadgkiss, you have the conn. I'm going down there."

"Sir! You can't..."

"Enough. Don't you tell me what I 'can't.'"

"But, respectfully, sir, I must object. We don't know what's going on down there. It would be highly irregular for you to go down before the area is secured. Allow me to send a team down first."

"Damn it, I know all that. But I'm... Damn." Rafael realized he should not be having this conversation on the bridge, in front of the crew. "Step into my ready room, Major."

When the ready-room door closed behind them, Zulak continued. "I know the regs, Dino. This is different. We're not even on an officially recognized mission, remember? It's all secret, off the record. And I'm the reason we're here at all—me and my Gods-blasted screw-ups, beginning with not terminating Soader when I had the chance. Two times now! So I'm going down. Now. Alone. Are we clear?"

"We're clear, yes. Your argument regarding the nature of our mission is sound, but I do *not* agree, and I officially protest your decision. I know better than to try to stop you, though. So, go ahead. Go get your girl and bring her back. But look—I'm going to have a team assembled, armed and standing by on a transbeam platform before you hit the ground. And if there's even a hint of anything going wrong down there, we're 'beaming at once. Are we clear on *that?*"

The commander regarded his old friend a moment, then smiled grimly. "Yeah, Dino. We're clear."

Ten minutes later, Rafael stepped up onto the platform in Transbeam Station 3, then turned to face the control console. "Ready?"

"Ready, sir," answered the tech on duty, Piccolo.

"Send me down, Ensign."

"Aye sir." He activated the 'beam and Zulak vanished. As soon as the commander cleared the platform, Piccolo feverishly punched in a new set of coordinates, touched the contact for transmission, and dashed onto the platform. Up came the 'beam's familiar swirling cloud of light, and Piccolo disappeared as well.

Meanwhile, in Transbeam Station 1, a landing party waited on the platform in full combat gear, weapons at the ready. The tech manning the console had already entered coordinates that would take the team to a location some fifteen meters from their commander's point of arrival.

Zulak emerged from the transbeam in an open space within a narrow canyon. Steep walls rose on either side. The ground between was level and sandy, but strewn here and there with rocks and boulders. The landscape was the least of the commander's concerns, however. Directly in front of him, twenty meters down the canyon, stood Soader, flanked by two Greys. All three had beam weapons leveled at him.

Soader glared at him for a moment, then leaned back and roared with laughter. "Harrrrrr! The look on your face, you puny, pathetic pile of crap!"

Zulak had half-expected something like this, and he was ready. While Soader howled in gravely mistaken glee, Rafael dove to his right and rolled, ending on his feet behind a boulder. Fortunately, Soader had ordered the Greys to leave the first shot to him, so even though both had ample opportunity to bring Zulak down before he reached cover, they held their fire.

"Soader! Where is my *daughter?!*" roared Rafael.

"In the hell of her nightmares, no doubt!" came the reply. "Harrrrr!"

Rafael leapt from cover, firing as he came. He hit Soader first, a clean shot to the shoulder, but the big Rept returned fire, grazing Zulak's left leg before the man could dodge back behind the boulder.

Their boss had taken his precious first shot, so now the Greys fanned out to either side, looking for a clear shot at Zulak. The one on Soader's right came into Rafael's view, and he brought the Grey down with a shot to the head. Then he dashed to the other side of his boulder, hoping for a shot at the second Grey—but the creature ducked behind another boulder before he could fire.

Soader, anticipating Rafael's move, charged straight toward the boulder where the commander hid. Only slightly hampered by his shoulder wound, he scrambled up the boulder's face like one of his lizard ancestors.

On the bridge of the ship far above, his eyes riveted to a monitor showing the scene at Zulak's beam-down point, Hadgkiss saw the first burst of weapon-fire. "Landing party, 'beam down! Shots fired!" he barked at his comm link. Before the first words were out of his mouth, the transbeam tech sent the team on their way.

The team arrived on the surface to see a running Grey tumble onto the sand, brought down by Rafael's shot. And there was a big half-Rept, clawing his way up a boulder. They swung their weapons toward him—but Soader, hearing the familiar hiss and hum of a transbeam arrival, was ready for them. Before they could bring their weapons to bear, he had gotten off three shots, each one finding its target. The fourth member of the party, Madda, dove and rolled for cover, firing as she went—but her hasty shots went wide.

Rafael, hearing shots from above, realized what must have happened and ran out into the open, looking for a clear shot at the Rept-hybrid. Soader caught the motion out of the corner of his eye; moving to the edge of the big rock, he brought his weapon up and fired just as Zulak turned to face him. The shot caught Rafael squarely in the chest. He dropped to the ground and lay still.

Soader roared in triumph, knowing no creature could survive such a hit. Then he leapt to the ground, putting the boulder between him and Madda. He tapped his comm pickup; "Transbeam me—now!" The Rept took one last look at the man he'd pursued in hatred for decades, then roared again as he vanished in the transbeam cloud.

Madda saw her commander go down; she screamed in rage, leapt up and raised her beam rifle toward the Rept atop the rock. He dropped out of sight before she could fire; then came the sound of the transbeam, snatching him away to safety.

Now the second Grey popped up from where he'd been hidden, hoping to eliminate Madda. He raised his beam rifle, hastily aimed for her chest and thumbed the trigger stud. His shot went low: it caught Madda in the hip, spun her around and dropped her to the ground. Thinking her down for good, the foolish Grey remained in the open; Madda rolled, brought her weapon to bear, and put a perfect pair of beam-shots between the Grey's oblong obsidian eyes.

"Commander Zulak is down!" called Madda into her comm pickup. "I'm wounded and can't get to him. 'Beam us up! The team, too!"

Rafael and Madda vanished in the beam. A second beam enveloped the other fallen team members.

Appearing on the platform, Madda shouted, "Medic! Medic!"—but medical teams were already hurtling down

the corridor toward the transbeam stations, just behind Hadgkiss and Chief Medical Officer Deggers.

Deggers ran straight to the platform, knelt beside Zulak's inert body and made a rapid scan with a hand-held; his heart sank. "Sick Bay," he ordered, "on the double." A pair of medics lifted the body, placed it gently on the gurney they'd brought, and raced toward Sick Bay. Deggers and Hadgkiss followed, a pace behind.

"Doc?" said Dino as they ran.

Deggers shook his head. "Not good."

"Hells," said Dino. "Oh, hells."

Bursting into Sick Bay, Deggers pointed to a rescue unit; the medics brought the gurney to a stop next to the unit and stepped aside. Responding to Deggers' terse commands, the robotic unit's sensors swung into place; their readings leapt to view on a monitor screen. Life support modules moved in, to re-start respiration and circulation and administer intravenous fluids and medications. But, despite everything the machines could do, the monitors' story remained unchanged: no sign of life.

For a fleeting moment, there was a tremor from the heart, as though it were trying to beat on its own again. Then it lapsed back to lifelessness, pumping only in response to the machines' steady stimulus. The brain function monitor showed no activity.

"Doc?!" Hadgkiss pleaded.

Deggers shook his head, tears welling. "I'm sorry, Dino. No."

Hadgkiss felt as if he'd been struck with a hammer. His captain was gone. And his closest friend since childhood. For nearly a minute he stood motionless, eyes downcast, focused on nothing. He was numb, but aware of massive grief mounting up: a black tsunami, rearing to engulf him.

And then he realized it: He was now captain. Responsible for *Asherah*, all her crew, everyone she protected and defended. He willed himself to the present and slammed an inner door tight against the grief-wave. Grieving would have to wait.

Straightening, Dino found himself facing Doc Deggers; several other crew were there, too—all waiting respectfully. They knew how close he and Zulak had been. "Doctor, place the body in a stasis tube at once. Now, what about the landing party?"

"All four were shot—they're already in treatment. Three are in critical condition, but we can save them. Madda was hit in the hip; it'll need major reconstruction and rehab, but she'll be okay. She says it was Soader down there."

"Thank you. Keep me briefed on their condition. I'll be on the bridge."

"Aye, Maj...Captain," said Deggers, his voice choked with emotion. He had been close friends with Rafael, too.

Minutes later, Hadgkiss strode onto the bridge and went straight to the captain's station. He tapped the intercom and switched it to ship-wide. "This is Major Hadgkiss," he announced. I am deeply sorry to inform you Commander Zulak was attacked, planetside, and suffered fatal wounds. He is no longer with us—may the Ancients rest his spirit. Services will be held as soon as practicable; for the moment, our task is to pursue his attackers and bring them to justice. As Commander Zulak's second, I have assumed command of this vessel. Despite the tragic circumstances, I welcome the opportunity to serve as your captain. I know you will continue to perform as the finest crew in all the fleet. That is all. Carry on."

Switching off the intercom, he addressed the bridge. "Signals Officer—a Rept was 'beamed from the planet after the attack. How can that be? There were no ships in the area when we arrived."

"I don't know, sir. On arrival, there were no ships on our monitors within 'beaming distance. None have appeared since. That can only mean a cloaked ship, sir."

"Cloaked!" exclaimed Hadgkiss. "Then it had to be a Fleet ship—or at least some branch of G.O.D. No one else has cloaking capability. Get me a list of all cloak-equipped vessels. I doubt it will be much help; they wouldn't be open about it—but it's a start."

He turned to the next order of business. "Security! Someone 'beamed off this ship immediately after the commander. I want to know who, and where they went. And get a party down there to collect the enemy casualties. I want to know as much about them as we can learn—where they came from, who they served—you know the drill. Get on it."

Minutes later, the lift doors slid open to reveal Madda. She sat in a hover-chair, her hip encased in an immobilizing brace. She steered the chair off the lift and straight to her duty station. "I didn't expect you so soon, Lieutenant," said Hadgkiss, "Welcome. Please join me in the ready room."

When the ready-room door slid shut, Dino and Madda faced one another. Each could see the grief in the other's face—along with the iron resolve to keep emotions in check for now, and carry out their duties. "All right," said Dino. "Report please, Lieutenant."

Madda appreciated Hadgkiss's careful formality. It

helped her focus in this horrible time. She reported what had occurred on Scobee, including her identification of the hostile Rept as Soader. "That ID has not been confirmed, sir—but I know what I saw."

"Understood, understood. I've no doubt you're right. Now tell me, did you see any sign of any other Human?"

"No sir. Just Commander Zulak. Why? Who else could have been there?"

"Someone 'beamed from this ship—from the same station the commander used—moments after he was sent down, and to nearly the same coordinates."

"But, who? Why?" Madda asked.

"It can only have been Piccolo. He was the tech on duty at that station, and he's now missing."

"Piccolo. Hm. He had his oddities, but I'd never have suspected him a traitor."

"Security is onto tracking him down. We know of nothing of interest in that area of the planet, so my guess is he's either in some well-hidden installation, or he was 'beamed by the same people who picked up Soader."

"Well, our security team's the best—we'll know soon enough. I hope they catch him fast. And alive. That's an interrogation I'd love to attend. Might have a few questions of my own," she said. Her green Rept complexion flushed to a deeper shade, signaling her fury.

"That makes two of us," answered Hadgkiss. "Anything else to report?"

"No, sir."

"Thank you, Madda. And thank you for bringing him back. Dismissed."

316   LORNA J. CARLETON

"Thank you, sir," she said, and left the ready room.

Dino leaned on his console, eyes closed, shoulders bunched. He'd worked for decades toward a command of his own. This was never, ever how he imagined winning one. He was ready, though. Ready for every responsibility but one: telling Remi Zulak her husband was dead.

CHAPTER 31

Bunker

At Hadgkiss's direction, *Asherah* returned to the deserted moon where she had rendezvoused with *King Hammurabi* less than a day before. There was the ship, just as they'd left her: powered down and tucked in the space-black shadow of a massive ridge.

Dino placed Jessup in temporary command of *Asherah*, with orders to continue their assigned "patrol"—in truth, to hunt down Soader, Piccolo, and anyone else connected with the ambush on Scobee, and search for any sign of Celine.

Dino and Madda 'beamed aboard *King Hammurabi* and laid in a course for the resort planet. They bore a tragic cargo: Commander Zulak's lifeless body, still in its stasis tube.

The moment *King* emerged from jump-shift, Hadgkiss activated her cloaking and eased into orbit over the resort planet. He called Remi and let her know he would be there shortly, and would brief her fully in person.

"Brief me about what?" she demanded, anxious. "Is Celine with you?"

"Please be patient, Remi," he responded, doing his best to sound calm and reassuring. "I'll be right there." He closed the comm link.

"This is going to be rough," he said to Madda. "I'll make it as quick as I can. Stand by to transbeam the four of us aboard." Madda acknowledged and followed Hadgkiss to the transbeam station. Though confined to her hover-chair, she behaved as though nothing had happened. Her calm efficiency was a comfort to Hadgkiss—a stark contrast to what he knew awaited him. He stepped up on the platform, turned, and nodded his readiness. Madda nodded back and activated the machine.

Dino arrived in the lounge of Remi's suite; she stood before him, her face a shifting mix of question, anxiety and impatience. He met her eyes, then lowered his gaze, overcome.

"Tell me," she said, struggling against the horrible fear welling up in her.

"Rafael..." he began, and she knew.

"No," she breathed.

"He..."

"No." She took a step back and fell into a chair, wide-eyed.

"He's gone," managed Hadgkiss, barely audible.

"How?"

"An ambush. We couldn't stop it. My fault—should never have listened, never let him go. I...I'm so sorry, Remi."

She groaned, and slowly shook her head.

"We were tricked—told Celine was there, given coordinates. Remote planet. He insisted on going for her alone. His argument made sense; I agreed. Soader was there, with backup. A trap. We had a team standing by, but they were too late. Soader killed him. And escaped.

"Someone aboard *Asherah* betrayed us—an infiltrator; a traitor. We'll find them. Someone got to Admiral Stock, too. He's the one who told us where to go. We should have known something was wrong—he acted strangely. Maybe drugged. We were so desperate to find her, we ignored it. And now... and now..."

"But, Celine! What about Celine?"

"She wasn't there. I don't think she ever was. Just a lie to lure us in. We'll find her, though. We'll find her. We have to."

He forced himself to face her. She stared back through her tears; stared in disbelief at Rafael's closest friend, the family's dearest, their Celine's godfather. She groaned again, lost.

The two fell together in surrender, let the crushing grief wash over them, held tight.

At last, with an effort, Hadgkiss forced back his sorrow, sealed it away. He gently withdrew and held her at arm's length. "Remi, it's horrible," he said, firm but gentle, "but grief must, must wait. We cannot risk staying here."

"But, this place is secure, isn't it?"

"Right now, there's only one place I would dare call secure. That's where we'll go. Now. We must. We have a secure ship in orbit; Madda is there, ready to 'beam us. We've got to get Mia and Hyatt and go. To minimize Mia's drama, it might be best if I brief them. What do you think?"

"Yes," she responded, rising to the need of the moment.

"They're by the pool. I'll call them in; you tell them."

"Right. I will not mention anything about Rafael. Not until you're all safe."

"Yes."

"All right, then. Bring them in. Just one more thing: thank you. Thank you for your strength. We will get through all this. I promise."

Remi fought down a fresh surge of grief, then nodded. "I know we will. I don't know how, but we will." She turned, wiped at her eyes and face, hurried out the suite's rear entrance and set off for the pool.

Dino watched her go, then tapped his comm pickup twice. "Aye, Captain," came Madda's voice.

"Remi is briefed, Lieutenant. She's gone to get Mia and Hyatt. I won't tell them about the commander until we've reached safety. Can't afford to stay here any longer than we must."

"Understood," she replied. "Standing by to transbeam four on your order."

Less than two minutes later, Remi returned, herding the bewildered couple before her. "Inside, inside—quick," she urged, "the major will brief you."

Dino stood waiting in the spacious lounge. Mia and Hyatt hurried in and stopped before him, their eyes full of questions. Mia opened her mouth to speak, but Hadgkiss raised a hand.

"I'm sorry, Mia. I know this is a shock and confusing. I'll answer all your questions as soon as I can." His officer's presence and tone calmed the girl. "It is imperative that we leave this place at once," he continued. "Your things will be safe here until we can return. I want you each to grab one change of clothes and a pair of shoes. You too, Remi. The most practical you have. A hiking outfit would be perfect. No time to change, no time for anything else; just get them and come back here, on the double. Go."

When the three returned, he tapped his comm pickup. "Four to transbeam, Lieutenant."

"Aye, sir," came the reply; moments later, the four appeared on the *King's* platform.

"This way," ordered Hadgkiss, and he led the new arrivals to a compartment adjoining the bridge. "Please take a seat and strap in," he said, indicating several flight chairs along the compartment's sides. "We jump for deep space in two minutes. Mia, Remi, I'll check to make sure you're secured before we depart."

When he was satisfied their passengers were secure, Dino joined Madda on the bridge and took his own seat. "Take us out of orbit," he ordered. "Engage jump-shift when we're clear. Resume full cloaking on arrival."

"Aye, Captain," came Madda's reply. Less than a minute later, they emerged from jump-shift above a nondescript, blue-green planet, painted here and there with swirls and streamers of white cloud.

"Two orbits, scan for hostiles, then request clearance," said Dino. "The station will know we're here, cloaking or no cloaking. I don't know how there could be any hostiles in this place, but we can't be too careful. I'll see to the others." He left his seat and rejoined Remi, Mia and Hyatt.

"Thank you for your patience," he began. "We've arrived at our destination. We're making a routine security scan before landing; you can leave your seats if you like, but you may be more comfortable right where you are. I know jump-shift can be unsettling. Once we're down, I'll brief you and answer your questions." Hyatt unbuckled and stood, but the women were happier to remain seated, still queasy from the jump. Dino activated a wide view-panel so they could see the planet below.

King Hammurabi swept round the planet twice, scanners at highest intensity. The world below didn't appear on any navigational chart, wasn't listed in any catalog of planets, moons, asteroids or stations. To all but a select few—extremely few—it simply didn't exist.

"Scans negative, Captain," Madda announced through her comm pickup. "Identification protocol with bunker station complete; we're cleared to enter."

"Thank you, Lieutenant. Take us in."

The ship arced down toward the surface, cruised over an expanse of gray-blue sea and approached an island, a few degrees north of the planet's equator and far from any other land. But for a low volcanic peak at its southern end, the island was densely clad in deep-green tropical foliage. Madda dropped the ship to within a hundred meters of the jungle and headed for the peak, then came to a gentle halt above the volcano's broad crater. Inactive for millennia, its contours were softened by time, weather and encroaching vegetation.

Hovering over the crater's center, Madda tapped an icon on her console. A circular opening appeared directly below: an iris door, cleverly camouflaged to match the natural crater floor. The iris dilated until the opening was a few meters wider than the ship was long. The vessel descended; down, down, settling at last on a broad platform, one hundred meters below the circular entrance. The iris silently contracted, leaving them in total darkness—but only for a moment. Lights flicked on all around the landing bay.

"All right," announced Dino, "we're safe, thank the Ancients."

"Thank the Ancients, yes," said Remi, as she and Mia unbuckled their restraints. "But the Ancients didn't build this place. Who did? What is it?"

"The Mentors built it," Dino replied.

Mia's eyes widened in surprise. Remi gasped. "The Mentors?" she said. "I've heard of them, but was never sure they really existed."

"Oh, they exist. They exist," said Dino, "though they prefer to maintain the lowest of profiles. It's crucial to their work that they be undisturbed, out of sight, out of mind. And, though few know anything at all about it, the Mentors' work is crucial to all life—all good and civilized life—in this universe."

"But, what do they want with us? Why would they allow us to come here?" asked Remi.

"Well, that's exactly what I've come to explain," said Hadgkiss, "on Rafael's behalf." Remi flinched at the name, but quickly composed herself, lest Mia notice. "It will be a relief to tell you, but I recommend you stay seated. Some of this may come as a bit of a shock."

Dino explained, in broad terms, the Mentors' nature—advanced, powerful, benevolent beings, dedicated to the nurture and advance of life and civilization, and protecting them against the all-too-real forces of evil.

"As you also may be aware, all people are, in fact, spiritual beings. Though our bodies pass away, we live on and on, animating body after body. When a body dies, the greatest majority of us choose to forget the life we've just lived. We obliterate its memory and start over in a new body, as though we have never lived before. I do not know when this became the custom, or why, but I am told it has a long history, and is almost universal in our modern times.

"The Mentors have no bodies, though they sometimes choose to animate one for a short time, to accomplish some purpose or other. They are also aware of the relatively few beings who, though they live their lives in bodies, maintain awareness of their spiritual identities, lifetime to lifetime. The Mentors guide and care for a select few of these people; they teach and train them, and encourage them to exercise and expand their abilities. Such people are good-hearted in the extreme, and happy to assist the Mentors in their work.

"Now we come to how we—you, Remi, and your family and those close to you—fit into the Mentors' scheme of things. As it happens, Celine is one of the beings I just described: one of those who are aware of their spiritual nature and their earlier lifetimes. One of those the Mentors teach, guide and care for."

Remi sat stunned, eyes wide in amazement. Hyatt, just as amazed, lowered himself back into his chair. Mia's face was impassive.

"This...this explains so much," said Remi. "When the admiral brought her to us as an infant, he explained Celine was special, and I could see that she was. Every being, every baby is special, but he said this child was beyond the usual. He made us pledge to safeguard and nurture her, just as we would our own dear child, Mia." She turned to Mia, smiled, and gave her daughter's hand a squeeze; Mia gave a perfunctory smile. Remi went on: "Elias promised one day we would understand better. I *do* understand now, though I expect there's still a lot to learn."

"All that's interesting," said Mia. "I guess it explains a few things. But what does it have to do with this place? I want to know why we're here."

Hadgkiss went on: "The Mentors established and hid this station years before Celine was born, as a secure refuge in case of severe trouble or threat to her, or those like her. Not long after they brought Celine to you, Remi, they briefed Rafael about this place, and how to access it if the need should ever arise. As Celine's godfather, they told me about it too, and allowed me to brief another, of my choice—someone I knew I could trust utterly. I chose Madda.

"I brought you all here because the resort planet, safe though it is, was no longer safe enough. We do not know where Celine is. We do not know that she is in any peril, but we cannot take any chances with her, or with those closest to her.

"A prime reason for our concern is that we know *Queen Asherah* has been infiltrated, and we have reason to suspect it has something to do with Celine. Of those still aboard, I can only be certain of Peggers, Jessup, Deggers, and Doyle. We can't fully trust anyone else—not in Fleet, not in G.O.D., not anywhere.

"Shortly, Madda and I will leave you here while we find Celine. To do that, we'll have to go to the *Queen*, but we'll operate on the assumption we're being spied upon, and that we can trust no one beyond those I just named.

"I estimate we'll be away for a week or less. In that time, we should be able to secure Celine, or know for certain she is safe. We should also have matters well enough in hand that you all can safely leave here and get on with your lives.

That's in plenty of time for the wedding, Mia. I haven't forgotten, believe me. However, you must also be prepared for the possibility that you'll be here longer, and that the wedding might be delayed. I'm very sorry even to say that, but we have to face the realities at hand."

"Yeah, okay, I guess," said Mia. "But hurry up and find Celine. If Miss Special-Special messes up my wedding, I'll never, ever forgive her. Ever."

"All right, Mia," said Hadgkiss. "Thank you for being honest."

Remi and Hyatt just looked at the girl, perplexed at such a self-centered response to Dino's revelations. A sad surprise, even coming from Mia.

Dino crossed the room and spoke into a comm link, set in the wall near the doorway. He turned back to the group and said, "I've called the staff to show you around and help you settle in. Madda and I will leave within the hour." Mia and Hyatt nodded. Mia sighed and looked away.

A young staff member arrived in a minute or so, introduced herself and invited the trio to follow her. Over the next half-hour, she led the three on a tour of the bunker station's facilities—everything they would need, including dining, hygiene, exercise, study and entertainment. She explained that the station's lighting and temperature cycled through regular days and nights, currently set to match Erra's, so their bodies would not be thrown off their natural rhythms. Finally, she showed the three their quarters—comfortable, well equipped and spacious—and showed them how to contact someone if they needed anything at all.

When the tour concluded, Mia and Hyatt went to the kitchen area to pick up a drink and a snack. Remi thanked

their guide, then returned to the lounge to talk with Dino.

"For a secret hideout, this is a pretty nice place," she began. "I guess I should be thankful it's here, and thank you for bringing us."

"You're surely welcome," said Dino. "It's what Raff would have wanted—what he would have done."

"You're right. But that brings us to the next thing we've got to do. It's time to tell Mia..." She fought down a fresh wave of grief; "Time to tell her Rafael is gone."

"Yes. And I'm willing to tell her. All things considered, though, it seems it would be best if she learned it from you. If you feel up to it."

"I'll never feel up to it, but understand what you mean—and I thank you. I'll just do it. Now."

"All right, Remi," he said. "I'll stay until it's done. I'll be right here—just call me if you need any sort of support."

"Thank you," she said, "just knowing you're here should be support enough." She hugged him quickly, then composed herself and headed for Mia's room.

Remi was gone for nearly an hour. Dino had just finished checking in with Madda when she returned. Without a word, she dropped into a chair, hunched forward, buried her face in her hands and sat, motionless, for a long moment.

Dino waited patiently.

She sat up, neatened her hair with a few flicks of her hands, and met Dino's eyes.

"As you can imagine, that was awful," she said. "She took it better than I expected, but still..."

"Was Hyatt there?"

"Yes. He was there when I arrived. It seemed best to tell them together. He's badly shaken—he sincerely admired Rafael—but I think he knew he should be strong, for Mia's sake. I'm glad he was there to support her.

"I didn't go into any details. Just said that Rafael had been killed in an ambush, and that it was Soader who did it. Mia knows Soader well, after our horrible experience with him.

"She screamed and cried, then just sat, numb and staring at the floor. We did our best to comfort her, but there wasn't much we could do. She'll have to work through it, like anyone does. Like we have to, too. After a while, she cried some more, then said just one word: "Celine." As if it were a swear-word. Hyatt and I just looked at each other; we knew what it meant. She blames Celine for her father's death. Absurd, wrong, but no surprise. I can only pray she'll come to see it's not true."

Dino went to the woman's side and rested a hand gently on her shoulder. "She'll see it. She'll come out of it, and go on with her life. She has you to help her through; that makes her luckier than she'll ever know."

Remi looked up at her old friend, grateful. "Thank you, Dino. She's lucky to have you to look after her, too. So am I. But now I believe Major Hadgkiss has duty to attend to, yes?"

Dino smiled. What resilience she had. Raff had been lucky to have such a wife—despite her occasional high drama. "Yes, that's correct," he replied. "The Major must return to his ship, and recover his commanding officer's daughter. Avenging his commanding officer's untimely death would be in order as well, though that may have to come later."

"All right," said Remi, rising to her feet. "I'll take care of things here. Update us if you can, without compromising security. But, return to us. Soon." Looking into his eyes, she took his hands in hers and squeezed them tight. "May the Ancients watch over you and guide you."

He held her look and echoed her squeeze—careful to be gentle with his bionic hands. "Thank you," he said. "Soon. Yes." Releasing her, he stepped to the room's center and tapped his comm pickup twice. "One to transbeam, Lieutenant."

"Aye, Captain. Activating transbeam," came Madda's voice.

Back aboard *Hammurabi*, Hadgkiss recounted all that had occurred. He admitted relief at telling Remi the whole truth about Celine. It had been a strain for him, and for Rafael, to withhold all they'd known for so many years. His one concern was having told Mia and Hyatt, too. He had no particular reason to distrust them; both were well trained at the Academy, and understood security's demands. It was just that the fewer who knew, the fewer could tell, in a weak or careless moment. Or, in Mia's case, he had to admit, a moment of spite. And the fewer who knew, the fewer he was obliged to monitor from this moment on.

CHAPTER 32

Capsule

S oader had a worlds-class hangover. He had been back in his quarters on Earth for nearly two days, following his trip to ambush Zulak. In a wild but solitary victory celebration, he'd consumed at least a week's supply of Earthling-blood elixir, his favorite imbibement—and it had thoroughly kicked his Rept-hybrid backside. Now he was sober enough to realize the Brothers' deadly deadline was almost upon him: the deadline for handing over Celine, Fianna and the Atlantean grimoires. "Oh, hells," he thought, rubbing his aching head. "Party's over; time to get back to work."

The first step in his grand plan was to visit Narco and Choy. When he arrived in the Dragon's lair, the big red sprang to his feet and squared off, heads lowered, curls of black smoke rising ominously from flared nostrils. He wanted nothing to do with his hybrid enslaver.

"Oooo, aren't we fearsome today!" Soader began. "What's

got you all fired up?"

"Is that supposed to be some sort of clever pun, you half-breed ass?" said Narco.

"Huh?" said Soader.

"Wow. Never mind," said Narco. "What do you want now?"

"As it happens, I am going on an important trip, and you are coming with me. So, settle down. We leave in an hour. Eat and crap and take a bath or whatever else you have to do to get ready."

"A trip? Where now?"

"To the moon—Luna."

"Luna! What in hells do you want with us on Luna?"

"I don't want *anything* with you on Luna. But when I finish some business I must conduct there, we will come back down here for an activity in which you will play a pivotal role. A role I trust you'll love. We are going to subdue and capture that lovely little slip of a white Nibiru Dragon. The one who kicked your sorry butt not long ago. This is your chance for at least a small measure of revenge. You should be grateful!"

"And how do you think we're going to 'subdue' her? She isn't much on her own, but teamed with that Human witch, she's damned formidable. The girl happens to be a far better aerial tactician than you—in case you hadn't noticed—and when she whips out her witchery, we're really in trouble."

"That is precisely why, next time we meet, I will be bringing along some magic of my own. Chemical magic, in the form of the most powerful paralysis drug known, loaded into a scatter-dart weapon. *You* are going to get us close enough for me to get off a decent shot. Twenty meters or so will do very nicely. I'll send a swarm of twenty-five darts their way. Each one can, on contact, inject enough paralytic to put them completely out of action for an hour or more. And these darts aren't ballistic; you don't just fling them out and hope your aim is good. They're smart darts—self-propelled and guided. The witch and her pale-winged mount don't stand a chance."

"Charming. It might even work, if you can manage to point the thing in the right direction and drug *them*, not us. But, why? What do you think you're going to do with a frozen Human and Dragon?"

"I don't 'think' anything, reddy-boy..."

"That's always been obvious," interrupted Narco.

"Shut your insolent yap and listen, ingrate. Once the two are down, we are going to transbeam them aboard a ship that's being provided for the purpose, and take them to the Brothers. In return, we will be compensated beyond your wildest dreams."

"You mean *you* will. Choy and I have no use for anything you'd consider compensation."

"Please! You know me so poorly! You *will* be compensated, with the one thing I know you desire more than anything else: You'll be returned to Kerr, where you and your brother Choy will have your own comfortable island paradise to enjoy for the rest of your days—and where your precious mother can live out hers, too. Do I have your interest *now?*"

"Interest, yes. Trust or belief, no. But we have no choice, so we'll go along with your ever-so-clever plan and hope you'll actually make good on your promise."

"Good choice. Sadly, sadly cynical, but a good choice, nonetheless. So, now that you know the plan, make your preparations. I will be back in one hour. We 'beam from right here."

Narco and Choy both snorted, with another black burst of acrid smoke from all four nostrils as punctuation.

Soader's next stop was Jager's cell, accompanied by four guards—two burly Repts and two armed Greys.

"Think you brought enough help?" Jager asked.

"Watch yourself, kid," said Soader.

"How can I help you this morning?" asked Jager. "Assuming you can be helped. Some things *can't* be helped, you know."

"Oh, you can help me all right," said Soader. "More than I imagine you'll like."

"We'll see, we'll see," said Jager.

"Yes, we will," the Rept replied. "We are going on a little trip. To TS...to Luna."

"Mmm. A pretty boring place, by all accounts," said Jager, "but whatever you like. What will we be doing on 'TS...Luna?'"

"Don't worry yourself about that. You'll see soon enough." He turned to the guards, pointed at Jager and said, "As you were briefed."

One of the Rept guards raised a beam pistol and motioned for Jager to move to the back of the cell. A Grey stepped to the door and keyed it open, then stood back as the Repts stepped into the cell. One grabbed Jager and jerked the young Human's hands behind his back. The other pulled out a restraint gun and bound the hands tightly. Then, gun still in hand, he grabbed Jager's feet, jerked them off the floor and bound them. One of the Greys raised a pistol-like weapon and thumbed a button on its side; a dart spat out and struck Jager in the shoulder, injecting him with a paralytic. He stiffened almost at once, a wince of pain on his face.

The first Rept lifted the immobilized ensign, threw him up over his shoulder like a piece of lumber and stepped out of the cell.

"Hmph," grunted Soader, "follow me." He led the way to the red Dragon's prison-cavern.

"Ready?" he asked Narco.

"Yes, master," the Dragon replied, sarcastic.

"Over there," he ordered the guards, pointing toward the Dragon. The Greys complied, though quaking with fear; even the Repts stayed as far from the Kerr as they could. Narco and Choy gave the group big, toothy smiles—as though sizing up a scrumptious buffet spread. One of the Greys nearly fainted.

Jager, though physically paralyzed, was fully aware of his surroundings. He recognized the Dragon as the one he'd seen on *Asherah's* monitors on the day of his abduction. "This gets more interesting all the time," he thought.

Soader tapped the comm pickup on his collar. "Ready for transport." Moments later, the scintillating transbeam cloud grew up around them, and the party dematerialized—Dragon and all.

STEPPING OFF A TRANSBEAM platform in TS 428, Soader looked around, growled and tapped his comm pickup. "Montgomery! Where are you? You were supposed to meet me on arrival!"

"Coming, sir! Right away, sir! So sorry, sir!" came Monty's strange, twangy voice. The hump-back dashed into the transbeam bay, dithering and trying to straighten his uniform collar. "Here, sir! Just prepping the equipment, sir. How can I help you, sir?"

"Don't be ridiculous—you already know what I'm here for. How long is it going to take you to get everything ready?"

"Right, sir. Uh, thirty minutes, sir?"

"You make that sound like a question. IS it thirty minutes, or isn't it? I'm asking YOU!"

"Right, sir. Well sir, I think thirty minutes, sir."

"Thirty minutes, then. I am waiting."

"Yes, sir. Waiting, sir. I'll hurry, sir."

Soader snorted and the little Human skittered from the room. The Dragon and guards stepped off the platform. The Rept carrying Jager propped the immobile Human up against a console and stood to one side, bored. The Dragon padded a few meters away from the group and settled to the floor to wait for whatever was next.

Jager, physically paralyzed but fully aware, weighed all he had just heard, everything Soader had said earlier, and what he knew of Luna and its transfer station. It all added up to just one thing, he concluded. Soader meant to transfer him out of his body. To where, he did not yet know. And he had no idea what twisted purpose drove the Rept. It didn't matter, though. He could not allow himself to be transferred. He'd invested too much of his identity in this body, used it in establishing too many connections, trained it in too many skills. And then there was his relationship with Celine and all the tremendous promise it held. No, there was too much to lose. He hated to do it, but he would have to exercise his only viable option. And he had less than half an hour to do it. He calmed and centered himself, and began.

In the end, the complex and spiritually arduous process took him only twenty minutes. They were twenty minutes he prayed never to have to relive or repeat. When he was finished, he had constructed a "capsule" or "cocoon" within his mental structure: a completely isolated mental and spiritual unit, walled off from the rest of his mind. It would be undetectable and unsuspected by any other being.

With the capsule created and ready for use, he next constructed a copy of himself—a near-complete duplicate of his mental and spiritual self, still inhabiting his body and capable of running the body as if it were actually its true owner/inhabitant. It would behave just as he would in any circumstance. No one interacting with it would suspect or detect that anything had changed, or that they were not dealing with the true Jager. No one but West or the other Mentors, or his soul-mate, Celine.

His work complete, he turned his body and all the business of daily living over to his new construct, "quasi-Jager," then moved inside the mental/spiritual capsule and sealed himself in. From within the capsule he could still perceive the world around him. He could still communicate mentally with Celine and the Mentors. Whenever needed, he could override quasi-Jager—or whatever being might be inhabiting the body—and control the body's functions, actions and responses completely, just as he had throughout the body's lifetime. And finally, should it become necessary, he could leave the body entirely and find a new one to animate. He fervently hoped it would not come to that.

Hoping the transfer station was not shielded against telepathy, Jager attempted to contact Celine. Success! She answered his call at once—and it seemed an eternity before the emotional rush of her communication subsided. When she calmed down at last, he explained where he was and assured her he was well and relatively safe— but that he needed to brief her on his current circumstances. Celine was alarmed anew, but perceived he was in a difficult situation; negative emotion would only make matters worse. She calmed herself and said she was ready to listen. He thanked her, then tried to reach West, meaning to brief both at once. He failed to make contact; Celine would have to brief the Mentor later.

He told the girl all that had taken place, what he suspected Soader meant to do, and how he had prepared himself. He vowed to maintain communication with her, brief her on any new developments and consult with her on his purposes and plans. She agreed, promised to remain always open to his communications, and to keep him informed as well. He thanked her, and the pair took a moment of silent communion, simply *being*, still and serene, in one another's presence.

Jager gently ended the moment with a spirit-smile, then said, "Soader is coming. You may not hear from me for a little while, but I'll get back to you again as soon as I can."

"Thank you. But don't keep me waiting too long, or I promise to show you what *real* trouble is all about!"

Jager laughed. "Okay! Okay! I promise! But look—there's one last thing I must tell you. Please listen close and careful. This is important."

"I understand," she replied. "I'm listening."

"Good," he said. "Here it is: I love you, Celine."

She was silent for a long moment. "Thank you, Jager. I love you, too. Always."

"Always," came his reply.

After another quiet moment, Jager spoke again: "He's here. Take care." And then there was silence.

Celine took a deep breath, let it out, and returned her attention to the world around her.

CHAPTER 33

Transfer

"All right, Jager-boy," said Soader. "I don't know if you're aware of it, but there are a lot of important people who are unbelievably eager to get their paws on that body of yours. Well, too bad for them—I got to you first, and here we are. And now Montgomery here is going to pop that soul of yours right out of that body's head and put it into storage. Then he's going to pop me out of this imminently handsome and capable body and transfer me right into your skinny little one.

"Not that I have any interest in the body itself, mind you. Who would? I'm really just borrowing it. It's your connections I'm after. 'You'—which is to say, me—are going to do some outrageously big, galactically important things in the near future. You'll be famous! Or infamous, but what's the difference, eh?

"Once I've executed my plans, I'll have Monty put me back

in my body, and auction yours off to the flock of bastards who've been fighting over it. I haven't quite decided what to do with *you* yet, but don't worry. Until I do, you'll be afloat in a soul containment chamber, utterly oblivious.

"But, enough jabbering. Montgomery, let's get this over with."

"Yes, sir," the little man replied. "Right this way, sir." He led the way to the transfer room he'd prepared. Soader followed just behind; the guards came next, one of the Repts carrying Jager's paralyzed body.

The party entered a big room that resembled a standard operating room, as might be seen in any hospital. Instead of one operating table, though, there were two tables, side by side and a few meters apart. The usual surgical lighting fixtures were replaced by what looked like large lamps, one over the head of each bed. Instead of lamps, though, these were the devices that would extract the soul from one body and transport it either into the body on the other table, or into a Universal Soul Containment Unit, where it could be stored for future implantation in a body. An array of four robotic arms also hung from the ceiling over each table, each arm tipped with a hypodermic, grasping "hand" or other implement.

Monty pointed to one of the tables and addressed Soader. "Please, sir, if you would just lie down on the table there, with your head at that end, where the little cushion is, then we can proceed."

"Unh," grunted Soader. He'd been through transfers before, and knew the drill. He hated the whole process, but it was a means to an end, so he'd endure it. He sat on the edge of the table and swung his feet up, maneuvering into position and lowering his head onto a low cushion that rose from the table's surface.

"Thank you, sir," groveled Montgomery. "But please, sir, I must ask you to remove your comm pickup, sir. When the process begins, it could arc and give you a nasty burn, sir, and we wouldn't want that, sir."

"Yeah, yeah," said Soader, unfastening the pickup and handing it to Monty.

"Thank you, sir. Now, if you'll have your people put the boy on that bed, sir?"

"Do what he wants," Soader said, and the Rept carrying Jager dropped the body onto the table with a loud thump.

"Hey, you clumsy ass!" yelled Soader. "Careful with that body, would you?! It's about to be mine, and I don't want it damaged, understand? Mess it up, and my first act with it might be killing *you*."

"Yes, sir," the Rept guard said, unimpressed at the threat. "That runt of a body killing *me*?" he thought; "Yeah, sure."

"Hmmmm," Monty said. "Sir, I believe I'm going to have to reduce the body's paralysis before we can continue. It needs to be lying flat for the procedure—right now it's bent at several joints, and the back is curved forward too much. With your permission, of course, sir."

"Whatever!" Soader barked. "Just do what you have to do. Let's get going!"

"Yes, sir! Of course, sir." Monty bobbed hurriedly away, returning moments later with a syringe. He eased the needle into Jager's neck and began slowly injecting the contents, pushing down on Jager's raised left arm as he did so. When the syringe was about half empty, the arm began to yield to Monty's pressure, moving slowly down toward the table. Monty halted the injection and withdrew the needle. Then, using gentle pressure, he adjusted each limb and the back and neck until the body was lying flat on the transfer table.

Next, he busied himself with the transfer equipment, positioning one lamp-like electronic disc above Soader's head, then the other over Jager's. Finally, he fiddled and fussed at a big control console behind the transfer tables, adjusting the machine's settings for the body types involved, and the characteristic wavelengths of the souls to be transferred.

At last, everything was ready.

"We're ready, sir. Shall I proceed, sir?"

"Yes, yes! I told you to get it over with, so do it, damn it! Do it! I don't have all bloody day!"

"Yes, sir. Proceeding, sir. Right now, sir."

As Monty worked the control console and watched, robot arms descended and injected both bodies with a sedative, lulling the occupants into a blank, deep-sleep-like state. Next, the center of the disc above Jager's head lit dimly, beginning with a dull, reddish light at its center. Other lights appeared, in a spiral pattern outward from the center, shifting upward through the visible spectrum as it whirled, faster and faster. At last the apparent motion ceased; a faint glow, deepest violet in hue, suffused the whole surface of the disc, pulsating almost imperceptibly.

Monty nodded, checked several monitor readings, then tapped a button. The violet glow swelled downward and enveloped the body's head; a high, piercing note filled the room, at the upper limits of human hearing. Then, abruptly, the machine went silent and the glowing disc went blank. The process was complete. Jager—or rather, the "quasi-Jager" near-duplicate the true Jager had created—had been drawn out of the body and transferred to the large cylindrical soul containment unit that stood in a corner of the room.

Jager himself, sealed within his self-generated capsule and firmly anchored within the body, had watched the whole procedure with detached interest. He had studied about soul transfer, but had never seen the procedure performed. He realized he must be the first person ever to experience a transfer in quite this way.

Monty rushed to the containment unit, tapped several buttons and examined the readouts on two monitor screens set into the upper part of the cylinder.

"Good, good," he said. "The boy's in there, all safe, all asleep. Oh, yes. All asleep." He was quite right—but the "boy" in the containment unit was just a copy of the real Jager. Monty returned to his console, picked up a microphone and rattled off a string of figures and procedural notes.

"There!" he said. "That step's done. Next!" He worked the console again, this time activating the unit above Soader's table. The process went through its sequence much as it had before, but with a crucial difference at the final phase: When the soul that was Soader had been withdrawn, it was not transported to a soul containment unit, as quasi-Jager had been. Instead, it was transferred to Jager's body. At the moment of entry, the body gave a single, brief twitch—and that was that.

Jager observed this process with even greater interest than the removal and transport of quasi-Jager. Now here he was, still in the body that had been his since its birth, but with another living being inhabiting and animating it. And that living being had no idea it was not alone and in sole command of the body. "Fascinating!" thought Jager; and then he laughed and laughed. "Fascinating" was exactly what that character from the old Earth entertainment program would have said—the character he'd mentioned to Celine a few days before!

"Celine!" he thought. "I've got to tell her what's happened." He reached out to Celine and briefed her on everything that had occurred since their last contact.

Celine was appalled at what Soader had done. "No!" she screamed, aloud. "No, no, no, no, NO!!!"

"Please, Celine. I understand how you feel. Completely. But please believe me: I have this under control."

To Celine and Jager's surprise, West suddenly joined the conversation. "Celine," the Mentor said, "your concerns are well founded, but please consider this: I believe Jager is fully capable of dealing with his situation. Indeed, I could not be more impressed with his course of action thus far. Bear in mind, Jager is orders of magnitude more powerful and skilled than this twisted brute, Soader. I would not suggest you dismiss your concerns, but dire as the situation may be, I have every confidence in Jager."

Celine was silent for a long moment. "Thank you, West," she spoke at last. "I'm glad to hear from you, and appreciate what you've said. You're right, there is no way in the universe I can be anything but worried and afraid. The thought of Jager so entangled with Soader makes me want to explode. I'll try to be calm, though, and help in any way I can."

"Thank you, child," West replied, "That is the best course to take. The two of you together comprise a more formidable team than Soader could ever imagine."

"I thank you, too, West," said Jager. "Thank you for your praise and your confidence; nothing could boost my own confidence more. And thanks for your concern, Celine. It *is* about as scary a fix as I've ever been in, and they sure don't teach you about things like this at the Academy. West's right, though. We'll get through it."

Jager completed his account, and assured Celine and West he would stay in contact as the situation developed. He pointed out to Celine the enormous advantage they now had: They would know Soader's every thought and scheme. They would be aware of his every move, before he even made it. They'd have to thank Soader for this, when it was all over!

Montgomery's next task was to rush Soader's now-uninhabited body to a preservation tank. There it would be eased down and down into a low, low level of functioning. It would be kept at that level, nourished, hydrated, oxygenated, cleansed of waste products and so on—just enough to maintain life and prevent deterioration until Soader returned to animate it.

With the Rept-hybrid's body secured, Monty returned to the transfer room. Working at his console, he initiated the recovery process, bringing Jager's body—now Soader's, as far as anyone but the true Jager knew—back to wakefulness and normal function under its new owner/animator.

CHAPTER 34

Inside Man

Awake and fully aware again, Soader began to get the feel of the body he now animated. First, he opened his eyes and looked around the room. Next, he attempted to move his hands, then his feet. Everything seemed to be functioning as expected, so he carefully sat up. His own body—the one he'd just left—was half-Human, and Rept bodies were constructed on the same basic principles and with the same general design as humanoids, so this new-to-him body wasn't so very strange. Its size and sturdiness surely were, though. "Ugh!" he thought. "These things are as light and flimsy as they look! I guess I'll get used to it, but I'm not going to like it. All the more reason to carry out my plans fast, so I can go back to a *real* body. My body."

Noticing Montgomery watching him, Soader/Jager yelled, "Hey! Have you got my body stored right? I'm going to want it again soon, damn it!"

"Yes, sir," answered Monty. "I can assure you of that, sir. All its needs are being met, and it will be monitored continually until you're ready to transfer back. We've done this countless times, you know, and never had a complaint. And you can be sure we'll be extra, extra careful and vigilant with *your* body, sir."

"Yeah, well, you better be. If it's not in better-than-perfect shape when I get back in there, I'll mash you up so bad, what's left of *your* pathetic body will be storable in a pill bottle. See?"

"Yes, sir. I understand completely, sir. Nothing to worry about, sir."

He had to admit, this body did feel quite agile and responsive; very much alive. That shouldn't have come as any surprise. He'd studied enough about Jager to know the young man had taken superb care of the body throughout its life—healthy food, rest and hydration, plenty of purposeful activity, and no harmful drugs or contaminants.

Jager, safe in his hidden capsule, realized he had a unique opportunity: He could observe Soader more closely than could ever be done otherwise, all undetected and unsuspected. He was quite literally inside Soader's head! "Or is it the other way around?" he thought, laughing. "No matter!"

Feeling a bit guilty—as though he were spying—Jager browsed through Soader's mind. Much of what he found appalled and sickened him. How could such a depraved person live with himself? He managed to glean—and make mental note of—a wealth of useful data. Here were the answers to a string of crimes that had remained unsolved for ages. Here were hideout locations, aliases, and all sorts of other useful information about scores of criminals and criminal organizations. There were even detailed plans for horrendous crimes not yet committed. Jager realized he was going to be outrageously busy when he re-took control of his body—and so were a whole lot of police forces and justice systems!

And then he hit on a true gem—information he'd searched and searched for, just days ago, without success: the secret to *Queen Morrighan's* universe-jumping! "Ah!" he thought. "Magic! I was so sure the answer had to be technology-based, I never even thought of that. Just like West has said over and over, 'Never discount the power of magic, young one.'" He laughed again.

Soader soon brought Jager's data-mining operation to a halt. He had made his way to the storage area where Narco and Choy waited, explained his new Human form, and began to brief them. "I hope you've enjoyed your little vacation here, with the nice low gravity and all, but there'll be no more lazing around. We're 'beaming back to Earth; it's time to collect our prize."

"Prize? The Dragon and her Human? How are they a prize?" asked Narco.

"They aren't the real prize—they're what we take to the Brothers. Then the riches and the real fun begin."

"All of which you'll keep all for yourself," said both Narco and Choy at once.

"Boys! Boys! You really should have more faith in Rept nature. I assure you, you'll share handsomely in all the wealth. Trust me."

"Ah. 'Trust me.' We've heard those words from you before. They've never led to anything good."

"You've no one but yourselves to blame for that. I'm not the one who got knocked out of the sky by an immature Human and a dainty little Dragon princess. I'm not the one who let a battered wreck of a blue Dragon escape from right under his nose. Noses. Whatever. Need I continue your catalog of catastrophes?"

"Never mind," said Narco. "I get the picture. You're never going to change, when it comes to responsibility. Or anything else. So, what do we do now?"

"Ready for action, eh? That's more like it. We are going to return to the transbeam platform and be sent back to Earth. We will locate the white Dragon and her Human. We will subdue and capture them, as I have already described. If they aren't still carrying the magic books they stole, we will force them to tell us where they are, and go collect them. Simple enough?"

"Oh, yes. Elegantly simple, in its utter lack of detail. Wonderful plan. Bravo," said Narco, with a snort.

"I'm so glad you appreciate it. Now, move your ass." Soader/Jager led off toward the transbeam station.

As all this was occurring, Jager reached out to Celine and West. "Hello! Just like we discussed, this is a heads-up on Soader's plans. Celine, he's promised the Brothers he will capture you and Fianna..."

"No!" Celine burst out. "Capture us? You can't let him try that! We couldn't fight back—we'd be fighting against YOU!"

"It's okay, it's okay," said Jager. "I understand what you're saying, and I know this sounds dangerous as all hells, but please hear me out. As I said, he's promised to deliver you two, and the Brothers have threatened him with some nasty consequences if he doesn't come through. Oh, and he's also promised to hand over the grimoires you and Fianna recovered. I guess he has no idea they're safe on Nibiru. Anyway, he'll never get that far in his plans, so no matter.

"It hasn't occurred to him yet, but aside from knowing you're on Earth, he has no idea where you are or how to find you. He was told you're on Earth by some spy he has in Scotland. We'll have to take care of that little detail later."

"Most interesting," interjected West. "I will look into that; but please continue."

"Thanks, West. Back to Soader, I do have an idea. First, please tell me where you are, Celine."

"We're in Germany—Vogelsberg, visiting Father Greer. I had some questions for him, and we wanted to thank him properly for all his wonderful help."

"Vogelsberg! That's perfect," said Jager. "Here's what I'll do. I can sort of whisper things to Soader—I'm now a real, live little voice in his head." Celine chuckled, despite her concerns. "Yeah, it is pretty funny!" said Jager. "So, at some point his little voice is going to bring it to his attention that he doesn't know where you are. Then I'll give him the hunch—the very strong hunch—that you and Fianna are where he last saw you: Vogelsberg. Oh! I'll also make it a 'gut feeling.' He's really big on 'trusting his gut,' even though it gets him into serious messes about fifty percent of the time."

"Perfect," said Celine. "We'll be ready for him. He's in for a major surprise. He won't just be up against Fianna and me. Ahimoth is here too—*and* another Dragon named Joli, who's smart and strong and well trained. I'll explain everything to them, so they won't be surprised when they see *you* on the red Dragon instead of Soader. And so they know to take the red Dragon down without hurting your body. That's going to be tricky, but we'll manage."

"Excellent, excellent," said Jager. "I didn't expect to meet such a force, and I know Soader surely doesn't either. There's one more factor in our favor, too: I'm here in his head…I mean, *my* head. Ahh, this is crazy! You know what I mean. I'm here, and I'll be dishing out every distraction and misdirection I can."

"An admirable plan," said West.

"It certainly is," said Celine, gaining confidence by the moment. "Barring any unforeseen complications, this should be… What is it they say on Earth? 'A portion of pastry?'"

Jager laughed. "'A piece of cake' is the phrase you're looking for. So appropriate! Some famous old-time aerial warriors used to say that. Real heroes, and they won against worse odds than we're facing."

"A piece of cake, then," the girl agreed. "Hmm. Don't Earthers like cake on special occasions, too? Like, oh, weddings and such?"

"Why, yes, they do, as a matter of fact. We'll discuss that later, though. Soader and Big Red are about to step onto the platform. Get ready—we should be there in a matter of minutes."

"All right, Mr. Littlevoice. See you in Germany. Love you!"

"Love you too, my warrior pumpkin!"

Soader/Jager and the red Dragon entered the transbeam station. Montgomery was there, waiting at the control console.

The Dragon shied away from the platform, but Soader/Jager nudged him forward—*gently.* Narco swung his head around in surprise. What was this? Soader being *gentle??*

Hidden in his mind-capsule, Jager realized his error at once. His natural inclination to be gentle and encouraging with another being in distress had slipped momentarily

into Soader's consciousness, and the Rept-soul had acted on it without any thought of its own. Much to Jager's relief, Soader hadn't noticed his own incongruous act. Jager vowed to be more careful. Soader had to keep on believing the body was now his, and only his.

When the pair were in position, Montgomery asked Soader, "Where shall I send you, sir?"

"Don't give me your damn problems—just do your job!" snapped Soader.

"Yes, sir. I'll be very happy to, sir. It's just that you haven't mentioned where you would like to go, sir. Unless you did, and I missed it. If that's the case, sir, I apologize, sir."

"Oh. Right. I was getting to that. You're to send me to..." For a moment, Soader was stumped. In all his clever planning, he'd forgotten to work out how to find his quarry. "Crap!" he thought. "Just a minute, just a minute," he growled at Monty, "I have to consult my notes here." He pulled his handheld from his pocket and pretended to study it while trying madly to decide on a location.

Then he heard a little voice in his head: "The place you saw them last," it said.

"Ah, yes. Here it is: the place I saw them last," he said to Monty.

"That's what your gut tells you," came the voice.

"My gut tells me that's where we'll find them again," said Soader. Behind him, Narco and Choy both rolled their eyes. They'd heard this "gut" nonsense before.

"Yes, sir," replied Monty. "Excellent choice, sir. And that place was...?"

"Germany—the Vogelsberg Mountains," whispered Jager.

"Germany, idiot," Soader snapped. "The Vogelsberg Mountains. Do I have to tell you *everything?!*"

"Vogelsberg Mountains, sir. Very good, sir. Just a moment, sir," said Monty, hastily calling up the coordinates for the place and loading them into the transbeam's controls. "All ready, sir. Shall I transmit now, sir?"

"Yes! Yes! Get on with it! You've wasted enough of my time already, with your inane questions and demands."

"Yes, sir," said Monty. He tapped the appropriate icon on his screen, and the transbeam did its work.

CHAPTER 35

Second Battle of Vogelsberg

The transbeam deposited Soader and the Kerr Dragon on a ledge, half-way around the mountain from the entrance to Father Greer's tunnels. Looking around to get his bearings, Soader quickly recognized where they were. He approached the red Dragon, clambered up into the saddle and pulled the dart weapon from its scabbard on the saddle's side. He checked to make sure the weapon was loaded, then unfastened the cover of the ammunition bag he wore at his waist. If he didn't get the girl and Dragon on the first shot, he'd be ready to reload quickly.

Satisfied, he jabbed the Dragon hard in the ribs with his booted heel. Narco had to suppress the urge to swing around and snap the head off the Human body Soader was using. "Huh," Narco thought. "I must have been dreaming when I thought the jerk had gotten more civilized." He stepped to the ledge's lip, spread his wide scarlet wings and leapt into flight.

"Here's what you're going to do," said Soader. "Stay on this side of the mountain and climb up into those clouds up there. If anyone's on that ledge where we saw the girl and the white Dragon before, we don't want them to know we're here. Once we're hidden in the clouds, fly around to the opposite side of the mountain. Then we'll dive down out of the clouds and surprise them, if they're there. If they aren't, we'll knock on their door and go back up to the clouds to wait a bit."

"What do you mean, 'knock on their door?'" asked Narco.

"I mean you'll swoop down close to that ledge where we saw them, and I'll take a couple of shots at their hidden door with my beam pistol. The noise is sure to bring the idiots scampering out of their hidey-hole to see what's going on. That will be their fatal, final mistake. Harrrr!"

"Mmmm. But I thought we were supposed to be capturing them, yes? Isn't that why you're carrying that dart weapon?"

"Don't tell me my business! I meant...I was...I was speaking figuratively! Of *course* we're going to capture them, but the Brothers will kill them eventually. You couldn't figure that out for yourself?"

"No, no—I'm not a master of strategy, like you," answered the Dragon, smirking. He flew up above the covering clouds, then circled around until they were high above the mountain's far side.

As the Kerr Dragon climbed, Jager called to Celine and told her Soader's plan. "I'll give you a heads-up when we're about to dive down out of the clouds," he concluded.

"Ha!" Celine replied. "We'll have a little surprise waiting for him!"

When the Dragon was in position, Soader shouted,

"Charge!"

"Here we come!" called Jager to Celine.

The Kerr tipped up his tail and pulled in his wings for maximum dive speed. In an instant they hurtled earthward, faster and faster and faster, down through the clouds. They shot through the bottom of the cloud layer, streaking straight toward Father Greer's landing ledge, Soader screaming as they came.

And then his scream stopped short. His jaw hung open in surprise—and fear. Instead of empty air above the mountainside, there were *three* Dragons: Fianna, Ahimoth, and Joli, hovering in a battle line between him and the mountain below.

Narco let out a deafening shriek and fanned his wings to full width, straining to halt their dizzying descent. The shock of it nearly tore Soader—in Jager's body—from the saddle.

"No! No!" Soader screamed, recovering from his initial shock. "Keep going! Head straight for the white one!" His desperate plan was to get close enough for a shot that would tranquilize Fianna and Celine, forcing the white Dragon to the ground. He was banking on the green and black Dragons to be confused at the sight of a young Human male in the saddle, rather than his own Rept-hybrid body. Even a brief hesitation on their part could provide the edge he needed to finish them off. Finish them off, and go down to collect his prize: a white Nibiru Dragon and her pet Human witch. His keys to fabulous wealth and power!

Thinking Soader had lost his mind completely, the red Dragon continued his effort to arrest their dive and avoid the terrible trio arrayed against him. Soader's hand shot to his belt, yanked out an electronic goad, and plunged its spiked tip into the red's flank. "Dive, damn you! Dive!!" roared Soader.

Narco and Choy screamed in pain, but leapt to comply, resuming their dive with three snap wingstrokes. Now they were streaking downward again, aimed straight for Fianna. Within seconds they would be in range for a shot at her and Celine. Fianna ducked and spun into a twisting, evasive power-dive, while Ahimoth and Joli leapt toward the plummeting red on vectors that would take them across their enemy's line of flight. Though it had all happened so fast that neither could fully block the streaking menace, each managed to rake the red as it passed, throwing it just enough off course to miss Fianna.

At the same moment the Dragons struck, Jager launched a mental blast of raw terror, focused to produce the strongest possible reaction in his/Soader's body and force Soader himself into blind panic. Body and invading spirit reacted instantly, in the greatest surge of raw horror either had ever experienced. Nearly every muscle in the body spasmed—including the muscles of the finger on the dart weapon's trigger. The gun released its swarm of black, tungsten-tipped homing darts just as the stricken red Dragon passed meters above the diving white.

Most of the darts flew harmlessly past their targets, but three lanced home and instantly discharged their payloads of tranquilizing drugs. Two struck Fianna in the neck and shoulder; one caught Celine square in the back. Almost at once, the drugs took effect. Both Dragon and girl felt a wave of fatigue, as if all their living energy were draining away. Their limbs—and Fianna's wings—went rubbery and unresponsive, then grew more and more wooden. They fell toward the earth, Fianna struggling to keep her wings outstretched enough to glide downward, not plummet like a bundle of lumber. Down and down they dropped, Celine now completely helpless and fading rapidly toward unconsciousness. At last, Fianna could fight the drug no longer. Her wings folded uselessly inward and the pair fell the last few meters to the ground, crashing with a sickening thud on a grass-covered slope. Though their respiration and circulation continued, voluntary muscular functions had ceased. They lay where they'd fallen, limp and completely oblivious.

In the skies above, the battle raged. After striking their red foe, Ahimoth and Joli swung around and down, intent on battering him again and again—strongly enough to sap his strength and will, and force him to land. At the same time, they had to act carefully, to keep Jager's stolen body from irreparable harm. The red Dragon fought back ferociously, unfettered by any such consideration. While Fianna and Celine lay helpless on the slope below, the three wheeled and clashed, raked and slashed, dove and collided again and again.

When it seemed the fight might go on indefinitely without resolution, a new element came into play—one unlooked for by either side. Out of nowhere, there appeared a swarm of strange, malicious entities. Having no material bodies, they appeared only as oddly pulsing, flickering distortions—as though the shimmering heat waves over a hot stretch of pavement had formed into distinct, wavering globes, each a dozen centimeters in diameter. They were clearly life forms or life manifestations, and their sheer malevolence was unmistakable. There were ten of the things, and they went straight for Ahimoth and Joli, clustering about the Dragons' heads, charging in close and then flitting away again. The air all around the entities was filled with an eerie, piercing, ululating sound that tore at the Dragons' nerves like a starving vulture.

Beset by these other-worldly beings, Ahimoth and Joli dodged and darted, shaking their heads violently, struggling to fend the things off.

Soader had no idea what the entities were or where they'd come from, but he seized the opportunity at once; he wheeled his mount and charged in to hammer at his opponents, first one, then the other, back and forth. Ahimoth and Joli countered as best they could, but the bodiless beings' torment was so relentless, they had no hope of fighting back effectively.

Having dealt Joli a crashing blow that sent her spiraling down toward the mountainside, with a crowd of entities still swarming about her, Soader turned his attention again to Ahimoth. He put the red into a steep dive, aiming to deal the black a vicious blow to the back, breaking his spine.

But now, a blinding globe of energy, like a huge sphere of blue-white lightning, burst into being around Ahimoth, enveloping and suspending him, motionless. Streaming downward from the brilliant globe was a thin bolt of the same blue-white energy.

Tracing the energy stream earthward, Soader saw its source: Standing on the ledge before the entrance to his mountain home was the tiny figure of Father Greer, feet spread wide and arms outstretched above his head.

Soader spun around again, looking back to where Ahimoth had just been. The energy globe was gone, the evil entities were nowhere to be seen, and the massive black Dragon was now diving straight toward him at terrible speed. Hauling violently at his steering straps, he pulled Narco and Choy around and down into a desperate dive.

Meanwhile, Father Greer had launched a second energy globe, down the mountainside to where Joli thrashed and twisted, struggling with the evil entities. The priest's globe burst into being around her, and with a last, furious shriek, the entities disappeared. Her struggles over, the green Dragon collapsed, exhausted. Exhausted and battered: Numerous bruises were darkening her back, neck and one leg, and her right wing had suffered a long, nasty tear.

Sensing Joli was distressed but in no immediate danger, Father Greer left the ledge and made his way down the mountain toward Fianna and Celine. As he went, he called out mentally to Jager, assuring him the girl and Dragon would be safe for the present.

High above, the Kerr continued his earthward dive at suicidal speed—but Ahimoth was moving faster still. In moments, the black overtook the red, and Soader braced himself for a blow he was sure would end his short life in the young Human's body. But, instead of smashing into the red brute with deadly force, Ahimoth slowed his dive—just enough to whip his long, powerfully muscled tail in a great arc, aimed at the middle of Narco's neck. The black tail struck, slamming Narco's neck sideways and straight into Choy's. The two red heads smacked together, knocking both unconscious. Now Ahimoth snaked his tail around the twin necks—once, then twice—in an inescapable strangle-hold. He had no intention of strangling the creature to death, though. Instead, he spread his wings wide and gave a mighty braking downstroke, slowing his descent and taking up the now-limp red's full weight. Soader/Jager hung helpless in the saddle, clinging for his life to the huge Dragon's back.

Struggling mightily to stay aloft, Ahimoth beat his wings

with all the strength he could muster, lowering himself and his enormous load earthward. Just before impact he gave a final, powerful wingbeat and unwrapped his tail from the red Dragon's necks. The creature dropped to the ground, and Ahimoth landed gracelessly at its side, utterly exhausted. Soader/Jager, still in the saddle, lay still. Soader himself was in shock, badly dazed; his left leg was pinned beneath the Kerr. Jager seized the opportunity: he assumed partial control of the body.

As Ahimoth lay where he'd fallen, eyes closed and panting, he heard a voice. "Ahimoth! Hit me in the head—knock me out."

Ahimoth had never met Jager in person, so he didn't recognize the voice. Looking around to see who could be speaking, he was surprised to see it was Jager—or at least, the voice was coming from Jager's body. "What?" he said, "Hit you in the head?? Is this some sort of twisted trick, Soader?"

"No, no. It's me—Jager. The real Jager. I've re-taken control of the body for a moment. I want you to hit it in the head. Not to hurt it—just enough to knock it unconscious. It'll be fine—you'll see." With that, Jager withdrew his control.

"Hmmmm. All right," said Ahimoth. "It *is* your head. Just a moment." He rose wearily to his feet, staggered to where Soader/Jager lay pinned, and drew back a paw to cuff the Human across the head.

The sight of the black Dragon looming above him, about to strike, jolted Soader to his senses; he screamed for mercy.

Ahimoth paused, cocked his head to one side, then bent down to within millimeters of Soader/Jager's face.

"Mmmm," said the Dragon. "Mercy, eh?"

"Yes! Yes! Please!! I *beg* you!!" Soader shrieked.

"All right, all right," said Ahimoth, in mock reassurance. "I shall show you all the mercy you would show another, in a situation such as this." He drew back his paw again and swung it, landing a glancing blow across the side of Soader/Jager's head. The merest tap for Ahimoth, but enough to ensure the vile body thief went out cold.

"Thank you, my friend," thought Jager. "Now it's my turn." He chanted a brief spell, and the capsule that had concealed him from Soader's awareness vanished. He seized total control of the body, then shoved the Rept-spirit straight out through the skull. No longer affected by the blow to the body's head, Soader popped to full awareness. For just a moment, he was utterly confused and disoriented. Then, seeing Jager's body—the body he had been animating just seconds before—gazing at him with an amused smile, he yelped in horror. Spinning around, he fled toward the sky, screaming.

Jager uttered a new incantation that brought the bodiless Soader to a sudden halt, frozen in mid-air. Next, he constructed a new mental-energy capsule, much like the one he'd made for himself. He drew Soader back, opened the capsule, shoved the Rept-spirit inside and sealed it off. "There!" he said aloud. "Safe, sound, and going nowhere. Not just yet, at least."

Jager reached out to Father Greer, who again assured him Fianna and Celine were safe and well. After a brief exchange, Jager thanked the priest and broke contact.

Now he reached down to the collar of his uniform and tapped the Fleet comm pickup—still in its place, just as it had been when he'd last "worn" this body. He made a call to Fleet headquarters, via a comm relay at the Luna transfer station.

"That's correct," he said, concluding his conversation with Fleet. "To reiterate: I have in custody at this location the soul of the criminal known as Soader. Until I can personally transport it to TS 428—Luna—I am entrusting it to the care of one Thaddeus Greer, at Vogelsberg, nation of Germany, continent of Europe, Earth—P444. Once I have transported the soul to Luna and sealed it in a standard Secure Soul Containment Vessel, I will forward it directly to the nearest Sector Justice Authority for processing. I will then arrange for my own transport to the closest Fleet vessel or base for full debriefing." He paused, listening, then spoke again. "Acknowledged. Ensign Jager C. Cornwallis, out."

CHAPTER 36

Together at Last

His immediate business with Fleet concluded, Jager turned anxiously to Ahimoth. "Celine and Fianna!" he said, "We have to go to them!"

"At once," replied the black Dragon, and he knelt so Jager could climb carefully up between his ebon-scaled shoulders. "Hold tight!" the Dragon said, and vaulted into the air. They landed a few wingbeats later, and rushed to the girl and white Dragon. They carefully inspected the fallen pair, looking for any sign of injury and reaching out to make mental contact—Ahimoth to his sister, Jager to Celine.

To their great relief, they found no sign of serious damage. And, although the two were unconscious and unresponsive to mental probes, the paralysis drug seemed to be wearing off: instead of being stiff and unmoving, both bodies were in natural, relaxed positions, breathing easy but making small motions—as if sleeping fitfully.

Jager reached out to Celine once again, probing more deeply. To his great relief, he perceived she was merely resting...and waiting. Waiting for *him!*

Jager stroked his love's bare arm, then took her free hand in his and squeezed it gently. The girl's eyes fluttered open; she turned her head and gazed up at him. "Celine!" he cried. "Oh, Celine; are you all right?"

"I think so," she said, groggily, "but, Fianna! What about Fianna?!"

"I am here, Little One," came Fianna's faintly shaky voice, "and I do not seem badly injured. I was able to arrest our fall until the very last moment; then I must have passed from consciousness. I shall be quite sore, I am certain, but there appear to be no broken bones or wing tears."

"Oh! Oh, I'm so glad, Fianna," said Celine, supremely relieved. "What about you, Ahimoth?"

"I am nearly unharmed," Ahimoth replied. "No wounds of any great concern. I have also spoken with Joli—she and I are able to ment. Though she has sustained some injuries, she assures me she will be all right again in time. By happy chance, she fell to earth quite close by, and will join us shortly."

"Oh, thank the Ancients," breathed Celine.

"Indeed, I thank them deeply," replied the white Dragon.

"And I!" said Jager and Ahimoth at once.

"Now, lie still and rest, both of you!" commanded Jager, still leaning close over his sweetheart.

"Aye, sir!" replied Celine, with the slightest of chuckles—and then a wince.

"I am not joking, Cadet," said Jager, though he smiled

broadly; he felt more relieved than he could ever recall.

After a few moments' quiet, Celine gingerly attempted to move: first her head, then her arms and legs. "Yes," she said, "it looks like I'm okay. Everything seems to work, anyway. I think my right leg must have hit the ground, though; it's sore, and I can sense it starting to bruise up in places." She paused, then fixed Jager with a suspicious look. "But wait a minute," she said, "How do I know I'm talking to Jager here, not Soader?"

"Ah," said Jager, giving his voice the faintest hint of a Rept's guttural tones. "An astute question. Excellent attention to detail. Sound security procedure. Yes, yes. A very good question...pumpkin!"

The girl chuckled, then reached out stiffly and cuffed him on the shoulder. "Okay, okay! I'm convinced. It's you!" She relaxed back into a resting position. "Now, would you be so kind as to bring me up to date? I seem to have taken a bit of an impromptu nap, and missed a few things."

"Yes, please do," agreed Fianna.

"Agreed!" called Joli, limping into view from behind a copse of trees.

The group greeted the green Dragon warmly. She thanked them for their concern over her injuries, but insisted she would recover in due time.

"All right, then. Now for the update Celine requested," began Jager. But his account was cut off before it even began, by the sudden appearance of a transbeam's swirling energy cloud.

When the glimmering display had cleared, there stood Vin. He was still weak, and his injuries were far from fully healed, but he could stand unaided.

"Vin! Vin!" cried the group, happily surprised.

"Hello, hello, my friends!" said the blue Dragon. "One of the Mentors caring for me said momentous events had transpired—events I should learn of without delay. She sent me here, though only for a short while. Can you tell me what has happened?"

"Certainly, friend," said Ahimoth. "Jager here was about to recount the details of the battle that has just transpired." He introduced Jager and Vin, and the boy launched into an account of the struggle. Others in the group chimed in from time to time, adding details and telling how things had looked from their own viewpoints.

The account was interrupted briefly when Father Greer joined the group. Those who knew him greeted the old priest, and Celine introduced him to Vin and Joli. He took several minutes to examine Celine, Fianna and Joli, confirming that although they should receive a healer's care—Joli especially—their injuries were not dire.

Jager continued his tale to its end. "Thank you, Jager!" said Vin. "I must admit I feel ashamed to have arrived only *after* the battle was over. I feel I have failed you all. Though I fear I would not have been of much use, I should have been here to fight beside you. I who have such a stake in seeing Soader brought to justice!"

"I understand," replied Ahimoth, "but no apology is necessary. We are glad to have you here at all—and gladder still to see you mending."

"Now that we've recounted today's victory," said Jager, "wouldn't it be fitting to bring Vin up to date on the many events and achievements that lead to it? He should know what his friends, old and new, have been up to."

"Yes! Tell him!" the group agreed.

"That would be wonderful," said Vin.

Jager marched down a list of recent events and accomplishments. As before, others pitched in with comments and details now and again, but for the most part they let Jager be their spokesperson.

There was Celine and Fianna's recovery of the ancient Atlantean spell books, and their rescue of Neal and Dini, King and Queen of Nibiru; Celine's miraculous banishment of the Brothers' hex, which had nearly extinguished the Nibiru Dragon race; Jager's discovery of a Fleet capital ship, missing for decades—and the secret of shifting any ship from their own Phoenix Universe to the Serpens Universe and back again. For Father Greer's benefit, Jager also recounted Joli's story, including her body's death on Nibiru, her new life on Earth, and her reunion with the long-lost companions of her youth. Finally, he told of Vin's captivity, liberation and impending recovery.

When Jager had finished, the group cheered, and happy hugs were exchanged all around. They hadn't realized how very, very much they had achieved. Laid out all at once, it was not just impressive, it was astonishing.

When the cheery celebration had run its course, Fianna spoke up. "It would be fitting that we all travel now to Scotland, to tell Nessie and her clan of the battle just ended, and these many other events of interest. None of what we have done would have been possible without the Water Dragons' contributions. Clearly, though, such a trip is not possible for all of us. I have a solution, however: I shall ment Nessie and recount it all, and she can relay it to her clan."

"Excellent idea," said Celine. "We should also find a way to send the news to Father Sinclair and his young apprentice in Glastonbury. They played a vital role, too."

"Exactly so!" agreed Fianna. "And then there is West. We owe her and all the Mentors our lives—as do the generations yet to come. Celine, can you contact her, and invite her to join us?"

Celine nodded. "I'll be happy to," she said. To herself, she thought, "West. Hm. She should *be* here." Then came an unsettling realization: She hadn't spoken with the Mentor, or even detected her presence, since their conversation before the battle. She called out to her lives-long guardian and teacher.

The girl stood quiet for a time, then addressed the group. "I just tried to reach West, but there was no reply. I spoke to North, her sister, and flashed her a full conceptual recounting of today's events. She thanked me, and asked that I give you all her love, admiration and congratulations. She also said she would relay everything to West, when she returns.

"It's too bad that West can't join us, but she must be attending to something awfully important. I hope we'll see her soon."

Just then, Jager heard a faint huffing noise; it seemed to come from a nearby mass of boulders. He held up a hand for silence, and listened a few moments more. "Ah! I know who that is," he said to himself. "Narco! Choy!" he called out loudly, "It's all right. You can come out. Soader's gone. Gone forever. You're *free*."

Two great scarlet-scaled heads peered hesitantly from behind the outcropping. "Free?" said Narco. "F-free?" echoed Choy.

"That's correct. Now, come and join us. It's okay. Really!"

said Jager.

"Yes! Yes!" the rest chimed in.

The Kerr Dragon padded out from its hiding place and approached the group. "But, I've done so much to harm you—all of you. You should hate me!"

"We understand," said Jager. "But let me explain. I believe I can speak for all of us here." The others nodded. "Yes, you have harmed us," he went on, "or attempted to. But, please consider this: did you do so by your own choice? Of your own free will?"

"I...I don't think so. But I don't know. I...I'm very confused," said Narco, speaking for himself and for Choy, as he most often did.

"May I add something, Jager?" asked Ahimoth.

"Yes, please do," the young man replied.

"Thank you. Narco, Choy, on the day I escaped from the caverns where Soader imprisoned us, I saw him speaking to you. I saw him hypnotize you, and force you to do his bidding. From all I could see—and from the honest goodness I sense in you here and now—I do not believe you have ever acted against any of us by your own choice. I believe Soader took evil advantage of the hurts and sufferings of your past, magnifying and turning them back upon you, to bend you to *his* will."

Narco and Choy were silent for a moment, then both burst into tears. The group stood quietly, allowing the Dragons to exhaust their grief. At last they grew quiet, then lifted their heads to face the gathering once more. They wore expressions of profound relief—and profound gratitude.

"What you have said is true," said Narco. "But I—we— find it hard to believe anyone could be so caring and kind as to help us see these truths and understand them. And so great-hearted as to accept us as we are, and despite all we have done. We know we can never thank you adequately, but we must try."

"Seeing you free—free from Soader's hideous prisons, physical and spiritual—is all the thanks we could ever want," said Fianna. "Is that not so?" she asked, addressing the group.

"Yes! Yes!" they called out. Then all approached the big red Dragon to express their acceptance and welcome in gentle words and touches. Narco and Choy cried again—this time in happiness, and this time not alone.

"Well!" said Jager at length. "Narco, Choy, you are welcome to join those of us who will be remaining on Earth. Or, if you prefer, you may return to your homeworld. Or go anywhere you wish! The choice is yours. The *freedom* is yours."

"We thank you again," said Narco. "May we stay with you here then, for a while at least?"

"Of course," answered Jager.

He turned now to Celine, putting his hands on her shoulders. "All right, Cadet Zulak. Group business having been concluded, the time has come to address some personal business. *Our* personal business."

After a long moment, eye to eye, intense and silent, they came together in a tight embrace, then kissed—long and deeply. The group stood quietly, sharing the moment and looking toward the future—their own, and this extraordinary young couple's.

Drawing back at last, Celine smiled her most brilliant smile. "It's about time you did that, mister!" she said. Everyone cheered and cheered as the lovers came together for another long, loving kiss.

The others watched, some mildly abashed, all delighted. Fianna stole a glance at Vin, and blushed to find him gazing straight at her, with a look that spoke volumes.

At last, the kiss came to a close. The young lovers drew apart, gazed once more into one another's eyes, and—to everyone's utter astonishment—vanished.

"What...?" "How...?" The assembled friends broke into wondering, anxious chatter.

"Listen, listen!" Ahimoth called out, then waited for the group to settle. "Think about it, eh? They are both masters of the magical arts. I am sure they have just put a bit of that magic to good use—to get away for a little time of their own. And surely they deserve it, after all they have been through, and all they have done for so many."

"Ahh!" "Of course!" "That's it!" most everyone agreed, their fears set aside and cheerful once more.

"Mmm, quite likely so," said Father Greer, quietly to himself. "I do hope you're right."

And, for all her joy at the couple's long, long-awaited meeting, Fianna couldn't escape a vague sense of foreboding.

About the Author

Lorna J. Carleton makes her home in Vernon, British Columbia. A BC native, Lorna is a Safety Advisor for a major utility, while also working toward a university degree. She's dreamed of being an author since childhood, and made several attempts at novel writing. *Dragons of Earth* is her second published work, and the second book in the Dragons of Nibiru series. She drew inspiration for the series from observations of life over the years; chief among them were clashes among diverse cultures, and the struggles of former cult members to get on with their lives and find happiness. While continuing the book series, Lorna is also planning a vacation trip to the Pleiades Cluster—providing she can find suitable transport (technological or otherwise).

www.lornajcarleton.com

Manufactured by Amazon.ca
Bolton, ON